SIMPLY IRRESISTIBLE

A COLLECTION OF IRRESISTIBLE ROMANCES

WILLOW WINTERS

LAUREN LANDISH

INKED

From USA Today bestselling authors, Willow Winters and Lauren Landish, comes a smoking hot standalone romance that'll have you wishing you had your own bad boy next door.

Little Miss Goody-Two-Shoes just moved in next door.

She's a good girl, the kind I want to ruin.

The problem is, she knows I'm bad news. I've always been trouble.

. . .

That's why she keeps pushing me away, even with her curvy body pressed against mine and those soft moans spilling from her lips.

But now that she's my neighbor, it's only a matter of time before I'll have her in my arms and clinging to me the way I need her to.

I may not deserve her, but I want her more than I've ever wanted anything.

She's not getting away from the bad boy next door.

*Inked is a full-length romance with an HEA, no cheating, and no cliffhanger.

PROLOGUE

MADELINE

I turn on my side and face my window, waiting for him to come into view. I feel so naughty. So needy. This is turning into a bad habit.

I bite my lip as he moves his curtains so he can see me.

Our eyes meet, and the hunger I see in his makes every doubt disappear. I want him, and he wants me. There's nothing wrong about that.

His lips turn up into a sexy smirk as his eyes roam my body. He takes his shirt off, his corded muscles rippling with the movement. He's the epitome of power and sex. His jeans are slung low, and the urge to lick the deep "V" at his hips makes my legs scissor. My hand dips down to my pussy and I love that he sees. I love that he watches me.

"Covers off," he mouths, and I obey. I'm wearing a tank top and a skimpy lace thong. He tilts his head and tsks. A small laugh escapes my lips as a blush creeps into my cheeks. I knew he'd want them off. But tonight I want him to take them off of me.

A few weeks ago I would've given him the finger and

[illegible] my curtains closed. But not tonight, not now that I've become addicted to the inked-up bad boy next door.

"Come over." I whisper my plea, and his eyes heat with desire.

"Get wet for me, peaches." I smile shyly at his command and slowly push my fingers against my clit, massaging small circles over my throbbing nub. My head falls back against my pillow, and a faint moan escapes from my parted mouth. I turn my head to the side and with my eyes half-lidded, I watch him watching me.

"More," he says in a deep, rough voice that makes arousal pool in my core. I make my movements faster and hold his heated gaze. His breath comes in shallow pants, and his hand pushes against the bulge in his jeans. I know he wants me. I want him, too.

"Please," the word tumbles from my mouth as I feel my back bow and a hot tingle take over my body. My eyes close as I almost fall and crash with an intense orgasm, but it escapes me. I'm on edge. I *need* him.

I open my eyes, and he's gone. I bite down on my lip and slow my movements. He'll be here soon. He'll fill me, stretching my walls with his massive cock and thrusting his powerful hips until I'm writhing beneath him and screaming his name.

When did I turn into a slave to his lust? I don't beg. I'm not that kind of girl, but he broke my walls down, and I've learned to love it.

He's bad for me. I know he is, but I still crave him. And now that I've given in, I'm all his. Until he's done with me, anyway. I know it's coming.

This arrangement isn't going to last, but I push the thoughts away and force myself to live in the moment.

For now, I belong to the inked-up bad boy next door.

CHAPTER 1

MADELINE - ONE MONTH AGO...

"I've never seen so many hot guys in my life!" cries Katie Butler, my partner in crime and childhood friend. We're standing in line outside of Club Dusk, the hottest nightclub in this town. As new residents to Grim Lake, a bustling town nestled in the lush Midwest, we've come to check out the nightlife scene on our last night of freedom. Not that the party scene is *my* scene.

Katie has been adamant all week that we go out and have a good time before we spend the next several years with our noses stuck in a book and stressing about exams. While I agree wholeheartedly with her, I'm just not sure if I want to spend the night with horny guys breathing down my neck.

I make a sour face as I survey the sea of young men standing in line in front of us. "Are you sure we're looking at the same people?" I say loudly over the bass of the music coming from within the club.

Honestly, I don't know what Katie's smoking. I wouldn't give a second glance to any of these dudes even if I was walking down the street, desperate to find a man.

And the few that are good-looking, already have a chick on their arms.

Not to mention I'm not here to find a boyfriend, I think to myself. *I'm just here to have a couple of drinks and unload some stress. That's it.*

Despite being the goal of maybe eighty percent of the women in attendance, I have no intention of getting sloppy-ass drunk and winding up in some strange asshole's bed the next morning, not knowing how or why I wound up in it.

Besides, after the way my last relationship ended, a boyfriend is the last thing on my mind.

Just thinking about my ex, Zachery Haynes, makes my stomach tense with a mixture of anger and anxiety. We'd been high school sweethearts who thought we'd be spending the rest of our lives together. Our endgame goals were even aligned. College degrees. High-powered jobs. White picket fence. A full-sized family. The whole nine yards.

That dream shattered when I walked in on Zach getting a blowjob from my high school nemesis, Jenna Stout. Seeing her there on her knees, slurping my boyfriend's dick felt like a spear piercing my heart.

Of course, being the egotistical, narcissistic asshole he was, Zachery tried to make it seem like HE was the victim. It was an accident, he claimed. He didn't mean to do it. It was all Jenna's fault for showing up on his doorstep looking hot as fuck in her cheerleader uniform.

She'd seduced him he said, she'd made his dick hard and made him take it out so she could slurp on it like a fucking cherry popsicle. The ridiculous explanation was more than I could take. I left him and Jenna right then and there to continue their oral session, and I never spoke to the bastard ever again.

I did suffer for it, though.

The whole trauma from Zach's betrayal put me in a deep depression, causing my GPA to fall. And by mid-semester, I was close to failing several of my classes. Luckily, with the help of Katie and my father, I was able to pull myself out of my rut in time enough to get my grades back on track to allow me to qualify to go to one of the best universities in the nation.

It's funny how things turn out.

There was one valuable lesson I learned from Zach's betrayal, and that was you could never trust a man.

Fuck a boyfriend, I think to myself. *I'll only enter a relationship when I'm good and ready. And that won't be for a very long time.*

I don't intend on dating until I've graduated and landed my dream job. Then, and only then, will I give the male species a second chance at regaining my trust. Besides, I certainly won't find Mr. Right in a club full of horny guys just looking for the next girl to fuck.

"I must be blind then," I say. "Or just plain stupid."

Katie tears her eyes away from the object of her affection and scowls at me. I must say Miss Katie's makeup is on point tonight, with false eyelashes that would make a drag queen jealous, rosy blush, glossy pink lipstick and dramatic eye shadow. Her hair isn't too shabby, either, styled into a trendy shoulder-length side bob that shimmers under the street light. A tight red dress that hugs her pear-shaped frame completes her look. "You really need to lighten up, Maddy. We came here to have fun, remember?"

I hold Katie's scowl for a moment before letting out a resigned sigh. "I know, I know, I'm just not looking forward to having a line of horny guys buying me drinks and reading me their lame pick-up lines in hopes that I'll sleep with them."

Katie looks at me like I'm crazy. "If you don't want that, then why the hell did you agree to come in the first place?"

It's a good question. If my goal is to relieve stress, there are a lot more relaxing things I could do rather than come to a rowdy nightclub... like enjoy a bubble bath with a chilled glass of wine, or cuddle up on the couch with a good romance book. I *love* wine now.

Last year, my twenty first, was all about hard liquor and beer. Simply because that's was the go-to for everyone else. Katie got me hooked on wine. First a White Zin and then a smooth Cabernet. It's easy to just have a glass and let the stress slip away. Especially when you're in the habit of avoiding the things that upset you. That's simply what I do, I steer clear of anything that could hurt me.

The truth is I've been avoiding the opposite sex since Zach's betrayal. Maybe subconsciously I wanted to see what it feels like to be desired again, even if it's by a horny guy looking to land his next lay. Yeah, that had to be it. I wanted a boost of confidence.

At five foot four, with green eyes, long blonde hair and a voluptuous figure, I've gotten enough compliments to know that I'm not bad-looking, maybe even pretty. But Zach's cheating had been a blow to my self-esteem. I mean, if I was so beautiful, why did he feel the need to cheat on me?

Stop it, I tell myself, something I do every time I find myself falling into the trap of internalizing my ex's actions. *Zach cheated because he was a narcissistic asshole that only cared about himself. It had nothing to do with my looks.*

It's a mantra I repeat frequently to keep myself from getting depressed. Lately though, I've been having trouble believing it.

"Are you kidding me?" I demand. "You're really going to act like you weren't bugging me all damn week to come out and have some fun?" I look at her like she's lost her mind. "I think your exact words were, 'Your face is starting to look like cracked asphalt because of the perpetual scowl you've had on your mug for the past month.'"

"You still didn't have to come," says Katie defensively. "And your face *was* starting to look like cracked asphalt."

I roll my eyes. "Get real. If I hadn't come I would've never heard the end of it." I put my finger to my lips and make a thoughtful expression. "Hmm, what was one of the arguments you were using to blackmail me to be your partner in crime? Oh yeah, that's right, 'I'm going to be so pissed off at you Maddy, if you don't come get shitfaced with me before we move into our new condo together.'"

"I did not say that."

I glower. "Yes, you did."

Placing her hands on her hips, Katie scowls back at me and admits, "Okay, maybe I did. Now what?"

"Nothing. Just letting it be known that I had no choice in the matter if I didn't want to deal with a pissed off diva for the next couple of weeks."

"I am not a diva!" she wails.

"Tell that to Vanessa! She's the prissiest person I know, and even she knows you're a diva!"

"Vanessa is a cat!" Katie protests.

"That's my point exactly."

"Ugh, whatever. I just don't know why you're giving me so much grief over this. What's so bad about me wanting you to come out and interact with the opposite sex for just one night, huh?"

I fall silent for a moment as the line moves up. We're only a couple of feet from being let inside the club, and I have to admit I'm feeling a little excited. "I don't know," I say finally. "I guess I'm still not over Zach."

Katie shakes her head, her bob swishing to the side.

"You're crazy. Why wouldn't you be over that ego-inflated douchebag?"

"I don't mean him per se, I mean what he did."

Katie frowns. "Oh. I understand... but we talked about that, remember? We agreed that Zach was an asshole who never cared about you, you were better off without him, and that you wouldn't let what he'd done bother you anymore."

"I know, Katie, and for a while I didn't let it get to me... but... I… lately I've been feeling like I'll never be able to trust guys again," I confess reluctantly.

"Who says you have to trust a guy to fuck him?" she replies with a shrug.

"Katie!" I object in horror.

Katie makes an innocent face. "Wha?"

"I'm not here for that!"

"Why not? Your muffin has cobwebs."

I cross my arms over my chest and threaten, "I'm going to leave."

Katie lets out a wild laugh at my exasperation. "I'm just playing! Sort of. You know, just because Zach cheated on you, doesn't mean you can't have a sexual relationship with someone."

"It does in my book. Besides, I'm not one to sleep around."

Katie snorts. "Why sell yourself short? There's nothing wrong with having sex with someone, no strings attached. Then you don't have to deal with all the bullshit that comes with a relationship, like what happened between you and Zach."

Katie has a point. Since Zach, I'd sworn off sex and probably would remain celibate for years to come. Why deny myself the simple pleasures in life because of the actions of one heartless bastard? What harm could come from fulfilling a primal need from time to time?

Because I want it to be special, I tell myself. *If I sleep with a guy just to satisfy an itch, it won't mean anything.*

"If anything," Katie continues while I'm lost in thought, "Zach's betrayal should make you want to use guys and leave them."

"No thanks," I say. "I won't stoop to his level."

"That's not stooping to his level; it's called empowering yourself."

"How is becoming the village slut empowering?"

Katie laughs. "Hey, guys do it all the time, and they're rewarded for it. We do it, and we're sluts. How is that fair?"

"You know I know it's not, but it just doesn't interest me."

"Won't you even consider the possibility?"

"Nope. I'm only here because you made me come… and because I want free cosmopolitans."

Katie giggles. "Don't we all? But seriously, if a smoking hot guy comes up to you and wants to have a little fun, are you really going to turn him down?"

"Yep."

"Liar."

"Just watch me."

I have every intention of keeping my word. I don't care if some guy buys me a dozen free drinks or is a clone of Charlie Hunnam and Channing Tatum put together, I am not going home with anyone.

We get through the line and into the club and the whole time I'm thinking, a few drinks, a flirt here and there, and then I'm going home.

No screwing whatsoever.

And then I see *him*.

CHAPTER 2

ZANE

I down the third shot of whiskey and relish the burn. It feels good to unwind after a long, hard day of work. Not that I didn't love it. I slam the glass down and lean back, cracking my neck.

I had a great day at the shop. Time flew by, and I loved every minute of it. I only had one client all day, but he was so fucking grateful and happy for the portrait piece I gave him. I used to love the challenge of tattooing portraits, but it got old real quick. It's so draining. Not physically, but emotionally.

When someone comes in to get a portrait tattooed, more times than not it's because they lost someone close to them. They cry when they come in, and then I have to hear all about it. I don't mind being a shoulder to cry on, but damn. Fucking sucks.

Some days I feel more like a therapist than a tattoo artist.

If it's not a person who's passed away, it's their boyfriend or girlfriend.

A few times I've even turned down requests. Yeah, I lose out on money when that happens, but I'm not going to tattoo a portrait of some chick's ex on her. Not gonna happen. Once a girl came in, only eighteen years old, wanting to get a profile of her "soulmate" on her shoulder. I asked her how long they'd been together. One month. Yeah, I'm not fucking doing that.

I know where to draw the line.

Not today though. A proud pop wanted his son on his bicep, and I was fucking thrilled to make it happen.

I smile to myself and wave at Tony, the bartender closest to me, for another beer.

Jackson's sitting next to me enjoying the club atmosphere. This is a normal night for the two of us. Usually we're surrounded by more of the guys, but tonight the club's packed, and they're on the prowl. He's had a cocky grin on his face ever since we got here, and for good reason.

Jackson's a playboy and every chick knows it, yet they fall right into his lap every night. He's got a classically handsome thing going for him, and he knows how to let charm and alcohol convince any woman to spread her legs for him. He's young and stupid, and going to knock up one of these broads one day.

He likes his reputation though. I don't get it. He's had more than one woman come up and slap him for fucking her in the back room and then leaving to go make out with someone else. He's a fucking asshole. Every time, he just takes the hit and smiles. Like I said. Playboy. Asshole.

I'd prefer it if Needles were sitting next to me, but he had shit to do tonight. So I'm left with Jackson.

He drums his fingers on the bartop and looks at me as he asks, "Hard day?" He's asking 'cause of the shots I'm knocking back, I'm sure. I'm not usually a heavy drinker. And if I'm being honest with myself, these shots aren't because of the pride I have from today's work. But I'd rather not think about the shit that's eating at me. It's not like I can change it.

Today's been a hard day, but not because of work. And no one here needs to know why. I school my expression and decide to focus on all the good shit going on in my life.

"Nah, fucking fabulous." He snorts a laugh like he doesn't believe me. "Not joking. Great day at the shop."

He nods his head as Tony pushes our beers toward us. Cindy, the other bartender, looks pissed that Tony was the one to give us the beers. I'm not sure if she's after Jackson's dick or mine. I couldn't really give two shits if she's after me though. I just wanna drink and be distracted enough to forget. I'm not interested in women tonight. I make a mental note to avoid her for the rest of the night.

If it's Jackson she's after, she can have him. She knows what she's getting into.

Jackson turns his back to the bar and faces the dance floor. The lights are dim, but the strobe and spotlights in the center of the room are enough to see all the women shaking their asses and putting on a show.

He stretches out and takes in the view. He does this shit all the time. Like it's a fucking buffet. He does get all the pussy he wants, but he could at least be modest about it. Shit, I'm way better looking than that motherfucker, and even I don't brag about tail as much as him. Being a playboy isn't my thing though. Maybe I'm just pickier.

"Which one tonight?" he says with his typical cocky grin.

The bass drowns out the sounds of all the chatter and clinking of the glasses behind the bar.

And that's when I see her. She's fucking stunning.

I notice the pretty little blonde the moment she walks in. She's curvy in all the right ways, and just my type.

I wasn't in the mood for a lay tonight, but seeing that gorgeous body, fuck yeah I am now. *She* could be the distraction I need. I know her body can take a punishing fuck. Thick thighs, and an even thicker ass. Her hips sway a little as she walks.

I find myself mesmerized as she takes a seat at the far end of the bar. I watch her for a minute, waiting for her to look my way. She looks everywhere but at me, and it's starting to piss me off.

My brow furrows, hating that I can't get this broad's attention.

She's fucking gorgeous and I already know I want her. Tonight. In my bed. I'm definitely taking this sweet little thing home with me. I watch as her clutch slips off the bar top and she lets out a little yelp, nervously looking around to see if anyone noticed.

A short brunette sitting next to her says something I can't hear, and then belts out a loud laugh and nearly twirls in her seat like the barstool is gonna spin for her.

I hadn't noticed her friend before; too busy eyeing up that ass. My girl looks embarrassed by her friend but smiles anyway, shaking her head.

I can see the two of them being friends. A sassy over-the-top chick with a trendy bob and a more traditional beauty who'd keep her in line. I bet between the two of 'em, the brunette will be the first on the dance floor. I can only hope her friend lets loose and I can squeeze in to take her spot on the barstool.

Her gorgeous green eyes finally catch mine but she's quick to look away with an innocent blush. I let a smirk kick up the corner of my lips. She's fucking cute. And she's got a pouty mouth and a heart-shaped face that add to the innocent look. I'd love to see those lips wrapped around my cock.

I stifle a groan as my dick hardens in my pants at that last thought. It's been a while, a long while since I buried myself in some hot pussy.

She looks like a good girl though, and I don't think it's an act. That could be a problem. Or maybe it could add to the fun.

I've seen girls come in here acting all cute and innocent, but what they really want is some thick gangster cock. Just so they can say they got dirty with a bad boy. A few shots and they're taking off their tops, letting anyone in here play with their tits.

I take another look at my sexy-as-fuck blonde and she's still a little stiff as she orders a drink. Right now I wish Tony would let Cindy take over that end of the bar. He's quick to get their orders and adds a little flourish to the pour of citrus vodka before adding some tonic or some shit to it. A girly drink. Yeah, she's definitely a good girl.

Her friend orders a Long Island Iced Tea, and I snort. Of course she would. I clench my teeth. That drink could put a wrench in my plans. I'm not sure I want her friend getting wasted. I need Blondie coming home with me, not babysitting her reckless friend.

Blondie cocks her head and her friend holds up one finger. I grin. Good. Well that solves that problem.

The two of them keep chatting, but it's mostly her friend doing the talking while Blondie just shakes her head and smiles. I can't hear a damn thing they're saying over the music.

I wish I could. I'm trying to think of how to cut in and lay on the charm. But I don't know shit about this broad.

My girl looks like she doesn't belong here. And she doesn't. Neither of them do. This is where the Koranav hangout. Everyone knows it in this town. The women in here are dancing to catch our attention. The men are Koranavs or prospects, or maybe associates. They're all men who are in on the business. Everyone knows what this place really is. Cops too, but they can't prove a damn thing.

Not that it matters. This is just where we hang out and relax, not do business. To be honest, I still don't feel like I fit in here. Not unless Needles is with me, or Nikolai.

I may be under the boss's thumb, but I don't like associating with most of these pricks. I look to my right. Like Jackson. I could do without this asshole. Still, it's nice to get a drink. And in this town, this is *the* place to go to unwind.

Plus it's expected of me. If I didn't show up… well, that's not a good look.

This sweet little thing obviously doesn't know shit. And it doesn't look like her friend does either. I want it to be true 'cause that makes it all the more challenging, and it means she doesn't already have an opinion of who I am and what I do.

Blondie twists in her seat to reach down from her spot on the stool. The sight of her bending over to pick up her clutch makes my dick jump in my pants. Her long blonde hair sways gently as she sits upright and finally relaxes a bit.

I catch her peeking up at me through her thick lashes, but I keep my gaze focused on the TV at the back of the bar. I watch from the corner of my eyes as she takes a sip of her drink and a small smile slips into place. She sets the glass down carefully on the napkin and takes another covert look around.

The guys have eyes on her even though she doesn't

know it. Plenty of cops have come in here. We don't do business here for that reason. It'd be fucking stupid to.

It's obvious to me she's not undercover, but the easiest way to tell if a woman is a cop is to try to fuck 'em. Jackson gets up from his seat next to me and licks his lips. His eyes are steady on the two of them.

That's not gonna fucking happen. Not her, and not her friend. He'd blow this for me for sure.

I strong-arm him, stopping him from getting all the way up and his ass falls back onto the stool. A few people look up interestedly, including Blondie, but I don't give a fuck. I shake my head with a grin, and the fucker actually pouts like I just took away his puppy.

She's mine, and he's not ruining this for me.

He looks me in the eyes and grudgingly gives in. "Fine, she's all yours."

I may not be high in the ranks. Shit they may not even think I really belong here, but I can sure as fuck call dibs on whoever I want. Simply because I'm a tough motherfucker, and everyone in here knows I could take them if I wanted. Shit, Vlad wanted me as a muscle man in the mob. Took a lot of guts for me to tell him it wasn't going to happen. I wanted my shop and my art more than anything else. I thought it was going to be a showdown. Thank fuck for Nikolai.

Either way, I'm all hard muscle and every fucker in here knows not to mess with me. A few had to learn the hard way. A few others picked fights with me just to see if they'd win. I'd be lying if I said I wasn't a bit cocky about going undefeated. Either way, Jackson has a reputation for fucking. Mine is for fighting.

If I want something, I'm gonna get it and no one's stupid enough to get in my way. Of course if it was Vlad or

Nikolai, it'd be a different story. The boss and the underboss are two people I don't fuck with.

But they aren't here tonight, and no one's gonna stop me from pulling that dress up and feasting on that delicious pussy I know is between those thick thighs.

I down my beer and get up, ready to find out how sweet and innocent Blondie really is.

CHAPTER 3

MADELINE

Trouble.

That's the only word I can think of when I lay eyes on the stranger dressed all in black. Tall, dark-haired and incredibly handsome, the dude literally takes my breath away. At the other end of the bar with one other guy and throwing back shots of what I think is whiskey, he's sitting there, staring at me with an intensity that makes me shiver all the way from across the room.

I can't get over how handsome this guy is, tattoos and all. Seriously, I'm not one for tattoos, but this guy is so sexy that his ink only adds to his appeal.

I stare back, challenging him to look away. He doesn't, and I'm almost spellbound by the way he continues to look at me. His gaze is so intense that I swear that my ovaries are doing the hokey-pokey.

But why is he staring at just me?

I know I'm not ugly, but there's a sea of beautiful women on the dance floor who are probably more than willing go home with this guy and ride him like a mechanical bull.

Who says he's looking at me because he wants to take me home and have sex? I wonder, even though I know that's what most men in the club are here for. *He might just think I look good.*

I'm comforted by the thought and feel a surge of confidence at being admired, but the look in the handsome man's eyes says otherwise. It seems to say, 'You're mine, and there's nothing you can do about it.'

I'm suddenly irritated. This is a guy, I feel, who's used to getting his way with women.

Well, he won't have his way with me, I vow. *I don't care how hot he is.*

I'm about to turn my nose up, you know, to give him the proverbial snub, when the guy sitting next to him jumps up. I hadn't noticed him until this moment, but he's a hot piece of ass himself, and I wouldn't mind it if he came over to say hi. But oh no, Mr. Sexier's ass isn't having it. He jumps up right after him and practically strong-arms the poor guy back down into his seat. The two exchange words before Mr. Sexier turns his intense gaze back on me. My heart thumps in my chest.

Oh no he didn't.

"Holy shit!" Katie exclaims over the heavy thumping bass of the music and gawks. Just a second ago she'd been laughing with some annoying douche who'd bought her a drink, but apparently she has her eyes on the two of them, too. "Did you just see that? Dude just made that guy sit down like he was in time out."

My mouth open and suddenly dry, I'm unable to respond because Mr. Sexier begins moving through the sea of undulating bodies toward our end of the bar. Even the way he moves is sexy, gliding forward with incredible swagger.

"I gotta go," I squeak suddenly, ready to make a run for

it. There's no way I'm sticking around to be accosted by Satan himself.

"Oh no you don't, missy," Katie growls, clamping an arm down on my wrist and holding me in place. "You're going to sit right here until Mr. Tall Bottle of Champagne gets to meet you."

"Let me go," I hiss, watching the man, who's almost halfway to us. I can't believe Katie is doing this to me. I'm totally petrified. "I don't wanna talk to that guy."

Katie scowls at me in disbelief. "You're crazy. Do you see how hot he is?" She stares right at him, and I wanna hide. She's making it so obvious!

"That's the very reason I'm trying to get away. Now let go!" I try to pry her fingers off, but Katie is a stubborn bitch.

"No," Katie refuses. "You're going to give this guy a chance. Live a little."

Bitch.

I tug sharply, trying to disengage from Katie's grip and run for safety, but she suddenly appears to have the super strength of Wonder Woman and I'm kept in place. I'm about to summon everything I've got to shove Katie off her barstool, but too late. Trouble has arrived.

"Mind if I have a seat?" asks a deep, sexy voice that sends goosebumps up along my arm. I almost close my eyes as my pussy clenches with need.

I turn to look up into the bluest eyes I've ever seen, and my breath catches in my throat. Now that he's up close, I can see he's even more handsome than he looked from across the bar, if that's even possible. His features are perfectly chiseled, with a strong jawline, sharp cheekbones and a cleft in his chin. The way his dark hair hangs down just above his eyes makes him look all the more enigmatic.

I can see the tattoo on his arm clearly now. It's a serpent, and it's a beautiful piece of art. It wraps around his arm in a tight coil. The rest of the sleeve is jam-packed with a combination of scrolls and intricate designs, with layers of colors that blend seamlessly. I find my eyes focusing on all the detail and wondering how long it took. Hours, no, days. And holy hell, it must've hurt.

Katie turns in her seat and smiles up at the stranger, acting as if she hasn't just held me hostage. "Not at all, Mr.…?"

"Zane," the handsome man supplies.

Fuck. Even his name is sexy. There's no way I'm going to survive this. This is what I get for spending so much time away from men. The first one that gives me any attention is knocking me flat on my ass.

Katie beams and offers her hand. "Nice to meet you, Zane. I'm Katie, and this is my friend Madeline."

I lean over and whisper in Katie's ear, "I am SO going to kill you for this."

Zane quickly shakes Katie's hand and then offers me his. I stare at it for a moment like it's a snake before taking it. The minute our hands touch, I feel a jolt of electricity go up my arm. Seriously, it's like a thousand volts just shot through my body and I swear my hair must be sticking up like I just stuck my finger in a power outlet. I wanna pull away, but I can't. I'm paralyzed.

"Nice to meet you, Madeline," Zane says in that deep, throaty voice of his, shaking my hand, unaware that his touch is doing some serious things to my body. After a moment, he lets go of my hand and I feel a twinge of disappointment.

"Nice to meet you, too," I manage, but I'm barely audible over the music and I'm sure Zane doesn't hear me.

He doesn't seem to care though, and his eyes continue to burn into me.

Katie suddenly jumps off her stool. "I was just telling Maddy here that I needed to take a tinkle." She motions at the packed bar. "You can have my seat until I get back." Oh. My. God. She did not just say tinkle. Kill me now.

Before I can object, Katie takes off like a speed demon, leaving me all alone with Zane.

Katie, you are dead, I send telepathically, wishing bad luck on my best friend for her treachery.

Zane nods at Katie's seat. "You mind?" I catch a whiff of alcohol on his breath. Whiskey. I don't drink whiskey. Personally, I hate it. But the faint smell of it on his breath combined with his unique, masculine smell makes me want to lean into him.

Do you even have to ask?

I'm actually kind of surprised by Zane's manners, considering that he looks like a fellow who takes what he wants without asking.

Not trusting myself to speak, I shake my head. Zane grins and sits down next to me. Being this close to him, I feel my body temperature rise. I almost feel like I need a fan.

Not noticing my discomfort, Zane signals the bartender, but the man who poured my earlier drink nods to the female bartender. She's a slim brunette with big tits. She's in the middle of serving some guy a drink, but I swear she puts on speed boots to get over to us.

"What will it be, honey?" she rasps breathlessly, looking like she's ready to bend over right then and there and let Zane fuck her in front of the entire crowd. Suddenly I'm wishing the other bartender were here, and not this bimbo.

I start to look away to give them some fucking privacy,

but Zane doesn't pay her an ounce of attention and replies, "A cosmo for my lady friend here."

What the hell? I wonder. *Is he a mind reader, too?*

"Nothing for you, *Zane*?" she asks, putting emphasis on his name. I'm reading her loud and clear, but if Zane is, he isn't showing it.

"Nah," he says, putting a hand on my barstool, a little too close to my ass. "Just my girl's drink." *My girl's*? I feel a blush rise up my chest and into my cheeks. I have to admit, being called his girl feels nice. But I'm quick to push those emotions down.

The bartender looks at me for a second with disdain, and then she looks back at Zane and winks. "One cosmo, coming right up." She sashays off to the mixer, swinging her hips with every step.

I decide to ignore both his hand and claim on me and instead I gape at Zane with shock when she's gone. "How the hell did you know I liked cosmos?"

Zane grins, a boyish grin that makes my inner voice scream at me to run away now before it's too late. "I'm good at reading women." His eyes seem to say, 'That's not the only thing I'm good at, either.' And I believe it.

"Can you read my horoscope, too?" I ask playfully. *You know, the one that says that if I don't get away from you now, I'm in serious trouble?*

"Huh?" he asks and I almost laugh.

Instead I smile and toy with the empty glass in front of me, running my fingers down the stem and leaning into the bar. I shake my head and say, "Nothing."

The brunette's back in a flash with my drink. "Anything else, handsome?" She's trying hard to get Zane's attention, practically sticking her tits in his face. But he only has eyes for me.

"Nah, that's all." He tries to give her a tip, but she pushes it away.

"It's on the house," she purrs as another patron calls for her service. She leaves with a wink, saying, "If you need anything else, just holler. It's always my pleasure to please."

I'm not absolutely certain, but I'm pretty sure Miss Minx was letting Zane know that she's down to fuck whenever he's ready.

"Do you get that all the time?" I have to ask, even though I already know the answer. He's fucking hot. Of course he does.

Zane shrugs as if it's no big deal. "I'm used to it." He stares at me. "You're not from around here, are you?"

Yep. He's a mind reader.

Shaking my head, I take a sip of my cosmo. I'm impressed. It's actually really good. I half-wonder if she spit in it though, just to spite me. "No, actually. Katie and I are new in town. We move into our new place tomorrow."

Zane looks very interested. "Oh yeah? Where at?"

Alarm bells go off in my head. *Don't tell him where.* I don't know why I don't want to tell Zane where I'll be living. It's not like he would stalk me considering he can have any woman he wants.

"1212 Candyland Road," I lie. And the drink must be hitting me, because that is a horrible street name to think up. This town isn't that big. He's gonna know.

Zane makes a face. "Candyland Road? I've lived here all my life and never heard of that street."

I gesture vaguely and take another sip. "It's near the edge of town."

"Oh, okay." From his demeanor, I can tell Zane knows I'm bullshitting, but he doesn't press the issue. He gives me a grin and leans forward, looking like my lie was more amusing than anything else.

"Aren't you going to order yourself a drink?" I ask. I really don't wanna get wasted while he's sober. I'm actually surprised he's not showing any signs of being tipsy with those shots he downed.

"Nah. I think I've had one too many shots of whiskey."

"I saw." I smile playfully. "How about something a little lighter, then? Like my cosmo?" It's not in my nature to share a drink, but the thought of this man taking a sip from this girly glass makes me smile. Shit, maybe I'm already a little tipsier than I thought.

"Nah. Not my style. Besides, cosmos are pussy drinks."

I know I should be turned off by his crude words and the diss on my drink, but the way he says it summons up the image of him down in between my legs and his powerful jaws clamped down on me.

Jesus, I haven't even known him more than five minutes and I'm already thinking dirty thoughts. Get a hold of yourself, Maddy!

"Hey, they're not that bad," I protest, hoping he's not clued in to the dirty image flashing through my mind. My nipples are hard, and my breathing is coming up short though. I clear my throat and take a quick drink. I need to get a grip.

"I'll stick with whiskey, or vodka," he replies as he shakes his head.

"You're missing out," I say as I take another sip of my drink.

"Doubt it. I'm particular with my intake of sweets." The way he looks at me drives home his pun.

I nearly spit out my drink into his lap. Holy crap. Did the bastard know I was just thinking about him between my legs? I try hard not to let on that I'm picking up what he's throwing down, but judging by the smirk on his face, he knows exactly what I'm thinking. Cocky bastard.

"So what brings you two to this shithole town?" Zane asks, looking as if he's trying not to laugh at my reaction. "Wait, let me guess. You're both going to the state university?"

I gulp, trying to keep my mind clear of that image of him eating me out. "Yeah."

He grins. "I knew it."

"What about you? Do you go to college there, too?"

A dark shadow passes over Zane's face and I feel like I've hit a nerve. "No," he says flatly after a second. That heat flowing through my body chills some. He obviously didn't like that question. Shit, I'm not buzzed enough not to realize his displeasure. It was just an innocent question though. I retreat to my drink.

The beats of the music fills the silence that ensues, and I wonder if Zane's decided I'm not worth his trouble. I figure the conversations he has with the women in places like these usually revolve around how soon can he take them home to his bed, not getting to know you type stuff.

"So, what do you do?" I dare ask when the silence between us stretches on for more than thirty seconds.

Zane seems to perk up at the question. "I'm a tattoo artist," he says proudly.

"Really?" Tattoos really aren't my thing, but I have respect for people with artistic talent. "That's pretty cool. I've never known a real artist before." I turn in my seat to face him. I really like that he has a job that's… different.

"Yeah. I own my own shop, Inked Envy on Second Street." He points at the serpent tattoo on his arm. "I gave myself this one."

I gawk. The whole thing is so beautiful. "You did this yourself?"

He nods. That's impressive. I know next to nothing about tattoos, but I know that had to be hard.

"How?" I can't even imagine how long that took. I look at his right arm and see there's no tattoos on that arm.

"I'm good at what I do," he says matter-of-factly, without a trace of bragging in his voice.

"Wow." Unconsciously, I reach out to touch his arm, feeling along the length of the tattoo. His muscles bulge underneath my touch, and once again, sparks seem to pop off his skin.

"Your hands feel so soft," Zane says, grabbing hold of my wrist and pulling me in close. He runs his finger up along my arm, shooting off more sparks. "I could fix you up, free of charge. Would you like that?" It takes a moment for me to realize he's asking about a tattoo.

I have an immediate urge to say yes, but I don't, and I stare at him, trembling in his grasp. In that moment, I'm more afraid than I've ever been in my life.

I feel like he has absolute power over me. His question could have been, "Will you come home and have sex with me?" and I would have said yes.

That's it. I have to get away.

"Sorry, gotta go!" Not giving him a chance to respond, I jerk out of his grasp and quickly disappear into the crowd of people grinding on the dance floor. I look around for Katie, but don't see her beneath all the flashing lights. Moving as fast as I can, I make my way into the club's hallway and stop to rest against the wall.

I breathe in and out, trying to get a hold of myself, my legs shaking. All I can think about is how close I came to losing control, and Zane had only asked if I wanted him to give me a tattoo!

"Where do you think you're going, sweet thing?" asks a deep voice that makes my knees weak.

Oh no.

I try to make a run for it, but suddenly I'm sandwiched between the wall and a rock-hard body.

Fuck.

"Did I say you could leave?" Zane growls in my face. His voice is soft and sexy, not meant to be a threat, only a dare to stay. The smell of whiskey is even stronger on his breath at this distance. Instead of disgusting me, it only makes me more turned on. His hot breath makes my nipples pebble. My core is soaked and my pussy is clenching around nothing. This isn't good. I fucking *want* him. Every inch of my body craves him.

"Y-y-you're not my daddy," I stammer, ignoring every instinct in me.

"No. I'm not." Zane gives me a cocky grin, moving in closer. "But I can be... if you want."

I'm almost on fire. My dress seems to be rising up my thighs, practically inviting Zane in. "What are you talking about?" I have to close my eyes and will the naughty images away.

"I think you know," he whispers in my ear.

I do know. And it would be so easy to give in, so easy to just melt in his arms. And he *wants* me. He *chased* me. That has to mean something.

"You know you want it." He says it as if his words are a dare.

He's right. I do want it. So fucking badly. My body is burning. Every inch of me wants him inside of me, even right here in this hallway. I don't care who sees.

Zane inches in closer as if coming in for a kiss. If his lips touch mine, I know it's all over.

I can't do this!

"Get the fuck off me!" I yell out as the thought of him sliding my dress up and fucking me against the wall becomes a very real possibility.

At the last possible second, I summon every ounce of self-control I can muster and shove Zane away from me. Then I take off like a jackrabbit down the hall, and out the club, not daring to look back.

CHAPTER 4

ZANE

I watch Maddy's back as she practically runs from me. Her hands grip the hem of her dress as she pulls it farther down her thighs. She's speeding off like I just told her I was a hitman and she's first on my list.

What the fuck?

I stand dumbfounded in a lust-filled haze. She's leaving? It takes a moment and the sounds of the club filling my ears to realize she's really gone. I was two seconds away from crashing my lips against hers and inching her dress up to give her the release she needs. Well maybe not here, where anyone could watch, unless she'd be into that.

She pushed me away. What the fuck did I do? I replay everything in my head, but I don't know where I crossed the line.

She had to know I'd follow her out here. Shit, I know she didn't think I'd let her get away that easy.

And she was loving it. I know she wants me. Or wanted me. Fuck!

By the time I think about chasing her and head out to the exit, she's nowhere in sight.

I push past the crowd and jog my way to the front. She's not here. I check every dark corner, but Maddy's fucking gone.

I search the dance floor and find her friend. Fuck me, but I can't remember her name for the life of me. Did she even tell me?

She's dancing with a group of women, having a blast and not paying attention to anything.

I have to grab her arm to get her attention.

She whips around like she's gonna bitchslap me until she recognizes me. Her eyes dart around me and she looks confused. Shit, that's not a good sign. I was hoping Maddy went to her before going wherever it is she went.

I scream over the music, "I lost your friend!"

"Fuck!" she yells out and starts pushing past me and everyone else, making a beeline for the door.

I follow her outside. Shit, did I really chase her off to the point where she felt like she had to leave?

I turn to look at her friend who's now got her cell phone to her ear. She's got one finger shoved into the opposite ear to drown out the sound of all the people still waiting in line. The bouncer's watching us, but I give him a quick nod.

"You good?" he asks with his brows raised. I give him a short nod. I'm not really good though. This fucking sucks. And I feel like shit for pushing her away like that.

"Goddamn it," her friend mutters after looking down the sidewalk and shoving her phone into her clutch.

She makes a move to go back inside.

"Did she leave?" I ask her.

She shrugs her shoulders and says, "Sorry." She gives me a sad look and a tight smile before making a move to open the door. Fuck.

I get it for her, opening it wide enough, but I don't go in.

"You think you could give me Maddy's number?" I ask her with a little embarrassment. I don't think I've ever asked for a chick's number before. And definitely not from her friend. She looks like she's considering it, but then she scrunches her nose and shakes her head.

"I'm sorry." She really does look apologetic. "I'll bring her ass back here though." She nods her head confidently.

"That's alright." I watch her go in as my hope of seeing Maddy again dwindles.

I stand outside the club feeling the crisp cold air of the night against my skin. The bass of the music beats in my ears and it pisses me off.

Anger replaces confusion. Not at Maddy, but at myself. I knew she was too much of a good girl. I needed to play it smooth and slow, and instead I went for the kill too fast and freaked her out.

But damn, I couldn't help myself. Feeling her body against mine… I stifle my groan.

I just had my hands all over that lush ass. I could practically feel how tight that hot pussy was gonna be cumming all over my dick. Speaking of my dick, the damn thing is currently hard as fucking steel in my jeans.

What the fuck did I do? She was all over me. She wanted me just as much as I wanted her. She felt so good with her curvy body pushed against mine. And she would've felt even better impaled on my dick. She was so fucking responsive, and I can only imagine what she'd be like under me.

I take another look around the crowd and then back down the sidewalk to the left and the right. She's not there. Fuck! I pushed too hard, too fast.

I run my hands through my hair and clear my throat.

Well, shit. That fucking sucks. I close my eyes and remember the soft, sweet sounds of her moans. My dick jumps in my pants and I have to turn and head back inside.

I need a drink.

I make it halfway there when a hot platinum blonde with a tight ass and perky tits stops in front of me.

"Hey handsome, I was looking to get out of here." Her perfect white teeth bite down slightly on her bottom lip, drawing my eyes to her mouth. Vixen is the first term that comes to mind as I take her in.

"I could use a ride," she whispers in a low, sultry voice.

Her lips are almost the same shade of red as her dress, and I have to admit that any other night with my dick this hard, I'd take her up on her offer, but not tonight. Not after Maddy.

"Not tonight." I give her a tight smile and move to walk past her. Her eyes narrow and she looks like she's gonna yell at me for some perceived insult, but then she remembers where she is.

"Fine, asshole," she grumbles as she pushes past me with her fake tits brushing my forearm.

I watch her walk off sashaying her ass and going right for another Koranav member. Yeah, she just wants to get fucked by a mobster. Doesn't matter who. I grit my teeth, feeling more agitated than anything else.

As I head to the back, all the thoughts I've been avoiding start coming to the surface. Fuck, I was feeling so damn good tonight.

Maddy took that away. She was a beautiful distraction. But she fucking took off, and with every step I take I want more and more just to drown myself in a bottle to forget this shit. She could've distracted me tonight. She could've taken that pain away, even if it was just for the night.

I walk back to the bar and my stool is taken by some

redhead who's got her legs spread and wrapped around Jackson's thighs. His tongue is down her throat and his hands are up her dress. Usually I don't give a shit, but tonight it pisses me off.

"Wanna buy me a drink?" I turn my head to the left as I rest my hands on the bar and see a second redhead standing there. She's sweet and cute, not like the viper in the red dress from a minute ago, but I can't get Maddy out of my head. I give her a tight smile, 'cause it's all I can manage.

"Sure thing." I keep my voice even and casual. A smile lights up the broad's face. She's gonna be real disappointed in a minute.

I yell at Tony, "Her next drink's on me!" and then turn back to her. "Have a good night, sweetheart." I leave cash on the bar and head out, ignoring the protests from the pretty little thing I'm leaving behind.

At least she got a free drink out of it. She'll find someone else. I'm just not in the mood.

I turn on my heels, giving Tony a curt nod when he catches my gaze. He looks like he wants to ask a question, but I'm not one who likes to talk. He should know that by now.

I walk out the back exit where it's less crowded and get in my Audi without a second thought.

Damn, tonight could've been so fucking good.

* * *

THE DRIVE IS AN EASY ONE. I live close to work, and play close to work, too. It makes life easy.

I twist my hands on the leather steering wheel and grip on tighter. I fucking hate today. Not what happened, just the fucking date. It always reminds me of things I'd love to never have to think about again. Every year it seems to get worse.

As if knowing I'm feeling like shit, Nikolai calls. His name and number pop up on my dash and whatever fucking music was playing is replaced by a ringtone. I push the button to answer as the streetlight turns green.

"Nikolai," I keep my answer short, and my voice even. He's the underboss, and in a way the one person who saved me. I hardly talk to him or to the boss, Vlad. But every year he reaches out, without fail. He's the only one who knows how much it affected me.

"I'm sorry, Zane; I forgot." His voice is etched with sincerity, and I believe him. "I went to the club expecting to find you there, but they said you just left."

I trust him alone out of all the Koranavs. He never shows emotion. Never. It's something that makes you appear weak in this line of business. Even Vlad's anger and hot temper make him look like a loose cannon in my eyes. But on this date every year, Nikolai always opens up to me. He's done this ever since it all happened.

"No need to apologize. I'm doing alright." As I say the words, the pain comes down harder on me. I twist my hands on the leather again and glance out the window as I come to another stop. I just wanna get home now.

"I'd believe you if you went home with some pussy, but they said you didn't." He says it with a touch of humor in his voice and it gets a short, rough laugh from me. I run my hand through my hair and stare at the stoplight.

I remember the feel of Maddy's ass in my hands, and my dick starts to harden. Yeah, I'll be fucking fine. As long as I can work and fuck, I'm fan-fucking-tastic. I try to forget Maddy and her soft curves. Fuck. I close my eyes, willing my dick to not get hard for a woman I can't fucking have. I haven't jerked off in years, not when I can get laid whenever I want. I'm sure as shit not doing that tonight.

"Promise you, it's all good," I tell him.

"If you say so." From his tone I can tell he doesn't believe me. I don't blame him. Anyone who was forced to kill his father would be fucked up. Even if his father was an abusive fuck like my old man.

It happened years ago, but fuck me, I can't let it go.

I was only ten or so when I started stepping in front of my mom to take the hits. I couldn't stand the way he hurt her. I tried to protect her. I thought I was doing the right thing. I thought she loved me.

I woke up one morning to him screaming about how "the bitch left." The beatings only got worse after that. Because of course to my father, I was the reason she left. It's hard to imagine it wasn't true. Why else did she leave me with him?

My old man was more than just an abusive drunk though. He was a degenerate gambler, and got into some serious debt with the mob.

Nikolai, Vlad and two soldiers who are probably long dead came for him when I was fourteen. They found him beating the shit out of me, but I was fighting back. I didn't have much weight to me since I'd barely hit puberty, but it didn't stop me from fighting back.

The mob doesn't like witnesses though, even if they are just kids.

Nikolai spoke up for me. Said he'd teach me. Vlad put a gun in my hand and gave me a choice. Kill my father and join them, or die with him.

It might sound like an easy choice, but it was harder to pull that trigger than I thought it would be. So many nights had passed where I wanted him dead. I swore one day I'd kill him for what he did to my Ma, and what he did daily to me. But when it came time, I almost chose to die with him.

He stared up at me and instead of telling me to do it to save my life, he called me every name in the book and spit on me. Maybe he did it to make it easier for me. But maybe he really did fucking hate me.

I think you always love your parents somewhere deep down inside. Even if they don't love you back. Even if they don't deserve it.

If it wasn't for Nikolai, I never would've survived.

"Yeah, I'm alright. Just wanna crash tonight," I tell him. "I've got an appointment tomorrow I wanna get up earlier for." That's true in a way.

"Good to hear. It's always nice to get lost in your work." I can see him nodding the way he does. I grew up with Nikolai as my only father figure despite the fact he's not even a decade older than me. It wasn't optimal, but at least I had someone.

It sure is fucking nice to get lost in work. He taught me that. I'm not gonna lie, I was a fucking punk kid growing up. I graffitied everything I could. Got in trouble a few times for it. The first time I went to jail wasn't for fighting, it was for tagging an abandoned building.

Nikolai was pissed. He said the mob doesn't need delinquents, and getting in trouble for dumb shit puts a target on my back. So he got me a job at a tattoo parlor. They smuggled drugs out the back of it. I didn't care though. I just wanted to get my art out there. And Nikolai said it'd be good for me. He told me not to fuck up, and to take it seriously.

I got a reputation pretty fast—a damn good one, and the family hooked me up with my own shop. I was eighteen with my own business, and had clients who fucking loved me. The only condition the mob gave me was that they would handle the books, and they were free to use the back for whatever they needed. I signed that day without thinking much on it.

A few weeks in, Garret and Vlad came into my shop and told me they needed me to cover up a tattoo on a body. I wanted to say no, but I knew better. She was a young girl, maybe my own age, and a member of an MC gang. Garret tossed her on my table and said the tattoo that could identify her needed to be covered. Her body was covered with bruises of varying colors, making me wonder how long they'd tortured her. But what was worse was that she was still bleeding. They'd used a knife on her and mutilated her.

I almost threw up looking at the poor girl. Vlad said they'd "had a little too much fun with her." I kept my composure and quickly added a layer of art to the dead girl's tattoo, but I knew then what kind of sick fucks they were, and that I didn't want anything to do with them. But it was too late. I didn't have a choice. The memory sends a wave of sickness through me. I thought then that I'd have to get used to that shit, but it's only happened the one time. Thank fuck. Other than that day, they stay out of my business, and I stay out of theirs.

I hate being under the mob's thumb.

I can't deny that they could have killed me. Nikolai saved my life, and gave me something to be proud of. And I do love my shop and my work.

I wish it was just mine. After all, people come to me for a reason. They want a Zane original. My art on their bodies.

Maddy comes to mind as I think about how I'd love to put my art on her. I start thinking about what I'd go with, but then I push that thought away. It's pointless to think about.

I pull up to my condo, coming to terms with the fact that I'll probably never see her again. To my left I see a car I don't recognize at the neighbor's place. I'm always aware of that shit. Just in case. You can never be too laidback when you're involved with the mob.

I guess they finally got the place rented out.

It's a cute little car. I'd bet good money a woman drives it. I check out the tags as I lock up my Audi. The locks slam down, and a small beep rings through the night.

Georgia.

Whoever they are, they're a long way from home.

CHAPTER 5

MADELINE

"Watch what you're doing with that!" Katie yells at one of the moving men who's attempting to pick up a heavy ornamental vase from inside the moving truck. It's the day after the disastrous night at the club, and we're busy moving into our new condo. Despite what happened last night, I'm pretty excited about starting a new chapter in my life. "That's a special gift my mom gave me as a graduation present!" she squawks.

"Sorry," apologizes the young guy, who looks barely older than eighteen. He gently picks up the vase and carefully walks off the van, moving as if he's carrying something worth more than gold.

Hands on her hips, Katie growls, "You better be."

"Jesus, Katie," I complain, shaking my head and wiping at the sweat on my brow. It's a sweltering ninety-five degrees outside and I feel like going inside and flopping down on the floor and enjoying the cool AC, but Katie insists I help her oversee the moving.

At least I'm not one of these guys, I think with sympathy. *They're doing all this hard work for less than minimum wage.*

And to make matters worse, they have Katie making their lives even more miserable.

To fight the heat, Katie and I are dressed in cutoff shorts and midriff-baring tank tops, but I'm still sweating like a dog.

"You didn't have to be so mean to the kid. He hadn't even picked it up yet."

Katie turns to scowl at me. "Did we, or did we not pay these guys out of our hard-earned student loan checks?"

I snicker at the thought of our student loans being 'hard-earned'. I guess I know what she meant though, since it's not like we won't be paying exorbitant interest rates after college. "Yeah, but that doesn't mean you can just treat them like that--"

Cutting me off, Katie turns to watch the young guy make it off the moving truck and onto the sidewalk with the giant vase. "Okay then. I can tell them whatever I want, especially when they're handling things that are dear to me."

"Psycho," I mutter under my breath, giving up.

"Hey!" Katie screams when the guy almost trips stepping over the sidewalk. Luckily, he regains his balance without dropping Katie's precious vase. "Watch it, clumsy!" After the guy makes it into the condo unscathed, Katie turns on me with a murderous glare. "See," she says flatly.

"Why are you being so bitchy today?" I demand.

"Because I have a nasty hangover." About time she admits it.

"Maybe you shouldn't have drunk so much." I don't know why I even bothered responding though. She never listens to me. At least she didn't wake me up at 3 a.m. by puking into the toilet.

"Maybe you shouldn't have run from the club and left me stranded," she says without missing a beat. Fuck, that hits a nerve. I do feel bad about that. But what the fuck was I supposed to do? She wasn't going to leave with me, and I *needed* to get out of there before I did something I'd regret.

I wipe at a trickle of sweat running down the side of my face. "You know what? I'm too hot to deal with your shit today. Can we not do this, please?"

Katie bites her lower lip and says, "Sorry," even though I know she isn't. "Speaking of hot, I can't believe you turned down that Zane guy!"

"I can. The dude was an asshole." I'm not sure why I'm lying to her. Zane hadn't done anything particularly wrong, unless you can call making me want to have sex with him a crime.

Just speaking about him brings up the memory of how hot I felt against his body, and how much I wanted him inside of me. When he pressed up against me, I could feel it. His cock was fucking *huge*. Somehow I get a little hotter thinking about what he could have done to me with a dick that big. I can't help but feel a little regret, but I know it was the right move to leave him there. Wasn't it?

"Who cares? If it was me, I would've fucked him every which way but sideways even if he'd slapped me around and called me his bitch." She thinks for a moment, and her frown morphs into a naughty smile. "In fact, I think I would rather enjoy that."

"Katie!" Thank God my face is already red from the heat so she can't tell how much the idea of him doing that to me turns me on, too.

Katie looks at me with typical feigned innocence. "Wha? That guy was the hottest guy I've seen in a long time. I would've killed to have him lusting after me like he was after you."

"He wasn't lusting after me," I argue. "He just wanted to buy me a drink."

"He wasn't? Remember how he shoved that other hot guy down in his seat just to get to you?" Fuck, that *was* hot.

"Nope." The word comes out easy as I shake my head.

"Liar. You said he had you up against the wall in the hallway, ready to bang your brains out."

The image of his lips being inches away from mine flashes in front of my eyes and I try hard to push it away. I wish Katie would stop going on about Zane. Thinking about him just makes my temperature rise, and it's already hot as hell. "What does it matter now anyway? I'll never see him again."

Which is a good thing, I think to myself. *He was nothing but trouble.*

Katie shakes her head at me in sympathy. "You just don't get it, do you? You're so scared to live a little just because of what happened between you and Zach that you're missing out on the simple pleasures in life."

"How is going home with a total stranger and getting screwed by him 'missing out'?" I demand. "If anything, it cheapens me."

"Are you kidding me? That guy was hot as fuck, with a big ass dick to match."

"And how would you know what he's working with?" Despite my question, I agree with Katie. When Zane was pressed up against me, I felt his bulge. And if the size of it was an indication of anything, he was hung like a horse.

"Did you see the size of his nose?" she says with a wink.

I roll my eyes. "You're impossible."

"And you need to get laid. Preferably last night. Hey!" Katie yells at the other mover. "Don't carry that like that!"

Katie begins badgering this guy about how to properly carry a box of her precious items of God knows what, even going as far to follow him into the condo, leaving me alone in the hot sun.

I'm about to follow her in when I see a box with my name on it on the back of the truck. If memory serves me correct, it's filled with a bunch of personal hygiene products that I don't want anyone to see. I'll take my tampons in myself, thank you very much.

"I'll just get that, and then I'm staying in the cool air until they're done," I mutter to myself. "I don't care how much Katie bitches and whines at me."

I jump onto the truck and grab the box. It's not that heavy, but it's awkward, and I make it off the truck before I have to set the box down to try to get a different handle on it.

"Need help with that, peaches?" asks a deep, familiar voice.

Oh my fucking God.

I look up into that cocky grin and those beautiful blue eyes. Instantly, images of last night are back in my mind and I'm filled with burning desire. Dressed only in a pair of blue jeans that are ripped at the knees, Zane is standing in front of me with his shirt off.

I can only marvel at his incredible body. Seriously, his abs looked like they were etched by a grandmaster mason, chiseled to perfection. To make matters worse, a sheen of sweat covers his entire torso, and droplets are running down the hardened lines of his stomach muscles. I have to fight an extreme urge to want to bend over and lick it off.

If I thought I was burning up before, now I'm in the fiery pits of hell.

"What are you doing here?" I croak with disbelief, trying to keep my eyes level with his face and not that washboard stomach of his.

Zane's grin grows wider and his eyes seem to assess my body, making me feel even hotter. He's pleased that he's shocked me. "I live right there," he says, nodding to the condo that's directly next to mine.

I gape with shock. Seriously, I'm fucking floored. What are the odds? What are the odds that I meet this guy at the bar and run away from him, only to find out that he lives right next door to me?

One in a billion, I think to myself. Fuck! I can't run away from him now.

"You're shitting me."

Zane chuckles. Fuck. Even his laugh is sexy. "Nah. Actually, I was surprised myself when I saw you guys out here. I was like, no way. Apparently fate's decided to bring us back together again." The way he looks at me conjures up the memory of running from his sexy touch. His eyes are telling me I've committed a crime, and he won't let me get away with it.

"Then fate must be fucked up in the head."

Zane throws back his head and laughs again. "You're funny, I'll give you that."

There's nothing funny about this situation. I ran away last night because I knew Zane was nothing but trouble, and now fate's put him right next door.

Almost as if to torment me.

"And sexy," he growls throatily, his eyes roaming all over my body.

I suddenly remember what I'm wearing, daisy dukes that hug my ass cheeks and a cropped tank top that bares my midriff, and I blush furiously under Zane's appreciative stare.

God, he makes me feel so sexy. Wanted.

"Yeah, somehow fate changed the name of my street to Candyland Road without even telling me."

My cheeks heat with embarrassment. "It's alright peaches," he winks at me.

Right then, Katie comes back out of our condo with one of the moving guys in tow. She stops and stares when she sees Zane, her jaw dropping. After composing herself, she walks over.

"Well, well, well. Look at what we have here," she says with a huge smile plastered on her face.

"Hey," Zane greets her politely.

Katie encircles her arm around Zane's sculpted waistline and looks up at him admiringly. "Sup, hot stuff?"

I roll my eyes at Katie's silliness.

Zane chuckles. "Not much."

"Can you believe he lives right next door?" I demand. For some reason the sight of Katie's arms around Zane is irritating me, though I don't know why. It's not like we're an item. Or like Katie would ever go after a guy I liked. My brow furrows at the thought. *Do* I like him? It's nothing. It's fine. Whatever.

"Nope. Can you believe these abs, though?" she marvels, actually running her hands along Zane's muscular lines that are slick with sweat.

"Get your hands off him!" I snap with so much venom it causes Katie to jump away from Zane.

"Damn, Maddy, I didn't realize he was your property." I bite down on the inside of my cheek and stare at the house.

She's right. I don't know what's come over me. I ran away from Zane like he was the devil last night, and here I am getting pissed because Katie's admiring his perfect body?

"I'm sorry," I apologize to Zane quickly, my cheeks burning from embarrassment. "I don't know what came over me."

Zane has an amused smirk on his face. He doesn't look bothered by my outburst in the least. In fact, I think he liked it. "It's cool."

"And you were calling me bitchy earlier," Katie complains.

"Well you were," I point out.

"Says the one who just screamed at me for touching our hot new neighbor." She raises her voice on the last words and gives him a wink.

I ignore how much I hate that I feel jealous. "I didn't scream."

"You didn't? I think they heard you on the other side of town."

I roll my eyes with exasperation and turn to Zane. "Do you see what I have to deal with?"

Zane chuckles. "I think it's cute."

Katie sticks her tongue out at me. "See Maddy, even Zane takes my side."

"Hey," Zane protests. "Don't put me in the middle of this."

"You sure about that? The three of us would make a good sandwich."

I blush. "Katie!" Jesus. She's so embarrassing. I know she's joking, but he might not!

"Wha?"

I shake my head. "Never mind." I cross my arms and lean back against the van.

Katie badgers him with question after question about the area and I watch them interact, only half-listening to what he's saying. He keeps looking back at me when he answers, even though I'm not the one asking. And as much as Katie loves pissing me off, she's at least keeping her hands to herself. With every move he makes, his muscles ripple and glisten in the sun. It's not fair. Fate really is a bitch.

"So, you going to help us out then?" Katie asks him. It's only when he answers he's more than happy to oblige that

I realize he's staying to help the movers. Which means he'll be in our house.

"I gotta go inside," I bite out and push off the van.

"You alright?" Zane asks.

I fan myself and walk backward. "Just need to cool off."

"You're telling me," Katie says with a smirk. I roll my eyes and nearly fall flat on my face as I try to turn around and walk normally. Fuck. I am not looking back. I refuse to check to see if he saw me.

Despite saying I was going to go inside and enjoy the A/C, I watch Zane at work, admiring his glistening muscles and washboard abs until they're done. Which happens all too quickly. I fucking hated packing, but I'd go out and buy all of Ikea if I could right now. I wish I had some new furniture I could ask him to assemble for me, giving me an excuse to check him out some more.

I grab a case of water from the kitchen and set it on the table for the guys. It's the least we can do.

It looks like Katie has set her sights on a new man and is chatting with one of the movers as the guys walk out.

I give them a wave and yell after them, "Thanks again!"

My heart beats faster as Zane, at the very end of the line, closes the door, rather than walking through it.

Oh, fuck.

I can't run now.

I grab a bottle of water and walk to the kitchen to start unpacking, completely ignoring the fact that he followed me in here. This is bad. I'm hot and sweaty and worked up. My lungs aren't even working right.

I stand near the fridge and consider bending down to open the closest box, but I know I need to say something. I look up and I'm trying desperately not to stare at him and his sweaty, hot body. Trying desperately not to think naughty thoughts. Trying, and failing miserably.

He's leaning against the sink, looking at me with hunger in his eyes.

"Would you like a drink?" I offer the bottle, holding it out to him. He has to know I'm so horny I can't think straight, and I can't stand being this close to him right now.

"No. I'm good." He pushes off the sink and takes a step forward. I'd take a step back, but the wall is right there.

"Why are you here?" I ask him.

"You know why." I do, but I lie.

"No, I don't."

He walks over and pushes me up against the wall, cornering me. His sweaty body is inches away from mine. My chest feels tight.

A feeling of déjà vu sweeps through me.

"You owe me."

His eyes seem to say, 'You won't be escaping this time.' His hand grabs my hip. Not a single part of me even thinks about pushing him away.

"Owe you what?" I ask in a hushed voice.

"This."

He kisses me, and my body comes alive with electricity. Everywhere he touches me sends sparks of desire straight to my core. I groan and lean into him. He can have me, right here. Right now.

No, Maddy! You have to stop!

I don't know how I do it, but I summon the will to shove him away. "Get out!" I gasp, stabbing a finger at the door. I'm shaking all over. Just a few seconds more and I would have been ready to have this man's babies.

Frustration flashes across Zane's eyes, but it's gone in an instant. "If that's what you want," he says.

It's not what I want. I want him to take me right there

and fuck my brains out. Zane knows it, too. My heavy breathing says it all. I'm barely in control of myself.

I can't let him do this.

"Yes," I say weakly. "Go, please."

It's for my own good.

"Fine." He opens the door, but turns to give me a cocky grin as he says, "But I know you're lying."

When he's gone, I slump down against the wall.

"Oh Maddy, what have you gotten yourself into?" I whisper to myself.

CHAPTER 6

ZANE

I pull up to the shop with a huge ass grin on my face.

I fucking love how much I shocked her. That flush I saw on her cheeks makes my dick jump in my pants. I can imagine that blush on her chest, rising up to her cheeks as I pound her tight little pussy. Fuck, I want that. I groan as my dick hardens and my balls fucking hurt. I need a release. This broad has me so worked up.

Peaches. My sweet Georgia Peach. I'm definitely getting her under me. I don't give a fuck how hard she pushes me away. She wants me, and I want her.

I almost had her in her kitchen. I'm surprised she let it get that far. She's definitely losing her will to fight this. I'm enjoying it though, breaking down her walls.

I'll have to wait and play this right. I wasn't sure if she was really that sweet innocent thing I thought she was pretending to be at the bar. But she is. A little uptight, too. Which makes it all the more challenging.

"Yo, Needles!" My partner in crime turns around at the desk when I come in.

He's young. Just turned twenty-two last week, which was a fucking fabulous night out. He doesn't look it though. He's got pale blond hair and a patchy beard that looks like he's going through puberty.

Poor bastard. The clean-shaven look only makes him look that much younger. He tatted himself up pretty good to add some age to him. He did a shit job on his left arm though. That's how we met. He had to come to a professional to fix it up.

Ever since then it's been the two of us running this place. There are a few other artists working out of our shop. But we're the only ones here open to close, and we're the reason the shop is so well-known.

At first Vlad didn't like it. It's not good to be in the spotlight. But then he saw it as the perfect opportunity to launder some big accounts through here. I don't know how big, and I don't ask questions.

I set my keys on the counter and take a look around. The place is everything I ever wanted. The entrance is spacious and open with floor to ceiling windows, and a large granite-topped counter in the center. The back wall is lined with art we've done. There are four sofas, two on each side, and a coffee table in between the two sets. Photo albums of what we've done in the past sit on the table.

Two hallways lead to a total of eight rooms in the back. We're always comfortable while we're working since the other five artists helped decorate our rooms exactly how Needles and I wanted. Room six is our stockroom, and the last two are for the mob. They're always locked, and I haven't even looked in them for nearly a year. I like to forget Vlad has his hands in my shop. Some days I don't even notice when the Koranav come in and out. For the most part, we ignore them, and they ignore us.

It makes it easy for us both, and that's the way I like it.

It feels like home in here. I fucking love this place.

"What's going on?" he asks, turning from organizing a station cart. We've got all sorts of products for aftercare that the customers can buy.

He looks back over his shoulder and then does a double take. "What's going on? Why the hell are you so fucking chipper?" he asks with a grin.

"What? I can't be happy?"

"At eight in the morning? No. You're a real unpleasant fucker this early."

I laugh at him and take a seat at the counter. "Met a girl who keeps pushing me away."

He chuckles and shakes his head. "She's smart." He stands up and takes a last look at everything he's refilled. Looks good to me. I trust Needles to handle this shit. He can handle the business aspect of things.

"You take a look at your first client?" he asks and I know why, too.

"Yeah, gonna be fucking boring, but I got something fun planned later on." My first client needs a touch-up and his ink refreshed. It's fading and looking an ugly shade of green as a result. It sucks because it's mindless work, just coloring in what someone else has done. I'm gonna do some fading on it though. I'll give it a professional touch, but it's still mindless.

I hate doing those jobs almost as much as those damn anchor and butterfly tattoos. Nothing's worse than when a young girl comes in and picks a generic tat out of a book, something that I've done a thousand times. I could draw them with my eyes closed at this point.

If only I could get my hands on peaches. I bite down on the inside of my cheek thinking about how fucking smooth her skin was. I wanna press my lips against her neck and kiss down her collarbone. Farther. I'd kiss down her breasts. I know just how they'd feel in my hands.

I could put something there for her, something on the underside of her plush tits. Maybe have it travel down her side. Fuck, she'd be so fucking sexy with a touch of ink. She's got a beautiful sun-kissed tan. She'd look even more beautiful with my art on her. Not that she isn't already gorgeous.

But she's a good girl. I bet if she has anything on her body it's just some sweet little butterfly on her shoulder. And I didn't see a damn thing on her shoulder. Her tight body's just the perfect canvas for my art.

Just as I start thinking about every inch of her body and what else I'd love to do with it, Marky comes in. He's a regular. He's retired and comes in here all the time just to hang out. When we remodeled a few years ago he even did half the work. He didn't want to be paid, just wanted to be useful.

I gave him a free tat and we called it even.

I like that he comes in here just to hang out and keep us smiling. He brings a good vibe into the shop. Adds to the comfort of this place.

"Zane, Needles," he says in a gruff voice as he sets down a carrier with four coffees. He's got his own in his other hand. Trisha and Logan will be in soon to snag their coffees. Marky's pretty fucking reliable for bringing in the morning brew.

Trisha wasn't into it at first. She's a picky broad. But Marky was determined to break down her walls and it started with getting her latte right, or whatever the fuck she drinks. Out of all of us, she opens up to him first when she has something she needs to get off her chest.

"Yes!" Needles grabs his cup and doesn't even check the temperature before guzzling it down. I take mine in my hand, but I don't like mine kissed-the-fucking-sun scalding hot like he does. I vent the lid, giving it a chance to cool off some.

"Thanks, man. What are you up to today?" I ask Marky.

"Not much." Marky grabs his usual seat in the chair next to the counter. "Just needed to get out of the house this morning." He lost his wife a while back. They'd been married for nearly forty years before cancer took her from him. I know it still hurts him to live in the house they'd had together since they got married. But the stubborn fuck won't leave.

Can't say I blame him, but I don't envy him either.

"What's new with you?" he asks. "You look too fucking happy for not having had your coffee yet."

Needles snorts. "See, told you."

I look between the two of them like they've lost their damn minds. "What the fuck?"

"Just saying, you're not much of a morning person is all." Marky looks at me expectantly.

"I can't be happy?" I ask.

"Quit fucking around," he says, rolling his eyes.

"Met a girl," I say with my grin spreading into an all-out smile.

Needles laughs at me, and Marky cracks a smile.

"She's that good in bed, huh?" Needles asks as he slaps my back and sets his cup down on the counter.

The smile leaves my face. I don't wanna tell them I haven't tapped that yet. But at the same time, some part of me also kinda does. There's something about having to chase her that I fucking love.

"She's not that kind of girl," I say before taking a sip of my coffee, trying to play this cool.

Needles looks at me incredulously. "You're hung up on a girl you haven't even had yet?" Marky chuckles at him and leans back in his seat. Needles has no fucking room to talk. I don't even know the last time he got laid. He's all talk, no game. So he can shove it.

"Fuck off," I say. "She's a challenge. I like that about her."

His brows raise. "Ten bucks says she's too good for you. Either that or she's stuck-up."

My jaw tics at his words. I don't like either of those thoughts. I also don't like that the first one is true. Yeah, she's too good for me, but good girls love bad boys. So I have a shot. Even if she thinks she can get away from me.

"What's her name?" Marky asks, snapping me back to the present.

"Madeline, but she goes by Maddy."

"Madeline is the name of a bitch with a stick up her ass," Needles immediately blurts out. He says the words confidently, and he's real close to getting his ass kicked. I don't like it. I don't like how he's thinking about her, and that it's so easy for him to talk about her like that.

"Your fucking name is Cody. I don't think you have much room to talk, you preppy jock, you." Marky laughs at the two of us. Cody Lewinsky is as far from a jock as you can get. He's lanky and goth as fuck. At first I wasn't sure I'd like him, to be honest. And he didn't talk much during our first session. Apparently, he doesn't like other people inking him. Can't blame him for that though, because I don't either. As soon as I was finished with the first session and he saw my work, he started talking and hasn't stopped since.

We bonded over our shared passion for tattooing and I really got to know him. He's a funny guy, but real standoffish. I like the fucker though. And his art is on point and on trend. That's what people go to him for, and it works out nicely for the business.

"Where'd you meet her?" Marky asks as Garret walks through the front door.

Garret Duncan is best described as Vlad's go-to henchman. He's tall and classically handsome like Jackson is, but he's fucking ruthless and coldhearted. One look at him and you can tell. What's worse is the fucker doesn't like me. He sees me as a threat because the rest of the mob is too fucking scared of me beating their asses to fuck with me.

I'm no threat though. I have no intention of being any more involved with the mob than I already am. I don't want to be Vlad's lapdog. But Garret does, and he thinks everyone's a threat to that goal. I'm just waiting for the day he steps up, thinking he can take me. I'll be ready though.

"Garret!" Needles calls out as he walks toward us. "It's in the back." He keeps his voice even, but he's tense. No one fucking likes Garret being in here. But once a week he comes to get the cash.

It's a necessity. An unfortunate one.

As Garret walks past us with a simple nod and not a single word said, I see Trisha walking toward the front door. She spots Garret and does an about-face. She fucking hates him. Trisha is short and petite, doesn't have an ounce of muscle on her. She also doesn't have any visible ink on her either. She's tatted up though. She's got a UV tat on her back. It's fucking gorgeous.

When people come in, they're surprised a cute little thing like Trisha is an artist. She went to school for ballet, for fuck's sake. She's an artist through and through. And she's damn good at her techniques. Her specialty is in unique tattooing methods. She doesn't work much because of it, but she's happy with that.

Trisha can be a strong force when push comes to shove, but she's a smart woman. She avoids conflict whenever possible. And for her that means staying away from Garret, and the rest of the mob for that matter.

She'll come back when he's gone, I'm sure. I feel for her though. She's a damn good artist and a real sweetheart. I hate that I put all of them through this shit. But I'm firmly under Vlad's thumb. There's nothing I can do to change this shit. Maybe someday if Nikolai ever takes over things will be different, but I'm not holding my breath on that one. Not with Garret in the picture.

"So?" Marky asks, and it takes a minute to remember what the hell he's talking about.

"So what?" I ask.

"The girl, Maddy?"

The tight feeling in my chest lets up and an asymmetric grin slips into place. I can't fucking stand Garret being in my shop, but I can get the fuck over shit I can't change. I don't let things I can't help keep me down. If I did, I'd be one real miserable fucker. Besides, we're used to this. It's coming on four years now of this routine. It's easier to just ignore it.

"Met her at the club the other night." I take a sip of coffee and stare at the label. "Turns out she's my neighbor." I don't tell them she took off that night and now she's stuck with me. My grin widens; her ass really is stuck with me this time.

Needles chuckles. "That's a real fucking tease."

"You're telling me." I think about how she pushed me away. She's teasing both of us. I fucking love it.

"She's a good girl and real fucking smart, too." I took a look at her books when I helped her unpack. I have to admit, the more I get to know about her, the more I like.

"Sounds like she's out of your league." Garret walks past us as Needles puts his two cents in.

Out of my league? Probably. But I still fucking want

her. Besides, I'm just talking about a fuck. Every good girl likes a little taste of the bad boy.

"If she's a good girl, and she's not slumming it for the night, my money is on her staying far away from you." It's like he read my mind and he's determined to put me in a bad mood. I know how she felt with my body pressed up against hers. I know she wants me.

"What's that supposed to mean?" My fist clenches, and my brow furrows. What the fuck? Needles is like my fucking brother. He's supposed to be on my side.

"I'm saying she's too good for you." He takes a look up from the books and realizes how pissed off I am. "Not that that's a bad thing. She's probably stuck-up and wound too tight anyway."

"All 'cause her name is Madeline?" He doesn't even know her.

"No," he says in a hard voice. "'Cause you wanted her, and she turned you down. She's the bitch from the club who left you hanging, isn't she?" Fuck, I wish I hadn't told him that.

"Watch it. She's not a bitch." My voice drops low and I narrow my eyes at him. Yeah, she turned me down. Nothing fucking wrong with that. I need to take it easy and slow with her, but I'm going to have her. I fucking know I will.

He puts his hands up in surrender and gives me a look I've never seen from him before. A look as if he's scared I'm gonna kick his ass. And he should be scared. I don't like the way he's talking about her. This protective nature in me is something new to me. But I can't help it. I don't want my best friend talking about her like that.

"I'm just saying, if she doesn't like you, then that loss is on her. That's all I'm saying."

I let it slide and try to get this tension out of my shoulders and just relax. He's only looking to defend me. He doesn't like her for running off, but he doesn't know enough to judge. If he met her, things would be different. Just that simple thought calms me enough to let it all roll off my shoulders.

"Who's that?" Garret asks. As far as I'm concerned, it's none of his damn business.

"Just Zane's neighbor," Needles answers, and I wish he hadn't. I don't want Garret knowing about her. Or Vlad, for that matter. They sure as fuck don't need to know where she lives.

Garret's brows raise and a crooked grin grows on his face. I don't like it. My stomach sinks, and I have to set my coffee on the counter.

"She givin' you a hard time?" he asks with a wicked twinkle in his eyes. Both him and Vlad have been known to rough up women. That, and fuck women a little *too close* to being *too young*. My first thought is to make it very clear that I want him to stay far away from her, but I can't say that. Knowing him, he'd go after her if he knew that's what I wanted. Just to fuck with me, and just to hurt her.

"Not at all. She's just making me work for it." I try to come off casual, and I think it works.

Garret lets out a humorless laugh. "Well if you need any help taming her, I'd be happy to join in." A sickness rolls through me and Needles is quick to look away. His face is pale, and he keeps his eyes on the floor. He forgets all the fucking time who we're dealing with, and what Garret's capable of. I'm the only one in here who's a member of the Koranav. I'm the one who has to deal with these fucks. I try to keep the two separate, but I wish Needles would shut the fuck up sometimes.

Marky starts to say something, but I cut him off. "All good," I say. I'm quick to just shut it down. "If I ever need anything, I'll ask for it. But on this issue, I'm all good on my own." I hold his gaze, daring him to push any further.

He tilts his head and grins. "Alright then." I hope I didn't tempt him. I don't think I did, but I'm sure as fuck gonna be keeping a closer eye on Maddy, and Katie, too.

"Catch you boys later," Garret says. I give him a nod, still holding his gaze until he turns away.

It's quiet in the shop for a minute. I take a sip and cut Needles off as he starts to apologize to me. I shake my head and reassure him, "It's all good."

"So about this girl?" Marky asks. I stare back at him, wondering if I should even go for her. She is too good for me. I shouldn't bring her into this shit. I'll look out for those two if Garret starts coming around, but I shouldn't bring trouble to her doorstep.

"You really hung up on her?"

I cluck my tongue against the roof of my mouth. It's not like I wanna marry her. I'm just intrigued by the challenge. And I know she wants me. I remember the way she molded her body against mine. I remember the spark between us. Fuck, yes. I need to have the broad.

I clear my throat and give Marky a small smile as my first client walks through the door. "She's a real good girl who's gonna find out what it's like to be with a bad boy like me." I give Needles a smile which finally puts him at ease.

He chuckles as he says, "Yeah, okay. I'll believe it when it happens."

CHAPTER 7

MADELINE

For the next week, I avoid Zane like the plague. Not that I have any time to see him. My class schedule is packed, and I'm usually awake by six a.m. and home by seven p.m. on most days. I don't have much time after homework to do anything but argue with Katie over dumb shit and then turn in for sleep.

She gets on my damn nerves, but I love her. I'd be lost without her, and the same goes for her.

The bus I'm on comes to a stop a couple of blocks away from my condo. I get off after thanking the driver, mentally cursing that I didn't just wait for Katie to get out of her class so we could have carpooled. Though, I could have just taken the car home myself and left Katie there to take the bus.

I would have never heard the end of it, I think to myself. *Besides, riding on the bus wasn't that bad.*

That's one thing I hate about sharing a car in a strange town. I can't move about like I want. I'd love to go find a coffee shop and open my books up and just relax as I study.

I used to do that all the time back home. The walkability in my town was fabulous. Not here though. For a state college there's literally nothing around it. Main Street has four stores on it. Four! I'm not used to being so far away from shops. I wanna get out and go somewhere to unwind.

I smile as I remember the purchases I made before I left campus. Thank God one of those stores was a liquor shop. A glass of wine will make this economics homework far more enjoyable. Or at least less miserable.

The whole ride home I'd been thinking about the scene in the kitchen with Zane. How hot his body felt against mine, how much I wanted him to take me right then and there, and how close I'd come to giving myself over to him totally.

That would certainly make my night more entertaining. And God knows I need some sort of release. Badly. And soon.

Now my panties are soaking wet, and I can't wait to get home to change out of them. Inwardly I curse Zane for my affliction. If he would just stay away from me, I wouldn't be spending half my time thinking naughty thoughts and fighting my desire for him. I'm starting to wonder why I'm even fighting him. It's not like it'd be the worst thing in the world to give in a little. He'd be a distraction though. Not like a coffee shop where I could just pick up and leave whenever I wanted.

I can already tell he'd be an addiction. And then when I was at his mercy and begging for his touch, he'd break me. Yeah, that's why I need to stay away.

By the time I turn the corner and the condo comes into view, I'm tired. I've been walking across campus all day and the bag I'm carrying feels like it weighs a ton. My shoulders feel sore.

I'm halfway there when I hear, "You look like you had a rough day, peaches." The deep voice sends a chill down my spine, and I have to close my eyes.

Is this guy a ghost or something? Seriously, he always seems to appear without warning.

I turn to see Zane standing there with that cocky smirk on his face. His hair is slicked back, he's wearing blue jeans, and a white, short-sleeved shirt that shows off his bulging biceps and tattoos. Tatted and ripped. That describes him perfectly.

I don't know what it is, but he seems to get hotter every time I see him, I think, practically salivating over the sexy bad boy.

I scowl at him to hide my lust, letting him know he's nothing special.

"Where did you come from?" I demand coolly. I'm sure as shit not going to let him know how he really affects me. He'd only try harder if he knew how I've started thinking about him at night. His bedroom is right across from mine, and I'm ashamed to admit how I've peeked through my curtains a time or two. I've already decided we need to move when this lease is up.

Zane twists his chiseled features into a mocking pout. "Damn, I don't get a 'Hi, how are you?'"

I cross my arms across my breasts. "No," I say flatly. I want to say, *I'm not going to be nice to you when you make me feel so... sexually frustrated.* "Sorry." I tack on the sorry and only partly feel like a complete bitch. I need to push this guy away. He's no good for me. If that means I have to be a bitch, so be it. He'll get the hint and leave me alone.

Zane lets out a mock sigh. "Damn, and here I was thinking that you couldn't wait to kiss me."

Despite pretending to be bitchy, Zane seems to sense I want to kiss him. Badly.

It only further irritates me.

"No, what I can't wait to do, is go inside and take a nice hot shower."

Zane's right eyebrow shoots up. "A *hot* shower, huh?"

I curse inwardly for making myself an easy target, my face flaming from his implication. "Yeah, now out of my way." I barge on past Zane, intent on leaving him in the dust. But he's not about to let me get away, walking me down in two quick strides. Come on! What do I have to do to get him to pick on someone else?

"Not so fast, peaches. Let me handle that load for you." Without asking, he removes my bag from my shoulders. My arms slip the loops before I can stop them, and I whip around to face him. I swear sparks penetrate my shirt when his hands get near me.

"Better now?" he asks.

I open my mouth to say a biting reply, but then close it. Despite his playfulness, Zane is only being a gentleman to me, and I'm treating him like crap. Maybe I should stop being so abrasive toward him and give him a chance.

But that's what he wants, I argue with myself. *For me to let my guard down so he can get in. If he's being nice, it's only because he wants to win this little game since I'm probably the first girl that's turned him down in years, and he can't handle it.*

I do have to admit my shoulders feel a lot better without the heavy weight on them.

"Yes," I say grudgingly as I roll my shoulders. "But you didn't have to do that. It's only a few more steps."

"I didn't *have* to, but I wanted to." He seems so sincere that I immediately feel guilty.

I look away and give him a small, "Thank you. I really appreciate it."

"Anything for a pretty lady," he says, lightening up the mood.

I snort. "Please."

"Why do you always give me such a rough time? I'm just trying to get to know you."

"Because you're bad news," I say, "and knowing you is probably more trouble than it's worth." I have to be honest. Maybe if he knows what I'm thinking, he'll respect my decision and leave me alone.

Zane makes a hurt face. "Why do you have such a low opinion of me? What have I done to deserve it?"

I gesture at him. "Just look at you. You look like trouble in the flesh, the good looks, the tattoos. You have such a... bad boy vibe."

"Hey, there's nothing wrong with that. And since when did being good-looking and having tattoos become a crime?"

"Don't try to sit here and act like you aren't a player that hasn't been with a billion girls and doesn't have several girlfriends right now."

"I don't," Zane says. I don't fucking believe that, and I don't do liars. I *hate* liars.

"Sure." *I bet he probably has ten packs of Trojans in his pocket right now. The extra large kind.*

"What will it take for you to believe me?" he asks, and I don't even look at him when I answer.

"Nothing."

"Come on, you can do better than that. Ask me anything you want about my personal life, and I'll give you a truthful answer."

As much as I want to grill Zane on his past, I don't want to seem like I'm too interested. Besides, I doubt he'll tell me the truth about his sexual escapades. "I don't have to ask anything. You're a player, and that's all I need to know." The scene from the other night with the bartender flashes in front of my eyes, the way she looked as if she wanted Zane to fuck her right then and there.

I wonder if he's already been with her. She knew his name. *He must be good if she wanted seconds.*

"Okay. You got me. Yes, I've been with a few girls, and yes I haven't been a model citizen. But I can swear to you that I don't have any secret girlfriends or anything like that. In fact, you're the first girl in a long time that's intrigued me."

"I'm the first girl in a long time that's resisted your advances, you mean," I say bitchily before I can stop myself.

"Yeah, that too, and I can't lie, it makes me want to get to know you."

I knew it, I think to myself. *He's only after me because I haven't fallen at his feet like all the other girls in his life.* The second I do, he'll drop me like a bad habit.

Decision decided. There's no way I'm letting my guard down for him.

"Thanks for proving my point." I don't know why, but I wanna cry. It hurts thinking I was right about him. I knew it though.

"That doesn't prove shit," Zane growls. He seems irritated with my assumptions about him. I must say, he looks even sexier when he's angry. "And it has zero to do with whether I'm looking for a quick hookup. Which I'm not."

"Bullshit. The way you've pushed me up against the wall, twice I might add, suggests otherwise." As annoyed as I am, just thinking about our close encounters sends goosebumps up my arm and makes my clit throb.

Zane gives me an intense look that makes butterflies flutter in my stomach. "But you liked it. And you wanted it."

I open my mouth to swear at him in denial, but then snap it shut. It's true. I did like it. And boy, do I fucking want it. But luckily, I have enough wits about me to know that nothing good would come from doing the sideways tango with him.

"Sorry, I don't know what you're talking about," I say. My cheeks heat and he smirks at me. Damn it. Now *I'm* a liar.

"Don't lie, peaches. You just need to give me a chance, get to know me. All I need is one night with you to change your perception of me."

"Never," I swear, though inwardly I'm trembling at the prospect of having one night with Zane.

We reach the doorstep of my condo and I stop to stare at him. "Well?" I ask. I just need to get my bag. Have some wine and study. I need to focus.

He knows exactly what I mean, but he plays coy. "Well, what?"

I hold out my hand. "Give me my bag back so I can go inside," I order flatly.

Grinning, he keeps my bag out of reach. "What's the magic word?"

"Now!" I growl.

"Eeenh. Wrong."

I place my hands on my hips and give him the most murderous scowl I can manage. "I'm not saying it, so you can either give me my bag back, or you can get the hell out of my way."

He studies me, and I have the distinct feeling that he's loving my sass, judging by that cocky grin on his face. "You're a stubborn little peach, aren't ya?" he remarks, his eyes twinkling.

I continue to scowl at him. "Will you stop calling me that? It's friggin' annoying."

"You know you love it."

I hate to admit it, but his little nickname is growing on me. I'll be damned if I let him know that though.

"In your dreams."

"Indeed." He lets out a mock sigh when I remain unmoved. "Alright peaches, being the nice guy that I am, and even after how rude you've treated me, I'll let you slide with no apology--"

"Good--" I say, interrupting before he can finish. I try to snatch my bag out of his hands, but he evades me easily and says, "If you go on a date with me."

My jaw drops like a bridge during a siege. Zane just isn't going to take no for an answer. "Are you serious?" I should be flattered, but instead I'm shocked. And maybe a little scared. How long is he going to keep pursuing me? If he just wants another notch on his headboard, he could easily find someone else.

He nods. "I'll take you somewhere nice and show you I'm not the bad guy you think I am."

"No," I say after a moment. "I don't want to go on a date with you. Not now. Not ever."

Zane is shocked by my refusal, though he tries to hide it, and he stares at me for the longest time before finally saying, "As you wish." He comes forward and gently places my bag in my hand.

I snarl, "Thank you. Now have a nice day." I move to walk past him, when suddenly he grabs me and pushes me up against the front door.

"I didn't say that you could go in yet," he growls, his breath hot on my neck. Apparently he's not as shocked as he looked by my rejection. I'm doing a shit job at hiding how much he turns me on.

Why do I keep winding up in the same position? I wonder. Once again, I'm sandwiched between Zane's hard body and a hard place. And once again, I'm turned on to the max.

Oh fuck, I can feel his erection digging into my side.

Shit, shit. My pussy clenches. A primal side of me wants him to take me like this and fuck me against the door for being so rude to him. I bite my lip and feel my core heat for him.

His lips are so close to mine and I want nothing more than to kiss them, suck on them. Devour them. Down below, my pussy clenches again with longing. I'd let him punish me with that thick cock of his. This is bad. Why does he keep doing this to me?

Zane stares into my eyes, and I'm suddenly lost in his. All I can think to myself is, *Why am I resisting this man? Just give in. Let him take me. All of me.*

Yes!

By now I'm hyperventilating, burning up with desire. I feel like all my defenses are crumbling, like I'm a few moments away from being totally his. And I want it. I want him.

Zane knows this too and he gives me an arrogant grin. He moves in close, bringing his lips close to my neck. I can feel his hot breath on it and it's driving me wild, making my limbs shudder with anticipation.

Take me, I groan inwardly. *Take me right here. Right now.*

Zane trails his lips up my neck, grazing my flesh, all the way to mine. This is it. This is the moment he kisses me and I give in to him.

Ready to finally surrender, I close my eyes and wait, my breathing ragged.

A second later, Zane lets out a mocking laugh and I pop them back open.

"Sorry peaches, but I gotta go," he says, releasing me and stepping away.

I gasp as fury twists the insides of my stomach. The bastard just made a fool out of me!

"If you want to take me up on my offer, you know where to find me," he says in parting. As he walks off, he's wearing a cocky smile that says, *Payback is a bitch.*

In anger, I watch him walk over to his place and disappear inside, leaving me feeling sexually frustrated. Again.

CHAPTER 8

ZANE

I lean my head into the spray of hot water and run my hands through my hair. The water feels good, but it's not doing a damn thing for this erection Maddy left me with. I rinse my body, feeling a million times better now that I have the sweat of the day off of me. I got in the shower as soon as I was done helping her loosen up some. But fuck, what I need is definitely not a shower.

I almost have Maddy where I want her. She was so close. But she would have regretted anything I'd done to her. I know she would have.

And that's something I don't want. She's gonna be right next door to me. She can't get away from me, but I also can't get away from her.

It'll be nice once I finally get her impaled on my dick, but I need to make sure she's gonna be happy about it afterward. I have to admit, it felt fucking good teasing her, too. It felt real good, knowing she wanted me and leaving her to suffer with her little pussy in need. My dick jumps with the need to satisfy that itch for her.

My sweet little peach is too fucking stubborn. I know she wants this. But something's holding her back.

'Cause I'm a bad man. And she's too fucking good for me.

Anger rises up as I have the thought.

Maybe that's true, but she still wants me. And I can give her the release she desperately needs.

I walk out of the shower and feel the hot steam that's filled the room. I grab a towel and pat down my face and dry off my hair. I'm too fucking hot. I almost move the towel to my waist to cover myself out of habit.

But then I remember that she's right there.

Maddy's condo is parallel to mine. Our bathrooms are right across from one another. I'm sure she could see me from her bedroom, too. I lift the blinds and open the window. There's a few feet between the buildings, so it's possible that someone walking by could see, but it's real fucking unlikely.

If my girl is in her room, I bet she could get a good look.

I look down at my cock and stroke it a few times, I need it to look good. I lean against the wall and pump my cock until it's hard as steel. I think about how her breasts felt pressed against my chest, those soft moans that spilled from her lips, and that's all I fucking need.

Shit, precum's leaking out. It's been weeks since I've had a release. I need one bad. If she'd just let me in I could be over there in a heartbeat and have both us cumming like we need to.

I open the blinds and smile wide when I see her on her bed with a large ass textbook in her lap. Yes! I open the window as far as it'll go, my thighs hitting the windowsill, and I smirk when I see her head turn to me from the corner of my eye. I pretend like I don't see her though. As if I just open my window stark fucking naked all the time. She doesn't know I don't.

Knowing how she's trying to push me away, there's no way she'd ever do this if she knew that I knew she was watching.

Damn it's hard keeping the cocky smile off my face. I turn to my side and stroke my dick once. I hear her little gasp, but I make sure I don't look out the window. In my periphery I wait for her to get up and close the curtains, but she doesn't.

Fuck yeah, my girl likes what she sees.

My forearm rests against the wall and my face is just barely showing in the window. Just enough to take a peek at her, but she can still see the goods. And judging by her face, she's happy with the merchandise.

I feel fucking cocky, knowing a girl like her is being so bad just so she can have a look at me. I let out a small groan that she can hear, and stroke my dick nice and slow.

Her eyes widen and search for mine, but I keep my face hidden in the crook of my arm.

I can practically see the wheels turn as she considers what she should do.

Be a good girl and touch yourself for me. Come on Maddy, be my sweet little peach and give me something to work with. Fuck, I wish. But that's way too much for me to hope for.

She's a smart girl, I bet she knows what I'm up to. I can see the hesitation, but more than that, lust. For a second I think she's going to leave, or get up and close her curtains. But she doesn't.

She watches as I stroke myself for her. I angle my body so she can see how I'm trimmed up and she can have a better angle of that sexy "V" at my hips. I've been told more than a time or two that it's my best feature. I'm pulling out everything I have to show her what I've got. Fuck, I'm peacocking like a bitch, but I don't care. I want her drooling over me and wanting me more than she's ever wanted anything else.

Seeing that heat in her eyes makes it worth it. No fucking shame at all.

Fuck me. She moves the book off her lap and leans back against the bed. Yes!

I stroke myself again as another bead of precum leaks out. I use it to rub along my head, and I swear to God her lips part with a moan and her tongue licks along her lower lip.

Yes, fuck yes. That's my girl. Let loose, baby. My peach needs to unwind.

I picture her licking the seam of my dick, and I stroke myself faster.

I see her hand slip under the covers and I almost lose it. Fuck, that's so hot. She's so goddamned turned on by what I'm doing she has to touch herself.

I imagine myself on top of her right fucking now. I'd slip that tank top off her body and suck her hardened nubs into my mouth. I wanna feel the weight of those tits in my hand. I can hear her moan as I twirl my tongue and bite down slightly. I keep up my strokes and rub the bit of precum over the head of my dick.

Fuck, she'd feel so good. Her mouth, her pussy. I want it all. I want to feel how good she is when she cums on my dick.

I look out of the corner of my eye and she sees me. Her hand stops, and her mouth parts. She's been caught in the act. I turn to her and stroke myself again.

"Pinch your nipple," I mouth to her and she stares back at me. Right now's not a time for teasing. I can't fucking take another standoff ending with both of us still hot and bothered. I need to cum, and she needs it, too.

I tilt my head down and stare straight into her eyes.

"Do it. Now," I tell her. I know she wants this. It's now or never, peaches. Don't disappoint me.

Her left hand moves to her tank top and she pinches her nipple quickly through her shirt and lets her hand fall after that. I smirk at her. I'm not letting her get off that easy.

I shake my head. "Let me see." I stroke myself again and her eyes fall to my dick.

Fuck me, she licks her lips and her hand moves under the sheet. I should let her have this. I know I should. I could scare her away by taking control, but I need to push.

I clear my throat, drawing her attention back to me.

"I wanna see." She bites her bottom lip as a flush moves up her chest and into her cheeks. She looks so vulnerable, so damn beautiful. She nods her head and slowly pulls the strap of her tank top down, exposing her plump, milky breasts and small, pert nipples. Fuck, I want my mouth on her right now. For a second I think about going over there. But I don't want to risk losing her. I feel like the second I lose eye contact she's gonna run far away from me. I need to make sure she gets off.

"Pinch it," I mouth. She's slow to move, but she obeys. That in and of itself is an accomplishment. Finally, she listens to me. She gently pinches her nipple, rolling it between her finger.

"Again." She keeps eye contact and pinches it again before taking the other strap down and doing the same to her other nipple.

Fuck, I'm so close to cumming. This broad has me wrapped around her finger and she doesn't even know it.

"Harder." I give her the command and she moves both her hands to her nipples, but I shake my head.

"One hand. Play with yourself." She stares at me for a

moment and I wonder if she heard me right. But then she slips her hand back down.

"I wanna see." That right there is the line. She shakes her head and the same fear I keep seeing in her eyes is there. I stop my movements and consider going over there right now and showing her how fucking good it's gonna be when she surrenders to me, but then I think twice.

This is a broad who needs time and space. I have to earn her trust. I can give her that. I can show her she can trust me.

I repeat my words, "I wanna see you." She shakes her head slightly and I don't push for more. "Don't stop, peaches." I stroke myself again. "Cum with me."

She's slow to move, but after a long moment she does. And I feel so much fucking relief that she does.

That's my girl.

I start pumping my cock, watching her ease back against her headboard.

She spreads her legs wider under the covers, but she leaves the blanket there covering herself.

Even covered, she's beautiful and tempting in every way. Maybe even more so since she's still hiding from me.

"Again." I give the command aloud and her eyes widen, darting to the narrow path between our buildings, but there's no one there, only us in this moment.

She bites down on her lip and pinches her nipple hard. Yes. Fuck, yes. I quicken my pace and give her another order.

"More." *More.* That's what I want from her. More of whatever she'll give me. I give her the command and watch as her back arches from how intense her touch is. I wish I were there. I wish I was the one giving her that pleasure.

I watch as her head tilts back, and her orgasm rips through her body. Her lips part and I faintly hear her moan as she cums from her own touch. It's the hottest thing I've ever seen.

My spine tingles and my balls draw up. Oh, fuck. *Maddy.* I moan her name as I cum. I cum violently, leaving a mess everywhere as hot streams pour into my hand.

I breathe out deep and look up just in time to see her pulling the curtains closed and I have to smile.

The next time I cum, it'll be inside her pretty little pussy, that's for fucking sure.

CHAPTER 9

MADELINE

"God, I can't decide what I wanna wear," Katie complains, twisting sideways to look at her ass in my bedroom mirror. I'm sitting on my bed, having watched her complain for the past twenty minutes as we get ready for class. I think what she's wearing, blue jeans and a colorful blouse, is fine, but for some reason Katie simply can't take my advice. She's tried on at least ten different outfits and each one has something wrong with it.

"For the millionth time," I say with exasperation, Just wear that. You look fine." I don't know why she insists on asking for my advice if she isn't going to listen to me. But then again I don't know why she keeps coming in here, knowing I'm going to say the same thing. She's looked perfectly fine in everything I've seen so far.

Katie is still twisted to one side. "I would, Maddy, but it makes my ass look flat."

"But it is." I hide my smile. She does have a flat ass. She's got a skinny waist and wide hips I admire though.

Katie turns to glare daggers at me. "What did you just say?"

"Your ass *is* flat," I clarify. "Flat as a pancake." I don't let on that I'm fucking with her, partly to get back at her for keeping me prisoner while she tries on her entire wardrobe.

Katie rushes forward, grabs a pillow off the bed and lobs it at my head. "Bitch."

I dodge it, giggling. "I'm only kidding!"

Katie crosses her arms over her breasts and scowls. "No you're not!"

"I am. I swear." I put my hands up in surrender, but apparently she's really pissed off.

"I don't believe you, Miss Evil. But you know what? Your ass isn't exactly anything special either, so there." Katie sticks her tongue out at me.

"Oh honey," I warn, "don't go there."

"Why not? You just did." Touché. But I didn't say it to hurt her. I'll try being honest with her, see if that doesn't make her less pissy.

"I only said it to get you to stop complaining."

"That worked out well, didn't it?" she asks with a bitchy tone. What the ever loving fuck? She better be kidding.

"It stopped you from complaining, didn't it?" I point out.

Katie sighs. "I knew I should have picked Vanessa for my roommate. She would have never had the nerve to tell me I have a flat ass."

"Hey!" I protest.

Katie sticks her tongue out at me again. "Now you see how it feels."

I cluck my tongue. "You need to get laid." She's either PMSing or seriously deprived of sexual gratification.

"*You* need to get laid. I can't believe you pushed Zane away for a second time."

If only you knew what happened last night, I think to myself. While I told Katie about my episode with Zane in the kitchen, she has no idea about our encounter the previous day, and I'm not sure if I'm going to tell her about that. *Or how close I am to having wild, crazy sex with him.*

"Have you seen him at all since moving day?" she asks, interrupting my thoughts.

Oh yeah. I've more than seen him.

Images of his naked, hard, chiseled body and big, fat fucking cock flash in my mind and my temperature starts to rise as I relive the events from the previous day. It felt so good to relieve some of that tension that had been building since we first met. Still, there's a lot of tension left, and down below, my pussy starts to feel moist and my clit throbs. In vain, I try to push these naughty thoughts away, cursing how horny they make me.

"Are you okay?" Katie asks, peering at me with concern.

"Huh?" I say breathlessly. I'm literally in a daze. Seriously, I'm about two seconds away from shoving Katie out of the room and spending some quality time with my rabbit, my favorite vibrator.

"I asked if you'd seen Zane."

"Oh. Nope," I lie. "I haven't seen him."

Katie frowns with disappointment. "It's a shame you won't give him a chance. I'd kill to have a guy that hot that crazy over me."

"Why would you? You'd be killing for a guy who probably has several different girlfriends that don't even know about each other." And that's it right there. I know he can have anyone he wants. There's nothing special about me except that I keep pushing him away. So the moment I sleep with him, it'll be over and I'll be crushed. It's a horrible fucking position to be in... because I *really* wanna fuck him.

Katie taps her fingers against her chin. "You know what? You're probably right."

"I know I am."

"I still wouldn't let that stop me from having at least one night with him. Shit, if I were you, I'd be over there riding him right now." She grins wickedly, as if imagining all the naughty things she'd be doing with Zane. "Some early morning foreplay before class."

"Katie!" I flush. Shit, I'd love that. And he's right there. He's so close.

Katie makes her customary fake innocent face. "Wha?"

I smack a palm against my forehead, and shake my head. "Never mind. I just can't with you."

Despite my objection, I can't help but think about what Katie said. How I would love to be over there right now, riding Zane's big fat cock, feeling him pump those powerful hips beneath me, thrusting deep inside of me with powerful force. My clit throbs in response to my fantasy, and I unconsciously touch myself.

"Maddy?" Katie asks, looking closely at me with curiosity.

I snatch my hand away from my lower stomach, my heart pounding, shocked by how close I've come to touching my myself in front of my best friend.

Screw you Zane, I rage, *for making me feel this way, for making me lose control.*

I have no idea how I'm going to get through the day with all these dirty thoughts running through my mind. There is no way I'll be able to focus. I might as well stay home.

This is why getting with a guy like Zane is no good. We're not even an item yet and he's already affecting my school performance. And my sanity.

"Yeah?" I say, trying to play it cool.

"You alright?" she asks with a cocked brow.

"Yeah, why?" I clear my throat and can't even look her in the eyes.

Katie shook her head. "I dunno, you started panting and looking all funny and then you were reaching down for your… umm... hoohaw. Got a yeast infection?"

I scowl with indignation. "Heck no!"

"Oh. Because I do," she says with a shrug.

"Okay, that's TMI."

"Why?" Katie complains. "Aren't we besties that are supposed to share everything together? Anyway, it itches like hell! I was scratching my stuff so much this morning that my labia turned all--"

"Katie!" I yell.

"Wha?"

"TMI!"

We spend the next ten minutes arguing over whether Katie should just wear what she has on or change into another outfit until I point out that if we don't leave soon, we'll wind up late for class. After a quick breakfast of Corn Pops and OJ, we walk outside.

It's a cool morning, the sun is radiant, and the sky is crystal clear. It's beautiful. It's so pretty here. It doesn't have the walkability of being in the city, but I'm starting to love this place.

"It's a beautiful day today, isn't?" Katie echoes my sentiment.

I'm about to respond when something that's even more beautiful appears out of the condo next door. His hair slicked back, Zane looks like he's stepped out of GQ magazine with his dark pants and dress shirt that's opened at the chest, exposing the tanned bronze skin underneath. I swear I can see my tongue rolling along the lines of his chest. His shoulders are so broad, the shirt stretches tight over his muscles. Fuck, he's so hot.

With swagger to die for, Zane walks up to us with a playboy grin on his face. It's hard to look him in the eyes. I just want to stare at his dick, as if it's out on display again.

I'm not sure what the protocol is for watching your neighbor masturbate, but my plan is to just ignore it and hope he doesn't say shit about it. I'm just going to pretend like it never happened.

He better not say anything. My heart beats faster in my chest. I can see him teasing me for it. Holding it over my head. Shit! And then Katie will know I lied. Fuck, he better not.

"Are you stalking me now?" I demand, trying to act cool and confident when I'm really shaking inside. All I can think about as I look at him is how hot he looks naked and about his big fat, pulsating cock.

"Hey," Katie protests, "you don't have to be so rude to Zane, Maddy. Geez."

Unperturbed, Zane chuckles, a deep throaty sound that does strange things to my nether regions. "Don't be so vain, peaches, I have to work, too."

I snort. "Well those are some pretty nice clothes just for a tattoo parlor."

"What can I say? I like looking good."

And you smell good too, I think to myself. Zane's wearing a spicy cologne that turns me on big time. I wanna know what it is. I think I read somewhere that we remember scents the most out of all the senses. I wanna remember this smell. It's like a masculine scent that was made just for him.

I'm stumped for a comeback. I'd be lying if I say he

looks bad, because he looks like sex on legs. Hell, he's practically a sex god, Zane Adonis Whatever-the-fuck-his-last-name-is.

Katie giggles. "Dude, you look more than good, like a million bucks!"

I shoot Katie a murderous glare for her treachery. She's supposed to be on my side.

Zane grins at Katie's compliment and then says, "But maybe I did decide to leave the second you came out."

"See. You're a stalker." I hold back my smile and the small thrill I get from him admitting it. It shouldn't make me so freaking happy, but it does.

"But I won't have to be one if you'd just hang out with me, preferably by watching a movie or something."

Katie leans in and growls into my ear, "Maddy, if you don't say yes, I'm going to possess your body and have violent sex with him." I have to laugh from her threat.

I'm silent for almost a full minute, my mind racing, before I finally say, "Fine. You win. I'll hang out with you."

Victory flashes in Zane's eyes, but he's not surprised. He knew I would give in eventually, the arrogant bastard. "A movie at your place it is. What movie would you like to see?"

"I heard Deadpool is good," Katie chimes in.

I turn to Katie and scold, "He didn't ask you!" I turn back to Zane and deadpan. "Deadpool."

Zane laughs while Katie mutters something under her breath about finding a place to hide a dead body.

After Katie and I exchange a few more feisty barbs, Zane says, "You girls are hilarious, but I gotta get going. Got a busy schedule up at the shop." He nods at Katie and says, "See ya." And to me, "Catch you later, peaches." I blush at his words and tuck my hair back behind my ear. Shit. This is not good. He's really affecting me now. Shit!

Katie squeals with delight as we watch him walk off. "Peaches! I just love that nickname. It's so frickin' cute."

I roll my eyes. "Oh please, it's obnoxious you mean." No it's not. I fucking love it. Damn it.

Katie turns to me, a big grin on her face. "You know why he named you that, right?"

"No, why?"

"Because he wants to eat you out."

I smack Katie on the arm and she howls with laughter. "I'm so done with you, Katie Butler!"

"I'm serious. He thinks you taste sweet, and he probably thinks about your juices, rolling down his chin while he's in between your…"

I plug my fingers in my ears. "I'm taking the bus!"

Katie laughs even harder, going red in the face.

"It's not funny!"

"Oh yes it is. You should've seen your face!"

I roll my eyes and walk off to the car. A few minutes later, we're driving down the road toward the university.

"Will you watch the movie with us and be my third wheel?" I ask, interrupting Katie in the middle of singing a Katy Perry song. It's gonna be bad if I don't have her there. I already know it. I'm ready to cave. I can't let it happen. I'm… I'm scared. That's the truth, and I'm embarrassed to admit it, but I am. I'm so scared that I'm on the edge of a cliff, and he's gonna fuck me and then throw me off.

Katie glances over at me. "Hmm. I dunno, Maddy. You've been pretty awful to me."

"I have? How?" She actually sounds hurt, and that worries me. I feel like I'm losing myself; I can't lose her, too.

"Well, let's see here, you said I have a flat ass."

"I already said that was a joke."

"And you didn't want to hear about my itchy vag." Okay, now I know she's joking. Thank fuck.

When I open to my mouth to curse, Katie holds up a hand. "Okay, okay, don't pull out your machete. I might watch with you."

"Might? What do you mean *might*?" I make sure to put a hint of a threat in my voice, because I *need* her there.

"I just don't understand why you would want me there. I mean, the guy is hot as all hell. I wouldn't want to share him in the least."

"That's the very reason why I need you to come. To keep me from doing something I regret. I mean, we're going to be in the living room on the couch together, all alone and in the dark..." My voice trails off as I think about how hot the setting sounds. I could just imagine us on the couch, Zane's lips on my neck, my hands stroking his rock-hard cock through his jeans. Just thinking about it makes my body shudder with anticipation.

"That sounds like the beginning of a porno movie."

"Katie," I growl.

"Alright, alright. I'll be there."

I lean across my seat and give Katie a brief hug. "Thank you, Katie." She really has no idea how much this means to me.

Katie looks over at me and winks as she says, "You're welcome... peaches."

I resist the urge to kill her and settle on a death glare.

CHAPTER 10

ZANE

Fuck, I don't think I've ever been nervous like this before. It's stupid. It's not like I'm some dumb kid trying to get laid for the first time. But that same anxiety is racing through my blood.

Maybe it's the challenge? The fact that I don't *know* this is going to end in a good fuck.

That's gotta be why I'm so damn nervous. I wanna make sure I do this shit right so she'll give me more. 'Cause I sure as fuck want it.

I did my homework. I've got a funny movie she's gonna love, Deadpool. I heard the guy gets pegged though, not sure how I feel about that. And I picked out some flowers for my girl. She seems like a girl who'd like sunflowers.

Something about her tells me she'd like them more than other kinds of flowers.

I almost went traditional with a dozen red roses, but I think she'd like these better. I fucking hope she does.

I knock on the door and wait. I look down at the flowers. Shit, this is stupid.

I've never fucking bought flowers for a girl in my entire life.

I almost chuck them behind the bushes, but then the door opens.

My jaw drops slightly and my heartbeat slows.

She looks fucking gorgeous. She's in a shift dress that fades from white to pink and ends mid-thigh. It's not hugging her body, it's loose. I could rip that up and off of her in a second flat. She's teasing me by hiding her curves under that dress, but I already know how voluptuous she is.

My lips kick up into a smirk as I ask, "You get dressed up just for me, peaches?" I have to tease her. It wouldn't be the same if I didn't.

She looks like she's going to say something smart, but then she sees the flowers. She blushes a bit and rocks back on her heels. "Did you really get me flowers?"

The way her voice softens and color rises into her cheeks, I think I struck something in her. A chink in her armor. Fuck yes, sunflowers are my new favorite flower. Not that I already had one to begin with. But if I can get her guard down with a bouquet, I'll get one for her every day.

I hold them out for her to take and then lean in. My hands grip the door jamb and I take a peek inside.

"You letting me in?" I cock a brow and wait for my words to sink in.

Her smile falls comically and she rolls her eyes before turning her back to me and walking straight back toward the living room. "I'll take that as a yes."

I take a step in and close the door behind me. Her place is the mirror opposite of mine.

Except it's littered with Ikea furniture and girly shit.

"Hi Zane!" Katie bounds down the stairs with a bright

smile on her face. "You're looking scrumptious today," she adds with a wink. This girl is ridiculous, but I love how Maddy whips around and gives her the evil eye. My girl's a bit jealous. Usually that's a turnoff, but on her, I fucking love it.

"Hey there, Katie," I greet. My brow furrows as I watch her swing around the staircase and head in the wrong fucking direction. What's this shit? She's gotta get her ass upstairs or preferably out of the house. The only reason I even suggested we do this here is because I knew Maddy would flat-out say no to a movie date at my place.

I walk back to the living room and find Katie taking a seat on a slipper chair in the far corner and Maddy walking into the room with the sunflowers in a vase. She sets it down on the coffee table and completely ignores my look as she walks back to the kitchen.

The look that's saying, *What the fuck is your roommate staying here for?* Katie pulls a throw blanket over her lap, completely ignoring me, too.

Maddy walks back in with two bowls of popcorn. They've got red and white stripes on them, obviously meant for movie dates. She hands one to Katie, who's apparently in charge of the remotes.

I follow Maddy to the sofa, choosing my battles. Specifically, choosing not to make this a battle. She's sitting under a blanket with a bowl of popcorn on her lap continuing to pretend she can't feel my eyes boring into her skull.

"You're gonna miss it if you don't sit down." Maddy doesn't even make eye contact with me as she says it.

If that's the way she wants to play it, fine by me. Katie's in for a show then.

I toss Katie the movie, giving in to this little battle. "All yours," I tell her.

She grins, loving that she gets to stay for this show-down. That girl is trouble and she fucking knows it.

I take my seat next to Maddy and spread my arms out over the back of the sofa. I don't even mention the obvious.

A few minutes tick by of Maddy and Katie exchanging small talk as Katie fast forwards to the start of the movie. I just watch, letting them get comfortable. The two of them take covert glances at me occasionally. I keep a smile on my face so they know I'm fine with this.

Honestly, it's fine with me. It's not gonna be fine for Maddy in a minute. But for right now, it's all good.

I try to look straight ahead and watch the movie. My peaches is leaning against the armrest, her feet are a few inches from me and she's got the blanket over her lap.

I have to figure out a way to play my next move right.

I'm sure as shit not gonna be a good boy and stay seated during the movie and have her kick my ass out as soon as it's over.

Fuck that! That's not a date. And she promised me a date.

I pick her legs up and put them on my lap. I have to hold in a laugh as a piece of popcorn falls from her mouth and lands on the floor. I've obviously startled her. She looks back at me nervously, eyeing me up and down. I keep my hands on her calves and start giving her a massage. My thumb kneads into her muscles, not too deep. Just enough to give her a soothing touch.

I wait for her to say something. To tell me to stop, but she doesn't.

Katie laughs at something we both missed. I look at the screen and a dude's getting shot.

I look back at Katie, that fucking psycho. She's cracking up.

I shake my head and grin. I look at Maddy and see she's picking at the bits of popcorn left in her bowl.

I'm quick to take it out of her hands and lay it down on the floor. She doesn't need another distraction. As I set it down I slide in behind her so my chest is to her back. She's stiff at first, but she gives in to me.

Yes, good girl. Progress.

She clears her throat and tries to lean away from me slightly.

That's fine, she can play like that.

I slip my hand under the covers and rest it on her thigh. I don't squeeze, and it's on her outer thigh and over her dress. As if it's just a simple touch and there's no intention of going further. Her breathing picks up, and she knows exactly what I'm doing.

She turns against me and opens that smart mouth of hers, but I cut her off before she says anything.

"Shh, the movie's on." I keep my eyes on the screen as Katie turns.

"Hush, Maddy." I can't help the rough chuckle and wide smile as Katie admonishes Maddy.

Maddy presses her lips into a tight line and backs her ass up hard into my dick.

Oh, damn. I bend over her body slightly and hold my breath for a second. "That was real fucking close, peaches," I whisper in her ear.

She turns back to give me some of that lip, but Katie cuts her off.

"Guys!"

Maddy looks back at Katie likes she's ready to snap. I fucking love this. It's more entertaining than any movie I could've picked out.

I take advantage of the two of them engaging in a stareoff and slip my hand up Maddy's dress.

Katie gets a sly look on her face and whips her head to the TV. I'm sure my girl gave it away. But I don't give a fuck.

She arches her back as I move my hand to her pussy. The sight of her pushing her breasts out like that makes my dick even harder.

Her eyes go wide and I lean in close to her, resting my head just behind hers.

"Shh," I tell her and plant a kiss on her neck.

Her breathing picks up, but she lets me. She looks back at me and bites her lip, but she doesn't say anything.

Yes!

I tap her thighs, waiting to see if she'll let me go farther, and she does. My girl must need this 'cause she's not fighting me.

That sassy mouth of hers is closed, and her legs are spread just enough for me to get her off. I chuckle in the crook of her neck.

My stubborn peach is at least willing to put her guard down long enough to let me get her off. Maybe she's thinking she'll just get off and leave me hanging, and to be honest, I'm fine with that. For now.

Her chest rises and falls with her heavy breathing and she licks her lips as I slip my fingers past her panties and circle her clit. My dick is hard as steel as I feel how hot and wet she is. Damn, she's good at putting on a front and denying herself what she wants.

I watch as her eyes go half-lidded and her lips part.

What I wouldn't give to be able to bite that lip right now.

I circle her clit and nip her earlobe as she whimpers. "Quiet," I whisper into her ear.

She tries to keep her expression neutral, but her eyes close as my fingers dip into her hot, wet cunt.

Fuck, she's going to feel so fucking good on my dick. I pump my fingers in and out, stroking her G-spot and press my palm to her clit.

I'm so fucking hard, I'm leaking precum.

I gotta get her off and try to get Katie outta here, cause I *need* to be inside her.

I feel it the moment she cums. It's fucking perfect.

Her pussy clamps around my fingers and her body trembles. She shoves her ass into my dick and I can't help but to rock a bit into that thick ass so she knows how much I want her.

An explosion on screen muffles her small gasp. She throws her head back and I catch her lips with mine.

It's fucking perfect.

And then I see Katie get up and tiptoe her way out of the room from the corner of my eye.

CHAPTER 11

MADELINE

Explosions jolt my body, and it's hard not to cry out as I throw my head back. Zane's thick fingers continue to assault me even as I spasm around his fingers and press my ass against his big dick. My breathing quickens, my vision blurs and the room spins as pleasure becomes my existence.

I don't know how much time passes before I come back to earth, but when I do, Katie is mysteriously gone from the room and Zane is staring at me with a big satisfied grin on his face.

Wow. I can't believe I just let him do that, I think with shock, falling out of Zane's lap and shuddering. But it felt good. Incredibly good. And I want more. But how could I let this happen in the first place?

It's Katie's fault, I blame. *She was supposed to keep this from happening.*

I search for her in a panic and find she's nowhere to be found. Shit! Did she see? Or did she leave before things got so heavy? Was it her way of giving Zane permission to have his way with me? I bet she fucking did. Whatever it was, she's gonna pay dearly for her treachery.

Damn you, Katie!

I decide to take my anger out on Zane. "You asshole!" I snarl.

Zane looks bewildered. "Huh? Why are you mad at me, peaches? I was just trying to loosen you up."

Oh, you loosened me up alright, I think wryly, trying to keep my eyes level with his face. I'm painfully aware of the huge bulge in his pants and my juices all over his fingers.

"Our date is over." I stab a finger at the door. "Leave. Now." I'm not sure why I'm being this way. This man just gave me the best orgasm of my life and now I want him to get away from me before...

Zane doesn't budge. "Come on. Our date can't be over, especially after that."

But *that* is the very reason our date should be over. Because I'm too fucking scared of what's coming next.

"Oh yeah? What do you think we should do then?" I don't give him a chance to answer and instead say accusingly, "I know exactly what you want to do."

Zane stares at me with a hunger that is palpable. "I ain't gonna lie, peaches. I want that sweet, tight pussy of yours cumming all over my dick. Right now."

His words almost make me swoon. Seriously, the way he says things, he could open up his own phone sex line. And the bad thing about it is, I want exactly what he wants. Even though I just experienced an explosive orgasm, I'm ready for another one. So fucking ready.

"I've wanted you since the moment I laid eyes on you," he continues. "You're smart, sassy, sexy and very funny. And I haven't ever met a girl like you, so how can you blame me?"

I stare at him, fighting my raging hormones, fighting

my emotions. With each passing second, I'm losing the battle. After just cumming all over his hand, it's hard to justify not giving in and letting him have his way with me. Fuck, I want him to use my body.

"Just give me one chance, peaches," he reasons, his voice dipping even lower than I thought possible. "To cherish you, worship you, and... be inside of you."

That's it. I can't take it. I want him to fuck me like he owns me. I want *him*.

I grab him by the hand and lead him upstairs. My heart pounds in my chest and my body heats with equal amounts of anxiety and desire. We fall back on my bed and he doesn't waste a moment to kiss me passionately. His hands roam all over my body as our tongues do battle, and I moan with need. Maybe I knew this was going to happen. I couldn't avoid it. He wants me, and he's a man who always gets what he wants.

Before I know it, my dress is being ripped over my head and I find myself in just my bra and panties. Zane moves to remove my bra, but I stop him, my heart pounding in my chest.

"Wait," I gasp.

"What?" His eyes are burning with fiery intensity, his breathing ragged. He looks like a man that's run a mile and is thirsty as fuck.

I tremble beneath that hungry gaze. "I don't know if we should do this." How I'm still resisting right now, I have no idea.

Zane is having none of it, and begins undoing my bra, his eyes promising pleasures beyond my wildest dreams. "Come on peaches, let me show you what you're missing." He brings his lips forward and kisses me up my neck until he reaches my lips, which he devours, sucking and gently biting on them.

It's over. I'm fucking done.

As he lays me back on the bed and begins to take off my last pieces of clothing, dismantling my resistance bit by bit, I finally surrender myself to him. And somewhere, through all the moaning, I hear him whisper in my ear, "And you're going to fucking love it."

CHAPTER 12

ZANE

I see her defenses fall down around her. I see the vulnerability in her eyes. Her lips part, and a soft moan escapes. Finally! I crawl toward her slowly and press my lips against hers. I'm not going to let her regret this.

I moan into her mouth, and slip my tongue in, massaging hers and enjoying her hands tangling in my hair. *Let go, peaches.*

She rocks her pussy against me and it's almost more than I can take.

I'm so fucking hard for her. She's all I've wanted for so long. I want this to last.

I gently pull her bra free of her arms. She shakes out her hair and tries to cover herself from me shyly.

"No you don't, peaches." I can see the hesitation in her eyes and the distrust. My girl doesn't like to be told what to do, but that's only because of another man doing her wrong. She'll learn to love what I do to her.

She'll learn to trust me. I'll show her.

"I wanna see you. I wanna see every inch of your beautiful skin."

I lean down and kiss her neck. She tilts her head, letting a soft moan of pleasure escape and exposing more of herself to me.

My fingers grip the edge of her panties and I'm slow to pull them down her thighs. I kiss my way down, loving the feel of her beneath me and the way she writhes from my touch. I plant kisses on her breasts, her sides, her hips. I look up at her and leave one on her clit.

She looks down at me with a vulnerability I'm growing to love.

I take a languid lick of her heat.

I groan and close my eyes. Peaches. "So fucking sweet." A beautiful blush colors her cheeks. I stare into her eyes as I suck her clit into my mouth and massage it with my tongue. She tries to keep my gaze, but her head falls back and her hands fly to my hair.

I suck harder and slip two fingers into her soaking pussy.

Fuck, she's so tight and hot. She's going to feel like heaven on my dick. I curl my fingers and stroke her G-spot, needing to get her off again so I can get inside her.

I *need* her.

I kick my pants off as she cums on my fingers. Her arousal leaks out of her pussy and I'm quick to lick it up. Her body jerks and trembles, and her eyes close tight as her release takes over.

I push my boxers down and cage her small body in under me.

I line the head of my dick up as the last of her orgasm flows through her. I dip into her pussy slowly, loving how tight and hot she is for me. I hold my breath as I push all the way in, making her back arch. Her nails dig into my back and her forehead pinches as she struggles to take all of me. I kiss the crook of her neck and give her a moment to get adjusted to my size.

She feels so fucking good. I knew she would. I groan against her neck. I knew she'd feel just like this.

I rock slowly and listen as her moans of slight pain become moans of intense pleasure. It doesn't take long until she's rocking her pussy and pushing me in deeper. Her heels dig into my ass, begging me for more. And I give it to her.

I don't hold back.

I thrust into her, holding her hips down so she forced to take all of me and everything I'm giving her.

Over and over I impale her with my dick. She screams out my name and it's the sexiest fucking sound I've ever heard.

I need to cum, but I don't want to yet. I don't want this to be over.

I've finally gotten a taste of her. I've broken down a wall I'm not sure she'll leave down for me. I know there's a good chance that the moment this is over, she's going to regret it. And I don't want that. I can't stand the thought that she'd ever regret being with me.

I push harder into her. I pound into her tight little pussy with everything I have, holding back my need to cum.

Her neck arches, and she screams out as her body trembles beneath me. The urge to cum is strong, but I don't. I won't. I want more.

I need to give her more.

I cover her nipple with my mouth and suck, keeping up my ruthless pace.

Her body pushes against mine as she screams, "Zane!"

Her scream is a plea. I know this is intense, but I'm going to give her everything I've got.

I pull back and release her nipple with a pop before doing the same to the other side. My blunt fingernails dig into her hips, holding her still as I pound away, taking pleasure from her, but giving her so much more.

"Cum for me, peaches," I whisper in her ear. And just like the good girl she is, she obeys.

The feel of her hot cunt pulsing around me is more than I can take. I erupt inside her, releasing wave after wave of hot streams. I cum harder than I ever have in my life.

I give her short, shallow pumps until I'm spent.

I look down at her, her eyes closed, mouth parted. Her skin is flushed with the most beautiful pink. She slowly opens her gorgeous green eyes and I can see everything in them.

She can't hide a thing from me.

I see her desire, her fear. I see her for who she really is.

And I want her.

I need her.

I refuse to let her regret this.

CHAPTER 13

MADELINE

I hear the door creak open and I become slightly annoyed. I don't like being woken up before my alarm clock goes off. Katie should know that by now.

"Go away!" I growl at her from under the covers, pulling them tighter over my head and burying myself in the warmth of the bed. It's too comforting. I'm not getting up.

If Katie knows what's good for her, she'll leave me alone and go on a run by herself.

A soft smile slips into place as I hear the door close and I'm able to relax slightly. I prepare to drift peacefully back to sleep.

But then I hear a sexy chuckle that causes my pulse to quicken.

"You're not a morning girl, peaches?" Zane whispers.

I have to blink a few times and lower the covers, but only enough to see him.

Crap, I have no makeup on. I'm in an old baggy t-shirt... I look like shit.

And oh my god. Morning breath.

No, he cannot be here.

I totally kicked his ass out last night for this very reason.

I mean I was as nice as I could be, but I don't want to ruin this before it even starts because of my morning breath!

I open my mouth to tell him to get out, but he crawls on the bed toward me with a heated look in his eyes. The look of a predator.

I shake my head and sit up slowly, backing away from him.

He smirks, like it's cute.

"How the fuck did you get in here?" I ask him, just to change the subject from you-can't-fuck-my-brains-out-when-I-have-morning-breath to anything else.

He smiles, and I'll be damned if he doesn't look completely doable right now. He hasn't shaved, so he has a sexy bit of stubble I want to feel scratching on my inner thighs as he eats me out. His hair looks wild, and it's begging me to run my hands through it. But I still haven't even processed what happened last night. He left me exhausted and sated. I kicked him out, took a quick shower and crashed. Hard.

"Katie let me in."

"That bitch!" Fucking Katie is going to be my downfall.

He laughs at me and cocks a brow as he says, "I can see why she said good luck."

I bite my bottom lip and look down at the covers. What happened last night was amazing. I can't deny that. I can't deny how alive I felt under him. But I'm too scared to fall for him so quickly. It's not safe. And I know that's what's going to happen if I'm not careful. I can't let it happen.

I have to protect myself.

"Zane, I--"

"Shh," he puts a finger to my lips. "Don't think about it." My lips soften against his finger and he pulls away. "I just need you this morning." He leans forward for a kiss and I reluctantly give in. I can't deny I want him. I'm tired of fighting.

"Let me make you feel good."

I try to talk, I have every intention to object, but the soreness between my thighs reminds me of last night. My clit throbs as if I've been primed and ready for him since he left.

He pulls me down under him by my hips and I let out a small shriek.

He grins at me as he says, "You need to be quiet, peaches." He lifts my t-shirt up high enough to kiss my belly. "In case Katie comes back," he whispers against my pussy. His thumbs loop around my panties and with a quick tug, he shreds them into nothing.

My eyes go wide and my mouth opens into a perfect O as he licks my clit and pushes two thick fingers inside of me. Yes! He feels so good.

My nipples harden and I remember pinching them for him. I remember how he came watching me. I quickly pull the t-shirt off and do it again. My fingers roll my hardened peaks and then I gently pull. There's a spike of pain that's hardwired to my clit and I fucking love it.

He taught me that. He gave that pleasure to me.

He looks up at me from between my legs with a hunger that makes my pussy clench around his fingers.

He groans, "Fuck, baby. I need to be inside you."

He sits up between my legs and moves his dick back and forth between my pussy lips, pushing in before I have a moment to even think.

Fuck, I barely think as my head falls back.

I hold in my breath as he pushes his rigid cock deeper and deeper.

The stinging pain of being stretched to my limit combined with the ache from last night makes it almost too much. But then his thumb rubs against my clit, and the delicious mix of pleasure and pain makes my body crave more.

He stills deep inside of me and kisses my neck, my jaw, my lips.

I arch my back and then tilt my hips. I need more of him. More.

As he thrusts his hips, I let out a strangled cry of pleasure.

My head thrashes, but he grips my chin and crushes his lips against mine.

I feel like I can't move; I don't even want to breathe.

I only want him.

He kisses me with a passion I thought I'd imagined last night.

I kiss him back with everything I have. No thought, only feeling. My body is moving on pure instinct. He devours my kisses like they were meant for him and him alone. My nails dig into his back, and I urge him on.

He pounds into me, taking more and more of me each time.

He pulls away and takes in a breath, pulling his shirt off. His muscles ripple, and the sight alone makes me clench around him.

He owns me in this moment. I know it. He knows it. He towers above me with power and lust. And I *love* it. I *want* it.

He doesn't ask, he merely flips me onto my knees and hammers into me from behind, taking me how he wants me. I can barely hold this position. My fingers dig into the mattress and I struggle to stay up as he fucks me ruthlessly. The wet sounds of him slamming into me again and again fill the room. I feel so weak and helpless, but more than that, deliciously used. And overwhelmed with a pleasure I've never felt before.

He leans down, pressing his chest to my back. His deft fingers find my clit and he rubs mercilessly.

Too much. Too much.

I bury my head in the pillow and he bites and sucks my neck and back, alternating with kisses. All the while fucking me with a relentless pace. I arch my back and he goes in deeper. Fuck! I moan into the sheets, biting down on them to muffle my need to scream.

And just when I think it's too much, and I can't take anymore, we both cum violently.

A blinding white light flashes before my eyes, and paralyzing pleasure flows through me.

He kisses my spine all the way up to my neck. He grips my chin in his hand and kisses me like he needs me. My heart swells, and I find myself kissing him back passionately. In this kiss I'm not holding back, I'm kissing him with the same intensity he's giving me.

As my orgasm leaves me and reality sets in, fear begins to overwhelm me. I didn't want this. I don't want to be in a position to get hurt again. And that's just what he'll do. Like all men do. My breathing speeds up, and the only thing I can hear is my heart pounding in my chest.

"You have to go," I tell him as the tears threaten to reveal themselves.

I've fallen too hard, too fast. I'm only going to get hurt.

"You okay, peaches?" he asks. He asks because he cares. But that'll change. I know it will. And I'll be stupid enough to believe he really does care about me. I'll be the one getting hurt, and it'll be all my fault.

"I'm fine, but Katie's going to be back soon." I wipe my eyes with my back turned to him. But he sees.

He grips my arm and makes me face him.

And I can tell by the way he tilts his head and gives me sad eyes, that he knows I'm going to lose it any second.

CHAPTER 14

ZANE

Fuck, I don't know what happened, I don't know what I did. But she's already trying to run from me. I'm not gonna let her.

"Come here." I pull her into my arms without giving her an option to leave me.

As soon as she's in my arms, she starts crying.

"Did I hurt you?" I know it's a tight fit and I was a bit rough with her, but I thought she was loving it.

I finally got her underneath me, and I took it too far. Fuck! I've never hurt a woman like that before, but I lose control when I'm with her. I can't believe I hurt her. I feel like such a selfish prick.

She shakes her head in my chest, and I don't understand.

"Tell me what to do," I say as I sit back on the bed and pull her into my lap. Our cum leaks out of her and onto my leg, but I don't give a fuck. I'll clean her up later.

"I'm scared, Zane," she whispers so quietly I almost don't hear her say it.

I smile gently into her hair. My chest feels like a

weight's lifted off of it. I didn't hurt her. She just thinks I'm going to.

She's too sweet. Too much of a good girl. But now she's *my* good girl. I'm going to make sure she knows it.

"You're scared I'm gonna hurt you?" I ask her.

"Yes," she heaves a breath and lifts her face away from me. Her cheeks are reddened and tearstained, but somehow she looks even more beautiful. Her vulnerability and raw emotion are things I find even more gorgeous. I fucking love that she's sharing with me. But she wasn't going to. She was going to push me away. That shit's not happening.

"I know how guys are," she says flatly. Huh? Where's all this coming from?

"What's that supposed to mean?" I ask her.

"Guys cheat--"

"Women cheat, too," I say as I cut her off. I'm nipping that shit right in the bud. I stare into her eyes, willing her to tell me what the fuck is going on in her head.

"Yeah, well, men are good at making up excuses for it and telling you that they love you and making pretty promises all the while thinking about fucking someone else." She's tense and on edge, and I get the feeling this isn't about me, and it's not about us. It's about something else.

"Women cheat too." I stare into her eyes, willing her to tell me what the fuck is going on in her head.

I pull her closer to me and tell her truthfully, "Whatever asshole did that to you, didn't deserve you." Her eyes widen slightly and I add, "I'd never do that."

I take her chin between my fingers and make her look at me. I brush my lips gently against hers and rest my forehead on hers.

"Listen to me, Maddy," I start to tell her. My heart thumps in my chest with anxiety. I'm making her a promise in this moment. But I know she'll be the one to break it.

"I'm here, and I'm not going anywhere."

She opens her eyes slowly and looks at me like she's afraid to believe me.

"I'll be yours and only yours, if you'll be mine," I offer her.

She wipes her tears away and searches my face. My heart stalls in my chest as she seems to take forever.

"Don't leave me hanging, peaches. Haven't you done that enough?" I ask her with feigned desperation.

That gets a laugh from her. I fucking love that sound.

"Deal," she says simply with a small smile and a spark of happiness in her eyes.

"You wanna go somewhere later?" I ask her to change the subject.

"Where?" she asks with a little pep in her voice that wasn't there a moment ago.

"The parlor," I suggest. I've been wanting her to come see it. If I give her a little more of me, maybe she'll relax and just enjoy this. My eyes roam her naked body as she tries to cover herself with her bed sheet. I'm tempted to rip it out of her hands, but I let her cover herself. She needs it.

"You mean where you work?" she asks, and my eyes snap up to meet hers.

"Can we bring Katie?" Maddy asks. "She's been wanting to check out a tattoo parlor for some time now." I think that'll make her happy, and if it means she'll say yes, then fuck yeah Katie can come. She seems better when she's got Katie around her, more at ease.

"Sure. I don't see why not. It'll give Needles someone to talk to."

Maddy frowns. "Needles?"

"He's a friend." I'm trying to be casual about it all, but

really I'm excited. This is my passion, and Needles is a good friend of mine. Really my only friend.

She seems a little giddy at the prospect of getting to see where I work.

"And maybe you'll agree to get a tattoo from me," I add.

Her eyes widen like I've lost my mind. "I don't know about that."

"Oh come on," I lean in and kiss her neck before whispering in her ear, "Tattoos are sexy."

She leans away and seems to consider it.

"What kind of a tattoo do you think I should get?" she asks and then purses her lips. I know she's the kind of chick who would detail out every curve of a tattoo before letting me put it on her. It's no fun for me, but that's just who she is.

"I have the perfect idea," I tell her.

She stares at me, waiting for me to continue.

I wink at her as I say, "Peaches."

She playfully slaps my arm and leans into me. It makes me feel good. Disaster averted. For now, anyway.

It's only a matter of time before she realizes how fucking bad I am for her. But I'll let her be the one to call this off. I'll let her walk away if it gets to be too much for her.

But until that day comes, I'm gonna enjoy her as much as I can.

She really is too good for me, and one day she'll realize it.

It fucking sucks, but I know it's going to end before I've had my fill of her.

CHAPTER 15

ZANE

"Wow, this place is pretty rad," Katie quips, looking all around as I open the door for the girls to the tattoo parlor. I feel that Maddy needs to see where I work to be at ease. I know she has her doubts about me, and I need to show Maddy that she doesn't have any reason not to trust me. Hopefully this'll do it. Or help at the very least.

"It is," Maddy agrees. Even though I know tattoos aren't her thing, I can tell she's impressed with the layout of the shop. We have squeaky-clean checkered floors, a lot of goth artwork on the walls, and framed pictures of clients with our most impressive tattoos. Maddy walks around, leisurely looking at all this stuff before she finds her way over to the counter.

"So is this where you give tattoos?" she asks as she runs her fingers over a photo album of our work.

"Yup," I respond. "I'll show you the back later, peaches," I say with a smirk at Maddy and give her a wink. In typical fashion she rolls her eyes, but I know she's dreaming about me fucking her on my table now. Fuck, I'd do it right now too if I could, but I don't want Katie to get the wrong idea about me. Right now she's on my side, and I wanna keep it that way.

Needles comes out of the back carrying some tattoo tubes in his hands. He's about to say something, but he stops when he sees us.

"Hello," Maddy says politely.

"Heya," Katie greets. She eyes Needles with curiosity, who's dressed in all black with his goth tattoos on display. I can tell that neither Katie nor Maddy are used to being around guys like Needles, and I wonder how this meeting is gonna go down.

Needles looks at them and then at me. "Who are these chicks?" he asks.

"Prostitutes," Katie says before I can respond. "The two dollar kind."

I chuckle. "These chicks are my girl, Maddy, and her friend Katie." I gesture at Katie and then add, "Ladies, this asshole is Needles." That gets a laugh from them and I expected the side-eye from Needles, but his eyes are focused on Katie.

"Oh, sup," Needles says. "Welcome to Inked Envy, where we hook you up with the best tattoos." He pauses then as if he just realizes something and looks at me with his forehead pinched. "Your girl? Since when did you get pussywhipped?"

"Since I broke up with your mom." I'm quick with a response, and I keep it light.

Katie snickers at my response, which I know she loves.

"Well that was bound to happen, considering mom's as loose as a sinkhole."

"God, show some respect, douche," I growl. Seriously,

Needles is making me wanna fuck him up. He's a shit wingman.

"Sorry," Needles says without a hint of authenticity. He turns to Maddy. "It's just that Zane hasn't been in a relationship in… well… ever."

"Is that a bad thing?" Maddy asks. She's side-eyeing me nervously, and I can only assume all sorts of dubious thoughts are running through that pretty little head of hers.

Needles walks over and sets the tubes down at his workstation. "I just don't see him settling down is all," he replies. "He's never been able to have a relationship that lasted more than a week.

Maddy grows quiet and I literally want to take Needles outside and curb stomp him. Does he have any idea that I'm trying to make Maddy feel comfortable with dating me? It's like he's going out of his way to shit all over my effort.

It's one of Needles' character flaws. He always speaks bluntly, even if it means offending someone. It's one of the reasons why he's my friend. He's real, not fake and phony like most of the people in my life. But right now his penchant for truth is annoying the fuck out of me. She doesn't need to know that shit.

An uncomfortable silence falls over the room, and I feel like I need to say something to put Maddy at ease, but I'm saved by Katie.

"One of you give me a tattoo!" Katie demands out of nowhere. "Right on my ass!"

"Katie!" Maddy protests. "I thought you hated tattoos."

"Not anymore."

"I'd be more than happy to if you're serious," Needle says, staring at Katie intently. He seems to have a thing for Katie, but I think she's out of his league. I'd give him less than an hour before he said something that would offend her and have her clawing him for blood.

"Well, I'm not," Katie admits.

"Damn," Needles says with disappointment. "That would've been the highlight of my week.

Katie blushes.

"How'd you two even meet?" Maddy asks, looking between me and Needles. She seems quick to keep Katie and Needles from getting a little too close, and it makes me wanna laugh at her. They're grown ass adults. If they wanna have a go, let 'em.

I look at Needles with a grin.

"So he came into my shop one day. Not this one, but a different one."

Needles is turning red, and I can't help but crack up laughing. "He got hammered one night and decided he'd give himself a tat."

I turn to Needles. "Show 'em."

Needles looks a bit pissed at me for even bringing it up. He's done all his tats himself, and he's good at what he does. But that night he shouldn't have done that shit.

"Nothing good happens after 2 a.m.," he says, lifting up his sleeve.

"Looks good to me," Katie says and shrugs her shoulders as she lets her fingertips graze Needles' skin. His lips turn up into a soft smile.

"That's 'cause he came to a pro to fix his shit work."

Needles' smile vanishes. "You were sober. That's the only difference."

I chuckle and wrap my arm around Maddy's waist, bringing her closer to me. She seems so much better now. So much happier.

"What about you and Katie?" I ask her.

Maddy looks with a scowl at Katie, who is grinning mischievously. “Don’t. Just don’t,” she warns.

God, this is gonna be good. I can already tell from the look on my peach’s face.

“Well, we’re kinder buddies,” Katie says.

“Kinder buddies?” I ask. My brow furrows, what the fuck is a kinder buddy?

“Yeah, we met in Kindergarten, so we're Kinder buddies. We were so young though, I don’t remember much.”

Maddy seems to relax and trust that whatever Katie has on her, she’s not gonna tell. But judging by the way Katie’s smile just grew on her face, she’s not gonna keep quiet.

“Except this one time, where Maddy--” Maddy runs to Katie and gets a hand over her mouth, cutting her off, but Katie manages to pull away and dodges Maddy's next grab. They're on opposite sides of the counter now. Katie's got a huge ass grin on her face, but Maddy just looks pissed.

“It’s not funny, Katie!” Maddy's shooting daggers at Katie, but Katie just keeps grinning and continues.

“She was on the playground,” Katie begins. Maddy darts around the counter, but Katie’s faster.

“And she fell from the top of the slide.” They look like two kids playing as Maddy chases Katie around the counter, trying to catch her. “And I went to help her. 'Cause you know, I’m such a nice person and all.”

I look at Needles, not believing this shit is really happening.

Maddy stops running, and the two try to catch their breaths. Maddy points her finger at Katie and says, “Just stop right now, and I’ll never tell--”

Before Maddy can finish her threat, Katie spits out, “And she had completely soaked her clothes!” She starts laughing hysterically, and Needles follows suit. "She literally scared the piss out of herself."

"I was like four!" Maddy yells. She still looks pissed, but more embarrassed than anything else. I wanna laugh, but I hold it in. Something tells me she'll never forgive me if I laugh at her for this right now. "I swear to God, I'm going to tell every story I can when you finally hold down a boyfriend," she mutters.

Needles stops laughing and looks at Maddy and says, "I mean, at least you were four. It could be worse."

I grunt out a laugh. "How old was that fucker that shit himself while you were giving him a tattoo?"

"Too fucking old!" he answers, and just like that Maddy relaxes a little.

"Oh. My. God. Are you for real?" Katie asks Needles with disbelief.

"I shit you not," Needles says, and I just shake my head, but it gets a laugh out of Katie.

"Oh my God!!" Maddy shrieks out of nowhere. I actually flinch. Grown ass men can't even make me flinch. "This is my song!" she yells out and takes my hand. I didn't even notice the music in the background. I generally just tune it out. It's more to help customers relax, not for us.

"What are you doing?" Needles asks as she pulls me in front of the counter.

"Dance with me!" she says. I stare into her beautiful green eyes, and I can't deny her.

"You're really fucking gonna dance!" Needles crows. He's having the time of his life with this shit.

I shoot him the finger behind Maddy's back as she sings along to whatever song is playing.

Katie whips out her phone to take a picture. Fuck, not a picture. Probably a video judging by the fact she's still got the damn thing raised.

Normally I'd just sit down and refuse to do this shit. But looking down at Maddy, she's so fucking happy, just having a good time.

Whatever, I can sway back and forth and let her have the time of her life over a song.

I push her away for just a second and she looks up, thinking I'm done. But I've got her hand in mine and I go for the twirl. I figure if Katie's recording, I might as well do something to make it worthwhile. Seeing Maddy smile makes it worth it.

She busts out a laugh and so does our little audience.

My heart swells in my chest as she gives me a wide smile and leans into my embrace again.

And then, in a split second, all the happiness is gone when I see Vlad walk up to the building with a scowl on his face.

"Needles," I call out even though my eyes are on the door. "You wanna take the girls out back for a second?"

Maddy's forehead pinches and she looks at me like I owe her an explanation. But she sees where I'm looking and turns in my arms.

"Just head out back, baby." I plant a kiss on her nose. I'm trying to keep it casual and not let on to the fact I'm pissed he's here. I don't want her around this shit. And I don't want him to ever lay eyes on her. But it's too late.

Vlad bangs on the door with his fist. Since the shop is closed, the door is locked. He fucking knows that.

"I'll be out in a minute," I say and give Maddy a smile as she looks at Katie, and then to Needles. She looks uneasy, and I know I need to settle her down some.

"It's just business." That's not enough to get the nervous look off her face though. Vlad's a scary ass looking dude. "I promise after this I won't be working any more tonight." I speak with a relaxed, easy voice as Needles starts walking them back.

"Let me show you guys the equipment I have in my trunk." Both women stop dead in their tracks, and I shake my head on the way to the door. Dude has no fucking game.

"I mean, my stereo system," he says.

Katie cracks up and asks, "What year is this?" She's joking, but Needles doesn't laugh. He knows how serious this shit is.

I walk to the door and pull out my key, listening as they open and shut the back door. I open the door wide and move to the side to let him in. "Vlad, nice to see you." It isn't really, but what else are you gonna tell the mob boss?

I've never liked Vlad or the shit he does. If it wasn't for Nikolai, I'd never feel comfortable enough to stay anywhere around these fuckers.

When the head of the mob is a cold-blooded killer with a taste for women way too close to being underage, it's hard to feel safe. He's backstabbed more than a few people. But I've always felt like I was on the inside. I guess that's only because I know Nikolai would give me a heads-up. He said if you don't know who's on the hit list, then it's 'cause your ass is close to being on it.

Every move Vlad makes is calculated. I've never given him a reason to even think about me. I stay out of his way and just let them take over the books for their laundering.

"You throwing a fucking party in here?" Vlad sneers. His cruel blue eyes stare back at me. He's a tall blond man with combed-over, thinning hair.

"I'm just showing a couple of friends the place is all."

Vlad's glare says it all. His eyes seem to say, *'What the fuck is the matter with you?'*

"Get those bitches the fuck out of here. Now."

Everything in my body screams at me to tell Vlad to go fuck himself, and I would, if I didn't think he would do something to harm one of the girls in retaliation.

"Okay boss." I turn my back on him and go right to the back. At least he doesn't follow me back here. I don't need him around either Katie or Maddy.

"You guys have to go," I say as soon as the door shuts behind me. Katie's leaning into the trunk of Needles' car messing with one of the speakers.

"Why?" Maddy asks; she's got concern written all over her face.

"We were having so much fun," Katie whines in protest.

"Just take my car and head back home."

Maddy looks like she's going to argue as I pull her a few feet down the street to where I parked. I need to make sure she doesn't. When it comes to Vlad and all this shit, I need to make sure she listens to me.

"It's just business, peaches." I open the door to my car and hand her the keys. "I'll be back as soon as this meeting is over."

It hurts to see Maddy's unanswered questions in her eyes. She wants to know what's going on. But I can't tell her. No fucking way.

I can see her starting to question everything, and I fucking hate it. I wanna tell her. I want to make sure she trusts me. But I can't. The more she knows, the worse it'll be for her. That, and she'll leave my ass.

"I shouldn't have brought you here with the chance of my old partner coming by," I tell her. It's a mix of white lies. It's true that I didn't know he was showing up tonight. But "old partner"... well that's just a flat-out lie.

But it does the trick. Her lips purse and her shoulders relax some. "So you're just settling *old* business?" she asks with her arms crossed, and the keys tapping against her forearm.

"Yup. And it'll be over with soon. So I'll be right behind you." That part's true. At least it better be.

This is my shop and if I want my girl here, she can come here. I just need to make sure I keep her ass away when *business* is going down.

CHAPTER 16

MADELINE

"So how's things with Zane?" Katie asks as we pull into our parking space in front of the condo. As we stop, I notice a car across the street that looks familiar, but I'm distracted and can't quite place it.

I glance over at Katie who's staring at me intently, hungry for juicy gossip. Dressed in a red tank top and white pants, her side bob is on point today and looks extra shiny underneath the bright sun. I have to admit, she looks cute. Too bad she hasn't been acting cute. For the past few days she's been pestering me with constant questions about Zane. How good is he in bed? Does he know how to work it? Did he have a monster dong? And so on and so on.

"Where they shouldn't be," I respond flatly.

Katie scowls, sensing my bitchiness. "What's that supposed to mean?"

"That I shouldn't have had sex with him, much less be talking to him."

"Oh, come on Maddy. Really? It can't be that bad. You've had a serious glow about you for the past few days."

"Seriously, thanks to you, I'm in this predicament." I know I shouldn't be doing this to Katie right now, but I'm about falling for Zane. Hard. When I'm with him, everything's great. And then I leave his side and doubt spreads through me. I just don't trust it. There's something off.

Katie eyes go large and her mouth opens so wide a giant trout could jump through it. "Me?!" she exclaims. "What the hell do I have to do with this?"

"You didn't protect me from Zane like you were supposed to," I accuse. She knows it, too.

"What the hell? What are you, two years old? I mean, what was I supposed to do, tell his big dick to stop wanting you?"

I roll my eyes. "You know I don't mean that--"

"Seriously Maddy, grow up. You need to have this experience with Zane. If nothing else than to teach you that not all guys are the same."

"That's the problem, he talks a good game, but in the end he's not any different from any other horndog out there."

Katie sighs, and places a comforting hand on my shoulder. "Maddy, I understand how you feel, I really do, but that's not the way to live life. You're supposed to have these experiences, so that you can grow. Shit, I'd rather have lived and smoked cock every once in a while than to never have smoked cock at all."

As serious as I feel right now, I have to laugh. "Really, Katie? Smoked cock? That's a horrible analogy!" Leave it to Katie to say some ridiculous crap to pull me out of a bad mood.

Katie scowls at me. "I never said I was good at it. I'm just trying to get you to cheer up and see reason."

"I know, Katie, I know. And I'm sorry about blaming you for what's happened. It's not your fault. I wanted this just as much as Zane. Maybe even more. I'm just feeling really scared right now and I guess I'm just freaking out."

Katie smiles at me. "Well, I'm glad you see that. And I think you should stop worrying. Now. Sit back, relax, and let this all play out. If Zane doesn't wind up being a good guy, you know what? Fuck him. Trust me, there are many more big dicks out there in the sea."

I giggle. I'm already feeling somewhat better. "Oh Katie, what would I ever do without you?"

"Probably never laugh and be a sourpuss all the time."

"Ain't that the truth," I agree, chuckling.

We gather our books, get out of the car and go into the condo. As soon as Katie swings open the door, my jaw drops at the sight before me.

"Daddy?" I ask in shock. "What are you doing here?"

There, standing in the middle of the living room, is my father, Kenneth Murphy. At sixty, his hair is white as snow, but that's his only visible sign of aging. He has a smooth, unlined face and crystal clear blue eyes. If not for the hair, he could easily be mistaken for a man half his age.

He's wearing black slacks and a white dress shirt with a tie, just a little too formal for a retired parole officer. There's a bulge on the side of his dress shirt letting me know he's carrying. Daddy never leaves the house without his gun. Ever. Now I know why the car outside looked so familiar. He could have flown, but knowing Daddy, he decided to drive so he could make a nice vacation out of this visit.

The bigger question though, is how the hell did he get inside?

"Well, hello Mr. Murphy!" Katie greets my father before he can respond, walking over to him and giving him a big hug. "Boy, do you get more handsome each time I see you, or what?"

Daddy chuckles at Katie's shameless flirting. "Thanks, Katie. It's nice seeing you, too. How's school been treating ya?"

"Oh you know, a little bit of that here, and a little bit of that there. I think I'd go crazy if it weren't for Maddy."

Daddy's eyes twinkle. He's always been one to play along. "So you two been getting along well, I take it?"

Katie nods. "Uh huh, except--"

I cringe, bracing myself for Katie to blurt out something stupid about me and Zane.

"She farts so loud when I'm trying to sleep."

My father lets out a goofy laugh and I roll my eyes while loudly protesting, "Katie!"

"I'm just kidding." She points at the hallway. "I'm gonna go take a shower and let you two play catch-up. It was nice seeing you again, Mr. Murphy."

"It was nice seeing you too, Katie."

When she's gone I ask, "How the heck did you get in here?"

Daddy walks over and sits down on the couch. "You two left the door unlocked. I figured after the door swung ajar when I knocked I'd better sit here until you two arrived back home."

How the hell was the door unlocked? I could've sworn I locked it when we left.

"You really should always lock your door," Daddy says with a disapproving frown. "There's all sorts of sick predators out there, waiting to prey on young, vulnerable women like you both. Have I not taught you that?" As part of law enforcement, my father was big on safety growing up, and he never failed to lecture me when he thought I was being careless with my welfare.

"We do lock the door," I object, trying to fight back irritation. I hate being scolded. But I know my father is only saying these things because he cares about me. "I just don't know why it wasn't locked today. That's all."

"Well you can't afford to not know, Maddy. One mistake can cost you your life."

I sigh in exasperation. "Daddy, I know--" He cuts me off before I can finish speaking.

"Do you always carry that can of mace with you like you promised me you would?" he demands.

I look down guiltily. "No," I reluctantly admit. "But I'm going to start doing it, I promise."

He shakes his head and stares me in the eyes with disbelief. "Damn it Maddy, it won't do you any good sitting at home!"

I'm taken aback by the venom in his voice and tears begin to well up in my eyes. I never have been able to take it when I felt I let him down. I feel sick to my stomach. I hate making my father unhappy and disappointing him. "I'm sorry," I choke out. My father never yells at me like that over something stupid. "I haven't been able to think..." my voice trails away as the image of a cocky, smiling Zane pops into my head.

Suddenly repentant, Daddy pats the seat next to him on the couch. "I'm sorry baby, come sit down over here. I didn't mean to yell at you."

Pushing back my tears, I drop my bag and go over to him. Damn, I'm just so emotional lately. With Zane and the stress from school, every little thing is getting to me. As soon as I'm there, he envelops me in his arms and kisses me hard on the forehead. "Will you forgive me?" he asks.

"Of course," I say. "I know you're just upset because you worry so much about me." He's a cop, and ever since mom died, all he does is worry about me.

Daddy nods. "Yes, I do." After a moment, he leans back

to study my face intently. "Is something else bothering you, or are you still upset with me?"

"Huh?" I ask, astonished at his unerring observation. I shouldn't be surprised, though. Daddy's an expert at reading body language, and he probably sensed there was something wrong with me the moment I walked through the door.

He gives me a knowing look. "Don't play stupid with me, Maddy, I know when something is on your mind."

I bite my lower lip and think. My father will know if I'm lying if I try to play it off. I don't want to tell him though. Daddy's overprotective as it is, and I already know he's going to hate Zane. I can imagine his disapproving stare already.

"Maddy?" he persists.

He's not going to stop until I tell him.

I let out a big sigh and admit, "I'm seeing someone."

My father's instantly back on edge. "Who?"

Taking a deep breath, I tell him everything, holding nothing back. He's been my voice of reason my entire life, and I can't lie to him. I don't want to. I even admit to my father that I'm falling for Zane. I don't know why, but I'm always able to confide in him.

When I'm done I feel relieved. It's almost therapeutic, telling my father about my feelings, worries and doubts.

"So let me get this straight," Daddy says slowly, "You met this fellow and you think he's a player, yet you still slept with him?"

Cringing, I nod.

He asks disdainfully, "And he's a tattoo artist?"

I nod again. Fuck, I should not have done that. Regret consumes me as my body heats.

He stares at me, his eyes boring into me so hard I can sense the anger behind them.

"What?" I ask, flinching at what's to come.

"Jesus, Maddy, a tattoo artist?" he snarls. "What the hell is wrong with you?'

"Daddy, I--" Again he cuts me off.

"Do you think I let you go off to school just to get involved with trash? You're supposed to be looking to go places in life. Not hanging around with some trashy, deadbeat womanizer."

Anger twists my stomach. "He's not a deadbeat," I say hotly. "Nor is he trashy. And he obviously supports himself well enough as an 'artist' since he has own place."

Daddy snorts with derision. "He might be peddling drugs on the side, for all you know. You've already said you don't even know if he has other girlfriends, so what reasons do you have to trust this guy?"

As much as I hate to admit it, he's right. What did I know about Zane before I slept with him, except that he was sexy as all hell and a tattoo artist? I know nothing of his past, don't even know how many sexual partners he's had. And with what happened at the shop with his *old* business partner, I'm beginning to have serious doubts.

Daddy's features soften. "I don't mean to be an asshole to you, Maddy," he says, sensing my inner turmoil. "I just care about your well-being. And I would prefer you not get mixed up with someone who obviously isn't a good fit for you. You need to let this fellow go so you can focus on your studies."

For a moment, I begin to seriously regret telling my father about my business. I have this sneaking suspicion he's going to start suddenly showing up on my doorstep unannounced just to check on me.

While I appreciate his concern, I won't be able to handle that. Whether or not Zane is bad for me, I don't need someone else dictating what I should do in this situation. As Katie said, I need these experiences to grow and mature.

"I know where you're coming from, really I do," I say softly, but then I harden my tone and add, "But I'm fine. You shouldn't worry about me. Whatever happens between me and Zane is my business."

He stares at me for a long moment, but I hold my ground. I feel like he wants to tell me that I'm forbidden to see Zane and that he wants me to move, but at the same time he's conflicted by the fact that I'm an adult who can now make my own decisions.

"Are you sure about this?" he asks finally, grudgingly.

"Yes," I reply, visibly relaxing. "Don't worry, if I do need you, I'll call you."

"Promise?"

I smile. "I promise."

I feel a sense of relief. We got through this discussion without my father demanding to see Zane so he could threaten him to stay away from me. Now all I need to do is to convince him that I don't need him to check up on me, and I'll be more than fine.

I open my mouth to ask my father about what's been going on his life instead of focusing on me, when the doorbell rings.

Right then, two words run through my mind along with a feeling of dread.

Oh no.

CHAPTER 17

ZANE

The door opens, and all I can think is, *fuck this shit.* A white-haired man dressed in black slacks, a dress shirt and tie stares back at me, and I watch his eyes as they take me in. Narrowing, judging. Yeah, I've seen this before.

I'm a beast, and I look the part.

I usually don't give a fuck, but my girl is standing by the stairs looking nervous as hell. My heartbeat picks up. My nerves buzz with an insecurity I'm not used to feeling.

I know this isn't going to last. We're just enjoying each other for now.

Shit, when she's done with school, she's gonna leave me far behind. I know it. I've accepted it. But I just got a taste of her. I'm not ready for this to end right now.

"You must be Maddy's father," I say as I reach my hand out to the old man. "Nice to meet you, sir." He lets it hover there for a moment, a moment that lets me know what he really thinks. Finally he takes it in his with a firm shake.

"You must be Zane." His voice is hard and unforgiving. "Maddy's told me about you."

I nod. "Yep. Zane Stone." I say this clear and proud. Although shit, I wish I'd known he was here.

Maddy clears her throat, and I can practically hear her heart pounding.

Maddy takes a few steps toward us and pushes him out of the doorframe so she can take my hand in hers. My heart swells in my chest.

"Daddy, as I was telling you, Zane is my..." she hesitates to finish, but looks right into her father's eyes with squared shoulders.

I've never been anyone's *boyfriend* before. But for her, right now, sure. I can be her boyfriend. "Boyfriend," I say the word with my eyes on her, but clear my throat and look up at her father.

He's fucking pissed.

It means a lot that she's willing to stand by me as her father clearly dislikes my existence, but I don't need to stay around for this shit.

I just came by to fuck you. I can't say that. But shit, it's the truth. I was looking forward to it too. "I just came by to see how your test went." She's been on and on about this damn test lately. But I'm sure she aced it 'cause she's a smart girl. And that sounds a fuck ton better than her dad hearing me describe all the ways I wanted to relieve her from all that stress.

She pulls me into the foyer and I resist, but she whips her head around and tugs harder. Her father stares at our hands and I wish I could just fucking leave. Fine. For her, I'll put up with this. Only because she stood by me. And that felt so fucking good. She'll never know.

I walk with the two of them to the dining room. Maddy's books are open on the other end, with her notebook out and highlighter.

She takes a seat at the other end and pats a seat for me. This ordering me around shit isn't my forte. But I'll let her take the lead on this. After all, it's her father. And I'm sure I'll get brownie points if he likes me.

I take the seat next to her and look up at the old man. Fuck, there's no fucking way he's gonna like me.

He's looking at me like… well, like I'm fucking his daughter. I can't help the grin that grows on my face.

I lean forward and give Maddy a smile. "How'd it go?" I ask her.

I can feel his eyes on me, but I ignore him. I usually don't take this shit. If a fucker's gonna give me a look like he's got something to say, I don't stand down till that shit is dealt with. But this is her father, I've gotta show some respect.

He gets this one moment. One day. That's it.

Maddy takes a deep breath and pulls her hair back. "Well, I think it went *okay*."

Before she can say anything else, her father interrupts. "So your real legal name is Zane?" he asks.

I turn to him and sit straight in my seat. "That's right, Zane Michael Stone." I don't like how he's looking at me.

"That's an interesting name." He says the words in a monotone, his eyes boring into my face. Also, what the fuck does that even mean? An interesting name?

I shrug my shoulders and say, "I didn't pick it." Maddy huffs a small laugh, but it's forced. The tension in the room is thick, and this is uncomfortable as hell.

"So, Maddy," he says as he looks at her like I'm not even in the room with them. "You didn't say Zane was a smartass."

I keep my mouth closed and let him have that one. Point one for Pops, I guess.

"Daddy, please don't do this now." Maddy's lips are pressed into a thin line and she's staring back at her father like she's ready to tear him apart.

Fuck, maybe I'm lucky not to have my parents around anymore.

Her father looks back at me, but before he can speak, Maddy tries to lighten the mood by saying, "So, I think we should all go out to eat. We could go to a nice restaurant," she suggests. She looks at me and says, "Besides, you owe me a date. And this way Daddy could get to know you." She sounds slightly hopeful and upbeat. I take a look at Papa Fuckoff, and I know that's not happening. My stubborn peach is apparently also delusional.

"I just don't get it. What do you see in him, Maddy?" he asks, leaning close to her with his elbows on the table.

I drop Maddy's hand and clench my fists under the table.

"Daddy," Maddy's tone takes on a hard edge. I'm not sure what the protocol for this shit is. I've never been in this position before.

"She's seen a lot of me, to be honest; she must've liked at least one part," I say with a straight face.

He looks fucking furious. I can't really blame him, but I'm not gonna let him talk to her like that. After a minute he shakes his head at Maddy like he's disappointed in her and that's the last straw, but before I can say anything, Maddy lays in on him.

"Daddy, I love you," Maddy says as her eyebrows raise, and I can see she's holding back that inner bitch she's unleashed on me a time or two. "But you need to stop this. Now."

I stare at my stubborn little peach who's all full of sass today. But this isn't the same shit she gives me. This is different. She's not playing a game, she's clearly upset, and I don't like it.

"Hey, it's alright." I take her hand in mine and rub soothing circles on the back of her hand with my thumb. "It's fine." I'm partially amazed at how well trying to calm Maddy down diffuses my own temper. So what if he doesn't like me? He's not the first. And I'm sure he won't be the last.

She doesn't need to get worked up over this. I mean, isn't a dad supposed to hate the prick who's doing his daughter? I'm pretty sure this is all normal. And her father's right. I don't look like the kind of man who she'd normally pick. Not that she picked me. I had to fucking fight for her.

My heart sinks a little, and I hate all these bullshit emotions that are hitting me. I need to get the fuck out of here.

I stand up from the table and give Maddy a small smile as she grips onto my arm. "I should give you two some time, peaches." I let her nickname slip, and see her father stiffen on my left.

"Nice to meet you, Mr. Murphy." I say it as a formality and don't look him in the eyes as the words come out hard.

"You don't have to go," Maddy says in a soft voice with her forehead creased. I bend down and give her a chaste kiss.

"I get to see you every day." I look back at her dad and give him a curt nod as I say, "You should spend some time with your father."

"I'll walk you out," Maddy says and tries to get up, but I stop her.

"I'm only next door, I can find my place myself." I have to repress my laugh as her father starts coughing. Maddy's mouth presses into a thin line and she gives me a look. I can't help the smile growing on my face.

"Talk to you later, peaches," I say and give her another kiss goodbye.

"Have a nice stay, Mr. Murphy." I give him a wave as I open the door and walk out.

CHAPTER 18

MADELINE

I spend the next five minutes scolding my father for his rude behavior toward Zane. Just because I have reservations about him, doesn't mean it gives Daddy leeway to be a total jerk to him and judge him like that.

He argues with me, telling me he doesn't like what he saw in Zane, and that I don't need to be messing around with him. Through it all, I hold firm. Despite my misgivings, I'm not leaving Zane without good reason, and that's final.

Eventually, Daddy gives up, but he does warn me, much to my chagrin, that he'll be watching.

As soon as my father's gone, I decide I need to go next door and apologize to Zane for his behavior. I feel anxious and embarrassed by what's happened, and want to make amends.

I walk over to Zane's and knock on the door. After a moment, the door swings open and my jaw nearly drops.

Zane's standing there in a pair of pajama bottoms hanging low, balanced precariously on his chiseled hips, that incredibly sexy V-shape at his lower abdomen fully on display. Down below, his bulge presses against the flimsy material, making my mouth water.

Good God, this man is going to be the death of me! I think to myself. He makes me want to be his sex slave.

Seriously, I want to fall to my knees and take that big fat cock out and start slurping on it like a straw jammed into my favorite milkshake. It's a nice distraction, but I can't help how my heart is squeezing in my chest.

I forcefully tear my eyes away and ask, "Are we okay?"

For a moment, Zane stares at me and my heart begins to pound with anxiety, but then he cracks that boyish smile of his. "More than okay, peaches." He reaches out, grabs me by the waist and pulls me into him. I melt into his body. Lower, I feel his cock pressing into me and I'm immediately turned on.

I'm so turned on that if he wants to fuck right here in this doorway for all the world to see, I won't have any objections.

Zane must have plans though because suddenly he pulls me inside, closes the door, and hefts me up onto his shoulders. I cry out with surprise, my legs trembling. "What are you doing?" I demand.

"We're better than okay," he says as he pulls my dress up and pushes his thumbs through my panties, ripping them off of me. Oh fuck. That's the sexiest thing I've ever seen. I push my head back against the wall and grip onto his hair as he licks me. Holy fuck. He's not wasting any time.

He says something about me being a good girl before dipping his tongue into my pussy. "Ohh!" I lean forward involuntarily as my legs tremble around him.

"Zane!" I call out, trying to balance myself. His blunt fingernails dig into my ass, forcing me to rock against his mouth. Holy fuck, it feels so good. My toes tingle and a low stirring of pleasure builds in my core. My back goes straight and my legs go stiff as he sucks my clit into his mouth, and then dives back to my entrance. Fuck, fuck, fuck.

I'm going to cum. It's the fastest I've cum in my entire life.

My breathing comes in short pants.

I rock myself against his face and grip his hair tighter, shoving him deeper. I'm so close. My nipples harden, and I want so badly for his dick to be inside me. I need him. My head rocks to the side. So close. He pulls away and I almost curse at him for leaving me on edge, but he quickly shoves two fingers inside and massages my clit with his tongue. Fuck yes! His fingers mercilessly stroke my G-spot and he bites down lightly on my clit. Oh shit! YES!!

My back bows, and I let out a strangled cry.

"Fuck!" I scream out as he acts like he's starving and my release crashes through me. My pussy clenches around his tongue, and he groans as I feel the pool of arousal leak down my thighs. My cheeks heat with embarrassment, but I feel so fucking good I'm not sure I care all that much. He keeps lapping at me until I'm limp.

He gently sets me down on shaky legs. I lean against the wall and catch my breath.

"My peach is juicy," he says with a smirk as he wipes my cum from his face. I feel that heat in my cheeks again and try to right myself.

I'm out of breath and shocked, and I don't know what to say.

"Come on, I want to take you somewhere," Zane says to me after our explosive oral session. I'm barely over my orgasm, my legs still trembling. It's amazing what Zane can do with his mouth and those powerful jaws.

Just remembering the way he suctioned my pussy

makes me want to experience it again... and again... and again.

"Where?" I ask, feeling completely off-balance.

"A date," he says simply. "You're delicious and all, but I gotta eat a bit more tonight."

I rock nervously on my heels, feeling stupid for even asking after *that*. "So we're good? My Daddy--"

Zane puts a finger over my lips. "We're good, peaches," he says and starts to say something else, and I can feel my heart beating faster. *I love you.* I know that's what he was going to say, but instead his mouth slams shut.

I feel a tinge of disappointment, but I shove it down.

I bite my lip, debating on saying it first. But no, that's not fucking happening. I pull up my bra strap and then pull my dress down.

"Dinner it is." I give him a small smile and I can tell he's waiting on me to say more. But he's not getting it.

If he thinks I'm going to be the first to say I love you, he's wrong about that. Just as soon as the smug thought comes to mind, I realize maybe he wasn't going to say that.

Insecurity sweeps through me. Fuck. When did I let this happen? I love him. The realization hits me hard, but it's true. It just happened so naturally with all the time we've been spending together lately that I wasn't even aware of it until now. I'm in love with Zane… but he's a bad boy. I'm sure he doesn't love me. Guys like him don't fall in love.

It's only a matter of time before he leaves me.

"Let's go, peaches." He wraps his arms around me and I do my best to forget my father's advice screaming in my head and ignore the painful insecurities telling me I need to end this before he breaks my heart.

He plants a kiss on my cheek and opens the door.

I know he's bad for me, and this is really going to hurt when he ends it. I won't tell him I love him, but I'm done pushing him away.

I may not say it out loud, but I fucking love him. How the hell did I let that happen?

CHAPTER 19

ZANE

"You're so bad," I whisper into Maddy's ear as we leave my workroom.

I lock it behind me like I do every day after my shift. But today we're leaving a little early.

She's been coming here every day to hang out while I work. It's our little routine. She goes to school, then comes here on Tuesdays and Thursdays. She's got all-day classes the other days of the week, which is perfect with my schedule. So on those days I meet her at her place later on, and fuck up her good study habits.

"We're gonna be so late now." Maddy's freaking out.

"Well you're the one who bent over in that short ass dress." That'll teach her to wear something like that out. Actually, knowing my girl, she'll probably wear them more often now. I smirk at her as she tries to fix her hair in the mirror behind the counter.

"You look good, babe." She does. She looks sexy as fuck. "How'd I get so damn lucky?" I wrap my arms around her waist and pull her toward me. I yank her up enough that her feet come off the ground and I bury my head in the crook of her neck.

"Stop!" she yells at me with a smile on her face while she's pushing off of me. I chuckle at her. I don't think she'll ever stop pushing me away.

"We gotta go," she says and grabs my hand the second I put her down. She starts pulling me toward the back exit where she's been parking.

I'm so caught up in how happy she makes me, I don't think about what day it is, or what time it is. I just let her lead me to the back.

As soon as she pushes the doors open and I see the van, I pull her back in, but it's too late. Four men are moving a pile of coke bricks onto a cart to take inside.

Fuck!

"What the--" she starts to ask, but I pull her to me and turn on my heels with her in my arms. My body heats with anxiety, and then I look up and see Garret walking out of the stockroom. I'm quick to pull Maddy to my side and walk past him.

"Whoa, where are you two headed?" he asks the two of us, but his eyes are on Maddy. She shifts on her feet and puts her body behind mine. I can tell she's not okay. She finally put two and two together.

My stomach drops, and I feel like shit. I feel like I lied to her, even though I didn't really. It was a lie of omission. Worse than that though, I put her in harm's way. Real fucking danger.

I'll do everything I can to keep her safe, but the way Garret's eyeing her is making me want to put a bullet in his head right now.

"Heading out," I answer him flatly. I know I look pissed. I can't help it. I can't school my features and play this off like she didn't see shit.

He gives me a crooked grin and nods. "See anything you like out there?" he asks Maddy.

She shakes her head, but doesn't give a verbal response. Her fingers dig into my skin, begging me not to let her go.

"See you later, Garret," I say and pull her to my other side. We walk straight out to my car. We'll come back for hers later. Right now we just need to get the fuck away from here.

I can't think. I don't know what to do.

This shit isn't good.

Witnesses don't live to be witnesses. I know that much. I know Garret's gonna tell Vlad, and then I'm fucked. I need to call Nikolai. But first I need to fix this shit between us.

I pull the passenger door open and gently push Maddy into her seat. I know she's still fucked up because she's not talking. She's chewing on her thumbnail and looking all around her. Shit, she doesn't even look like she's breathing.

I reverse and pull out without saying anything. The silence stretches between us for way too fucking long.

I need to say something, do something to make this right. But I don't know how. This just drives home the fact that I'm all wrong for her. I'm trouble, just like she said I was.

"You alright?" I finally ask her. I can't look at her though. My hand grips the steering wheel tighter as I slow to a stop at a red light. My heart beats frantically and my lungs won't fill. But none of it matters, because she's not looking at me. She's not saying shit.

Her walls are up, and she's looking out the window as silent tears fall down her cheek.

Fuck! I can't stand this. The light turns green and I step on the gas to get us home.

A lump grows in my throat and it stays there until I park the car.

She's quick to unbuckle her seatbelt and try to get out, but I don't let her. She tries to smack me away, but I'm not letting her leave like this.

I pull her into my lap and let her beat her fists on my chest. A sob rips up her throat. Her face is red and her cheeks tearstained. She's fighting my hold on her, and I take it.

I take it all. I fucking deserve it.

When she finally seems to give up and collapse into me, I tell her, "I'm sorry, peaches." I don't know what else to say.

"You--" she tries to speak as she wipes under her eyes, but she can't. Her gorgeous green eyes stare out the window as she tries to calm herself.

"I'm sorry," I tell her again, but I know apologies don't mean anything to her.

"You deal drugs?" she asks with an accusatory tone. She doesn't look at me. She's staring at her condo.

"No. The mob does." That gets her attention. She faces me with her brows raised in both fear and surprise. Her voice goes up an octave as she says, "You're in the mob!"

I shake my head and say, "It's not like that."

She shakes her head and hunches her shoulders, wrapping her arms around herself. "I need to go."

I grip her hips, I can't lose her. I know if I let her go right now, she's gone forever. But it needs to happen. Fuck, as the realization hits me, my chest seems to collapse with pain.

"Peaches, don't--"

"Don't call me that!" she yells at me, and looks at me with a raw sadness I've never seen on her face. I hate it. I hate what I've done to her.

"I'm sorry, Maddy."

Her composure breaks, and I can tell she's holding back more tears.

"I'm sorry. Just, just tell me that you won't say shit." That's all I need from her, and I'll let her leave me.

She looks at me with fear in her eyes. "I didn't see anything."

"Good girl." I try to kiss her, but she pulls away from me. I should expect that.

"I'm sorry, Maddy." I know this is the end. But I don't want it to be over. "Is this it?" I ask her, hating how I'm leaving it in her hands.

Her body shudders with a sob, and she falls limp against me.

"I don't know," she answers with her head buried in my chest, and I hate it. I hate that she's making me be the one to pull the trigger. We need to be over and done with though. I can't let this shit I'm in get to her.

I'll make sure no one comes after her. I'll call Nikolai. I'll get this dealt with. I knew I was going to be bad for her. I never should've let it get this far.

"I'm sorry, Maddy. I'll leave you alone now."

She cries harder against me. But only for a moment.

"Fuck you, Zane." She pushes against me and opens the driver's door, climbing out. She angrily wipes the tears away and walks to her door with her arms crossed over her chest. I sit in the car way longer than I should. Wanting to chase her, but knowing I shouldn't.

CHAPTER 20

MADELINE

I walk up the stairs, each step feeling heavier than the last, my breathing labored. I'm feeling an array of emotions; anger, sadness and rage. Unspeakable rage. I want to hit someone, preferably Zane.

I knew it! I rage, holding on to the anger and ignoring the pain in my chest. *I knew he was no good for me. Why did I have to be so stupid?*

I tried to fight him. I can't deny I knew this was bad. I brush the tears away and hold on to the railing as I slowly walk up the stairs.

He's a drug dealer! I want to scream, but if I open my mouth, I know I'll just cry. *A fucking drug dealer!* A shudder runs through my body. That man was no good. My heart freezes remembering the way he looked at me. I nearly fall on the step remembering the man from a few weeks ago. Fuck! The signs were there. I'm so stupid. He lied to me! How could he?

If my father only knew. He'd be fucking furious. He all but warned me not to trust Zane, but even with my misgivings, I went along with the bad boy anyway. How stupid am I? How stupid could I have been to not see what was in front of me this whole time?

I make it up the stairs and to the window of my bedroom. I peer out and see Zane's car still parked by the sidewalk. He's sitting there, staring straight ahead. A part of me wants to run back out there and scream at him, accuse him of lying to me, but another part of me just wants to remain away from him. Far away. It doesn't matter what I do though. No matter what, I'll be hurt. And if I run to him, he'll only hold me and try to make me feel better. And then what will I do? When I'm in his arms, I'm a fucking idiot. I'm weak and stupid when I'm with him. I slam the curtain closed and turn my back on him. I put my hand over my mouth and try to stop crying. It just hurts so much.

My bedroom door opens and my heart stops, thinking it's Zane.

"Maddy?" Katie asks with astonishment. "Maddy, what's wrong with you?" She's quick to run to my side and I lose all composure.

I collapse in her arms, sobbing like a baby. "Zane," I wail. I try to tell her what happened. About the drugs, the man, the breakup. I try, but even I can't understand my words.

"Huh?" Katie asks in bewilderment. "Maddy, stop crying, you're babbling and not making sense."

It takes great effort to get a hold of myself. I sit up, wipe at my teary eyes and focus on Katie. She's looking at me with shock, probably wondering what the hell is going on. "It's Zane," I manage to choke out over a sob.

"Zane? What did he do? Cheat on you?" Katie scowls darkly. "If he hurt you in any way Maddy, I swear to God, I'll twist his dick until it's curved."

"No, not that," I say and gulp back another sob. "At least

I don't think so." But he's a fucking liar. *What else did he lie about?* Even as I think the nasty thought, I know it's not true.

"Then what? What did he do that was so bad that you're in here acting like a maniac?"

"He's a drug dealer. Or at least he deals with people that deal drugs." It's the second one. It has to be the second one. I refuse to believe he's any more involved than just owning the place. A million ideas run through my head.

Katie's jaw drops. "A drug dealer? Are you serious?" she squeaks.

Sniffling, I nod. "I saw these guys unloading it at his shop."

"Holy shit!" Katie exclaims. She pauses and then asks, "Are you absolutely sure?"

"Yes! I don't know what's going on, but I'm sure they're using the parlor as a front. Zane's reaction after confirmed it." I rub my eyes. They feel swollen and tired. I feel exhausted. And most of all, broken.

Katie shakes her head. "I can't believe it. He even brought us by there and let us meet Needles."

"I know, right?" I sniffle and try to hold on to that anger. "What a fucking fraud." I give her a pleading look. "What do I do, Katie?"

Katie takes a long time to respond, but she finally says, "The only thing you can do. Stay away from Zane. Far, far away."

CHAPTER 21

ZANE

I wanted so fucking bad to go after her. I watched her close the door to her condo and I stared at it for a long time. I could've begged her to take me back. But what could I promise her?

I can't leave the mob. They'd hunt me down. They'd hunt *us* down. Marky's there now at my place, keeping an eye on her house for me. I refused to leave until I had eyes on her. I called him the second I had the strength to get my ass back here and confront Garret.

I have a sick feeling in my gut. I may be overreacting, but I'd rather that than risk her safety.

It can't have been more than an hour since we left, but the shop's deserted. I walk to Trisha's room, but it's locked. Needles' is open though.

"Yo," I call into his room, holding onto the jamb of the door. "When did they leave?" I need to know. Once they pick the shipment up it takes a few hours to drop it off. But then they'll be free to do whatever. I was hoping I'd catch them and make sure Garret stays away and leaves her the fuck alone.

Needles looks up at me from his drawing pad and opens his mouth to answer, but then his expression changes and he stands up, letting the pad fall to the floor with a dull thud.

"Bro, what's wrong?" he asks me and I back up, running my hands down my face.

I keep telling myself it's alright. I keeping thinking she'll be fine.

But I can't fucking lie anymore.

This shit isn't right. I'm not alright.

My heart twists in my chest. *She's* not alright.

"Maddy," I start to tell him, but my throat closes. I shake my head and pound my fist into the wall.

"How long?" I ask him again. My words come out harder than they should.

"Like fifteen minutes." I nod my head and swallow thickly. "What happened?" he asks again, and I know I need to tell him.

"I gotta call Nikolai," I tell him as chills run down my arms.

Fuck, having to make this call makes it that much more real.

I pull my phone from my pocket and dial his number. I shouldn't. I shouldn't be calling to talk about this shit. It's against code. Nothing is ever discussed on the phone. It's the reason I drove here.

I press the buttons and put the phone to my ear. Every ring makes me worry more and more, like he's avoiding me. Like maybe they're gonna take a hit out on me and keep me in the dark about it.

It's Nikolai, I tell myself. He wouldn't do that to me. He was everything to me growing up. He's not gonna fuck me over like that. Right?

Finally, he answers, "Yeah?" Hearing his voice answer

the same way he always does is a good sign. A good fucking sign.

"Nikolai, I got a problem." I pinch the bridge of my nose and close my eyes. Fuck! I wish this weren't real. I wish I could just take it back. I'd take it all back to save her.

"You need me?" I can hear him move the phone and I'm guessing he took it off speaker.

"You don't know?" I ask him.

"Know what?"

"Something happened today at the shop."

"How bad?" he asks.

I shake my head and reply, "Not bad. It's just, my girl." I swallow thickly before continuing. "She was here and went out the back when the van was here."

"That's not good, Zane." Nikolai's voice is low. There's a pause before he asks, "Did she see anything?"

I can't lie to him. "She saw a bit, but she knows not to say shit." I say the last words with conviction. "She's not gonna say shit to anyone." I start pacing the room with my hands in my hair. Needles is watching me like he's ready to go to war with me. He's always been a loyal friend like that. But he's nervous as fuck. "She's good for it. I'd put my life on it."

"Just calm down, Zane." He's talking like there's nothing wrong with what happened.

"I think Garret's gonna want her," I say, and I have to pause. I can't finish the sentence. I shouldn't, first of all. This is all going down on the phone and I can't say shit like that. But that's not the reason I can't get it out. The thought of them going after her makes me physically sick, almost unable to speak.

"We won't touch her. *He* won't touch her." He's quick to answer, and his words are absolute.

"I have a bad feeling, Nikolai." I'm telling him the truth.

I really do. Something in my gut is telling me she's not okay, that she's still in danger.

"It's me, I got your back, Zane." Hearing Nikolai's voice telling me it's alright calms me down a good bit. Maybe it's all just in my head because I had to end it with her. Maybe that's why I feel so fucked.

I did need to end it though. She can't be around this shit. I'll never be able to bring a good girl into this shit life. I should've known better.

"She's a good girl, Nik," I tell him simply.

He chuckles low and rough on the other end. "I'm sure she is, and she's fine."

"Do you need anything from me?" I ask him. I can't imagine it's that easy. That she saw some shit, but they're just gonna let her go.

"Nah, it's all good." It's silent for a moment. "You alright?" he asks.

No. I'm not alright.

"Yeah, I'm good." I nod my head and look out the small window in Needles' room. "If it's all good and she's safe," I feel the need to clarify so he knows exactly what I'm saying. "Then I'm good."

He hesitates on the other end and my heart stops in my chest. But finally he responds, "It's all good. And I give you my word that she's safe. Go calm your ass down."

I wait another moment, letting the words sink in before I end the call.

"What'd he say?" Needles asks. I shove the phone back in my pocket and try to calm down.

"He said she's good... It's all good."

We stare at each other, neither of us saying shit, but I'm sure we're both thinking the same thing. *He's lying. She's a witness, and that means she's dead.*

"Needles, help me take her car back, man." I can't even look him in the eyes.

"Yeah, sure," he says as he takes a hesitant step toward me. "It's gonna be alright." He nods his head weakly, barely keeping eye contact with me.

Even he doesn't believe it.

CHAPTER 22

MADELINE

I shouldn't be here.

It's been days since I last saw Zane. Yet, he's been on my mind ever since. Every waking moment has been spent thinking about him. I can't get him out of my head. The more I think about my situation, the more I begin to rationalize. So what if he's mixed up in a world of crime? Does that make him a bad person? He said he didn't sell them. That it wasn't like that. Maybe they pressured him. Maybe *he's* the victim.

I raise my hand and pause right before I knock on Zane's door, thinking, *I should leave.*

But I can't. All I can think about is Zane. I want to see him again, that cocky smile, that chiseled body. I want to feel his strong hands again, touching me, feeling me, caressing me.

I want to feel better, and I know he can make me feel good. I know he can. He's like a drug made just for me.

Taking a deep breath and gathering my courage, I knock. There's no answer. I knock several more times. My knuckles rap against the wood and each time the hollow sound makes my heart squeeze harder and harder in my chest. Still no answer. I stand there for what seems like eternity before finally giving up.

He's not coming to the door. Bastard.

Feeling tears well up in my eyes, I turn away and walk back over to my door.

It's a good thing he didn't answer, I tell myself as I storm back inside feeling mad as hell. *I should stay away. I always thought he was bad for me, but now I know for absolute sure.*

As much as I want to believe those words, I can't stop thinking about him. Maybe right now he needs me. God, I wish this ache in my chest would just go away. I wish we could get lost in each other and just run away. I think about how well we went together, when the world would disappear around us. How much I miss his touch, his hot lips, his naughty words spoken in my ear.

Goddamn it, Maddy! Be strong!

But I can't. Just thinking about Zane makes me weak.

"Are you okay, Maddy?" Katie asks with concern as I brush by her.

I ignore her and continue on to my room. There's nothing she can say that will make me feel better, and in a way, I blame her for my misery. After all, wasn't she the one that encouraged me to see Zane?

Katie follows me down the hall and up the stairs, but I pretend she isn't there. When I reach my room, I close the door on her. Before I can lock it, she pushes her way in.

I turn my face to the side to hide the tears. "Please, just go away!"

Kate walks in and closes the door. She crosses her arms across her chest and defiantly says, "No, Maddy. I refuse. I'm not going to let you walk around and treat me this way."

"I'm not treating you in any way," I deny.

"Bullshit. You're taking what happened with Zane out on me."

"No I'm not." My words sound hollow. Empty.

"Keep telling yourself that." Katie pauses and then accuses, "I saw you go over there."

"So what?" I reply defensively. "I wanted to talk to him."

"What the hell are you thinking? I told you to stay away from him." She's angry, and her words are like venom.

"You know that's funny, Katie, when you're the same one that encouraged me to give him a chance."

"Yeah, I did. I'm not ashamed of it either. How was I supposed to know he was involved in that shit?" I want to argue with her, but I bite my tongue. She's right. I can't blame her for not knowing the truth about Zane.

"You weren't," I admit grudgingly.

"Okay then. Now that I know the truth, I want you to do me a favor. Don't see him. *Ever*."

My heart twists in my throat. It hurts. It hurts just thinking about it.

Seeing my tormented expression, Katie presses on, saying, "He lied to you."

"He didn't really," I find myself saying, "He just kept the truth from me. Which isn't exactly the same thing as lying."

I can't believe I'm defending him, I think to myself. *After all I've said about guys being no-good dogs, and now I'm taking up for someone who's been dishonest to my face.*

"Maybe I can change him," I say, trying to convince Katie as much as I'm trying to convince myself. "Maybe he'll stop."

"Are you even listening to yourself?" Katie asks with disbelief. "Is the same Maddy I grew up with, or did aliens abduct her and stick me with this clone? 'Cause you can't be serious."

"I know it sounds stupid, Katie, but... maybe Zane will change for me… I mean, I feel like he would…" I trail off weakly.

Kate raises a finger sharply, cutting me off from whatever I might say next. "Stop it, Maddy, just fucking stop. You tried this very thing with Zach. And did that work?"

"No," I admit reluctantly. Katie's right. It's just that I hate how I feel inside. I hate how I feel my very existence depends upon being with Zane. Being with him is intoxicating beyond words. Being without him is like being in a dark, lifeless abyss. "I just don't know what to do."

"It'll take a while, but get back involved in your studies and try your best to stop thinking about Zane. I'll even do whatever it takes to help you keep your mind off him. After a while, it'll be easy."

Katie's being overly optimistic. The guy lives next door and we're stuck in our lease for the rest of the year. How the hell am I going to stop thinking about him when I can look through my bedroom window and he's right there?

"You'll find someone else somewhere along the line in the future, someone who loves you and that'll treat you right."

I can't take it. I break down and start sobbing. I feel Katie's arms wrap around me a second later.

"Shh," she coos. "Everything's going to be alright." She comforts me. It feels good to be held. I just feel so damn alone without him.

When I finally stop sobbing she says, "Come on girl. Pull yourself together. We got class in the next thirty minutes. That jerk-off is not about to ruin you like Zach did. Just be happy that you found out what you did before the relationship went any further."

After Katie's sure I'm okay, we take off to school. When

we arrive, I'm a cauldron of bubbling emotions I can hardly contain.

I don't know why I agreed to come to class today, I think to myself as Katie pulls in between two trucks on the west side of the parking lot. *I'm a total mess.*

Katie gathers her books and begins to get out, but pauses when she sees I'm not budging. "What are you doing?"

"Sitting here," I say, trying to hold back tears.

Katie frowns. "Aren't you going to get out?"

"In a minute."

Katie opens her mouth to protest but I sharply say, "Katie, not now. Please. I need a moment to collect myself."

Katie stares at me long and hard. "Fine," she says reluctantly. "But don't stay in here too long. You'll just be making it worse." She climbs out of the car. Before she shuts the door she adds, "I'll be sending you a text to check on you. Answer it. And I'm taking the keys."

Then she walks off and I watch her for a moment before breaking down into tears. Luckily, this crying fit only lasts a few minutes, and after a few sobs, I'm able to pull myself together.

One day it'll stop hurting. I know it will. I just need to live through the pain and it'll go away. One day.

I gather my books and then check my makeup in the mirror. My mascara is all runny and smudged. I quickly fix it and then step out of the car. I'm about to round the car when I hear the sound of running footsteps.

Before I can turn around, rough powerful hands clamp down on my mouth. I try to scream, but there's a rag pressed to my face. I try to shake the hands off of me. I inhale deeply, and then belatedly realize I need to hold my breath. The rag is obviously laced with something to knock me out. Fuck! I struggle against the man. Or is it men? But my body feels weak. I'm losing control of my limbs.

Then I go unconscious.

CHAPTER 23

MADELINE

I come to with my hair in my face. When I try to push it out of the way, I realize that my arms are pinned behind my back. I groan. I feel sore all over. Slowly, I open my eyes and experience a jolt of shock.

This can't be happening.

Though I'm bent forward with my hair in my face, I'm able to distinguish my surroundings. I'm in a chair, in a dark room and it's very quiet. Panicking, I struggle against my bonds, my fingers grazing against the rough material. Rope. Fuck! They tied me up. I pull harder, but I only succeed in burning my skin. It's tied too tightly. *Damn it!* Tears flood my eyes. Nausea twists my stomach.

Please tell me this is all just a dream.

But it's real. Very fucking real.

My mind is rushing with all sorts of doomsday thoughts. Who kidnapped me? Why was I kidnapped? And worse of all, what do they plan on doing with me? The latter thought terrifies me and chills my body.

Is it because of Zane?

I don't want to believe it. Zane wouldn't do something

like this to me… would he? It's a scary thought. If it's true, it means I never really knew him all along. I try not to despair.

"Vlad, I have a gift for you," a deep, familiar voice says, startling me. Up until that moment, I thought I was alone. I turn my head slightly to get a visual on who's talking. My blood goes cold when I see who it is. Standing in a darkened corner is Garret with a phone pressed to his ear. He's staring at me in a way that makes me want to writhe against my bonds and get the fuck out of here, but the fear is so strong that I'm paralyzed.

"What do you think, boss, eh?" Garret asks on the phone. "She's older than what you're used to, but she's just your type." Garret laughs and then adds darkly, "The fighting kind." He smiles, a sick and disgusting sight that turns my stomach.

I can hear a voice on the other end and then silence, but Garret doesn't respond and keeps staring at me with those dead, chilly eyes.

I go dizzy with terror. "Zane!" I yell, tears streaming down my face. "Zane, please don't let them hurt me!" I shake violently in my chair, struggling in vain to break free.

Garret's handsome face twists with rage and he walks over and backhands me in the face. I gasp with pain as my head whips to the side, and he snarls, "Shut up, you stupid bitch! That piece of shit ain't coming to save your ass."

The taste of metallic blood fills my mouth as stinging pain shoots through my face. Fuck, that hurt.

"Thanks to you, he's good as fucking dead." My heart stops beating. No. No!

Garret gives me a wicked smile at the look of confused distress on my face. "Yeah that's right, bitch. Zane is dead because of you."

"I-I-I didn't do anything for Zane to deserve this," I stammer. "Please don't hurt him.

"Lying whore!" Garret backhands me again and I cry out with pain. Hot fluid pours out of my nose. Blood. "You saw us unloading. Ain't no way we're gonna let you live after that."

"I won't tell anyone!" I try to yell, but my mouth hurts so fucking bad. The small cuts sting, and I spit up blood. "I swear," I say weakly as tears prick my eyes.

Garret chuckles evilly. "No amount of begging or lying is gonna save you, cunt. If you didn't want to end up like this, you should've never got involved with Zane."

I start sobbing incoherently. This isn't fair. Not for me. Not for Zane. Not for anyone.

I feel a hand touch my shoulder, and my heart nearly stops.

Oh no. Oh God, no.

Garret chuckles at my terror, guessing my worry. "Don't worry, bitch. We're not going to rape you... yet. I gotta wait for the boss and the camera so we can give Zane a nice parting gift." His fingers touch my chin and I rip my head away. He smiles down at me as he says, "I want him to be able to watch."

"Fuck you!" I scream at the top of my lungs, no longer caring about what happens to me. At this point, I feel like I have nothing to lose. They're not going to spare me, and I'm not going to give him the pleasure of seeing me beg for my life.

Garret laughs at my rage. "We'll see how much shit you'll be able to talk when I have my dick in your mouth."

I sneer. "Fucking try it, and I'll bite your dick off."

"Fucking cocky bitch!" Roaring with rage, Garret shoves me and my chair topples over backward. My head slams against the floor, and I see stars. Through the pain I smile, pleased I made the evil fucker mad.

Garret lets out a snarl of frustration. "I can't wait to fuck you, bitch," he growls from somewhere above me. "You won't be talking shit after I get done. You'll be begging me to end your life."

As defiant as I've become in this predicament, I don't offer a response because I'm filled with terror.

When it's obvious I have nothing else to say, he mutters something I can't hear and leaves. I hear the sounds of footsteps, followed by a door closing. I'm left alone with my thoughts and the knowledge that I only have minutes or possibly even hours left to live.

Please God, help me! I plead within the depths of my mind. *Please don't let my life end in this way!*

But God is either deaf or not listening. The truth is, no one is coming to save me. Not Katie. Not Daddy, and definitely not Zane.

I feel like there's only one thing left to do.

I close my eyes and pray for the end to come swiftly.

CHAPTER 24

ZANE

My chest hurts so fucking bad. It hasn't stopped hurting since she came to my house the other day. I had to ignore her while she knocked on my door, but hearing her crying was like a knife to my heart. I wanna talk to her. I wanna explain everything. More than that, I wanna leave this life behind and take her away. But we'd have to run. We'd always be running.

You can't leave the mob.

Fuck, I can't handle it. But it's for her own good. I know it is. I've been keeping an eye on her. Marky has, too. I can't be around her all the time, and I trust him. He'd tell me if there was anything going on.

I can't sleep. Every time I hear a car pull up, I instantly think it's someone coming to take her. I've dialed up Nikolai's number at least a dozen times, but I never hit send. I need to know she's gonna be alright, and she's not on their list.

He told me she's alright. I have to believe him. I trust him.

But at the same time, I don't.

And Marky's still watching her when I can't. Just in case.

As if reading my mind, not ten minutes later I get a call. I stop working on the mock-up of the tat I'm doing later and calmly pick up my phone.

I'm trying to keep the worrying down to a minimum. Every time he calls my heart rate picks up, and dread runs down my spine. But each time it's always been to tell me she's fine.

I answer it and try keep my voice even, but before I can ask him about her, he's yelling on the other end.

"They got her." My blood runs cold. "I wasn't sure, Zane. I didn't want to freak you out." He's talking rapid-fire, practically shouting, and it's hard to hear. I stand up and pace the room as my body goes numb with fear. "I didn't know what to do so I just watched, but it was them and they took her. I tried--"

"Stop. Stop." It can't be true. My lungs refuse to fill. "Who has her?"

"Garret. That fucker and two others. I wasn't sure if it was him. It wasn't till I was pulling in and they got out. I wasn't fast enough. I followed them as fast as I could, but I lost them."

My blood races with adrenaline, anger takes over the fear. I'm gonna kill him. I'm gonna slice his fucking throat open.

"Where?" I ask him as I try to keep my hand from tightening on the phone to the point where it feels like it's going to break.

"I followed them onto Washington and then they went past--"

"Where?!" I scream into the phone. I'm barely able to breathe, my vision's going white. I need to get there now. Right fucking now. Every second away from her is a second he could hurt her. Fuck, my heart sinks. He's going to. I know he is.

"I lost them going north on Market Street." Market Street? What the fuck is on Market Street? I don't know. I don't know shit about the mob's operations. Fuck!

I hang up the phone and immediately dial Nikolai. I'll fucking kill him. I'll kill all of them.

He answers the phone, and I don't give him a second to give me his bullshit.

"You lying motherfucker," I seethe into the phone.

"Whoa!" he yells on the other end, but I don't stop. I'll never stop.

"You told me she was safe. You're fucking dead."

"Zane!" he yells out.

"All of you are dead." I'll start at the top and work my way down.

"Zane! Who has her?" I pause in my oath to make all them suffer. I wasn't expecting him to deny it. "Who has her?" he asks again, but I don't answer. I don't know if he's bullshitting me. My body's shaking with anger, and I'm not sure what to do. I don't know if I believe him. I don't know what to believe anymore.

"It's not us, Zane! I didn't lie to you. Zane!" He's quiet for a second. "Zane! Are you there?" He sounds panicked, and his voice is filled with concern.

"You didn't know?" I ask him while trying to calm myself down. A shred of relief goes through me. But only a shred. This will be easier if it's just Garret. So much easier if I have Nikolai's backing.

"It's not us--"

I cut him off. "Garret took her."

He's quiet for a second. I let it sink in, but in my head I hear the *tick tick tick* of time passing.

"Are you sure?" he asks.

"Yes," I'm quick to answer.

"Do you know where?" he asks. My phone beeps, and I'm sure it's Marky calling back. I pull the phone away from my ear and see I'm right. I ignore the call.

"They went down Market, but that's where we lost them."

"Give me her cell. They're probably at the warehouse." I rattle off her number and pace the room, feeling like a caged beast.

"What's the address?" I ask him. That's all I need. Just the address, and I can go.

"Hold on Zane, we need to know who's there."

"We'll find out when we get there."

"It only takes a minute, hold the fuck on," he scolds me, and I can't stand it. I need to move; I need to go to her.

"Fuck!" he yells into the phone, and it stops me in my tracks.

"What? What?" I ask him. Fear runs through me. Not Maddy. Please, fuck, don't be about Maddy.

"Vlad's there." His voice is hard and devoid of emotion.

"Vlad and Garret?" I ask him. My head feels dizzy and I have to lean against the wall. Pain tears through my heart.

"He's fucking dead." Nikolai's voice is cold. I nod my head at his words.

"How many others?" I ask him. He's tracking their cells to locate them. I've seen him do it before. Thank fuck for Nikolai keeping me from going in with no plan.

"I only see four of them. But there could be more."

"Do you have anyone?" I ask him. I can't ask Needles or Marky to come with me. They aren't trained for this shit. They wouldn't know what to do.

"Yeah, I do, but you need a vest, Zane." I don't fucking want to wait on a vest. "We have the element of surprise on our side. They won't see us coming. But we need to be smart." I don't care about being smart or being prepared, I just need to get to her.

"If I ever meant anything to you, you'll help me keep her safe."

"Zane, I'm on your side." He sighs into the phone and says, "We'll get her back. I promise you."

My throat closes as other emotions take over, but I hold on to the anger. I picture what I'm gonna do to them when I get there. They're dead. Every fucking one of them.

"Garret's mine."

* * *

"You need to be smart about this, Zane," I hear Nikolai speaking, but I'm not listening. We're close, so close to getting her back and keeping her safe.

"You can't go in there guns blazing," he says. The fuck I can't.

"Nik," I say as I look him square in his eyes, "If you think I can go in there and not put a bullet in every one of their skulls, you've lost your mind."

"That's fine by me," he replies as he keeps my gaze, "But we need to go in quietly."

My jaw clenches. "I don't like it." He wants me to sneak in and find her. He wants me to wait for his call. I'm not fucking waiting. If they're in there… if they're with her. My throat closes and my fists clench at the thought. "I'll fucking kill them!" I slam my fist on the dash.

Nik looks at me like he's not sure what to do. "If it was up to me, Zane, you wouldn't be going in," he says quietly. "And you don't have to like it. But you need to respect my plan. I promised you we'd get her back, and I fully intend to keep that promise."

I bite my tongue as he continues. "You need to be quiet.

You can't let them know we're there." He's right. Logically I know that. But logic can go fuck itself right now for all I care.

I hold his eyes and nod once. "Done." I'm lying. I'm not holding back. I refuse to stand by and watch and wait.

Nik looks behind me and asks, "Lev, Alec, you two loaded?"

"Damn right, boss," Alec answers. Lev nods. I look behind me at the two men. I've seen them before--hell, I've grown up with them. But I don't trust them. I don't trust any of them. I barely trust Nikolai.

For all I know, this is a setup and they're going to stab Nik in the back.

I'm going in and grabbing my girl, and getting the fuck out. If I can kill those fuckers who took her on my way out, that's what I'll do. She's all that's important. I need to get her out of there.

"We'll head in through the back," Nik says and starts giving orders. We're parked in a lot just behind the warehouse. He said there's no cameras here. I'm taking his lead, but I don't like waiting. I need to make sure she's safe.

Nik looks at me while he talks. "This hotheaded fuck is staying with me." He turns back to look at the other men while my eyes bore into his skull.

"You two need to make sure the place is secure. Sweep the place and kill anyone in there. Every single one of those fuckers is a traitor. He's not the boss anymore." They nod and agree, and with that I'm moving out of the car and I don't stop until we're there, staring at the steel double doors to the warehouse.

Nik is slow as fuck compared to me, but he's quiet. The other men are also quiet. All I can hear is my heavy breathing, and the sound of blood rushing in my ears.

I move to open the door, but Nik stops me. His hand flies to the handle and he rips my hand away.

Nik puts his finger against his lips and stares me in the eyes.

I nod my head and back away, following his lead. My heart's beating so fast and loud. I can feel it pounding against my chest.

As soon as I'm in, I hear her. The warehouse is nearly empty. To our right, I can see half a dozen folding tables with boxes piled high in two rows in front of them.

This must be where they pack and ship the product.

In an instant my head whips to the left.

I can hear her muffled cries for help. They echo off the wall. I move straight back, to the left. There's one hallway on this side, and her voice is easy to follow.

Keep screaming. I need to hear you, peaches. I need to know which door. My feet move of their own accord, and I'm only half-aware of Nik moving behind me.

I hear her cries from the far door, and I'm on it instantly. I'm there. She's still alive. I'm here. I can save her.

I go to grab the door handle, but Nik pulls me back. My fists clench and I almost knock him out. But his attention isn't on me. It's on the door.

My shoulders heave as I wait for him to get going. I hear her scream out, and it's too much.

Nik's hand settles on the doorknob, gently turning it. I resist the urge to kick it open. I need to get to her. Her cries are louder now, and I don't know what's happening to her. My hands grip my gun and sweat pours down my face. My heart's beating too fast.

Maddy. I'm here.

Nik gently and soundlessly pushes the door open enough for us to creep through. As soon as I'm in, I see her in front of a desk, on the ground tied to an overturned chair. Vlad's standing above her with a large knife in hand. There's plastic wrap and duct tape on the desk. Their *equipment.*

Maddy's struggling against the ropes, trying to pull her hands free as she bucks off the ground. She's helpless and trying to scream through a gag. Tears are running down her face. My heart pangs in my chest.

Vlad's got a sick smile on his sunken-in face as he cuts her leg with the knife. Behind him, Garret's setting up a video camera.

Sickness threatens to take over, but more than that, anger. How dare they touch her? My body trembles with barely contained rage. Those sick fucks!

I can't let him touch her. I won't. In the distance, I hear gunshots. Alec and Lev must have found other people in the warehouse. But now we've lost the element of surprise as Vlad and Garret look up and realize we've come for Maddy.

I hear Nik yell as I run out to the middle of the room, my gun pointed at Vlad and firing. My hand's shaking so hard, I miss. The bullet sounds off and barely grazes Vlad's back. Garret comes from my left and throws a chair at me. The fuckers aren't armed.

Good. I aim my gun at him as the chair flies through the air.

It hits my calves and trips me up as I try to run to Maddy. I try to cover her, but I fall and the gun slips from my hands. It lands on the ground with a loud clank next to me, and I brace myself. I'm quick to get up and move to her side.

At the same time, I hear another bullet go off and see Nik go after Vlad from the corner of my eye. Garret's quick to run into Nik, knocking the two of them to the ground. Vlad's focused on Nik, and I can tell Nik is his target. I reach up to the desk and grab the knife.

Maddy first. I have to save her. Before I do anything else, I need her to be safe. I need to give her a fighting chance at least. I crawl to her and quickly cut the rope from her wrists. The knife saws back and forth.

I hear the sound of bones crunching and fists slamming into flesh. By the noises echoing off the walls of the small room, I know Nik must be putting up a hell of a fight.

Finally, the rope breaks and I hear Nik call out for me. "Zane!"

I put the knife in her hands, knowing she needs to cut the rope on her ankles. "Run, Maddy!" I yell at her. "Run!"

I grab the gun on the floor next to me and turn to aim, but I can't fire. I could hit Nikolai. I move quickly through the room, kicking the chair and aim as soon as I have Garret lined up. He lifts his head and sees as I pull the trigger. He ducks and kicks off the ground, shoving his weight forward and pushing his body into my thighs.

I fall hard and the gun goes off as I crash to the floor. My hand hits the floor hard and I wince as Garret punches me in the gut. The gun slips from my hand and he reaches for it. I grab his waist and yank him down and away from it. He kicks my thigh and reaches for the gun again, practically climbing up my body. I headbutt his stomach, and he keels over in pain. I slam a fist in his jaw and it sends him sliding away from me, away from the gun.

I reach for the gun. I can feel the barrel with the tips of my fingers.

I see Maddy using the knife to cut the rope around her ankles from the corner of my eye. I need to kill him. I can't let him get to her. I need to get the gun first.

Maddy's screaming, and keeps looking at me. She needs to

get out. Just save herself. But she's not running. She hurls her body at Garret with the knife in her hand. But he's too quick. He kicks her hard in her face, sending her flying backward. Fuck! "Just run Maddy!" I scream to her, but she ignores me. I'll never forgive myself if something happens to her.

The knife slices his leg, but doesn't do anything more than slow him down for a moment. It's a moment I'm able to scoot closer to the gun than he is though.

Garret grabs my leg and tries to pull me away. I kick him. Hard. I miss, but on the way down my foot hits his jaw and he slips off of me. I kick against the ground watching Garret, and look up to see Maddy crawling on the floor and pushing the gun to me. I take it in both hands and roll onto my back, steadying it down my body and just as Garrett looks up, I shoot.

Bang! Maddy shrieks. *Bang! Bang!* I keep shooting until the gun's out of bullets.

Garret falls to the ground lifeless, but the fight's not over. I turn to my left and see Nik and Vlad both grappling on the ground, both with their hands at each other's throat. I aim my gun and fire, but it's empty. Fuck! My body's hot and my heart feels like it's racing to climb up my throat.

I search for another gun, but I can't see one. There's nothing.

I watch as Vlad puts all his weight on top of Nik and tightens his hands around his throat. Nik doesn't let up, but he's losing the fight. I can see it happening.

I run toward them and slam my body against Vlad's. He falls, and his hands slip. Nik takes in a heavy breath, coughing as his lungs fill for the first time since Vlad started choking him. I struggle to get up as Nik pushes against me and tries to pin Vlad's heavy weight down.

Nikolai's hands wrap around Vlad's throat. Vlad tries bringing his legs up to pin Nikolai to the ground, but I'm quick to grab him. I leave Maddy behind me and grip onto his calves. I push all my weight down and pin him. I don't let up until I see Vlad's hands move from Nik's throat to the hands strangling him.

The blood vessels in his eyes pop and his face turns red. Maddy screams. She doesn't stop screaming. I leave Nik and scoot backward to hold Maddy. She's on the ground, knife in her hand with the cut rope on the floor next to her.

Her clothes are torn, and the cut on her leg is bleeding pretty bad. I grab her in my arms and push my hand against her cut to stop the blood from flowing. I try shushing her. Her body shakes in my arms.

"I've got you. You're safe." I try petting her hair, but she's pushing me away.

My eyes focus on Alec and Lev as they come into the room with their guns out. I start to push her behind me, but they take in the scene and lower their weapons.

I hold Maddy closer to me as I see the life drain from Vlad's eyes. Lev walks over and holds a gun out to Nik as Vlad's body goes limp.

I turn Maddy's head away and watch as Nik puts the gun to Vlad's head and pulls the trigger.

Bang! Maddy jolts once in my arms, but she doesn't scream.

A clean shot in the skull. Blood spills from the wound as the head turns slightly and Nik moves off his chest.

"It's over, peaches. It's alright," I whisper into her hair, but she doesn't respond. That's when I notice she's not holding on to me anymore. She's limp in my arms.

"Maddy?" I give her body a firm shake as my heart races with panic. She's breathing, she's alive. But she's not responsive.

CHAPTER 25

ZANE

She won't stop shaking. I hold her closer to me. I think she's in shock. "It's alright peaches, I've got you." I repeat the words over and over, holding her tighter to me.

I look up at Nikolai. "I need to take her to the hospital." She needs help. She needs it now.

He looks back at me with hesitation. That's something the mob doesn't do. At the hospital they ask questions. Questions are something for snitches.

I grind my teeth. I'm not going to let her go without a fight.

"I'm done with this shit, Nikolai." I nearly spit my words out. I look up at him, holding my girl closer to me.

He's the only one I had in my life for the longest time. But that's over now. I'm ready to move on. And this isn't the life I want. It's not the life of a man she deserves. And more than anything, I want to deserve her.

"What's that, Zane? You're done with what?" he asks with a small threat in his voice, but I don't care. I'm not letting go of Maddy, and her and this life simply don't mix.

"I'm out. I don't want this anymore. Take the shop, do what you want. You're the Don, and I'm asking to go. I'm asking for peace."

Nikolai looks at me and then back at his men. They heard, but they keep their heads down. Nikolai is the boss now. He holds the power.

He takes a few steps back and runs a hand down his face. "Get these fuckers out of here now!" he yells at his men.

"You need to wait till it's clean." I nod and agree, but I don't like it. Nik passes me the plastic wrap and duct tape and it takes me a minute to realize it's for her cut.

I take care of it and keep an eye on her as time passes. I rock her in my arms and watch her breathing. She seems to be doing better and not worse, so that's a good thing.

"She'll be alright," Nik says. I look up at him and his eyes move from her to me. "She's alright."

"I wanna take her to the hospital."

Maddy nestles into my chest, she's quiet and still trembling. This was too much for her.

Nikolai nods his head at me. "Call 'em."

I don't hesitate to reach in my pocket and dial up the ambulance. I'm short and to the point. "I have a young woman in shock on 32 and Sussex." They ask questions that I don't answer. "She needs an ambulance." And with that, I hang up the phone. I may want out of the mob, but I'm sure as shit not going to give them any information.

I'm not a rat.

A long moment passes. "You okay, peaches?" I whisper into Maddy's ear. She nods her head and offers me a small murmur, but her eyes aren't focused.

"What's the shop worth?" Nikolai asks, bringing my attention back to him.

"No clue," I answer him. I don't fucking know. I don't handle the books. "You can check the books."

Nikolai looks at me for a moment. "I'll give you the money, whatever it's worth, and you go where you want." I hold his gaze, feeling a weight lift off my shoulders.

I nod my head as I hear the sirens coming. They're always fast when you hang up.

"It's been a long time coming," Nikolai says. "I'm proud of you, Zane."

I don't know why, but it hurts to hear him say that. My eyes water and I'd feel like a little bitch if Nikolai's weren't all glassy-looking, too.

"It's over," he says.

I nod my head and lean down to give Maddy a kiss.

"It's over, baby; we're safe now."

CHAPTER 26

MADELINE

"I think she's awake, Mr. Murphy," I hear Katie say. Her voice sounds muffled, almost as if I'm under water. I hear other people talking too, but their voices are too distorted to understand what they're saying.

Groaning, I struggle to open my eyes. They feel heavy, like they weigh a thousand pounds. On top of that, my body is sore all over and I feel incredibly weak. After a moment, I'm able to lift my eyelids enough to see. Everything is blurry. There are several people, I think, standing over my bed. I blink rapidly to clear my vision, and slowly the room comes into view.

I'm lying in a hospital bed, surrounded by Daddy and Katie. Katie is holding my hand and looking down at me with a mixture of relief and love. Daddy looks like a man who's been told he's won the lottery.

As grateful as I am to see these two, I notice one person missing.

Zane, I think with panic. *Where's Zane?*

I try to lift my head to look around, but it's too much for me and I fall back. Seeing my distress, Daddy rushes forward and places a hand on my shoulder to calm me. "I'm here, baby," he reassures me, leaning down to plant a gentle kiss on my forehead. "No one is ever going to hurt you again. I swear it." For a moment, I feel comforted by his words.

"We're both so glad you're alive," Katie adds, her voice filled with joy. She places her hand over her chest. "For a while there, I thought you wouldn't make it. You almost gave your father and I a frickin' heart attack."

I smile briefly at her, so she doesn't think I'm an ungrateful twit. "Where's Zane?" I croak. My voice sounds raw, like I've smoked a hundred packs of cigarettes.

"He had to leave," Katie says, glancing apprehensively at Daddy.

"Why?" I demand, sensing something's not right. Why would he leave me like this?

"Because I told him to," Daddy replies sternly, his smile morphing into a scowl. "I told him to get out and to never come back. He's the reason why you're here, and he can go to hell for it."

Anger swells up from the depths of my stomach. "Why would you do that?" I snap. "Zane saved my life!" I can scarcely remember the events following my rescue, but I clearly remember being held in Zane's loving arms before I lost consciousness. My father was wrong to send Zane away when he'd risked his life to save me.

He snorts. "Saved you? Had you never met the lying bastard, you wouldn't be in this situation."

"I'm only alive because he saved me!" I yell, my voice croaking like a frog. Through the large doorway, I see several nurses stop to stare at me, but I don't give a damn. I'm fucking pissed.

"You have no idea why you're alive," Daddy says.

"You're clearly delirious, so I'm going to forgive how you're acting toward me."

"I am not delirious. As soon as they say I'm well enough, I'm out of here! And the first thing I'm going to do is find Zane to tell him how much I love him."

Daddy's face turns red with fury. "You're going to do no such thing, young lady!"

I glare back at him, pretending not to notice Katie fidgeting and looking uncomfortable. I know she must feel pretty conflicted right now, stuck between her best friend and my well-meaning father. "I'm a grown woman. You can't tell me what I can or can't do!"

He glowers at me, the veins standing out his neck. I swear if I wasn't already half-dead, he'd strike me. He takes a deep breath, as if to calm himself and opens his mouth to speak. "You know--"

"Mr. Murphy," Katie says, quietly interrupting him. "I think Maddy and I need a second alone."

He turns on Katie, and at first I think he's going to cuss her out, but he just stares at her.

"Please?" Katie pleads. "Just a few minutes, and I'll let you take the helm."

Daddy turns his gaze back on me for a long moment before grudgingly saying, "Alright. You have five minutes." Not saying another word, he bends down and kisses me on the forehead, and then he walks out of the room, gently closing the door behind him.

"What happened?" I ask her as soon as the door clicks shut. Katie grabs a chair from the corner of the room and drags it over to the bed. She sits down and takes my hand.

"Are you okay?" she asks, her eyes filled with concern.

I shake my head, tears welling up into my eyes. "No," I sigh. "I'm not." Tears roll down my face as I relive the trauma of my kidnapping, and it's an effort to wipe them away. "I need Zane," I say.

Seeing my distress, tears well up in Katie's eyes. "Oh Maddy," she sighs. "I can't imagine what you went through."

My throat feels like it has a lump the size of a bowling ball in it. "They were going to…" I can hardly get the words out. "Rape me... and kill me." I'm grateful my father isn't in here to hear this part of my story. I fear he might blame Zane and go find him and shoot him.

Katie places a hand over her mouth in horror. "Oh God, Maddy, no."

I nod. "It was so awful, Katie. I didn't know if I was going to live or die."

"And Zane really saved you?" she asks in wonder.

"Yes," I reply. "Against all odds, he found me. And then he killed them. He saved me."

Katie's eyes go wide with shock. "He killed the guys who kidnapped you?"

I nod. "And they fucking deserved it," I snarl, half-rising in the bed, my eyes blazing with hatred. "They deserved to be fucking dead!"

Katie's taken aback by the venom in my voice and the savage scowl on my face. I know she thinks that this behavior isn't like me, but she wasn't there. She didn't live through the horror like I did. It changes a person.

"When was Zane last here?" I ask, looking all around as if he's about to pop out of thin air.

"Yesterday, when you were admitted. He called me and told me to get your dad. I did, and then when I got here he told me you had been kidnapped, but everything was fine now. He didn't say anything about killing anybody, though." She bites her lower lip anxiously.

"He didn't tell you because he didn't want Daddy to

know. Daddy hates him, so imagine if he knew what Zane did, even if it was to save me."

"He'd arrest him."

I nod. "Exactly. So I need you to promise me, Katie. Promise me you won't tell a soul about what I've told you."

Katie is a long time in responding, and I fear she's going to run out and tell my father, but finally she nods. "I promise, Maddy. You don't have to worry. I won't tell a soul." She bites her lower lip again and then looks anxious. "But there's something you need to know."

I hold back a groan. I've had enough surprises to last me a lifetime.

"The cops interviewed your dad and me, and I'm sure they're going to interview you as soon as they think you're well enough."

"Ugh," I groan. "That's the last thing I need right now."

"You're going to have to lie to them, Maddy."

"I know that."

"I hope you know you could get into serious trouble for that."

"I don't give a fuck." I don't care what crime I'll commit by covering for Zane, I'm going to stand by him until the very end.

"Just making sure you know that."

"Thank you," I say sarcastically.

Katie scowls. "Bitch."

I don't miss a beat. "Ho."

Katie laughs and leans down to hug me. "Maddy, I'm just so happy you're alive!"

I wish I could rejoice with her, but I feel sick to my stomach. "Damn, I really wish there was a way I could get out of being interrogated."

"You know, you don't have to talk to them right now. You're the victim in this, you can stall them by saying you're not ready to talk about it. And then when you are well enough, you can lawyer up first before saying anything, if you have to say anything at all."

"I'll just say I don't remember shit, that I fell and hit my head, which I did, and I'm having trouble recalling anything." They can't make me talk.

"You always were sort of brain-damaged," Katie agrees, and we both laugh.

"Do you really love him?" Katie asks me in a serious tone after a moment of silence.

"Yes," I reply with conviction. "I do. I don't know if he loves me, or if he and my father will ever get along, but I do love him. Very much."

Katie looks at me with a proud gleam in her eye. "That's good, Maddy. I'm so happy for you, and I'm glad to know you've finally given a man your heart." Then she wryly adds, "Even if he had to murder two guys to capture it."

"Katie!" I protest.

"Wha? You know I'm just pulling your leg. You know, I talked to Needles too, during all this."

"What did he say?" I ask.

"He told me that they're moving shop. That Zane's out of the mob for good and moving on. When you're well enough, if you still want, I'll take you to Zane."

My eyes brim over with tears. "Thank you so much, Katie."

She rubs my arm affectionately. "That's what friends are for."

I feel so much love and appreciation for Katie right now. She's been my rock throughout my life, and I'm honored that she's going to stand by me and my decision to cover for Zane. I'm not even worried that she'll ever talk about what I've shared with her.

Still there is one last thing that is bothering me. "Katie,

am I wrong?" I have to ask. "Zane killed those people, and I'll have to live with that knowledge for the rest of my life. But even knowing that, I still love him and want to be with him. Do you think that makes me a bad person?"

Katie snorts with derision. "I think you refusing to tell me how big Zane's dong is makes you a bad person."

"Katie!"

Katie laughs, and a moment later, I'm laughing right along with her. We laugh and laugh until our sides hurt. When we're done, Katie's expression turns serious and she grabs my hand and rubs it. "No, I don't think you're a bad person, Maddy. You're the best friend a girl could ever ask for."

"Thank you." My eyes well up with tears, and I'm truly touched. I know then that Katie and I will be friends for life. Our bond is stronger than ever.

Katie smiles at me with great affection, the same that I feel in my heart. "Besides, you can't help who you love."

Grinning and filled with happiness, I squeeze her hand and reply, "Truer words have never been spoken."

CHAPTER 27

ZANE

"You sleep at all last night, man?" Needles asks as I place the machine in the cardboard box as carefully as I can.

"No." I don't mean to be short. But I'm worried about her, and tired as fuck. I stayed up in the waiting room downstairs.

I just can't get the image of her tied up and helpless out of my head. I wish they were alive so I could kill them again. I never wanna leave her side ever again.

I know she left me. I know this shit is my fault. But I couldn't leave her. I respected her father's wishes, but I wasn't going to leave.

The nurse on duty was nice enough to keep me posted. I know she's awake now. I know she's alright. I keep checking my phone, thinking she'll call me. But nothing yet.

I wouldn't even be here if Nikolai hadn't told me the shop needed to be cleared out today.

"It's gonna be alright." Needles slaps my back and gives

me a reassuring look. He has no fucking clue how I feel though.

"As soon as this shit is packed up, I'm going back to her. Her father can't stay in that room forever." I don't know if she'll want me. But I have to try.

"Even if he does, so what?" Needles says with a scrunched nose. "Fuck him."

I give him a sad smile. I thought about just being an ass and refusing to leave. But he's her father, and I know she doesn't want us fighting.

"It'll hurt her," I tell him. I know she didn't like it when we fought before. Who am I to go in there causing problems when she's recovering from that shit? The shit I caused her.

I want her though. I need her.

I have to try.

I breathe out deep and get back to loading my shit into cardboard boxes.

I hear the door open behind us and I assume it's Trisha. She's got a box in the back that she needs to move to the new place.

But then I hear Katie's sarcastic mouth. "You better not be leaving town."

I clench my jaw and try to hold in everything I wanna say. I need to know how my girl is. I wanna tell Katie there's no fucking way I'm leaving her. Instead I slowly turn around, and I'm speechless.

Maddy's standing there with a bandage on her leg and a bruise on her face. Her gorgeous green eyes are staring at me with so many emotions shining through.

I drop the shit in my hands and stare back at her, taking her in. I wanna run to her, take her in my arms, and kiss her. I'd drop to my knees and promise to make it up to her. I'd spend the rest of my life doing it.

She looks so uneasy. Like she doesn't know why she's here.

Fuck it!

I only have one life to live, and I wanna spend it with her.

I take large strides across the room to take her in my arms. And thank fuck she wraps her arms around me in return. I bury my head in the crook of her neck and kiss every inch available.

"I'm so sorry, Maddy."

She doesn't say anything which makes me nervous, but she holds me tighter.

"Is it true?" she asks in a voice that tells me she's scared to know the answer.

"Is what true?" I pull away and search her eyes. My heart races with panic.

"Are you done with that? *All* of it?" she asks me. I slowly nod my head as I realize what she's asking.

"I am. It's over. I swear to you."

I hear her sob, and it breaks my heart. I brush her tears away with my thumb and hold her face in my hands.

"I'm sorry, peaches. I'm so fucking sorry." I take her lips with mine and kiss her with all the passion I have for her. I want her to feel it, and to know it, never doubting me again.

"I'll make it up to you," I whisper with my forehead resting against hers. "Every day for the rest of my life." I kiss her again and she leans into my touch. My hand splays across her back and braces her against me. I don't want to ever let go.

"I love you, Zane." She whispers her words and my heart swells in my chest, but I'm still worried. I wait for a "but". After a moment she pulls back and looks at me, her eyes searching my face and then I see her vulnerability.

She's just waiting for me to say it back.
"I love you too, peaches. Forever."

CHAPTER 28

MADELINE

"Yes!" I scream out as pounds into me. Fuck, he feels so good. Every time is like the first time. He groans in the crook of my neck.

"That's right, peaches," he says as his callused thumb presses against my clit, and I fall hard against the bed. My back bows, and my pussy spasms with an intense orgasm.

"Cum on my dick, baby." He continues fucking me through my release as waves and waves of heated pleasure light every nerve ending on fire.

He thrusts into me, forcing the headboard to bang repeatedly against the wall.

The haze of lust clears for only a moment.

I push up against the wall as if I could stop it, but it's useless. Zane is lost in pleasure and overpowers me, caging me in and fucking me as though he needs his release more than his last breath.

"Fuck!" I scream out as the waves dim and the tips of my toes and fingers tingle. Again. Slight fear overwhelms me as my body heats. My head thrashes, and I try to push him away.

I almost say the words, *I can't*. But Zane's lips find mine. He kisses me with such passion, I'm forced to give myself to him.

His hips pound against mine, each time pushing against my throbbing clit, once, twice, three times and he explodes in me. The feel of his massive cock pulsing inside of me sends me over the edge again.

And we find our release together.

After a moment, my breathing evens and Zane pulls out of me. I wince from how sore I am. We finally moved in together, seriously this time. Not just one of us staying at the other's place. No more roommates. Just us. And he's taken advantage. Not that I'm complaining.

Shit! The headboard.

I peek up at the wall and cover my face.

"Damn it, Zane," I groan into my hands.

"What?" he asks all innocent-like. He knows what he did. He hasn't even sanded the spackle from the last time he dented the wall.

"We need a new headboard." I concede. I fucking love this one. It's beautiful. But Zane is a beast, and there's no way this is going to work.

He chuckles, all rough and low. And sexy as sin. My clit throbs, and my legs scissor. I can't get enough of him.

"Already?" he says and grins. "You're insatiable." I playfully push him away as he tries to crawl on top of my body.

I giggle and lie on my side, facing him.

I was so scared only weeks ago that we were ruined. That everything that'd happened was just too much. I didn't think our relationship would survive.

Especially when my father came over and saw us together on the sofa. I stood up, ready to tell him not to say anything, but Zane and him took it outside.

I'd be lying if I said I didn't eavesdrop.

My heart nearly leapt up my throat when I heard Zane tell him he killed the men who put their hands on me. He told him everything.

My father still isn't sure that I should be with him, but at least he has some respect for my decision to stay with him and he keeps his mouth shut when he sees him.

The truth is, I needed Zane, and he needed me.

Without each other, we wouldn't have healed like we did. My fingers trace the snake on his arm. It's my favorite thing to do while we're in bed.

"When are you gonna let me give you a tattoo?" he asks me.

I've been thinking about that a lot lately. We have a fresh start. A new home all to ourselves. I want everyone to know I'm his. I'd be proud to wear his art.

But I'd be prouder to wear something else.

"When you put a ring on it."

He gives me a panty-melting smirk and crawls on top of me. "Is that so?" he asks, cocking a brow and chuckling.

"Hell yeah. Haven't you heard the song, if you like it you shoulda…" My voice trails off as he reaches over to the nightstand.

Oh hell no. No. He. Did. Not.

He pulls the drawer open and pulls out a small black velvet box.

I cover my mouth with both my hands as tears well in my eyes.

"Madeline Murphy, be my wife." He doesn't ask, of course. I roll my eyes and sniffle before letting out a small laugh.

"You didn't even ask." I look into his eyes and feel so freaking loved.

"Last time I asked you for something, you gave me the runaround for weeks." My shoulders shake with a soft giggle, and my eyes go glassy with tears. “I wasn’t willing to take the risk this time.”

“I fucking love you, Zane.” I wrap my arms around his neck and kiss him with every ounce of passion I have.

He looks into my eyes and smiles wide as he says, “I love you too, peaches.”

EPILOGUE

ZANE

"Are you sure it's not going to hurt?" Maddy asks me again. I've told her it's gonna fucking hurt. Tattooing over any bone isn't a walk in the park. But somehow she keeps getting it in her head that I've told her it isn't going to hurt.

"Just a little, but don't worry, I'll make it up to you."

She looks up at me warily and takes in a deep breath. "Alright. Let's do this."

She opens the door to the new shop and walks right in like she owns the place. And I guess she does, since what's mine is hers, now that we're married.

"Hey Needles, do you guys have cosmos here?" she asks Needles, and I can't help but laugh as he gives her a look like she's crazy.

He looks past her and right at me. "She for real, bro?" he asks.

"Give her what she wants, man. She's getting my mark on her."

Needles gives her a big smile and Trisha walks out from the back. She must've heard us come in.

"I got something in the back you'll like." She grins at Maddy, and I get the sense that the two of them have talked about this before.

"Whatever you're drinking, take it down fast, baby." I pull her into my arms and hold her tight to me. "I've been waiting for this for a long time."

"What'd you decide on?" Needles asks Maddy.

She looks back at me with a small smile and then to him and says, "I told him whatever he wants. I trust him." That's almost true. She told me she wanted peaches. Her confession nearly knocked me on my ass.

She said she needed it. She needed me to make my nickname for her permanent, so she can't run from it.

I think I'm going to throw in some sunflowers too. She lights up every time I get them for her now. If she's having a bad day, it's real easy to put a smile on her face and then take her to bed and help her forget whatever's bothering her.

Needles snorts a laugh as Maddy pulls away from me and grabs a small pink bottle of something from Trisha. "Well, it's your funeral," he says under his breath.

"Kinky?" Maddy asks.

"Fucking delicious," Trisha says, shooting back her own tiny ass bottle.

"You on the clock?" I ask her.

"Nah, me and Katie are going out tonight."

Maddy rolls her eyes and sets her empty bottle down. "Don't let her get you into trouble."

"Us?" she asks. "Never."

I pull Maddy into the back as I nod to Trisha and Needles. "See you guys later."

She squeezes my hand and takes a deep breath as she sits on the table.

I decide to give her a little laugh. She's too stiff, too worked up.

"How about on your inner thigh? Right near your pussy. Since it's so fucking sweet."

She smiles a bit and bites down on her lip, but she's still nervous.

"You don't have to do this, you know?" I've given her so many chances to back out of this. I know she's not into getting a tat herself. I wouldn't blame her if she never got one. I've been trying to hide my excitement just in case she did want to back out.

She shakes her head emphatically and says, "I want this, Zane."

She lifts her shirt and leans back on the table.

"Make me yours forever," she says.

I bend down and kiss her stomach. Faint stretch marks are still there from when she carried our little man, Gabe. He's safe at home napping with the sitter while we go on our first "date" out. She could do anything she wanted, and this is what she picked.

She took a chance on me. She loved me, married me, and gave me a family.

I look into her gorgeous green eyes and know I'm cherished.

"You are mine forever." I wait for her to look up at me before I say, "I love you, peaches."

She gives me a sweet smile and says, "I love you too, Zane."

* * *

TEMPTED

From *USA Today* bestselling authors, Willow Winters and Lauren Landish, comes a sizzling and tempting romance about the bad boy you can't resist.

I lived my life with no regrets.

Until she showed up.

It started with her old man. That stubborn bastard set me up.

He knew what he was doing, and I fell for his daughter before I even heard her voice.

. . .

What was he thinking, trying to set her up with a prick like me?

She's too good for me. I should've walked away, but every time she told me no, it only made me want to chase her more.

I shouldn't have brought her into my life. I'm trouble, that's all I am, and I brought that to her doorstep.

But I can't let her go now, even if she hates me for it.

She tempted me; now she's mine.

PROLOGUE

LIAM

That old man knew exactly what he was doing. He fucking set me up. All those times he talked about his sunshine, Elizabeth. All those pictures he showed me? Not to mention all the stories he'd tell me when I was keeping him company. Of course I fell for her before I even heard her voice.

And now I'm fucked. *She's* fucked. What was he thinking, trying to set her up with a no-good asshole like me? She's too fucking good for me. He had to know it.

I'm trouble, that's all I am, and I brought that to her doorstep.

Those gorgeous blue eyes stare back at me with something deeper in them than lust. I've finally won her over. Every bit of her.

I'm a fucking prick for doing it. I know I should've let her down easy. I should've walked away and turned my back on her. Shit, I should've never chased her.

She's a smart girl; she knows I'm no good for her. And it's true. I've got a death threat in my back pocket in the form of her picture, and it's all because of me.

What was her father doing pulling this shit? He knew the hard truth about me. I shake my head, hating how I'm blaming him. The old man's dead now. I'm such a piece of shit, trying to put this all on him and throw the blame on someone other than me.

I pushed her to cave to me. I just needed a taste. And now that I've got her and a good fucking reason to leave this life behind, it's all crashing down around me. But she's here now, and she's in danger.

"Whatever you're thinking, Liam, you need to stop it," she says, and her soft, sweet voice is so damn soothing. Her small hand cups my cheek and I quickly nip her thumb playfully. She lets out a cute squeal, and her eyes quickly heat with desire. I try to give her a small smile, but I can't force it.

She bites down on her bottom lip and softly says, "You worry too much." She looks up at me through her thick lashes. I can't deny her. I'm addicted to her touch.

I take her curvy body in my arms, feeling her soft, lush frame melt into me. "Only when it involves you," I respond with more honesty than she'll ever know.

She gives me a sweet smile and nudges her nose against mine with her eyes closed. She wants me to take her right now. And I can't deny her that wish. I take her lips with my own, and press my tongue against the seam of her full lips, as she yields to my touch with a kiss. She parts easily for me, spreading her legs and straddling me. She gives in so easily now.

She's learned to trust me.

She's learned to love me and everything I do to her. *If only she knew.*

"You don't have to worry," she says, and she's nearly panting now, her voice trembling with need. "Just take care of me."

I know what she means by that.

Fuck, it's like a bullet to my heart how much she trusts me. I run my hand down my face and stare into her eyes. Her forehead is slightly pinched, and her mouth is parted. Her haze of desire is starting to be replaced with a look of confusion. She doesn't know why I'm hesitating.

I have to tell her. She's going to fucking hate me. She's going to know she was right about me all along.

I nip her bottom lip, and my dick twitches as she closes her eyes and moans. Her hands tangle in my hair and I decide right then--I'm not going to let her go. Even if she hates me. I can't risk it; I can't risk *her*.

One more night with her. Just one more night between us. And then I'll tell her. She's going to fucking hate me. But she's not leaving. I can't let her.

They know she's gotten to me. I can't leave her now, it's too late.

She tempted me; now she's mine.

CHAPTER 1

LIZZIE

The somber chime of church bells greets me as I step out of my car, a red 2015 Toyota Camry. My legs feel shaky as my shoes touch the ground, and for a moment, I'm hit by a surge of weakness as I lean against the car for support.

I can't do this.

But I have to.

For daddy.

Every moment is a struggle, but I manage to stand up straight and close my car door. I take a moment to gather myself, breathing in deeply and fighting back tears before looking up into the dark clouds above.

Why did you take him from me? I demand angrily. *What did I do to deserve this?* As if in response, there's a deep rumble in the distance, a dark foreboding sound that threatens to take even more from me. But I have nothing left. I feel numb and hollow.

A loud crack splits the sky. He didn't deserve to die! My stepfather was a good man. It's not fair.

Bitterly, I tear my eyes away from the unforgiving

heavens and begin making my way through the parking lot. A cool breeze sweeps the area, causing the hem of my black dress to lift up around my thighs and goosebumps to rise on my flesh. Numbly, I ignore it and continue on.

Ahead, I see people walking up the church steps and anxiety tightens around my heart. There are a lot of familiar faces, a few faces I'd rather not speak to, and some I don't know. Even from this distance I can already see the pity in their eyes and hear their empty condolences. It angers me. A lot of them couldn't give a fuck about my father. Or me. They're just here to see me break down.

I vow to put on a strong front, not let them see me cry.

They're all frauds, I think disdainfully. *Half of these people disliked my dad when he was alive, and now they want to pretend like they care.*

It irks me, makes me angry. And I cling to that anger to keep me from being consumed with grief. I'm certain some of these people weren't invited to the funeral, and yet here they are anyway.

As I make it to the church steps, a familiar voice pierces my awareness. "Lizzie?"

I spin around, my dress swirling around my legs, and see my childhood friend, Natalie Doubet, standing there with a large, silver tray of cookies in her hands. Garbed in a black lace dress, her dark blonde hair is pulled up into a severe bun and she's opted for subdued, conservative makeup.

I'm awash with relief. Of all the people I recognize filing into the church, Natalie is the only one I'm happy to lay eyes on.

"Nat!" I cry. I wish my lips would turn up into a smile, but they refuse.

"Hey Lizzie," she says, and her voice is soft, soothing. I just want to melt in her arms.

I run up to her, my arms outstretched.

"Whoa!" Natalie snaps, twisting her body to protect her delicious cargo. "Watch the cookies!"

Despite feeling like shit, I laugh and gently reach out to stroke her arm. Good ol' Nat and her testy temper. "Sorry."

"Don't be. I didn't mean to snap at you, I just didn't want you to get sugar cookies all over your dress." Natalie nods at the church. I can see the sadness in Natalie's eyes as she looks at me, and I fight back the tears that threaten to stream down my face like a waterfall.

"Let's go find the reception so I can put these down and I'll walk with you."

"Okay," I manage.

As we make our way into the church, I'm greeted by distant relatives and past acquaintances. I do my best to hold it together, fighting back tears as each person hugs me and offers their condolences. It's impossibly hard, especially enduring the comments of the more fake and phony guests, and several times I almost start wailing with grief. Somehow, I survive the group without breaking down and then Nat and I head farther into the church.

In the reception room there's already a small crowd milling about, chatting in hushed tones. I lock eyes with more faces I haven't seen in years, and then look away. I know it's only a matter of time before I'm surrounded and barraged with false sympathy again. I'm dreading every second of it.

"I'm so sorry for your loss," Natalie says as soon as she sets the tray of cookies down on the refreshments table. She gives me a big, warm embrace, and once again, I'm fighting back tears. Will it ever end? "I knew Turner was getting up there in age," she remarks, pulling away, "but he looked fine every time I saw him come into the bakery."

It's a struggle to even speak. "He was here one day, and then gone the next," I croak.

Natalie shakes her head solemnly. "I know, right? It's crazy."

A tear escapes my right eye and trails down my cheek. "I don't understand," I moan, angrily wiping away the offending tear with the back of my hand. "I thought cancer took time. I thought there were signs." It hurts. It hurts so much to think there was nothing I could have done to save him. If only I could go back in time.

Nat clamps a hand on my shoulder, her eyes clouded with sympathy. "I don't know what to say, Liz, except... sometimes these things happen."

But why did it have to happen to him? I want to scream out. *It's not fair!*

"If you need anything while you're in town, I don't care what it is," Nat continues, pulling me into another warm embrace, "I'm here for you."

"Thank you," I say simply, swallowing the huge lump in my throat.

After rubbing my back for a few moments, Natalie pulls away and peers at me. "You look good at least, like you lost a lot of weight." She pauses and then adds, "I'm so sorry, I didn't mean to come off like that."

I brush away her worry. "You're fine. I wasn't eating much before the news, and I ate even less after I heard it. Stress, you know?" I had just finished with finals when I got the news. I have two semesters left until I'm done with my masters. There's a two month break before I have to go back. Until then, I'm here. Back in my hometown, mourning the death of the only family I ever had.

Natalie gestures at her tray of goodies. "You should try one of my sugar cookies. I guarantee they'll get you back on track." She gestures to her stomach and adds, "They're a bit fattening."

I snicker at her little joke and roll my eyes. "You're beautiful." She giggles and straightens the tray with a small smile.

I glance at her baked morsels. While I'm not hungry, they do look delicious. Each cookie is a rich golden color, iced and dusted with multicolored powder. "I shouldn't," I say. "I've been trying to stay away from sugar. It only makes me feel jittery."

"Nonsense." Natalie gently prods me toward the cookies. "Depriving yourself at a time like this isn't going to help anything. You need something to help you feel better."

I take a cookie and take a small nibble. My eyes go wide a moment later. "These are delicious!" I exclaim before taking another bite, this time a larger one. My appetite has been in the shitter lately, but even I have to admit how tasty these things are. I don't know if it's because I'm starving, but I swear they're the best cookies I've ever eaten.

"Aren't they?" Natalie beams proudly. "They're a customer favorite. I can hardly keep them on the racks. Within twenty minutes of putting out a fresh batch, they're gone."

"What are they made of?" I have to ask; I'm still marveling at how rich and sweet they are.

Natalie crosses her arms, her eyes twinkling. "Can't tell ya. It's my super secret recipe."

I savor the taste. I'm really loving this cookie. "I figured you would say that."

Natalie winks. "You know me."

I close my eyes, relishing the delicious flavor assaulting my taste buds. "My God, I always knew you could bake, but never this good." My eyes pop back open as something occurs to me. "Wait a minute, a customer favorite?"

"I took over my grandma Eva's bakery," Natalie explains. "I now run Sweet Morsels Bakery full time."

I'm shocked. I had always pictured Natalie going to law school, settling down after a few years and having a bunch of babies. I didn't think she'd stay in town. "You're kidding!"

Natalie shakes her head. "Nope. Grandma Eva got too old to run it and wanted to retire. Since mom was too busy with her daycare business, that left me to take the reins."

"Wow," I say, impressed. "That's amazing. Head of your own business at twenty-three."

"Ain't it?" Natalie agrees. "I never thought that I'd be doing something like this, but here I am." She frowns, as if a sudden unpleasant thought occurs to her. "It's not all cupcakes and ice cream though."

I finish chowing down the delicious treat. Unconsciously, I grab another and pop it in my mouth. "What do you mean?"

"I didn't inherit the business for free. I owe grandma Eva fifty grand."

"Mmm," I say, shaking my head.

Nat nods. "And if that's not bad enough, I also took out a loan to buy the house right around the corner from the bakery so I could oversee the shop. So I'm up to my eyeballs in debt."

The word 'debt' brings up my own worry. Before my stepfather died, I took out a large student loan of forty grand to cover living expenses while I get my master's. And as massive as that debt is, it doesn't even include the student loans I have from my time in undergrad. At the time, I wasn't worried because daddy assured me he had the money to help me pay for it. Now he's gone. My heart twists with pain. I shouldn't be worrying about money. But it's there in the back of my mind. I feel guilty even thinking about it.

"But I'm okay," Nat says quickly at my frown, as if afraid I'll fall into pieces at any more bad news. "Business is brisk, and within a few years I should own the shop free and clear."

"That's good," I say absently, still munching away. Nat's right. The cookies are helping. Maybe I'll just eat the whole fucking tray. "How's the town been otherwise since I've been gone? Anything change?"

Nat shakes her head, watching me. "Nope. Still the same ol' same ol'."

I'm not surprised. Everything looks the same. The town, the people. This church, the exact same one mom used to take me to for Sunday school every week until she passed away. It still looks to be in the same condition since I last saw it. I can still remember the days mom and I used to walk up the steps. When daddy would come, they'd playfully swing me back and forth, holding my hands as we entered the iron-wrought doors.

As I gobble down cookie after cookie, tears burn my eyes and I have to push away the memory. I'm so fucking tired of crying.

"That's enough, Lizzie!" Nat hisses, snatching the next cookie out of my hand, breaking me out of my recollection.

"Hey!" I object. "That was my last one."

"Right," Nat growls.

"You're the one who told me to eat them," I point out.

"I told you to indulge a little, not eat the whole damn tray!"

I open my mouth to protest, "I didn't eat the whole--" I stop and stare in horror at the cookie tray. Of a dozen, only four are left. Eight. I'd eaten eight cookies without even realizing.

Shaking her head, Nat stuffs the cookie she'd taken from me into her mouth. "Look Liz, I know this is a terrible time for you, and it might seem insensitive to say right now, but I am not going to let you develop any kind of bad habits in order to cope with Turner's death, do you understand me?"

I stare into Nat's face. She looks so serious while chewing that cookie I burst into giggles. "Yes, Ma'am." My laughter draws curious glances from people around the room. A few give me sympathetic looks as if they're thinking my giggles are a fit of hysterics borne from my grief, and start making their way over. I quickly morph my smile back into a frown. *Oh God. Here they come.*

"Good," Nat is barely able to say before she's swept out of the way by a throng of well-wishers.

Before I know it, I'm overwhelmed by everybody talking at once.

"It's a shame about your stepfather, he was one of the best men this town's ever had."

"How are you doing, Lizzie?"

"We're so sorry for your loss."

"Did you know your father was dying?" Really?

"Who's going to watch over the house while you're at school?"

Nat looks on with sympathy while I'm being mercilessly interrogated. She knows I can hardly tolerate some of these people, and I'm just trying to keep it together.

Luckily for me, Nat intervenes right when it feels like I'm about to pass out. "Okay, that's enough," Nat says sternly to the group. "Lizzie's really tired and would like to go inside the chapel to see her father before sitting down."

She grabs me by the hand and begins pulling me toward the chapel doors.

"Thank you," I whisper with gratitude as we leave the group behind.

Nat shakes her head. "No problem. I'm not even you, and they were about to give me a stroke."

I let out a dry chuckle.

My legs are trembling like jell-o as we enter the chapel. The crowd seated inside goes silent as I enter the room. Though it's the last thing I want, several people get up to greet me in the middle of the aisle. Some give me sad faces, and tell me everything will be alright, that God will take care of me. Others take my hand and tell me they're sorry, while others embrace me and put on an act of crying.

By the time I make it down the aisle with Nat, I feel like I'm being suffocated. I can only hope the service ends quickly. I don't know how much more of this shit I can take.

Then I see the coffin.

Oh daddy, I cry inwardly. *I'm so sorry.*

There he is, lying in front of me, devoid of color. Lifeless. My legs feel as if they're going to buckle as I walk over to the coffin. I peer down into daddy's face. He looks rested. Peaceful. Still, I can hardly take looking at him. He's gone. Never coming back.

Slowly, I touch his hand. His skin feels cold as ice.

I can't take it anymore. I lose it. My shoulders shake as I sob uncontrollably. Somewhere in the back of my mind, I feel anger. I promised myself I wouldn't break down. But here I am, bawling like a baby.

I hate it. I hate that the vultures can see me crying, that they can see my pain.

All I want to do is go home, curl up in daddy's favorite chair and take in the smell of his cigars. If I could, I'd lay there for days, talking to him, remembering all the good times. But I know I can't.

He's really gone.

At some point, I don't know when, Nat wraps her arms around me and leads me over to my seat. She's rubbing my back and quietly shushing me. I'm handed a handkerchief, which I gratefully take to blow my nose.

The procession has begun, and people are beginning to line up near the coffin to view my stepfather.

"Are you okay?" Nat asks, her eyes filled with concern.

"I'm mad at myself," I say angrily, wiping at my nose.

Nat frowns. "What on earth for?"

"I promised myself I wouldn't break down."

"Don't be. You're only human."

"Yeah, I know I am, but some of these people aren't. I gave them the show they've been waiting to see."

Nat glances scornfully around the room. "Look, don't worry about them. If there's anyone here that's happy to see you cry, then they can lick my asshole."

Even I have to laugh. She's ridiculous. I roll my eyes, but I have to admit, I do feel slightly better.

After I pull myself together, I dare a glance around the room. No one seems to be visibly showing glee at my breakdown, but I know better. I catch a few tight smiles and waves as my eyes scan the room, and I'm about to turn back to Nat when my breath catches in my throat.

Who the hell is that?

There's a man I don't recognize, but he's staring at me. To say that he's handsome is an understatement given his chiseled bone structure and slender, but muscular physique. His short dark hair is a little longer on top and styled in a way that makes it seem messy, yet polished. Like he just woke up looking that fucking hot. He's dressed in a black suit I'm sure cost a couple grand; he looks like he stepped right out of GQ magazine.

Underneath his hypnotic gaze, I'm suddenly feeling self-conscious of how I look. I'm sure with all the crying I look a hot mess. It annoys me that I even care at all. My dad is dead. Looking good is the last thing I should be worrying about. Still, I can't help it. I wipe under my eyes and take in a steadying breath.

"Who's *that?"* I'm forced to ask Nat against my will.

Nat looks around the room until her eyes fall on the handsome gentleman and they light with recognition. "Oh," she says casually. "That's Liam Axton. Your dad's neighbor."

A jolt of shock runs through me. Daddy's neighbor? Nat has to be mistaken. "You mean he lives on the corner, right?" I clarify. "I can't believe the Bernards would have moved from their home. They've lived there all their lives."

Nat shakes her head. "No, I mean he literally lives next door to your dad's house. In twenty-two Wyoming."

I can't help it, but I'm fucking floored. The house at 22 Wyoming was my dad's rental property. It's right next door to our family home, 20 Wyoming. Growing up, he said it was his cash cow and vowed he would never get rid of it. How could he have sold it to this... stranger?

I'm struck silent by this revelation. I steal a glance of Liam. My heart jumps in my chest. He's still staring at me. Hard. Boldly. His eyes seem to be assessing me, burning into me with an intensity I find unnerving.

It suddenly feels very hot in the room, and there's only one question on my mind.

Who the fuck is this guy, and how the hell did he know daddy?

CHAPTER 2

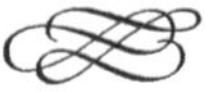

LIAM

I don't know why the fuck I'm here. *The law office of Allen Douglas, Esq*. I'm alone in this cramped office, waiting on the lawyer to come back in here. I wanna get this formality over with as soon as fucking possible.

My eyes dart around from his desk to the old dusty bookshelves, and I want to get the fuck out of here. I need to get away from people. The funeral was enough to make me bolt, but I owed it to Richard.

I already said my goodbyes and laid him to rest, but I had to attend. I can't deny that part of the reason I went was to see *her*. Elizabeth.

He talked about her constantly. Day in, and day out. Everything reminded him of her in some way. I know he had regrets about not telling her everything. I told the old man he should've let her know. She's a grown woman, and she deserved to know the truth. He was a stubborn man though. He refused to let her see him as he lost more and more of himself. It's not my place to say he was wrong for doing it, but I don't know that I could've kept it from someone I loved.

So she constantly weighed on his mind. I've heard more about her than anything else from the old man. I feel like I know her. When I saw her crying over his coffin, it broke my heart to see her in pain. I guess I can see why he didn't want her spending weeks crying over him. He couldn't stop the inevitable, but he tried to protect her from it until the end.

I wanted to comfort her and tell her how much he truly loved her.

But that's just not who I am. And even though I know all about her, she doesn't know shit about me.

I almost did it though, just because I fucking wanted to. I almost walked up and took her in my arms and shielded her from all those prying eyes. She didn't need them watching her break down like that. I could tell it was bothering her. If it wasn't for her friend being there with her, I would've stepped in. She needs someone. I don't know why I feel so strongly about it, but I want to be that someone.

I make a point not to show emotion around anyone. Acting on emotion gets you killed in my line of work. But she looked so fragile and so damn torn up. Her pain called to a part of me I hardly know, one I rarely even acknowledge. I wouldn't have been able to help myself. I don't protect people; in fact, I do the opposite. But she's different.

I have a feeling she would've pushed me away, even if she wanted me to hold her.

A humorless laugh huffs from my chest. If she did, that'd only make me want to hold her more.

My dick stirs in my pants and I feel like a damn pervert, but imagining all the ways I could comfort her has me craving her touch. She's gorgeous and curvy. I can just imagine how she'd feel in my arms. I'd pull her into my lap and kiss every inch of her body. I'd take away her pain and make her forget. That's what I want.

Fuck, my dick's hard as steel. I groan and adjust it before anyone comes back in.

What the fuck is wrong with me? I run my hands down my face and through my hair. I crack my neck and push down all the shit I'm feeling. I'm used to doing that, ignoring whatever bitch emotions are getting to me. I just need to get this reading of the will over with. Then I can move on and get back to the way my life used to be before Richard showed up.

I have to concentrate on work. That's what I need to do. I need to get back to my office and get my shit straightened out.

Instead I'm in this tiny office, waiting on this reading that should have nothing to do with me.

I told that old man not to leave me anything, so for the life of me I don't know why I'm even here.

I purse my lips and realize she should be here soon. His Elizabeth.

I'm in a leather wingback chair, and I settle back before taking my phone out of my pocket. At least I can give his daughter her house back.

He never should've given it to me in the first place. I'm not sure if she'll sell it or rent it out like he used to. Shit, she might even sell her family home that's next door for all I know. Whatever she wants to do, it's up to her.

I wake my phone up and look at the time. *Time for this shit to be over and done with.* I've got a few emails and some texts I need to respond to.

It's only a few more minutes until the door behind me opens, and I'm quick to put my phone away and sit up straight. I take a look over my shoulder as the old lawyer rounds the desk and sits in his chair.

Elizabeth closes the door behind her with a soft click. She stills for a second when she sees me, caught by surprise. But she seems to ignore me more than anything else. Her eyes are on the empty chair to my left.

Her long hair barely moves as she walks slowly to the seat and settles in without a word. She leans down to set her purse on the floor and runs her fingers through her hair. I can just barely smell a hint of vanilla and something else, something sweet. My eyes roam her curvy body as I take her in.

I can't help it.

Our eyes meet, and there's nothing but animosity in hers.

That sweet, sad vulnerable look that was in her eyes at the church is fucking gone. Maybe I imagined it. Or maybe she just doesn't like the fact that I'm here at her stepfather's will reading.

That's not my fault though, so she can get that dirty look off her face. I push down my irritation and give her the benefit of the doubt.

She pulls her long hair over one shoulder and nervously twists it around her fingers.

Her pouty lips are turned down into a frown, and her eyes are a bit puffy. The sight of her still so worked up over her stepfather's death makes my heart clench. She's in so much pain.

He said she used to light up his world with one look. But those baby blue eyes aren't filled with any emotion that conveys happiness.

"My condolences," I offer her in a low voice so I don't startle her. She bites down on her plump bottom lip and turns to look at me. She noticeably swallows and bites out a small thank you.

She's tense and unhappy--I get that. But I didn't anticipate her being so cold to me.

Maybe she's pissed I'm here at all. I have to keep reminding myself that she doesn't know me. I feel like we have a connection that's just not there.

Shit, it's not like I want to be here. Usually I'd blow this kind of shit off; I have more important things to do. But if Richard wanted me here, then I'm here.

Fuck, I was with him every day until he died. I could use a little sympathy, too.

I close my eyes and clench my jaw, hating that I even had that thought just now.

I only knew her old man for a few months. Yes, his death was like a bullet to my chest, but I knew it was coming and he wasn't my father. This isn't about me.

If this is her way of dealing with his passing, then so be it. I'll be her punching bag. I can do that for her, and for him. My foot taps on the ground as I wait to get this over with.

"I know you're dealing with a lot right now," the lawyer says as he reaches across the desk and places a wrinkled hand on top of Elizabeth's hand. "I'm so sorry for your loss." He sounds sincere, and I have to look away and down at the floor for a second. My heart sinks a little. The old man is really dead.

She turns her hand over and grips his like it's her lifeline. For some reason, it pisses me off. I want to be the one giving her that comfort.

But she doesn't know me. I let the anger roll off of me. If he's making her feel better, that's all that matters.

I grip the armrests and sit back. I must be worked up more than I thought over Richard's passing. I don't like it.

"All right, let's go through this as quickly as possible,

shall we?" Allen raises his bushy white eyebrows and gives Elizabeth a pointed look.

She squeezes his hand once and sits back, taking a deep breath. She lets go of his hand and lets hers fall to her lap. My eyes catch the movement and my fingers itch to reach out and take her hand in mine, but I don't. I clasp my hands together and wait for the lawyer to get this shit over with. Whatever the old man left me, I'll be more than happy to keep as a reminder of him.

Maybe it's an old watch or a trinket, I don't know. Whatever it is, I'll pocket it and move on. Knowing him, it could be his favorite DVD. I huff a small laugh thinking about it. It puts a smile on my face, but then I remember where I am and I feel like an asshole. Neither of them seem to notice though.

"Let's begin. Richard Francis Turner's Last Will and Testament." The lawyer shakes out the pages and starts reading down the lines, completely oblivious to the fact that Elizabeth is stiff at his words. She's not crying or breaking down like she was at the funeral, but I know hearing those words shook her up. She's not alright.

Allen's words turn to white noise as I watch her clutching her necklace and staring straight ahead with a grim look on her face.

If Richard could see her right now it would fucking kill him.

I usually don't think twice about other people's pain. That's life. But watching her trying to hold herself together is breaking something inside of me.

Suddenly, her composure changes into confusion and then anxiety.

I look back to the lawyer, trying to pay attention to whatever he just said.

"Hmm." Allen looks lost as he goes through the pages.

He flips through them and repeats back what he just said. "It all goes to Mr. Axton."

My forehead pinches as I take in what he's saying. That can't be true.

"All?" *All of what?*

"Everything Richard owned or is in his name, with the exception to the family home, 20 Wyoming and its contents, is to be given freely to Mr. Liam Axton. This includes all other properties, and financial investments, and all the remaining balances in all of his bank accounts. The house, 20 Wyoming, and its contents is to be given to his only surviving heir, Elizabeth Turner." My body goes cold as he says the words and then looks back up at me, waiting for a response.

"What? No!" Elizabeth grips the chair with both her hands before standing up so fast she nearly sends it flying backward. The chair rocks on its back legs before gently settling.

"That can't be right!" She shakes her head. "Daddy wouldn't leave me with nothing."

"I'm sorry, Lizzie," Allen says, looking back down at the papers in his hand and gripping them harder, wrinkling the pages. He looks back through them as though he read them wrong. "The deed and title for your family home have been put in your name, but all other belongings have been left to Mr. Axton."

So all he left her was his house, the one right next to the one he gave me, but nothing else. What the fuck?

I remain still, and I struggle to accept this is even real. It must be a mistake. She's right, there's no way he wouldn't have left everything to her. He loved her. He wouldn't have done that to her.

"This man didn't even know my father!" Elizabeth

points her finger at me for emphasis and chokes on her words as tears prick her eyes.

I reach up for her hand to calm her down and try to explain as I stand, but she rips it away from me. Her wide eyes look at me with worry, and I put both my hands up in surrender.

Her breathing is coming in frantic pants; she looks like she's on the edge of having a panic attack.

I sit back down, not knowing what to do. I don't want to make her angry, but she sure as shit doesn't want me to comfort her right now.

"I'm sure there's been a mistake," I say evenly and calmly. She looks like a wounded animal. My heart hurts for her, so I let the offense slide. *She's just hurting,* I have to remind myself.

"Yes," she says in a high-pitched voice as tears roll down her face. "There's a mistake."

"There is no mistake; it's all been left to Mr. Axton."

The room is quiet for a moment. Why the hell would Richard do that? I open my mouth to let them know I'll give it all to her. I don't need his money. I hadn't expected this either. I wanted to give the house back to her, too. But before I can say anything, Elizabeth turns all her anger on me.

"Who the hell were you to him? What'd you do, threaten him?" she says accusingly. That really fucking pisses me off. I'm ready to beat that ass of hers for talking to me like that.

"Whoa! Whoa!" I don't like that she thinks so little of me.

He told me not to tell her everything that happened. He doesn't want her to know about the shit he did when his insurance wouldn't pay up for his treatments. Richard confided in me. He put the house in my name without me knowing. He did this bullshit with the will without telling me. And on his deathbed he made me promise not to tell her that he kept all this from her.

I don't know what he was thinking, but if he wanted his only daughter to fucking hate me, then mission accomplished.

"I don't want it," I say simply, ignoring her eyes boring into my head with hate.

My heart twists with pain. I don't want her to hate me. What the fuck was Richard up to, doing this shit? "There's obviously a mistake."

"Obviously." Elizabeth sits back down and leans forward, looking back to Allen. "If... *Mr. Axton*," the way she says my name makes me cringe, "doesn't want the inheritance, then everything's fine, right?"

"Well, there are some legal issues we can work out." Allen has a tense expression on his face as he looks between the two of us.

"Good, because that's *obviously* a mistake." Her voice hardens as more tears fall down her cheeks. "He didn't know shit about daddy."

That's it. Something inside of me snaps. I was planning on just letting this all go, but the way she's looking at me with pure hate is just not gonna work for me.

I want comfort, too. I want her to give me a god damned chance.

"I want a date," I say, and both sets of eyes whip over to me.

"Fuck you!" Elizabeth sneers. "I'm not for sale, asshole."

That mouth of hers is pissing me off.

I gotta get up before I do something stupid.

She's making me wanna pin her ass against the desk and settle her down the best way I know how.

Without another word, I walk out of the office in a mix

of rage and sadness. I storm out, ignoring her screaming at me, and Allen trying to calm her down. I walk straight out to my car to get the fuck out of there. I'm mostly just confused though by the time I swing my car door open and settle down in the seat.

I grip the leather steering wheel and twist my hands. My heart's racing, and I just want it all to stop. I hate this pain in my chest that just won't let up.

What the fuck was Richard doing giving it all to me?

I told him he didn't owe me. I didn't help him out for the money. It wasn't about that. At least to me it wasn't. I hate to think he even thought that about me.

And now his baby girl fucking hates me.

I clench my jaw and start up my car.

I'm not letting this go. She needs that money. I know she does.

She's gonna have to sit down with me and show me that sweet side I know she has if she wants it. I don't care if that makes me a dick. She brought this shit on herself.

CHAPTER 3

LIZZIE

"There must be something wrong," I insist, holding back an ocean of tears after the handsome bastard storms off. "This can't be right." I don't care if I pissed him off, but even as I think it, my heart sinks. I don't want to piss anyone off. I'm just so damn tired of crying and being in pain. And then this? I don't understand it. Why would daddy do that?

Allen looks at me from under his bushy white eyebrows and shakes his head. "I'm sorry, Miss Turner, but the will is right here, clearly in your stepfather's handwriting." Allen slides the crumpled papers across the desk. "See for yourself."

I snatch it up, causing Allen to mutter an ominous warning, "Careful with that. If you damage the will, Liam can hold you accountable."

Fuck Liam.

Ignoring the old fossil, I scan the document. Sure enough, it's daddy's handwriting. I'd know his distinctive scrawl anywhere. My heart starts pounding like a sledgehammer, and my head spins. My breathing becomes ragged and I feel like I'm going to faint.

How could he? I wail within the depths of my mind. *How could he do this to me?!*

I can't believe it. This can't be true. I want to pinch myself, make sure I'm not stuck in a nightmare.

A total stranger! He left everything to a total stranger!

I can't figure out why on earth he would do this. He knew that I'd taken on massive debt. Debt he had promised to pay so I could live a better life. Then he goes and dies and leaves everything to some random cocky bastard with no relation to him?

What. The. Fuck.

I'm hurt. And beyond fucking mad. To say that I feel betrayed doesn't even begin to express how I feel. My body heats with anxiety, and I don't know what to think about anything.

"He can't do this," I find myself protesting. I want that smug bastard to come back here so I can claw at his arrogant mug. "He can't withhold my inheritance like this!"

Allen reaches across the desk and gently pulls the will from my hands. I instantly regret not ripping it up in his face. Who gives a fuck if Liam takes action against me? The bastard doesn't deserve anything. He didn't even know my father. "I'm sorry to tell you this Miss Turner, but he most certainly can. Liam Axton is the sole heir to your stepfather's estate and he isn't legally obligated to share anything with you, even considering your close relationship with Richard."

I stare at Allen's lined face for a long moment, feeling sick to my stomach. My mind races, searching for a reason why my father would do this to me. What could I have done to deserve such a terrible punishment?

Be a shitty daughter. Every inch of my skin pricks with a

chill at the thought. Was I really? I loved him. I should have told him more often. No, I should have showed him. I loved him so damn much. How could he not know that? He was my world.

After all, where was I when my daddy was dying? At school, too busy with my studies to care about keeping in frequent touch with the man who had loved me as if I was his own biological daughter. A man who had died heart-broken and alone, without me to care for him.

Maybe I do deserve this.

I can't take it anymore. I burst into tears, my shoulders shuddering violently from powerful sobs.

I'm so sorry, daddy, I cry inwardly. *Had I known you were sick, I would never have gone so far away for school. Never! I would've stayed at home and taken care of you. Really, I would. You must believe me!*

I rock back and forth in my seat, the pain crushing my heart. "I wish I had known," I cry, tears pouring from my eyes. "I wish I could take it all back!"

Allen must think I'm going mad with grief, but he gets up from his seat and comes around to my side. "There, there, child," he coos, patting me awkwardly on the head. "Everything will turn out alright."

I continue to sob and Allen is forced to wrap his frail arms around me, letting me cry on his shoulder.

After what seems like an eternity, I sob my last sob and I'm able to pull away. My cheeks burn with embarrassment when I see Allen's expensive dress shirt is soaking wet from my slobber and tears.

"I'm sorry I got my snot all over you," I sniff, wiping my nose with the back of my hand. I'm such a pathetic mess. But I don't care.

Allen brushes away my worry with a dry chuckle. "You'd be surprised. You're not the first person to break down in my office after a will reading, and you most certainly won't be the last." He reaches across his desk and grabs a couple of tissues and then hands the bunch to me. "In fact, I'm just happy there wasn't any violence between the two of you," he says, as I take the tissues and blow my nose. "I've had to replace my desk at least ten times."

I look at him through bloodshot eyes. "Seriously?" I say and sniffle.

Allen nods. "Usually will readings deteriorate quickly when certain family members find out they've been left out of the will. I've actually had all-out brawls take place in my office."

I shake my head before blowing my nose again. "That's crazy."

Allen makes it back behind his desk and I feel a twinge of guilt. The poor old man is going to have to smell my slobber all the way home. "Indeed. I find that a death in the family always brings out the worst in people if they think they can end up with something of value."

"Isn't that the truth," I mutter, sitting there feeling numb. I really don't know what to do. I'm heartbroken I've been left with nothing. Something occurs to me. "Do you know if my stepfather knew Liam at all, like *really* knew him?"

Allen shakes his head. "Sorry, I do not."

I frown. It all seems so strange to me. Why would daddy hand over his will to someone he hardly knew? Unless… he really knew him?

He couldn't have known him, I think to myself. *I never saw this guy while growing up. He has to be some last minute actor that showed up when daddy grew vulnerable.*

Maybe that was it. Maybe daddy had come down with a sudden onset of dementia, forgotten who I was. Then this Liam character had taken advantage of him. The idea makes my chest burn with anger, though it seems an unlikely scenario. Still, it makes me feel uncomfortable even thinking about it.

I shake my head. It's impossible. I talked to daddy fairly often. That's not it. I feel ashamed for even thinking it. But then again, he never mentioned Liam. Who the hell is this guy?

I'm full of confusion and grief, and thoughts of Liam are doing things to my body I'd rather not admit to. *A date*. Did he really say that? I take in a short breath, thinking about doing it. It's just a date, and it's with *him*.

My eyes glaze over as my mind goes back to the funeral and I remember the way he looked at me. Like he wanted me. Like he needed me. Desire burns in my lower stomach, and my cheeks redden from heat.

Allen clears his throat. "Miss Turner?"

I jump in my seat. "Uh, yeah? Sorry," I say, my face on fire. I quickly grab my purse and stand up. I think it's time to go home. "I thank you so much for your service, Allen. I'll be going now."

Allen gives me a nod. "Should you work out something with Liam, I'd be glad to offer my advice."

I touch a hand to my chest. "Thank you. That means a lot to me." *But I won't be doing shit with that bastard, except busting his ass for being a filthy thief.* I walk over to the door and place my hand on the knob. Before I open it, I say in parting, "Sorry for ruining your shirt."

"It's no loss." Allen grins. "I've got thirty more just like it at home."

* * *

ON THE WAY back to the home I grew up in, my father's home and now the only thing I have left of him, I keep running through different scenarios in my head. Liam forced daddy to will everything over to him. Liam drugged him and made him sign everything over to him. Liam blackmailed daddy and made him sign over his estate.

Each scenario fills me with rage. But not toward Liam, just at myself. There's no way any of that is true. But still, who is Liam?

Something is absolutely wrong with this scenario.

Whatever Liam did, I intend to get to the bottom of it. I'm not going to let this man get away with what's rightfully mine. I vow that Liam will pay with everything he has if I find out there was any foul play involved in my father's death.

As I pull up, I spot Liam's car, a red fucking Porsche, in the driveway next door. I stare at the car angrily, as if willing it to blow up from my gaze alone.

I'm going to find out who you are, Mr. Asshole, and what you did to make daddy leave everything to you, I think to myself as I glare balefully.

Enraged, I jump out of my car and slam the door. I stomp across the yard, my yard, and to the front door. Balling my fist, I pound on the hard wood like a maniac. It's been raining off and on since the funeral, but right now it's cold and my knuckles hurt as they slam against the wood, but I'm just happy to feel anything at all.

I only get in several thumps before the door swings open so fast that I almost punch Liam in the face. Good.

He moves to the side, easily avoiding my wild swing. "Whoa! There's a doorbell, you know."

I hate to admit it, but I go weak in the knees at the sight of him. I can't figure out why. He's dressed in the same outfit he had on at the lawyer's office, except now his shirt's unbuttoned down to his chest, showing the hard, tanned skin underneath.

God, he's so fucking handsome, I think to myself.

Slowly, I lower my hand and glower at him, though I feel desire twisting my stomach. I hate how it makes me feel. This guy, this *fraud,* is my enemy, yet I can't help but notice how good-looking he is.

How is that even possible?

"Yes, I know there's a doorbell!" I snarl indignantly.

"Then why didn't you use it?" he asks with a cocked brow. It makes him look even sexier, and that only pisses me off more.

"Maybe because I didn't want to." I say nastily.

"I see. You just came here to yell and call me an asshole some more," he says with a twinkle in his gorgeous green eyes. It's almost as if the bastard is looking forward to a showdown with me.

I ignore his playfulness. "What did you do to him?" I demand in the most accusatory tone I can manage.

The corners of Liam's lips pull down into a frown. He's mad now. *Good.* "What do you mean, 'do to him'?" His voice is lowered and all traces of teasing are gone.

"You know exactly what I mean." It takes everything in me to keep my voice level and not let it crack. Just the thought that he did something to daddy makes my body tremble with anger.

"No. Sorry, I don't." He holds my gaze, daring me to suggest something.

Bastard.

"You should be ashamed of yourself!" I snap angrily. "Taking advantage of a dying man!"

Anger flashes in his beautiful eyes like a violent storm. "Are you fucking serious right now?" he growls. "I was a good friend of your stepfather's, and had nothing but respect for that man."

"Bullshit!" I spit out the word. "Why should I believe

you? You're a fucking liar!" I don't even think about what I'm saying, I just let out my rage.

"Who the fuck are you to tell me I'm lying, huh?" He takes a step toward me, towering over me in an imposing manner. I tremble slightly, but stand my ground. "You weren't there to see how close we'd gotten."

You weren't there. His words hit me like a punch in the gut. I almost double over from the pain it summons.

"So knock it off with that bullshit, okay? I didn't do shit to your stepfather, or make him do anything against his will. But I don't give a fuck if you believe me or not." There's hurt in his voice, but more than that, there's anger. And it pisses me off. I'm the angry one here. I'm the one who lost her only family.

Unthinking, I lash out, my hand whipping his head to the side. "Fuck you," I whisper.

I hear a guttural growl. Next thing I know I'm up against the wall in the foyer, right next to the door, my hands held above my head. "You shouldn't have done that," his deep voice rumbles in his chest, his breath hot on my face. "You should really be careful with the way you speak to me." He glares at me with a look that is murderous, yet drenched with desire.

I struggle against his hold on me. I don't know why I bother; his biceps are bulging, corded with toned muscle.

He keeps me rooted in place easily, staring at me with fire in his eyes. "You need to settle down. Your mouth is going to get you into trouble."

I tremble beneath his gaze, practically spellbound by his intensity. Below, I can feel his hard, throbbing cock pressed against my lower stomach. I'm breathless, feeling it pulsate against me, and my temples pound from my racing pulse. My nipples pebble. Seriously, I can probably give

Madonna and her cone bra a run for their money right now.

Fuck. My panties are soaked. I'm embarrassed, and I have to close my eyes for a moment to calm myself down.

"Let me go," I order when I finally feel in control again. I try to sound strong, commanding, but my words come out painfully weak.

He shakes his head and keeps my gaze. "Nope. I think I'll hold you here until you check your attitude."

"You can't do that," I say, my breathing ragged. I try again to tug free from his powerful grip, but I might as well be trying to move a mountain.

"Sure I can." He presses into me a little harder and I can practically feel his heartbeat pump through his massive cock.

Dear God. My pussy clenches with need. The thought of him fucking me right here, right now, races through my mind. Thing is, it'd probably make me feel a lot better right now. And shockingly, I want it. I want him. I am really fucked in the head.

Seriously, the close proximity to his hard body and throbbing cock is making me tremble with insatiable need.

I can't believe this. This is the man that stole my inheritance from me. Get a hold of yourself, Lizzie!

"I know you want it, too," he continues, bringing his lips dangerously close to mine. "In fact, I bet that pussy is soaking wet for me right now."

My heart flutters in my chest. The bastard is right. I'm going to need a new pair of panties.

"Don't flatter yourself," I croak. I hate how weak I sound.

Liam grins in response. "You sure about that? How about you drop those panties and prove that I'm wrong?"

It's crazy how much I want to please him. I actually

consider doing it. The thought of feeling something other than this hatred and sadness is tempting. My lips part with the need to kiss him. Luckily, a loud sound from outside, like a car door slamming shut, breaks me from the lust clouding my better judgment.

This is a line I can't cross.

"Get your fucking hands off me," I say with as much force as I can muster. This time tears prick my eyes and I break eye contact with him. I need to get out of here and away from him.

He knows I'm serious.

"Fine," he says as he slowly lets me down. He keeps his hands on me until I'm balanced and I think about shoving him away, but I don't need any more physical contact or threat of *punishment* from him.

I sulk as I head to the door and turn to face him to say one last thing. "I don't care what you say. I'm going to find out what you did. And when I do, you're going to pay."

I turn and tromp across the yard to my family home, the shitty mood only bringing my mood lower. I can't believe this fucking asshole is right next door. I wish I could put more distance between us, but I can't. I struggle to get the key into the lock and I fight the urge to scream out, feeling so helpless and pitiful. By the time I get inside, I'm soaking wet from the cold, spitting rain. I slam the door closed and lean my back against it, my breathing ragged.

I'm so angry. I'm angry at being attracted to such a bastard. More than that, I'm angry that I have no idea how I'm going to find out how he knew my stepfather. I need to know who that man is. I just don't know how to find out other than asking him. But after today, I know I need to stay far away from him.

CHAPTER 4

LIAM

I feel like shit. I was harsh with her, and I shouldn't have been. I know she's upset. Shit, they just put him in the ground today.

She may think I'm some crook, but if she'd stop hating me for one damn minute she'd see what a mistake she's making.

Her anger and the way she's been talking to me are starting to affect me. I didn't expect that. I was curious before, but now I'm close to being fucking obsessed. I've got a hard-on that's just not going down. Maybe that would shut her up. I huff a laugh thinking about her down on her knees with those plump lips wrapped around my cock. She'd probably do it just so she could bite me. I wince at the thought and walk back to the living room.

If she wasn't Richard's baby girl I'd make sure I fucked this broad out of my system. I run a hand through my hair and walk over to the boxes I was putting together. I've gotta pack everything up.

I grab the clear packing tape from the coffee table and make sure the bottom of this box is secure. I've got a lot of shit over here. I didn't even realize that I'd practically moved in here. It's been nearly three months. I guess I just slowly moved things over here.

To this shitty little house. Well, not shitty I guess. It's old though and small compared to my place.

Richard didn't have anyone though. He was too damn stubborn and he outright refused to tell Elizabeth anything. He didn't want help, but I wasn't gonna let him die in that house all alone. I couldn't let that happen. Not after what happened with my own father. I wasn't gonna just walk away from him.

I wanna tell her everything. I saw the hurt in her eyes when I said that shit about not being there. I didn't mean for it to come out like that. She has to know that. I don't want her to think I was there for him when she wasn't. Even though it's true. It's not fair for her to think that way.

He didn't even really want me there. Well, at least that's what he said. But he never sent me away, and he was always happy to have the company. I remember how even toward the end, he always prepared coffee for us. Stubborn bastard. He always had to beat me to it, even when things got to the point where he could hardly do a damn thing for himself. He never wanted her to see him deteriorate like that.

I throw the tape down on the hardwood floor and cover my eyes. I'm not an emotional man, but I remember the way he talked about it. How he said he'd never put her through that.

He had a hospital bed in the living room. By the end he was hooked up to machines, and the stubborn man still wouldn't tell her. The last conversation they had, I was there at his side. I was waiting for him to tell her so she could at least say goodbye. But he didn't.

I take a deep breath and steady myself.

It gets to me though.

Richard reminded me of my own father. I was young when my parents got in the car crash. I remember my pops in the bed at the hospital though.

I thought he was gonna make it.

I didn't understand how he could survive the crash, only to die a few days later.

Shit, Richard even looked like my pops.

I remember when he came into the office to put in his first bet. I did a double take. He was wearing faded jeans and an old flannel shirt just like my old man would've worn. Richard had greying hair that was thinning out some, and his hands were worn from all his years of honest labor.

We see a lot of clients day in and day out. Even though most only show up when they have to pay. They're never happy then. Instead they're usually scared and wishing they could take it all back.

I'm not gonna lie, I make good money off their bad bets. I run the business with my brother and cousin. I guess it's a family business, considering my uncle's the one who raised the three of us and taught us the ropes.

When the clients come in to place the bets though, they're giddy. Happy and excited. They feel like they can't lose.

But not Richard. I'd seen that look on his face a few times before, and I could tell right away what it meant. He was a man who *needed* the money.

I almost didn't take it. I watched as he placed the bet with Zac, my brother. He was obviously new to placing bets, but he pulled out a piece of paper with his notes on it. He'd done his research at least.

When he lost, he came in to double down. He'd placed a shit bet. He looked worse off than he'd been before.

Tyler brought me in to see what I wanted to do about it. Zac takes the bets, but Tyler makes sure they pay up. And I make sure shit runs smoothly. It's a nice system we have going. Tyler could tell something was off with Richard, too. When you don't come in with the money you owe us, there's a problem. Tyler knows how to deal with that shit, but the desperation coming off Richard was something else.

I told the old man that making bets he couldn't pay would get his legs broken. Richard just gave me a smile and told me I'd get my money either way. He just needed the money fast.

Colon cancer's a bitch. And expensive.

His days were numbered; it was already spreading. He said he had to try though. His insurance disagreed. They gave him less than twelve weeks and said the treatments probably wouldn't do anything. So they refused to pay. But he wasn't giving up hope. He had to live. He had a daughter who needed him, and he wasn't going to go down without fighting.

I don't listen to sob stories. I don't care about personal shit. But for some reason I had to help this guy out. I grabbed the cash from the vault and handed it over to him without thinking twice. Two hundred and twenty grand.

At first he refused. He tried giving it back to me. That's just the kind of stubborn asshole he was. But after I gave him an ultimatum, the cash in my hands or nothing, he finally left with the money.

The next day he came back with the deed to a house and the key.

He said the real estate agents couldn't sell it in time, but if he could, he'd have the money he needed, easy. But he said after he was gone, I could sell it and it should be worth a bit more than the money I gave him.

I could see the pride in his eyes vanish when I shook my head and told him I didn't want it. It hurt him to be given the money. So I grabbed the deed just to make him happy. He nodded and shook my hand.

I didn't know what to do with it. I don't need shit from anyone. And I sure as hell don't need a house in the suburbs.

That night I drove by the address on the deed and saw him there. It took a good ten minutes before I realized it was the house next door that he'd given me.

Maybe it's because I could never do anything for my pops, I don't know for sure, but that night I stayed in the house and made sure I saw him every day that followed.

The doctors were right; the treatments didn't help, and I was there when the life left him.

It fucked me up pretty good. One minute, the machine was beeping, the next it was just a single tone.

I wish he hadn't made me promise not to tell anyone. Especially Elizabeth. She'd feel so much better if she knew the truth. I know she would.

I told that old bastard he should tell her. But he looked me in the eyes and said he didn't want her to remember him like that.

Tears prick my eyes and I have to stop thinking back to him and all that shit. I place my phone in my pocket and try to get back into work. I need a damn distraction from all this. But that's fucked, too.

Ian's making threats and being a pain in my ass. He's our competition in a way. And he's slowly losing his clients to us because of his shit business tactics. My cousin, Tyler, should know to take care of this shit and nip it in the bud. Intercepting clients and making deals to pay off their debts with me is a no-no, and Ian knows it. I already know I'm gonna have to step in before shit gets out of hand. I don't feel like it though.

I'm so damn exhausted. I get up and make my way upstairs. I just need to sleep this off. All this stress and no outlet to relieve it is making me tired beyond belief.

I remember Elizabeth's soft body against mine. I fucking want her. She tempted me, and now all I can think about is punishing her tight pussy. I'm surprised with how much restraint I had.

As I collapse onto my bed upstairs, I can faintly hear Elizabeth. Her childhood bedroom is right across from my bedroom. Only ten feet or so separates our houses. But from my window, I can see straight into hers. I know because I've looked out this window staring at Richard's house, waiting for this all to end so many damn times.

I hear another small sob and it breaks my heart. She's crying again. Fuck, it hurts to know she's right there. If she didn't want to hate me so much, I could take away her pain, mine too, if only for a moment. It's better than having to deal with all these shitty emotions.

I wanna go over there.

I wanna ease her pain.

I want her to take mine away, too. I already know how good she'd feel.

I wanna make this right. I don't know why this is all fucked. But I'll make it right. I shouldn't have been such an asshole. She doesn't owe me shit. It was selfish of me to do that shit today. I did it out of anger and pride, and took advantage of her mourning her father. I'm such a fucking prick.

First thing in the morning, I'll let her know it's all hers and that I'm gone.

I'm a bad man, but I'm not so bad that I wanna hurt her like that.

She's too good for me anyway.

I should've known better. I never should've chased something I can never have.

CHAPTER 5

LIZZIE

I can get through this. One step at a time.

I take in a slow, trembling breath, fighting back the pain twisting my stomach. After a moment, I let out a sob and bury my head in my pillow, muffling my cries. Smothering the screams.

It's so hard being in this house. Memories of daddy keep flashing through my mind, filling me with grief-tinged nostalgia. I can still see him now. His weathered, but charming smile. The gentle way he always treated me. How dearly he loved me. Fuck. I'm even seeing mom, too. It's been so long since that pain has felt so raw.

I'm trying hard to keep myself together. But I feel like my soul's been shattered into a million tiny pieces.

Fight it! I shout in my mind, trying to deny the tidal wave of pain surging through my limbs, making me want to wallow in my grief. *Be strong!*

That's what daddy would want. He'd want me to fight, be strong for him. Not indulge in my misery. I have to do it. I have to make him proud.

After what seems like an eternity, I'm able to quiet my

sobs, though the tears and pain remain. I sit up on my bed, sniffle, and wipe at my tearstained face. I look around my room, noting that everything is exactly how I left it. Ryan Reynolds posters adorn the pale pink walls, and there's a big fat ass purple Barney stuffed animal in the right corner of the room. I thought it was funny to keep him, but now all it does is remind me of how my father won him for me at a carnival. It fucking hurts.

Emotion threatens to overcome me again, but somehow, I manage to push it back.

Last night wasn't good. Not at all. I thought I'd be productive. I thought with how angry I was at Liam I could handle going into daddy's room and packing up some of his things. I was wrong, for two reasons. One is that I'm definitely not ready to say goodbye yet. The second is that daddy had already done it. Tears leak from the corners of my eyes, but I don't bother to brush them away. He knew he was dying. He cleaned up everything so there wouldn't be as much work for me. The tears come harder, and I press my palms to my eyes. It hurts so much. I wish he'd spent his last moments with me and not doing shit like that.

It takes a moment for me to calm down. A long moment.

"Pain, pain go away," I whisper, "Don't come back for any day."

I sit there for a while, staring at my posters. Numb all over. Then a thought occurs to me.

Maybe I should just give Liam what he wants. I'll have to sell this house. I know I will. I have so much debt, and no job. I haven't had any income while I've been in school. Grad school doesn't leave time for anything else other than hitting the books. School. I huff a humorless laugh. That's a pipe dream now.

The idea of giving in to Liam is so appalling, I almost let out a bloodcurdling scream of fury. Seriously. It pisses me the fuck off to have to rely on the handout of a stranger. But the stakes are high. If I can't dial back my ego, I'll lose my house. My father's house. The one thing I have left of him. And if I give in to Liam, I'll lose my pride. Pride's the only thing I have left at this point.

I have to decide which is more important. And that's an easy choice. I can't let go of this place. I can't say goodbye like that.

A date will give me a chance to know him more. And I do want that. I need to figure out who the hell this man is. I wish I wasn't so attracted to him though. It makes things complicated.

Shit. *I hate it.* I hate how he makes me feel, how he makes me want him. It's not right. It's not right how I want him to bend me over and fuck me like I'm his. How I want him to own every inch of my body.

I should tell him to fuck off. To go to hell. Fight the will and contest it. Take him to court, sue him for everything he's got. But deep down, I know it's not worth the fight.

The smug, handsome bastard has me in the palm of his hand.

And he so knows it, I think angrily.

If I accept his offer, I don't know how I'll get through it. Good God, how can I survive being around a man I want to kill and fuck, all at the same time?

This house. I need to focus on keeping this house and just being able to live. I have no money without doing this.

That's it. *My inheritance.* What's rightfully mine. What he stole from me. If I keep my mind on that, I should be good. He'll never get to lay a finger on me. One date, and then it's all over.

I wipe my face one more time and rise from my bed.

I've got dried tears and slobber all over my face and night-gown. A cool shower will do me some good.

I make my way into the bathroom. I grab a towel and place it on the sink. Then I disrobe and look in the mirror. A haggard-looking young woman looks back at me. Even with a pound of foundation on left over from yesterday, I can see the bags under my eyes. Days of no sleep and constant crying spells are really showing.

Hopefully I'll look more refreshed after a long, hot shower.

I turn away, open the shower stall and turn the knob. I place my hand under the stream and wait for the water to turn lukewarm. When it's tolerable, I step inside and close the door.

I let the water hit my face and drench my hair, imagining it washing away my pain and worries. I grab the pouf hanging off the showerhead and lather it with a lavender-scented body wash. I lift it to my nose and inhale deeply, focusing on soothing my battered soul.

As I begin to lather my body, naughty thoughts about Liam begin invading my mind. Suddenly, I'm back in the moment of being pushed up against the wall, his cock pressing against me. Desire burns through my lower stomach and my legs tremble slightly as my pussy begins pulsing and clenching uncontrollably. I let the pouf drop and the water rinse everything away.

Unconsciously, I begin rubbing myself, imagining Liam here in the shower with me, his hard cock pressed against my lower stomach and demanding entry.

"Oh fuck," I moan, the image making me dizzy with lust.

I move my hands faster between my thighs, rubbing my throbbing clit in a circular motion. Pleasure courses through my limbs as my nipples stiffen like stone.

God. I want him here now. Taking me. Fucking me.

My breath quickens, becoming ragged. I slump against the shower wall, moaning and groaning. In my mind's eye, I imagine his chiseled body drenched with water, thrusting his powerful hips against my ass, plunging his huge cock deep inside my needy pussy.

Pressure builds inside of my core, threatening to explode.

I'm going to cum. All over his big fat cock.

Gasping, I snatch my hand away from my aching pussy.

What the fuck are you doing, Lizzie?

I'm shocked at how close I've come to having an orgasm. Fantasizing about Liam, no less. *My enemy.*

My thighs are trembling, and I'm shaking all over. I'm not sure if I'm shaking from my near-orgasm, or how frightened I am at just having lost control. Probably both.

Ashamed, I quickly finish my shower and then step out into the steamy bathroom.

As I dry myself off, I vow to forget what just happened. It was just a mistake. An anomaly.

It will *never* happen again.

Done drying off, I slip into an old favorite pink bathrobe. I locate my blow dryer under the sink and plug it in. I still can't think straight; I'm just going through the motions. I flip my hair to the side and am about to turn the blow dryer on when the doorbell rings.

"Shit," I mutter, wondering who it is. After a moment, I figure it's just a well-meaning family member, come to check on me. I have neither the temperament, nor the patience to deal with that shit right now. I'll just ignore it. Whoever it is can come back later.

I press the power switch, and the loud hum of the dryer fills the room. I purse my lips when I think I hear the doorbell ring again. I turn the dryer off for only a second and sure enough, there's another chime. I ignore it, turning the blow dryer back on and let the hot air run through my hair, enjoying the sensation. I can faintly hear the doorbell ring again, this time repeatedly.

Whoever it is, isn't going away anytime soon.

I blow out a sigh of frustration and turn off my blow dryer.

I'll just go answer the door and tell them I can't deal with visitors right now. I check my appearance in the mirror. My hair is wet and disheveled. I look a mess. But I really don't give a rat's ass. The person outside has no business harassing me like this. I can't wait to give them a mouthful.

I rush out of the bathroom, down the hallway, and down the stairs. *Ding-dong. Ding-dong. Ding-dong.*

"Just a minute!" I yell in annoyance. Good God. Whoever's outside is going to regret doing this. Don't they know I'm grieving for my father? Why would someone be so rude at a time like this?

Breathless, I reach the door and snatch it open, ready to do battle. And then I know why. My heart does a backflip. *Liam.*

He's looking like he stepped straight off a modeling shoot, dressed in simple blue jeans and a buttoned white shirt that shows off his corded biceps. His hair is slicked back, and his chiseled profile makes my heart flutter.

His eyes widen as he sees me, wet from my shower, only clad in my flimsy robe. His gaze travels down my body, to my breasts and then my legs which stick out from the slit in my robe. In an instant, he catches himself and brings his eyes back to my face.

Too late. I saw him check me out. Hard nipples and all.

My cheeks burn with embarrassment and I pull my robe tighter around myself and cross my arms across my chest to hide my erect nipples. "What are you doing ringing my doorbell like a maniac?" I demand angrily. "Come to assert your male dominance some more?"

Liam swallows hard and then clears his throat. "I came over to tell you something." He doesn't seem at all bothered by my bitchy put-on in the least.

Images from the shower flash through my mind, causing my pussy to throb. *Sweet Jesus.* "Tell me what?" I ask, casting those naughty thoughts back to hell where they belong. My voice sounds strained. I hate it. And I feel guilty. If he only knew what I'd been doing in the shower before he showed up.

Whatever he has to tell me must be pretty damn important, leaning on my doorbell like that.

Liam pauses as if thinking about what he wants to say. "That I'm sorry about how I treated you yesterday," he says finally.

My jaw nearly drops to the floor. "You? Sorry?" I snort with derision. "That's a good one."

Liam carefully keeps his eyes on my face. "I'm serious. I shouldn't have come on to you like that. You just lost the most important man in your life, and were just acting out your emotions. I should've had enough empathy to realize that instead of behaving like an asshole."

I'm at a loss for words. Seriously. I've been building up Liam as my enemy since I first learned who he was. Our last two exchanges didn't go well. And now this? I don't know what to think.

Yet looking at him, I don't doubt his sincerity. He appears to be truly sorry.

"Well, uh... that's nice of you to say," I mumble, not knowing how to take this sudden turnabout in behavior. "Thank you for telling me." I'm practically whispering, and I can't even look him in the eyes.

The corners of Liam's kissable lips curl up into a soft smile. "Just nice?" he asks.

"Yeah," I say. "Sweet. Really sweet of you." I clear my throat and add, "I'm sorry, too. I was out of line." It hurts to admit it, but it's true. I just want to hate someone. I want someone to blame. And Liam's a good target.

Liam chuckles. "You're really cute, you know that?"

My cheeks burn again. "I've been called worse."

"Only by fucking idiots," Liam growls.

I'm taken aback. Liam has not only apologized to me, but now he's taking up for me. Now I'm really not sure what to make of all of this.

For a moment I'm stunned, unable to come up with a suitable response. I have too many conflicting emotions. Anger. Sadness. Lust. To make matters worse, all I can think about is how it felt when Liam's hard body was pressed up against mine.

I look Liam in the eyes. I see sincerity there. And... desire. He wants me. I know it. I could invite him in right now for a passionate tango, and I'm sure he'd jump on the chance. I just can't let that happen. I need to have some self-control.

I begin to part my lips to reply... I don't know what. A part of me wants to demand he sign over my inheritance to me, another part of me wants to yell at him to go away, and yet another wants me to let him have his way with me.

I bite my tongue, not trusting myself to speak. With all the dirty thoughts and emotions raging through me right now, I'm afraid of what might come out. Besides, I'm not sure if Liam is trying to play me. By giving in to my desire, I could be playing right into the palm of his hand.

I have to be on guard with this man. I don't know him at all.

"I didn't mean to disturb you when you were so..." He pauses as his eyes flicker down my robe, and a shiver runs down my spine. "Indisposed." He gives me a cocky grin, signaling he's lying. Of course he'd meant to disturb me with the way he'd spammed the doorbell. But at this point, I don't care anymore.

Suddenly, I feel as if I've made up my mind about my situation. I just hope it won't end in disaster.

He runs his hand through his hair and turns to look back at the house next door, *his* house, and then starts to say, "About that date--"

Heart pounding, I blurt out, "About that." I cringe at the note of desperation that enters my voice.

Liam turns back to me and appraises me with a furrowed brow. "Yeah?"

Dear God, Lizzie. I hope you don't live to regret this.

I take in a deep breath and reply, "I think I'm willing to take you up on that offer."

CHAPTER 6

LIAM

That was unexpected. I don't know how to feel about this broad.

The last day or so, I've gone back and forth with how I feel about her.

The way she said she accepted my offer should tell me everything I need to know. This is a business deal for her, nothing more. We go out, and I give her everything that was left to me. A simple transaction.

I don't fucking like that. That's not what I want. I want to go out with her, the real her… shit. I twist my hands on the steering wheel, and grip it tighter. My knuckles are white.

I'm a liar. I wanted to fuck her. That's why I said that shit. I know that's why.

I was hurting, she was hurting. And she was pissing me off. She didn't even try to get to know me. My heart pains in my chest. Yeah I wanna fuck her, but I want her to know that I did care about her old man. My relationship with him was short-lived, but I know the pain she's going through.

I fucking need someone, too.

I park my car in the office parking lot and look up at the highrise. It's a sleek steel building with large, dark glass windows. It's intimidating and masculine. And I own the entire building. I had it built just for our business.

It's an odd feeling going from the cozy rundown house that Richard used to rent out and then handed over to me, to walking into this building.

It feels colder and lonelier than it ever has before. I don't like it.

I don't talk to anyone on the way in. I don't need to. Most don't know who I am anyway. I'm just a man who rents the top floor, or so they think. They don't need to know what I do, or why I do it. My clients come in through the back of the building via an elevator strictly for my business' own use. Not this one. I prefer coming in through thc lobby and taking in the condition of the place. I'm a silent partner, I am in all my investments, but I like to check in and make sure everything runs smoothly.

Everything is separated between my business and the other businesses here, even the parking lot. It keeps things neat and clean. I own everything, and that way I can control it all. This is why my brother and cousin need me.

We have high-end clients because of me. It doesn't stop some of the Joe Schmoes from coming in and risking all they have on their favorite team because it's their lucky day, but it does make this business a commodity.

I stand by the elevator and walk in, trying to shake off my feelings about Elizabeth agreeing to my proposal. It wasn't meant as a business deal. I stretch my shoulders slightly and breathe out my annoyance. A few people walk in after me and I wait for them. I stand quietly at the back of the elevator. There are doors behind me and I have one of only three keys that will open them.

The bell dings, and the elevator cart comes to a halt.

I adjust my crisp white shirt sleeves and crack my neck as I wait for the two women in pencil skirts to stop gabbing and get off. There's only one man left and he's in a nice navy suit with thick blonde hair that's styled professionally. He keeps eyeing me like he's wondering what I"ll be doing on his floor. He thinks I'm stopping on his floor since I haven't pressed another button, but I'm not.

I give him a tight smile as the cart stops on the thirty-eighth floor and he exits. He looks back over his shoulder with one last curious glance as I push the button to make the doors close. I take out the key and slip it in, pushing in the code and wait till it reaches the top floor.

I rock on my heels.

I used to think nothing of this. Going into work was just a daily chore.

I enjoy my job. There's always something to do and new ways for us to improve. But my heart isn't in it today. That's for damn sure.

The doors slide open and I walk into the airy space. It's one large, open concept area. The back wall is covered with 110-inch ultra high-def televisions. There are sixteen of them, spaced evenly on the back wall. The majority of the space is divided into four seating sections with sleek black leather sofas. And in the very back, there's a bar stocked with top-shelf liquor.

I head to the left though, past a buffet station used for catering and walk straight through to my office. It has the same masculine feel as the den. But I like staying in here because it's closed off and soundproof. I don't have to listen to that shit that goes on out there, but they also can't hear whatever it is I'm doing back here.

If Elizabeth saw this, I wonder what she'd think. I doubt she'd think I was a bookie, maybe a party planner instead. Since we do throw what I guess you could call parties. It's a live betting arena. And the thrill of watching it happen gives our clients an aspect to our business they don't get anywhere else.

Every month I get more and more clientele because of the unique features we offer. And that's a problem for some people, like Ian Dracho. Many of our customers come from him. He's a lowlife who I know for a fact has rigged games to get out of holes he dug himself.

To take the bets, you have to know the odds. You have to be good with numbers and statistics. My brother's damn good at that, but Ian isn't. So he rigs the games, or offers shit bets that only fools would take. I don't blame his customers for leaving him. But he sure as fuck does. And he blames us for taking them.

My ass doesn't even touch the leather in my Herman Miller Aeron chair before my brother Zac and cousin Tyler walk in. The three of us make a good team. I know I haven't been around much lately, and they've been bugging the fuck out of me because of it. I'm not surprised they were on me the second I got here. It's not like we're going to have anyone coming in for an appointment until later anyway, so what else do they have to do other than give me shit.

I sink back into my seat and try not to be irritated.

Zac looks like me, but with a baby face that makes him look approachable and charming. The sharp features only I inherited from our father, well they give you a hint that I may be dangerous. But Zac could fool anyone into thinking he's Mr. Right. He takes the seat across from mine at the dark walnut desk and angles it so Tyler's included in a circle of sorts.

Tyler's all muscle, and that's why he's good at his job. His broad frame fills up the wingback chair in the corner of the office as he sits back and sets his right ankle over his left knee. He's a quiet man and doesn't say very much. But when he does, you listen and right now he looks like he's got something to say.

"'Bout time you came back." Tyler's voice is deep and has a hint of humor. That, combined with the smirk on his face makes me think he's not quite as upset with my absence as Zac's been.

"You done being on vacation?" Zac asks sarcastically. Yeah. Zac's pissed. I'd spent a lot of time with Richard. I shouldn't have. But what's the point of having your own business if you can't take a break when you need one? Although, I have to admit, it's been a little over twelve weeks since I've had my head in the game, and that's a long fucking time.

I fiddle with the engraved silver fountain pen on my desk. It always sits here. My father used to keep it in his pocket. He liked to say that it was his good luck charm. Always had this damn pen in his pocket... except for the day of the car crash. I'd begged him to let me hold onto it that day when he'd left. Zac was too young to remember, but I'll never forget. "It wasn't a vacation," I say simply before righting myself in the seat and leaning forward. I set the pen back down and straighten it, putting it right where it belongs.

I clear my throat and continue looking my brother in the eye as I say, "Give me an update on the numbers first." The bottom line is what matters. Our expenses are immense and they pay off well. But a small dip one month could mean a decline overall if something's not right.

"Numbers are good." Zac adds, "They're actually a bit up."

My eyebrows shoot up in surprise. "I wasn't expecting that."

"We got in a few more clients that like to have fun more than they care about the bets." I nod my head and smile.

"That's what we want," I say with a cocky grin. We want them to enjoy the experience, so even if they're losing their money, they'll keep coming back.

Tyler huffs a laugh and says, "Gotta admit, I like those clients more." Tyler's more of a bouncer than anything for those clients. For the most part anyway.

Put enough men in a room, add alcohol, and shit's bound to get out of hand. I give Tyler a nod, but turn back to my brother. Although I'm a bit relieved to hear we don't have problems on the money front, there's still some serious shit that needs to be dealt with.

"There's still an issue that needs to be taken care of," I say and gesture to Zac, who's nodding his head like we're on the same page. I'm the problem solver. I fix shit, and I develop our brand. That's my job, and I'm damn good at it. And right now, we've got shit that needs fixing.

"Dracho is a fucking problem," he says flatly.

"I'm gonna need more than that, Zac. How many clients has he taken?" That's really what this is about. He sees us as a threat, and we are, but there's no way he can beat us. Not with the shit operation he's running.

"None of the top earners, but a client is a client and when they owe us, I don't like getting a call from him. He can't reach out to them and take on their debt. It pisses me off." Zac's angrily tapping his fingers against the chair. He's on edge and pissed. He adds, "He's pushing us by doing that and interfering with our business."

I clench my jaw and crack my neck. Zac's got a point, but if the people who owe us go somewhere else looking for a loan, we can't stop them. I look back to the pen on the desk and run the tip of my finger along the engraved lines. It's a habit I have. This is tricky.

The guys are quiet while I try to think of a way to stop this shit from becoming a bigger problem. I'd say we could just stop doing bets with the clients that know of him, but there are a lot that have come to us after dealing with that prick.

"How much of our business came from him?" I ask.

Zac shrugs his shoulders. "How the fuck should I know?"

I imagine it's a lot, considering his name is brought up in our circles with regularity. He's got a right to be mad since we took his business, but if he was better at his job then that wouldn't have happened. That shit is on him.

"The only thing I can think of is requiring the cash up front." I settle on a solution, although I don't really like it.

Tyler whistles in his seat, and his eyes widen. Apparently, he doesn't like it either.

"We'll lose a lot of business that way, Liam." Zac's right. We would lose a lot of business, but that's the only way we'd guarantee not having to deal with that asshole.

"Do you have any alternatives?" I ask him.

"We could take care of him," Tyler says flatly. It turns my blood to ice. Tyler's father, my uncle, was a member of the mob. It doesn't mean much to Tyler if someone's gotta go, but I don't like it. It's best to avoid that situation in the first place by preventing it from happening. I shake my head and nod at Zac.

"Okay, not our high-end clients. But the others, the ones we know came from him. We're going to require their payments upfront. How much business do we stand to lose from that?" I ask Zac.

Zac looks up to the ceiling and taps his fingers on his knee for a moment before he looks back to me. "I'd really have to check the numbers, but it's probably as high as twenty percent."

I lean back and say, “Problem fucking solved. We can take that hit. Our profit margin can handle that, and it'll get that prick off our backs and out of our territory.”

Zac’s face finally cracks a smile and he nods, looking at Tyler and then back at me. “Alright, I’ll let ‘em know.”

“We could’ve used that answer a month ago, Liam,” Tyler says from the corner.

“Yeah, well, I’m here now.”

“So no more sneaking off?” Zac asks.

I take a deep breath and look away. I don’t have to answer to either of them, but I’m not gonna lie to my brother. “I’m going back tonight, actually.”

“You moving into that place?” Tyler asks with disbelief.

A rough chuckle rises up my chest, “No. No, I am not moving into Twenty-two Wyoming. I’m giving it back to the old man’s daughter.”

They know all about him. And for the most part they gave me some time and space while I was away. Zac was younger when pops passed. But they know it took a toll on me.

“Why you going back then?” Tyler asks.

Zac butts in with a smile as he says, ”Let me guess, the daughter.”

My lips turn down into a frown.

“I’m right, aren’t I?” Zac says, happy as a fucking snot-nosed kid in a candy shop. “Tell me I’m right.”

“Fuck off,” I say with a bit of humor.

“You for real?” Tyler asks.

“I knew it!” Zac slaps his knee. “You’re such a bastard, Liam.”

I shake my head, not wanting to tell them anything. Besides, it’s not like I’ve been fucking her.

“Who is this broad?” Tyler’s asking questions, and Zac’s making assumptions. I don't like either.

"No one. Unless you two have any more business to discuss, I suggest you get the fuck outta here." They don't need to know about her. All the stories Richard told me flood back to me. But in an instant they're gone and replaced by that look on her face when she accepted my offer.

She looked so fucking beautiful with her skin all flushed from just getting out of the shower. She's a natural beauty. But she'd look better if she wasn't wrecked from exhaustion and stress. And I could tell she wasn't happy to go out with me.

I want it though. I'm a selfish asshole, so I'm going through with it. A small piece of me is still hanging on to something. I don't know what, and I don't know why.

She thinks I'm bad news, and she's right.

But I just want a taste of her sweetness.

I want her to know me like her father did.

More than that, I want to know the woman Richard was always talking about.

I need to make sure she doesn't regret this.

CHAPTER 7

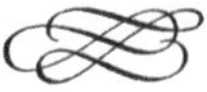

LIZZIE

I peer at myself in the mirror, staring critically at my figure. I'm wearing a red dress with spaghetti straps that looks nice, but lacks impact. The lush curves I usually enjoy when I'm at a healthy weight are somewhat diminished.

Damn, I think to myself. *Nat was right. I've really lost a bit of weight. But it's not my fault I don't feel like eating.*

Nat has tried everything to get me to eat, with no success. I can't even stomach her delicious sugar cookies anymore.

Still, I like what I'm wearing. It's classy, but it shows off my womanly figure. The weight loss hasn't taken that from me at least.

As I stare at my appearance, I tremble with excitement. It's been a few days since I accepted Liam's offer. I've expected to see him since then, but he's been gone. I'm all worked up and nervous that he's changed his mind. But he hasn't. And for some odd reason that makes a small part of me giddy.

In a few minutes, Liam will be here. I'm not sure if I made the right decision by taking him up on his offer. I know practically nothing about him. For all I know, his apology was designed to get my guard down so he can con me, like how maybe he conned daddy. If I'm not smart with this guy, I could end up in a lot of trouble.

I need to be careful. I take a deep breath, trying to gather my wits, but my eyes pop open wide as the doorbell rings.

Cursing my luck at not being completely ready, I run out of my room and down the stairs. I make it to the door and realize… *Shit! I have no makeup on.* Thinking quickly, I unlock the door and run back up the stairs.

"It's unlocked!" I yell from the top of the stairs. "You can come in now!" I dart around the corner as I hear the door creak open.

"Elizabeth?" I hear Liam call. It's odd hearing my full name. No one calls me Elizabeth.

"I'll be down in a minute!" I yell from the upstairs hallway, my heart pounding. "Can you wait in the living room?"

"Sure." I hear the door close and then his heavy footsteps as he walks through the hallway to the living room.

Thank God.

Five minutes later, I have my war paint on. I'm wearing a light layer of foundation, rosy blush, smoky eyeshadow and a shiny lip gloss. I've done a rush job on my hair, styling messy curls going down the right side of my face, but it's good enough. I make my way downstairs and stop before I enter the living room, anxiety washing over me.

I wonder if he'll think I look good, I worry. For a second, I have the urge to run back upstairs to change outfits and mess with my hair again. *Stop it right now, Lizzie Turner,* I scold myself. *You're going on a date, not marrying the man. Pull yourself together. And this is only to honor my end of the deal he offered and to find out what he meant to daddy.*

A twinge of anger runs through my veins, but it's dimmed. I haven't felt the same about Liam since he apologized. It's harder for me to be angry as the days wear on. But I hold onto it, because without it, there's only sadness.

After a moment, I gather my courage, take a deep breath and walk into the living room. Then I nearly swoon.

Dressed in black slacks and a bright white, crisp dress shirt that's open at the chest, Liam's sitting on the couch, legs planted wide, watching TV. The way he's relaxed there, his hair a bit messy, looking hot as fuck, is driving me wild. Seriously, I've seen guys sit like that before, but he's making an art form out of it. He looks like he owns the place, like he's the fucking king of the world.

The image of walking over and straddling him, smothering his neck with kisses while his hands roam all over my body run through my mind, making me shiver with need.

Liam seems to sense my presence. He tears his eyes away from the TV and they settle on me. "You look beautiful," he says in a deep, husky voice, not appearing to notice my inner turmoil. Hunger flashes in his eyes as he says those words.

"Thank you," I say softly. "You don't look so bad yourself."

Liam grins.

That's when the theme song on the television hits me. It makes my heart jump. As I walk farther into the living room so I can see for myself, I gesture and ask, "Is that MacBoys you're watching?"

Liam glances at the screen and then grabs the remote, turning the volume down. *He knows how to operate the remotes. They're a pain in the ass. One to turn the TV on and off, another for the volume and a third for the channels. And he knows how to use them. Has he been here before?*

He nods. "Yeah, it is." He seems to sense that him watching daddy's show has gotten to me. I can't help it.

I fight back the tears that threaten to spill from my eyes. "That was daddy's favorite show." It's hard to keep my breathing steady at the reminder.

"Yeah, I know," Liam says in a soft voice. "He's the one that got me hooked on it." He starts to say something else, but then he stops, looking a bit choked up.

Liam sounds so sincere that it's hard not to imagine him and daddy being friends.

It's just an act, I tell myself. *A ruse just to gain my trust.*

A part of me wants to call him out on it. Call him a liar. Accuse him of making up stories so that I won't go after him for taking my inheritance. Yet when I look at Liam's face, all I see is real, raw emotion. It's easier for me to think he's a liar than to accept he and daddy were friends. Because if that's true, where did that leave me in my step-father's eyes? And without focusing my energy on hating Liam, my mind goes straight to my father.

"He must have meant a lot to you," I find myself saying. *I can't believe I just said that.*

Liam nods. He clears his throat uncomfortably. "He was a good man." He nods his head, but doesn't look me in the eyes.

I grow silent. I stare at the man I thought was a liar. A man I treated like shit and took my anger out on, rather than hear out.

"Let's go, shall we?" Liam says abruptly. He turns off the

TV and stands up. He runs his hand through his hair and I can't help but be slightly distracted.

I should say no. I should tell him I'm sorry. I'm so damn sorry I ever questioned daddy's will. I feel like shit. Daddy left everything to him for a reason. I should just be happy I have this house. Tears prick my eyes, and I wish they didn't because Liam's quick to come over to me and try to comfort me.

I awkwardly laugh and brush the tears away, shaking my head. I hate how he's seeing me like this.

"I'm sorry I brought him up," Liam says as he starts to reach for me, but then stops.

He doesn't even wanna touch me. I breathe in deep and look at the ceiling with my eyes wide to prevent the tears from coming and ruining my makeup.

"Hey, it's alright." Liam leans in a bit and rubs his hand down my back. I want to lean into his touch. But I know I shouldn't. I feel weak. If I give him an inch, I'll be begging him to take a mile. And that's a mistake. Even with my head clouded in lust and sadness I know that much at least.

I let out a heavy exhale and get ready to apologize and take it all back, but he beats me to it.

"I wanna take you to dinner," he says simply. "Come on, let's just get out and relax." I stare deep into his sparkling green eyes and wonder if I can really do it. *Relax*. Like it's just that easy.

He sees my hesitation and pouts comically before saying, "You said you would; don't back out on me now."

I laugh and sniffle a bit.

"Alright then. Let's go." I give him a soft smile, and something eases in my chest when he flashes a handsome, bright smile right back.

"Perfect," he says and leads me to the door, as if this is his house. As if he's been here a thousand times. I start to think about this house and all the memories it holds and why I'm here, but I shut it down. I take one last deep breath and leave it all behind as we start our *date*.

We walk outside and he holds the door open for me.

"Thank you," I say softly, clutching my wristlet in my hands.

"You like Italian?" he asks smoothly. As though this is easy for him.

"I do." Lasagna is one of my favorite dishes. My mom used to make it a lot growing up. Well, really any pasta dish. Daddy used to say she loved carbs a bit too much. The happy memory turns the corners of my lips up for a moment. Just a small moment.

"Good, because I know the perfect place to go." I'm snapped out of my memory by Liam's words as he opens the passenger side door for me. I give him a small nod and slide in.

He drives me downtown to the strip, a place where the hottest clubs and restaurants are. The entire drive, neither of us talks. We simply listen to the music on the radio. It's hard to keep my mind from wondering if he's even interested in me. We pull into the parking lot of a restaurant called Di-Italio.

I've heard of this place. The cheapest plate is a hundred bucks.

I really don't feel comfortable with a guy dropping several hundred dollars on me on a first date. Especially a guy I'm not sure I trust yet. A guy I'm not sure I really want to be on a date with. I stifle my objections and carry through with the plan. It's just a date. Just one date.

He comes around the car and lets me out. He's being a perfect gentleman, and I'm doing my best to accept it without feeling like a fraud.

"Thank you," I say softly.

"Of course." His deep voice calms me and settles my worries. He splays his hand on my lower back and leads me to the door. My heart blossoms. I've never been courted this much before. And especially not by such a handsome man.

What's a man like him doing with a woman like me? I try to push my insecurities away. Aren't I worthy of a man like this? A man who admires and respects me? I start to speak, but I can't finish.

As the man at the front entrance opens the door, I turn and face Liam. "I think this is really very nice of you, but--"

He puts a finger to my lips, completely catching me off guard. The act is intimate. And he seems to realize it only after he's done it.

He slowly pulls his finger away and clears his throat.

"I just wanna feed you," he says. "Just sit down and let me meet the daughter Richard always talked about." Hearing him bring up my father makes my heart swell. I search his face for the real reason why he could possibly want to be here with me. But I can't think of any other than he genuinely wants this date.

I nod my head in agreement. I can do this.

My lips part slightly as my heels click on the travertine tiles on the floor of the restaurant. It's beautiful. There's a rustic feel to the decor that seems to take me to another place.

Soft sounds of a soothing violinist mingle with the murmurs of chatter in the large venue. There are sconces on the walls, and candles on the tables that provide dim, but intimate lighting.

The deep reds and off-whites of the linens adds to the romantic feel. It's nearly overwhelming.

"I've never been somewhere so nice before," I quietly admit to Liam, looking up at him through my lashes as the maître d' leads us to a circular booth in the very back. It's in its own corner and it's more secluded here; the noises are even quieter, the lighting even darker.

"Well then," Liam says as he smiles down on me. "You're in for a treat."

CHAPTER 8

LIAM

It was hard to keep a straight face when Elizabeth said she's never been somewhere so nice before. Her father said the same thing when I took him here.

I own this place. Well, technically I own fifty-one percent of it. I'm a silent partner though. It was a damn good investment. And it makes me happy to be able to take whoever I want here, whenever I want. Food's good, and so is the atmosphere.

I'm happy I brought her here. I finally have a moment with her where she's not trying to claw my eyes out.

I can tell something's really bugging her. To be honest, it's a bit awkward. Almost like a blind date. Except that I already know so much about her, and she hardly knows a thing about me.

"Listen," she starts to say, but then a waitress comes with a pitcher of ice water and fills our glasses. The young woman sets the pitcher down gently on the table and presents the menus. She starts rattling off details that we don't need to hear.

She offers some Shiraz for tasting, but I already know what I want. "Could we have a bottle of Screaming Eagle Cab?"

Elizabeth looks at me from the corner of her eyes with a smirk.

"I know it doesn't sound quite right, but it's from Napa Valley and you're going to love it."

The waitress nods her head in agreement and adds, "It's delicious. It'll go wonderfully with whatever you choose from the menu."

Elizabeth gives me a tight smile and says thank you. She reaches for the menu and tilts it slightly. Her lips fall open after a moment and I watch as her eyes go down the rows of items.

I take a sip of water, not bothering to look at my menu. I know exactly what I want. I get the same thing every time I come here.

She purses her lips in disappointment, and I have to ask, "What's wrong?"

Her eyes fly to mine and she shakes her head as she says, "Nothing." She's so tense and obviously not feeling alright.

"I thought you liked Italian," I say simply. I'm not buying that 'nothing' response she gave me. If only she'd tell me what's wrong. I hate that she's so standoffish. I need to remember she doesn't know shit about me.

She sets her menu down and looks away before looking back at me. "I'm just stupid. I was going to get lasagna. I don't know what some of these other things are." Her voice trails off, and she looks away again, markedly embarrassed.

I reach out and turn her menu over. I tap on exactly what she wants. "It's right here. You'll love it." Finally, her lips kick up and she seems to relax a bit.

"Thank you," she whispers. She reaches for her water and takes a sip. Her eyes still don't reach me.

She's not pissed at me anymore, which is nice. But there's nothing there in its place. She's shy and seems uncomfortable.

I think she needs a fucking glass of wine. As do I.

I take in a deep breath and decide I need to get this weight off my shoulders and just tell her something about me and her father. Something to ease her worries about me. But I'm not sure what to say. I don't want to break my vow to Richard, and I also don't want her to know what I do for a living.

But before I can say anything she turns to me and asks, "So what do you do, Liam?"

Fucking hell. I look her in the eyes as I tell a white lie. Not even really a white lie, just a lie of partial omission. "I have a few investments." I take a drink from my glass as she eyes me skeptically. I can practically see her desperately trying to keep the disdain off her face.

I need to give her a little more than that. "This place is one of them."

Her eyes widen with surprise as the waitress comes back and pours a small amount of the cabernet sauvignon into my wine glass. I take a sip and nod. I already knew I'd like it. I'm just going through the motions.

When the waitress leaves, Elizabeth leans in and asks, "You own this place?" The surprise in her voice is evident.

"Only part of it. I don't do any of the work. I just put in the money and get a return from it each month. Nice and easy." She considers my words and takes a sip from her glass.

"Mmm," she says as she starts to set it down, but then puts the glass right back up to her lips. "That's really good." My chest fills with pride.

"I told you." I give her a cocky grin.

She looks down at the table and then pushes her hair behind her ears. "How did you meet my dad then?" she asks.

I wish she hadn't. I don't want to lie to her, but I don't want to break the only promise I made to a dying man.

"He found me," I say as I start talking without thinking.

She gives me a sad smile and says, "Daddy was good at doing that. He liked to talk a lot."

"Yeah he did," I add. "He was a good man."

She looks up at me like she wants to ask more, and my heart beats faster with anxiety, but she doesn't.

I need to get off this subject and get it on her. Women love talking about themselves.

"So what are you going to college for?" I ask her, even though I already know the answer.

She turns her shoulders toward me and answers, "Well, I'm getting my master's in psychology." She stops talking and looks down at the table. She pinches the tips of her fingers and looks away for a second, but I don't understand why.

"You doing alright?" I ask her. Richard said she was. She could've been lying to him, though I don't think she would have. He said she was doing great and that she'd be done soon. I don't understand her reaction.

She looks back at me uncomfortably. I thought I was making progress with this broad, but every turn I hit a damn brick wall.

She starts to answer but then reaches for the glass and takes a large gulp. What the fuck?

She finally faces me and answers, "I can't really afford to go back… now."

My heart sinks in my chest. I need to put that shit to bed.

"Elizabeth," I start to say, but she flinches like I hit her. I'm thrown off guard.

"No one calls me Elizabeth," she says with a hushed voice.

"Your father did."

"I know." Her voice croaks slightly, and her eyes glass over with tears.

"Hey," I reach out and take her hand in mine and rub soothing circles on her wrist with my thumb.

She shakes her head and pulls her hand away slightly. "It's fine. Ignore me. I just need a little time." She breathes in deeply.

"It's gonna be okay. I'm sorry, Elle."

She tilts her head and shakes it slightly as she says, "Lizzie." She tries to correct me, but I don't think of her as a Lizzie.

"Lizzie's a kid's name." I like Elle. It suits her. *Elle*.

She considers me for a moment, thinking about something, but not giving me a clue as to what it is. "What were you saying?" she asks, forcing the tears back and putting on a front of calmness.

It takes me a second to think about where I was going with all that, but then I remember. I decide to just go for it, like pulling off a damn bandage.

"Everything is yours. What your father left to me in the will, and the house he gave me. I don't need it, and I don't know why he left it to me. But it's all yours. I called the lawyer yesterday and you'll have it all in your name as soon as possible."

Her entire body seems to sag with relief. She looks back at me with disbelief. I can tell she doesn't know if she really believes what I'm telling her.

"It's yours," I say simply.

It's quiet for a moment before she says, "Thank you."

She takes the napkin off the table and folds it in her lap neatly, focusing on it.

"It's yours, not mine. Your father loved you. You were all he talked about. I don't know what he was thinking."

She looks back at me with skepticism and then sadness as she asks, "He wasn't angry?" It throws me off.

"Angry?" I ask her. I don't know why she'd think he was angry with her.

"At me. For leaving, or for not calling enough..." Tears fill her eyes, and she's quick to put the napkin over her face.

I respected Richard. I may have even loved him. But right now I hate him. I never agreed with his decision not to tell her, and looking at her now I wish he'd made things more clear for her. She shouldn't be thinking this shit.

"He loved you more than anything." I don't know how much to tell her. I scoot closer to her in the booth and gently pet her back. "He said you were his sunshine."

A small sob rips from her throat, but she's quick to settle herself.

"I'm sorry," she finally says as she pulls herself together.

"Don't be," I tell her. "You can let it all out."

She gives me a small, humorless laugh and drinks down her water to calm herself. I think about moving away, but I don't want to.

"So, tell me something," she says out of nowhere.

"Like what?" I ask her.

"Anything," she answers. Her big blue eyes look back at me with sincerity. "I just wanna talk."

I'm quick to remember one of the stories Richard told me about her sneaking a bottle of peach schnapps into her room. I tell the story the way he did. He thought it was funny as hell. The entire time she's got a wide smile on her face and her eyes are glassy, but full of happiness. I smile back at her and in that moment it hits me. This is what I wanted. This is what I thought we'd have together.

* * *

THIS IS SO MUCH BETTER. Almost an entire hour has passed since we've gotten our wine, and my little Elle is really warming up to me. I fucking love it. This is exactly how I imagined it'd be between us. This is how I pictured her.

"Tell me more," I say. She's been talking all night. It's like she's got all these memories, just pouring out of her. I'm happy she's sharing them with me.

"Well, the one time when we were at the dealership, daddy said he didn't like the car." Elle takes another sip of wine. It's her third glass, and after this one I'm cutting her off. Mostly because she's nearly drunk, but also because the bottle's empty. "And the salesman looked so sad. Daddy had been talking about seeing that car for weeks, but when he finally saw it in person, he changed his mind." She moves her hands in the air, talking animatedly.

I grin at her, she's so into this story. She's so cute. "So I felt really bad for the guy, you know? He'd just lost his sale."

"Yeah, I can see that."

"So I started talking up the car to daddy. Saying how much I loved the color, and how the leather seats were nice and really comfortable." She slaps her hands onto her lap, adding, "And they were heated."

I chuckle at her.

"Well, I talked it up so much, daddy bought it." She lets out a small giggle with her shoulders shaking. "He gave it to me a few years later when I got my license." She takes another sip of wine and adds with a laugh, "I hated that damn car. It broke down like eight times."

"How old were you?" I ask her.

Her forehead scrunches up. "Gosh, like fourteen?" She says it like she's asking me. Like I'm supposed to know the answer.

I give her a small laugh and shake my head slightly. "You really are a sweetie, aren't you?" I ask her.

She giggles a little. "Daddy used to say I was sweet as Dixie." Her fingers trace the edge of the wine glass and although her smile dims, it's still there.

"Yeah, you were real sweet to me," I say sarcastically to lighten the mood before picking up my own glass and finishing it off.

She busts out a laugh a little louder than she should. It's a beautiful sound though that fills my chest with warmth. She takes the glass of wine in her hands and runs her fingers along the stem before finishing the glass. That's the entire bottle. I don't even have a buzz, but she's a little more than tipsy.

She needed that wine. That's for damn sure. And a good meal. She ate her entire plate of lasagna, and more than half of the lava cake I ordered for us to split.

She takes a spoonful of the remaining chocolate syrup and half of a strawberry and spoons it into her mouth. Her plush lips close around the spoon and she moans softly. My dick instantly hardens. The date may be close to over, but the night's just getting started.

"Hey, why don't we get out of here?" I ask her. I've got a million things I wanna do with her. A million and one I wanna do *to* her.

Her eyes light up with excitement and she sits up straight, leaning into me. "And go where?" she asks with a hint of excitement.

"Let's go back to my place. We can play some cards." Richard told me how she'd always bug him to play when she was younger. He swore she'd grow up to be a professional blackjack player.

A beautiful smile stretches across her face. I've never seen her smile like that. It looks beautiful on her.

I love it. I love that I put it there even more.

"Yeah, okay," she answers softly. She bats her thick lashes and bites down on the tip of her tongue. A blush rises to her cheeks. "That could be fun."

CHAPTER 9

LIAM

I can tell Elle's buzz is starting to wear off as she shifts in her seat in my car, and I'm thinking she might change her mind about coming back to my place. I don't want that.

I'm driving like crazy to get back to 22 Wyoming. I'd take her to my place, but it's farther away and I don't want to give her more time to change her mind.

I think she'll be happier close to home, too. She'll have an escape if she wants it. Although, my place in the city would impress her more. I wrestle with which place I wanna bring her to, but really, 22 Wyoming is closer, so that's where we're going.

Elle lays her cheek against the seat of the car and says, "I owe you such an apology." Her crystal blue eyes look up at me with sadness, and I don't like it. I don't wanna take a step backward. We don't need to go back there.

"You don't owe me anything--"

"Yes I do," she says as she nods her head and leans forward, cutting me off. "You're just a nice guy, and I was so mean to you."

She's getting all worked up, and I don't like it. I want the fun girl at the restaurant back. And I'm not really a *nice guy*.

She starts going on and I cut her off as we pull up to my place. "Stop it." I put the car in park and grip her chin in my hand so she has to look at me. "You don't owe me anything but a night out."

"It's been really fun," she says haltingly, as if the date's over. My heart pounds in my chest. I finally got her, no way I'm letting her get off that easy.

"Fun's just getting started," I say as I push my door open and walk around her side to open hers. But she's already got her door propped open.

She places one foot on the ground, a bare foot, and gets out with her heels in her hand. I reach for her other hand and she waits a moment before putting her small hand in mine.

I try to lead her around the car to 22 Wyoming, but she plants her feet on the ground and looks over at her family home next door.

"I think I should go home," she says in a small voice. I should've taken her to my place in the city. Damn it.

I keep my expression neutral. "If you wanna, that's fine. I just thought it'd be fun to kick your ass in a little card game."

Her expression changes instantly. "You think you can beat me?" she asks with a small smile. "Like it's gonna be that easy?" she scoffs, then looks back at her house.

I shrug and say, "I mean, I'm good at what I do." I lean against the car casually, not letting her see how bad I wanna get her inside my place. All through the night I kept picturing her under me. I'm so close. I can't fucking stand it. "Just a drink and a game of cards." I'm lying through my teeth. I want so much more than that.

Elle looks at the ground and purses her lips before looking back up at me and saying, "Okay, just one drink *and* I deal."

I smirk at her. "If those are your conditions, I accept." I already know I'm gonna guilt her into letting me deal. She may look like a hard ass, but she's a pushover. I can practically guarantee this night is going to end with her in my bed.

* * *

"I DON'T KNOW how you're kicking my ass this bad," I say comically as I lean back in the old chair at the kitchen table. This set was here when I moved in. I do know how I'm losing; I've been purposely busting my hands to build her up. She's got all the black chips in front of her, and most of the reds and whites. There's no way she can deny me dealing out a few hands; I'm really working up the sympathy. 'Cause I wanna start betting more than chips.

"I thought you said you were good at this?" she asks me with a sly smile as she shuffles the cards.

"I used to play all the time with my brother." I start to tell her about my own father and how he taught us to play, but then I stop. She doesn't need to hear all that. I don't want her sympathy for my loss just days after putting her own father to rest.

"He used to kick my ass, too." That's true, but Zac's a special case. He's good with numbers and he could kick anyone's ass at cards. She doesn't need to know that though.

"Can I deal this one?" I ask her with a cocked brow. She clucks her tongue, but easily passes the deck to me.

I reach behind me to the fridge. I don't even have to get

up, the kitchen's so damn small in this place. I could practically cook a meal while still sitting at the head of the table. I swing the door open and grab a beer. "You want one?" I ask.

She scrunches her nose and shakes her head no. "Oh yeah?" I say in response. "My beer's not good enough, it's gotta be expensive wine?" I tease.

She sticks her tongue out. "I just don't like beer."

"Alright then, you wanna shot?" I ask her. Her buzz is completely gone. I certainly don't mind it, but I wanna push her boundaries a little.

She looks down at the cards before looking up at the clock on the stove. I expect her to use the time as an excuse to get going, but instead she looks back at me and nods. "Yeah, just a small one."

I give her a wide smile and get my ass up to grab a bottle of vodka. That's all I've got. I take two shot glasses out of the cabinet and pour a *small* one for her and a full one for me.

I place hers down and get ready to throw mine back, but she's just staring at the shot glass like it's going to bite her.

"What is that?" she asks.

"Vodka. It's not gonna bite you, Elle." She rolls her eyes and tips it back. She slams the glass down with a scrunched-up face.

"Okay," I say as I sit back down, setting the bottle on the table, "If I win this hand, you do another teeny tiny shot. If you win, what do you want?" I ask her.

Her eyes twinkle with a little mischief. "You wanna up the ante?" she asks.

I smirk at her. "What are you thinking?" I ask.

She bites down on her lip and whispers, "Can it be strip blackjack?"

My dick has never been this hard. I swear to God if I don't cum tonight, I'll die from blue balls.

"It most certainly can, Elle," I answer with a straight face and she bursts into laughter.

Now I'm regretting that shot. I need to win this hand and every hand after this. But I've still got my wits, and it'll take some time for the alcohol to even hit me. I'm quick to shuffle the cards and deal them out.

She's got a twelve showing with both her cards up. I smirk at her, feeling cocky. This is gonna be an easy win for me. She doesn't take the hit, and sits back like she's not worried. But I know she's gotta be.

I've got a ten up and flip the bottom card. It's a five. Shit, that's not good.

"You gotta take it," she says with a smile on those beautiful plush lips. All I can think is regardless of who's naked first, those lips are gonna be wrapped around my cock. The sooner I get this done with, the sooner I can get what I really want.

I get a seven and bust.

I push the cards to the side, unbutton my shirt and toss it on the floor.

Elle looks calm and collected, but a blush rises up her chest and into her cheeks. I stretch a little and her eyes dip to my chest. She clears her throat and sits back in her seat, trying to act like she's unaffected. I know she likes what she sees though.

I shuffle the cards and grin at her as I say, "You can smile all you want Elle, but that dress is coming off next."

Her cheeks flush a violent red, but she doesn't respond as the cards are dealt.

She gets two face cards. "Twenty, stay," she says with a smug attitude.

I deal myself an ace on top and that sweet smile on her

face falls. I flip my bottom card over, and my dick twitches when I see the jack of diamonds. "That dress has gotta go."

She purses her lips, but slips her straps down and shimmies out of it. I slowly shuffle the cards while taking in those gorgeous breasts. The cards almost fall out of my hands, but she doesn't notice. Thank fuck. That bra needs to come off though. I wanna see those nipples right now. They're hard, and I wanna see them. Right fucking now.

Her chest rises and falls with deep steady breaths as I quickly lay out the cards. She's dealt a sure loss of a hand.

"What's it gonna be?" I ask her with a brow cocked.

"Hit me," she says in a voice laced with lust as she signals a hit and busts at twenty-four.

I expect the bra to fall, but she shifts in her seat and my eyes catch a red lacy pair of panties fall to the tiled floor. I close my eyes and hold back my groan.

Shoving the cards to the side of the table, I deal out what I hope is the last hand.

I smile when I see an ace up for me, and she's got a seven and an eight.

"You wanna see?" I ask her with a hand on my bottom card. I fucking hope it's a ten or a face card. She bites down on her bottom lip and nods. Her eyes are focused on the card.

Ten of clubs.

"Dealer has blackjack," I tell her with my eyes on hers even though I'm dying to look at her chest.

She reaches behind her and then pulls the laced bra away slowly. Her tits are perfect. They're large enough to be held in my hand, and those nipples are tiny little buds with a pale pink color.

I lock eyes with hers and say, "Come here, Elle." It's bold of me, I know it is. But I've been pushing her all night, and she's been with me every step.

All of a sudden she looks nervous, but she gets up and walks over to me, completely naked and looking all sorts of shy. I turn in my seat, and the legs of the chair scrape against the floor. That's all I can hear along with her heavy breathing, and the blood rushing in my ears.

I'm surprised there's blood anywhere in my body other than my cock. It's pressed against my zipper, hard as fuck and ready for her.

As soon as she gets to me, I grab her hips and pull her closer. I stay in my seat and lean forward, taking her tiny nipple into my mouth and swirling my tongue around it. Her head falls back and her hand flies to my hair. Her nails scratch my scalp as she grips on to me.

Her soft moan fills the room, and it fuels me to pick her ass up and set her down on the table in front of me.

I let her nipple pop out of my mouth and plant a kiss on her belly before pushing her to lie down.

She looks at me with wide eyes before bracing herself on the table. "Lie down for me all the way, and put your feet up here." I tap my hands on the table right where I want her feet and wait.

Her lips part slightly and she's slow to obey, but she does it.

She does what she's told, bending her knees and spreading herself for me. I look down at her pretty little pussy and instantly start leaking precum. She's so fucking wet, she's glistening. I don't hesitate to push two thick fingers inside of her. Holy fuck, she's so tight.

She gasps and her back bows, but I'm quick to push her hip down and hold her in place. I pump my fingers a few times, and her pussy clamps down. Fuck, she's going to feel so good. I stroke her G-spot until her legs are trembling. My eyes stay on her face the entire time. Her eyes are closed, and her lips parted in utter rapture. She needs this. She needs me.

"Cum for me." She shouts out her release on my command, and her pussy tightens and then spasms on my fingers. Fuck, yes. I pull out and taste her. So fucking sweet. I groan as her heavy breathing starts to settle.

I move my hands to my zipper and kick off my jeans as I lean down and get a better taste of her. I suck her clit in my mouth as the jeans drop to the floor. They make a loud noise as they fall and it makes Elle's head pop up. I look back up at her with my mouth still latched onto her clit, but she's shaking her head.

What the fuck? I release her and wipe her juices from my mouth as she tries to say something, but her voice is too low. I'm guessing she wants a condom. That's fine for tonight, but I want her raw as soon as fucking possible. If she wants paperwork I'll have it faxed over for all I care. I don't give a fuck. I need to feel her pussy pop on my dick with nothing in between us.

"What's that?" I ask her, pulling my dick out of my boxers and stroking it once.

She shakes her head again and then leans back, looking at the ceiling. "I don't... I don't..."

I raise my brows and lean forward a little. "I can't hear you, Elle. You don't what?"

"I don't want to have sex." She spits out the words fast and refuses to look at me, her eyes still focused on the ceiling.

What? Why the fuck… What? I can't even put a coherent thought together.

"I'm sorry, I just…"

I sit up and give her a little space and she closes her legs. Fuck, I feel a weight on my chest. I pushed too hard, too fast. "Nah, it's okay." I gentle my hand on her thigh and give her a soft smile. I don't want to scare her off; I'm afraid I already have though.

"I could," she says as she shrugs a little and doesn't look me in the eyes. "I could do other stuff?" She says it like it's a question.

"Let me take care of you again." I look down at her pretty pussy and stroke my dick. I'll take care of both of us.

"You don't have to," she says in a small voice. Her forehead is pinched and I know she's anything but happy about telling me no. I get it though. That's alright. I can wait.

"I want to," I tell her and then kiss her thigh. "I want you to ride my face this time."

She looks back at me with surprise, and I keep my eyes on her as I lower my tongue to her pussy again.

I take a lick and wait for her to relax. She does instantly. Good girl.

I don't waste a second.

I shove my face in between her legs and lick up her tight cunt, spearing my tongue into her pussy. My fingers grip her ass tightly to keep her in place.

"Oh yes!" she screams out as her back bows. That's it. She just needs a little more to get her going. This time I'm not letting her get off so easy. I smile into her pussy at my little joke and then suck on her clit until she's writhing under me and moaning my name.

My chest fills with pride. That's right, my name. I wanna hear her screaming it soon as she cums on my dick.

I flick my tongue across her clit and pull her ass closer to me. "Ride my face," I command her as I push my tongue flat against the top of her opening and her clit. She rocks her hips, and her hands move to her breasts. Oh, fuck yeah.

I watch her and stroke myself under the table as she pinches her nipples. Holy fuck, she's so hot. I stop paying attention to her pussy and just suck on her clit as her body trembles.

Her toes curl, and her legs push inward. I've gotta take my hand away from myself to push her leg back, and as I do she screams out my name and pushes my head into her pussy, rocking herself shamelessly against me.

It's the sexiest fucking thing I've ever seen. My balls draw up and I cum instantly and without warning. I reach my hand down as quickly as I can to try to catch the hot streams of cum as her arousal leaks down my face.

My spine tingles, and I groan into her pussy as more comes out of her. The vibrations from my groan send a shiver up her body. She slowly lets go of my hair, and her body goes limp.

Holy fuck. I came just watching her get off. Watching her cum is by far the sexiest fucking thing I've ever seen. But there's no way I am letting her know I got off under the table. I'm quick to get up and shove my dick in my boxers as I step out of my jeans. Her head turns, and she starts to move.

"Stay." I give her the simple command without thinking. Shit, I don't think she'll like that. I expect her to react to it with attitude 'cause who the fuck am I to talk to her like that, especially when she doesn't even wanna fuck me, but she just lays back down. I wash my hands in the sink and grab two handfuls of paper towels. One of them I run under the warm water.

I bend down quickly as I get to the table to wipe up the floor as fast as I can. I don't want her knowing what I'm doing. As I get up, my head hits the table. Fuck! That hurts. I hit it hard. I wince and grab my head where the pain is pulsing.

She pops up as I try to play it off, and her eyes go wide with worry. "Are you okay?" she asks.

I'm still holding my head, but I answer. "Yeah."

"Did you hit your head?" She looks confused, and her eyes are looking on the floor.

"Yeah," I answer and don't elaborate. She laughs a little and lies back down, but she's looking at me like I'm a lunatic. At least she's smiling.

As I wipe between her legs, she starts to look a little uncomfortable again and says, "I'm sorry." Her mouth opens to say more, but I stop her.

"Don't you dare apologize. I fucking loved it." She has no reason to be sorry, and I don't want her to have any regret over this.

"I can--" she starts to say as her eyes look to my boxers, but she doesn't know that's already been dealt with.

"No, you don't need to do that." Her eyes go a little sad, and she bites her lip.

"I'll wait for you, Elle." I give her a small kiss on the lips. "When you're ready, I'll be here."

CHAPTER 10

LIZZIE

The next day all I can think about is Liam down in between my legs, eating my pussy out like a starving man. The sensation of his powerful jaws clamping down on my clit had been mindblowing. I'm still getting shivers from the out-of-this-world orgasm he'd given me.

Yet one thought keeps bugging me. *I should've gotten him off.* Like, what was I thinking?

That I didn't want to give myself to him yet.

It's true. I don't want to play my cards too fast, even with how hot he makes me. But I wanted him. And I'm the one who initiated things with the strip blackjack. I was playing with fire, and I knew that. Still, I can't understand why he didn't want me to at least return the favor. It doesn't make sense.

Thinking about it, it makes me feel self-conscious. Was it because I was drunk? Maybe, but I wasn't sloppy, falling-on-my-ass drunk. I was just a little tipsy, and I definitely knew what I was doing. I didn't even wake up with a hang-over. If he was so concerned about that, he wouldn't have gone as far as he did.

For a moment, I wonder if I made a mistake in playing the blackjack game with him at all, but then brush the feeling away.

It was definitely better than just coming back here, running upstairs and crying my eyes out in my bed, I think to myself. *Anything would be better than that.*

Looking around the cold, empty house, I feel incredible sadness, which confirms I made the right decision.

I really should stop worrying. I'm reading too much into the situation. Liam provides a useful distraction from all the pain and grief I'm going through. An outlet for my emotions. I need him.

Or maybe he's the last thing I need.

I need another opinion, I think to myself.

I pull out my cell and dial up Nat. It's been a while since I've dated. It's just not something I'm really comfortable with. I don't know why. I'm just not interested. Well, I wasn't. But now I am.

"Hello?" she answers, sounding out of breath.

"Hey Nat!" I say, trying to sound cheerful.

"Lizzie! I'm so happy to hear from you!" She sounds so chipper and like she really is happy. It brings a smile to my face. I'm really lucky to have a friend like her. We've been apart for years, but every time we see each other, it's like we pick right back up from where we left off.

"Are you busy?" I ask.

"No, not at all. I just need to put a fresh batch of cookies in the oven and then I can talk. One sec."

I feel relieved. "Ok."

I wait and hear the sound of metal banging in the background. I lie back on the sofa and laugh at what I've done. It's like I'm at the psychologist's office. Nat's my shrink. I roll my eyes. I am so fucked if she's the one who's going to walk me through this. I can't help but silently laugh.

Nat is on the phone again a minute later. “Back. What’s up?”

I pause before telling Nat my dilemma. Would she think less of me if she knew I was fooling around with a man so soon after my daddy had died? I subconsciously start biting my nails as my smile falls. I hadn't even thought of that. I think back to my studies, and I know it's normal to seek out a pleasurable distraction when you're upset, especially when mourning. But that doesn't change the fact that she may think worse of me.

“Hello?” Nat presses when I don’t say anything.

“I need your opinion,” I breathe out. I need someone to talk to. I can't keep all this in anymore. I take a deep breath. I need a friend. And that's what she is. She's a good friend.

Nat sounds intrigued. “Opinion on what?”

I freeze up again, worrying Nat will not like what I have to say.

“Lizzie?”

Screw it, I think to myself. *Nat isn’t going to judge me. I hope.*

Taking a deep breath, I tell her everything. About the house and the will, our date, the blackjack game and our foreplay.

“And he didn’t want you to, like, at least... take care of him?” Nat asks when I’m done.

I feel relieved that she didn’t immediately jump to judging me.

“No,” I say. “And I don’t understand it.” The self-conscious feeling increases. I hate it.

“I don’t know, Lizzie. I don’t think there’s anything wrong with that, if you ask me. In fact, I would kill for a guy who got me off and didn’t expect anything in return. Lord knows, I fucking deserve it with how hard I work.” She snickers. “Maybe I should start offering sugar cookies in exchange for some mind-blowing cunnilingus."

I laugh. "You're cray cray."

Nat continues, "I'll put a sign out front that says, 'Will Bake For Sex'."

After a short laugh I reply, "I've tasted your cookies. You might get a lot of action with that offer."

"If only!" Nat snorts. "Really though, you better tattoo your name on that tight ass of his. Claim him before anyone else finds out and there's a line of chicks waiting around the corner for him. "

"Please," I say and laugh. "I can't do that." That's not what we are. There's nothing about him that's screaming commitment. My brows furrow, and my heart sinks a little. I'm not even sure if we're dating. Is that a thing still? Do people still call it dating?

Nat snorts again. "The hell you can't."

"Not happening," I repeat. "But seriously, I still can't believe what happened. Yesterday, all I wanted to do was go on a date with this guy so I could fulfill my part of his deal and move on. Instead, I wind up laying naked on his table."

"There are worse things in life," Nat says. "In fact, I think you need Liam right now, Liz. He might be just what you need to help you get through..." Nat's voice trails off, but I know exactly what she means.

"Maybe," I say softly. Maybe. Possibly. God! I hate how wishy-washy I feel about this situation.

"So shouldn't that solve it?" Nat asks. "Spend more time with him, get to know him more before going further. Maybe it's a good thing you two didn't have sex."

"That's the problem. I'm afraid to get to know him."

"Why?" she asks.

"I'm afraid I might find out…" *He's a fraud,* I finish in

my head. I don't want to believe he is. But I still don't understand how he inherited everything. I put a hand over my face, feeling like a greedy bitch. Seriously, why would daddy do that? But Liam is giving everything to me. God, I feel like a bitch for questioning any of this.

"Might find out what?"

"Nothing," I say. "All I know is that daddy left everything to him. Why? I don't know. I can't even begin to understand the reasons why."

"Maybe your father just wasn't in the right mental state as he got closer to death," Nat suggests. "And since Liam was the only one around, he gave him everything."

"Wouldn't that mean Liam took advantage of him, though? If he knew my father wasn't right in the head, he shouldn't have accepted anything from him." This train of thought makes me uncomfortable.

"Hmm... possibly," Nat says slowly. "Then again, you can't be sure what happened." Nat pauses as if something occurs to her. "But if you had these concerns all this time, why did you go that far with him?"

Her words make me sick to my stomach. I feel cheap all of a sudden. "You're right, Nat," I say weakly. "I had no business going that far with him, and yet I did. I feel like such a whore for putting out on the first date."

"Please," Nat snorts, and I can practically hear her roll her eyes. "I don't know any whores who get paid to get eaten out. And if you aren't happy with that, I'd be overjoyed to take your place."

"Oh Nat," I say and laugh. "Leave it to you to say something like that."

"Seriously, Lizzie, you're overthinking this way too much. Do you really like this guy?"

"I do... well, at least I think I do."

"Hmm. Well let me ask you this--do you like the way he makes you feel?"

I think about the sweet side of Liam, how much of a gentleman he was on our date. How fun he was, back at his place. "Yes," I say finally. "I really do. He makes me feel... good."

"Okay then. Just have fun with it. No matter what happens. Just have fun."

The way Nat says it makes it seem so easy.

Maybe it is that easy, I think. *If I just give it a chance. Besides, I have time. I don't have to leave here to go back to school for almost two months.*

But what would happen after those two months? I feel a twinge of pain in my heart at the thought of leaving.

After a second, I push those thoughts away. I need to stop worrying and just let things happen. It's not like I'm in a committed relationship with Liam. For all I know, we're not meant to be anything more than fuckbuddies.

Maybe he's just in my life to provide me with a distraction to my grief, and that's it.

"What harm can it do?" Nat presses. "It's just a little fun."

I decide I'm going to heed Nat's advice. After all, what harm could it do?

I smile and finally reply, "I can do fun."

CHAPTER 11

LIAM

"Where were you last night?" Zac's on me as soon as I walk in the office.

I sigh heavily and walk right past him, answering, "What's it matter?" I went out and saw my Elle last night. Just a movie date. No sex, nothing. Just the two of us cuddling on the sofa and watching *Up*. It's a stupid kids' movie. But she picked it out. She said it was sweet. She cried in the beginning a little, and I wondered why she'd pick something that would do that to her, knowing how the beginning starts. But I think I know why. And it made me happy to hold her and be there for her.

I'm really starting to like this broad. A week later, and I'm still interested in just being around her. It's different for me. But then again, recently a lot of things have been different. Starting with her old man.

"You're just gonna keep running back to the 'burbs to get laid, is that it?" Zac asks me with contempt. I don't like the way he's talking. I give him a hard look and he settles down a bit.

"What the fuck is up your ass?" I snap back at him as I take a seat in my chair.

"We got a threat last night." My jaw clenches. I fucking hate some of the assholes we do business with. I look up at my brother and wait for more.

"From Ian?" I ask him. He wouldn't be the first. It's common for guys who place bets they can't afford to threaten us later, rather than pay up. It doesn't happen often, but it does happen. It's useless for them to do it. We always have collateral, and we always get paid. We'd be stupid to take a bet that can't be repaid. That's why we look into our clients. So those threats get muted pretty fucking fast.

But for Zac to be this pissed and this worked up, it's gotta be Ian's doing. He nods his head, confirming it. I run my hands through my hair. Fucking hell. My first thought is that I don't wanna deal with this shit. I'd rather be back with Elle, holding on to her and kissing up her neck. I might be warming up to her, but she's heating up for me, too.

Zac clears his throat and gets my attention again.

"Why the fuck is he bothering us now?" This fucking asshole needs to get out of our business. I'm done with him. He's a fucking nobody.

"He didn't like that we were giving him a bad name."

"What's that supposed to mean? His name doesn't come out of our mouths."

"A couple of the guys were pissed they had to pay up front and asked why," he replies.

I give my brother a hard glare. "And what'd you tell them?"

"It wasn't me," he answers defensively.

"Fucking Tyler." Why's there always gotta be something? "We shoulda just cut those clients."

"Some of the high rollers come from Ian, too."

"Yeah," I say and let the anger slip away easily; my brother's got a point, and there's no point in thinking that way. "What's the threat?"

"That he's gonna 'gut us like the fucking pigs we are and bleed us out'."

"What a fucking prick." The threat doesn't even faze me. I've heard worse from more capable people.

Zac pulls out his phone and shows me a video of fat fuck named Gino Stalone shoving a note into the mailbox we have around back. I recognize him. He's one of the assholes that tried to work me over when they first heard about us. He's still walking with a limp because of me. He should've done a better job. Instead he came at me with a punch and took a bullet to the kneecap for his troubles.

"You know that saying, don't shoot the messenger?" Zac asks me.

I grin at him as he adds, "I told Tyler it was a shit saying."

"So he's taking care of it?" I ask Zac, just to make sure we're on the same page.

"Yeah, Ian should get the message loud and clear tonight." I don't like that it's coming to violence. But some things are only resolved this way.

"Good." I sit back in my chair, but I'm tense knowing a war is coming. I'm not backing down. My eyes fall to my desk and I see a manila envelope. My heart races in my chest with a hint of anger.

"What the fuck is this?" I ask.

Zac looks at it with a frown and then recognition crosses his face. "It came from some lawyer. He said you were expecting it."

I nod my head and try to calm the fuck down. Not everything is a threat. It's a note from Richard. When I called to tell the lawyer to do whatever paperwork had to be done to transfer it all to Elle he told me about it. I left the reading before he could give it to me.

I slowly pick up the envelope and consider opening it. I see Zac stand from the corner of my eye.

"We good?" he asks.

"Yeah, it's all good." He watches me for a moment and then glances to the envelope. "He said it was from that old man."

"Yeah," I say, and my chest tightens with pain. We don't show emotion much. Well, except for anger. That's one we see a lot. But for him to be checking on me like this, it's unusual.

"It's all good," I repeat, and my brother nods and makes his way to the door.

Before closing it he asks, "Is she good, too?" It catches me off guard. A part of me relaxes though. I like that he's asking about her.

I stare him in the eyes for a moment, considering what he's asking. "She's doing okay. She's working through it." It's gonna take time for sure. But she's doing good I think.

He nods his head and looks at the floor before taking in a deep breath. "If you need anything, let me know." With that, he leaves.

I'm lucky to have my brother. Poor Elle doesn't even have that. I don't know how I survived my father's death, but it definitely had something to do with the people who surrounded me. And she has no one. Except me. And I'm basically using her for my own selfish needs.

I feel like a fucking asshole for thinking it, but it's true. I'm using that poor girl to make myself feel better. I throw the envelope down on the desk and cover my face with my hands. I'm a fucking bastard for it. She's clinging to me to help her get over her father's death. And I'm just counting the days until I can get her underneath me. I'm such a fucking prick.

She's a good girl; she didn't even wanna fuck. She has morals and virtue. And here I am sifting through fucking threats and making sure pricks get what they deserve.

I've been working my ass off to make the operation legit and avoid this kind of shit, but it keeps coming back to me.

The image of Gino or Ian or any of those assholes coming up to me while I'm with her, or shit even while I'm next door to her, makes my blood boil. I'll kill them all before they touch her.

My heart beats faster, and my gut twists with pain. I should leave her now, before anything gets out of hand. Who am I kidding though, it's already out of hand. If they knew about her… my throat closes with worry. I know they're going to come after us. I can't give them an easy target. I can't let her get caught up in this shit.

I know I should end it with her today. I'm not good enough for her. I never will be.

I *need* to let her go. She's doing better. She'll be fine without me. Fuck, I don't want to. I haven't wanted anything in so long. I run my hands in my hair, not knowing what I should do. I'd be a selfish prick to keep her.

I already know that. I never should have chased her. My heart clenches in my chest. She's got a life, she's got schooling to go back to so she can have a real career. She'll be alright without me. She'll be *better* without me.

I've been living in a fantasy world with her, and this is my reality. I need to wake the fuck up before I get her hurt. Or worse.

I look down at the envelope on the desk. Maybe Richard left it all to me so we could meet. Or maybe he thought he truly owed it to me. I snort and refuse to look at it.

The reason doesn't matter. He was a fucking asshole for doing that. For teasing me with a woman I never stood a chance at being good enough for.

I take a deep breath and pick up my phone. I do the right thing before I can stop myself. I type in the message and send it. It fucking shreds me.

CHAPTER 12

LIZZIE

I'm sorry. It's over - L.

I stare at the text blankly, feeling a lump form in my throat. The words repeat over and over in my mind as I sit on the couch. *It's over.* I shake my head. I can't wrap my mind around this. Didn't Liam claim that he wanted to get to know the real me? And now he's breaking it off? I thought everything was going great. Like better than great. It was perfect. I thought we were perfect together. I feel blindsided. I didn't have a clue that he felt differently.

I tear my eyes away from the text, anger threatening to overwhelm me.

He's breaking up with me because he's mad I didn't have sex with him.

Or maybe it was because I still haven't gotten him off? In a way, I feel bad that I didn't. He made me feel incredible. Gave me a mind-blowing orgasm. I actually feel guilty over it, which is bullshit considering how I offered to... take care of it. But that was over a week ago!

And now he's breaking up with me. Fucking asshole.

There's no use going over the shoulda coulda wouldas, I think to myself. *If Liam really cared about me and wanted to get to know me like he claims, he wouldn't break up with me over something so trivial. He said he'd be there when I was ready. More bullshit.*

The more I think about this, the angrier I get. He had no right to do this. Come into my life. Get me addicted to him... and then just leave.

Fuck this! I rage. *I'm going over there right now to give that bastard a piece of my mind.*

I've been thinking about it all day. I know he's there. His shiny car is right there in the fucking driveway, taunting me.

You know what? I'm doing it. What do I have to lose? Nothing. Nothing to fucking lose.

I march outside and walk next door. Instead of using the doorbell, I ball a fist and pound on the door as hard as I can. It hurts my knuckles, and the cold weather doesn't help. It's only then that I realize I'm in my thin nightgown and it's freezing out here.

As the realization hits me, Liam yanks open the door.

My breath leaves my lungs at the sight of him. He has no shirt on, his chiseled abs proudly on display, and he's only wearing a pair of basketball shorts. Shorts that show off his huge cock imprint. I whip my eyes back up to his and ignore my need to look back down.

At first Liam looks shocked, and then hurt. He's quick to cover it with anger though. "Didn't I tell you last time that there was a doorbell?" he growls.

I haughtily reply, "I didn't feel like using it."

Liam responds with a tight voice. "I can see that." Why is he so pissed? He has no right to be pissed.

"It's over?" I demand. "It's over?"

Liam doesn't reply and just looks at me stoically. God, it fucking hurts. It feels like my heart is just splitting in two. Am I really that big of a fool?

I do my best to hold back the tears that threaten to spill from my eyes. "Hello?" I persist. I hate how my voice is about to crack. How I feel like bursting in tears and collapsing in his arms.

Liam scowls, making me feel even worse. "Look, what do you want from me?" he growls. "You got your fucking house. You should be happy to be rid of me. After all, I'm a fucking dirtbag asshole."

"That's not true--"

"Those words came from you," he says.

It hurts because I did say that, but I apologized and it was so long ago. At least it feels like it was long ago. "I called you those names in a moment of weakness." I try to defend myself, but he just crosses his arms in front of him. His entire stance is aggressive and standoffish, but his eyes are pained. I don't know what I did. I don't know how to fix this. I didn't mean it when I called him that. He has to know that.

"I'm sorry." He just stands there still, waiting for me to leave.

"Is that why you don't want me?" I practically whisper. My anger is nonexistent now. Instead I'm just heartbroken.

His hard features soften, and he looks apologetic for a moment. He takes in a deep breath and says, "I'm not good for you. You already know that. You don't want me." He shakes his head slightly and looks at me with sympathy. It only makes me angrier.

"I can decide what I want for myself!" My body starts to shiver, and I look back to my house and then past him into his living room. It's so fucking cold.

"Go home, Elizabeth."

He begins to shut the door, but I wedge my foot into the opening before he can close it. I'm lucky he didn't slam it. I would've lost my whole fucking foot.

"If you wanted me to suck your dick, then you should've just let me!" I scream at him out of anger.

"Do you think that's what this is about?" he asks me, and suddenly I feel sick. My cheeks burn with embarrassment and my heart clenches in my chest.

He takes a step closer. "You think I don't want you 'cause you didn't suck me off?" He looks at me incredulously.

"I wanted to! I wanted to fuck you, too! I was just scared!" After screaming at him and taking several deep breaths, I finally register what he asked. "It has to be that," I insist. He doesn't respond, he just looks back at me with a look of disbelief. "I can't think of any other reason..." My voice trails off. God, I feel like an idiot. My insecurities run rampant.

"You deserve better than me." He tries to back away again, and it pisses me off. The whole 'it's me, not you' routine? Yeah, whatever. He can shove that excuse up his ass.

"You're not running away from me that easy!" I snap. "You're going to tell me what's wrong or so help me God--"

"Or what?" Liam says with a menacing threat. "What are you going to do about it?"

Anger swells within my chest. I grasp at that anger for dear life. I'd rather feel that than the hollowness of being dumped. What have I done to deserve this treatment? Liam can't treat me this way. I won't let him.

Unthinkingly, I lash out, slapping Liam across the face as hard as I can. His head whips to the side. Damn. That felt good. It's like déjà vu, only this time, it's warranted.

Liam slowly turns his head back to face me. There's a red mark where I've struck him. And anger. Incredible anger in his eyes.

"You don't think I want you?" He grabs my hips and brings me inside his house, slamming the door closed. "Oh, I fucking want you."

Growling with anger, he grabs me and slings me up against the wall. He presses his hard body into me, letting me feel how hard his big cock is. "You want me, Elizabeth?" he grunts. "You sure this is what you want?"

"If you want me, then fucking take me!" I scream at him.

"You're about to get fucked, Elle. If that's something you don't want, now would be the time to say something."

"I told you I want you--" Before I can finish, Liam's lips are pressed against mine. I instantly part my lips and deepen the kiss. His hot tongue mingles with mine as his hands travel down my body.

He pushes up my nightgown, and then pulls my panties off of me, exposing my swollen pussy. My clit throbs, and I push my pussy against his hand.

"Fuck, Elle. You're dripping wet for me." He breathes out the words as if I'm torturing him.

I look into his eyes and tell him again. "I want you, Liam." I do. I want him so fucking bad. I need his touch. I need him. Can't he tell?

The word *please* is on the tip of my tongue, but he jams his fingers inside of me, probing, thrusting before I can get it out.

Oh fuck, he feels so good. The heels of my feet dig into his ass, pushing him closer to me as he fingerfucks me.

I groan and arch my back against the wall. Yes! My nipples harden and the sadness of him pushing me aside before diminishes as the pleasure burns low in my belly.

"I want you," he whispers in the crook of my neck as his fingers stroke my G-spot, bringing me closer and closer to my orgasm. He kisses my neck, my jaw, and then my lips. All the while pleasuring me. Yes!

He breaks our kiss and looks at me with heat in his eyes. "You have no idea how much I fucking want you." His confession confuses me, but I don't have the energy to think about it. There's one easy answer that's begging to spill from my lips.

"Then take me," I moan out and then gasp as he removes his fingers, leaving my throbbing pussy unsatisfied.

The high I felt as I approached the edge of my release vanishes as he backs away from me.

I blink several times, not understanding why he pulled away and then glare at him. I swear to God if he's leaving me high and dry like this it'll be the cruelest thing anyone has ever done to me.

"How much do you want me?" Liam asks in a husky voice as he shoves down his shorts and strokes himself.

My mouth waters and I lick my lips as a bead of precum forms on the seam of his head. If that's what he wants, fine. I want him. Even more, I want him to know how much I need his touch. I have no shame in giving him the pleasure he gave me.

I try to get down on my knees, but he stops me, grabbing my wrist. I see hesitation in his eyes as he searches my face. "I told you, you don't have to do that."

"But I want to," I whisper. He takes a step forward and grabs my ass in his hands, picking me up and pushing my back against the wall.

"This is how I want you," he says, looking deep into my eyes. My heart races in my chest. He lines his dick up as his lips crash against mine with desperation. In one quick thrust, he's buried deep inside of me and I scream out with pleasure.

My body heats as he slowly pulls out and then hammers his hard cock into me. His large girth stretches my walls, but he doesn't give me a moment to adjust. My breathing halts, and my head thrashes. My nails dig into his shoulders. I want him closer and deeper, but I also need him farther away. It's too intense. It's too much. But it feels so fucking good.

"I fucking want you," he growls as he picks up his pace. My back pounds against the wall with his merciless pace. A strangled cry is ripped from my throat.

I scream out his name as he ruts between my legs, kissing and biting my neck.

My nails scratch along his bare back as I try to escape the intense pleasure, but he has me pinned. My chest heaves, and my head slams against the wall as an overwhelming pleasure paralyzes my body. My toes stick out straight and I fall recklessly over the edge. My mouth opens with a silent scream as my body tenses and then my nerve endings come alive all at once, exploding with indescribable pleasure, and I find myself screaming out his name.

He groans my name in my ear and thrusts short shallow strokes, each one rubbing against my throbbing clit and prolonging my orgasm. My nails dig into his back and my teeth press down on his shoulder as my pussy clamps down on his dick and waves upon waves of pleasure rock through my body.

I sag against him, catching my breath, and he holds me for a moment before setting me down on the floor. I feel so weak. My entire body is limp and heavy.

I lean panting against the wall as Liam pulls his shorts up and heads down the short hallway to the kitchen. My pussy is sore, and my clit is still throbbing. I close my eyes and rest my hot cheek against the cool wall and try to calm my racing heart.

I pick my panties up and pull them into place. There's a bit of cum on my thigh, but I try to ignore it.

The lust-filled haze quickly dissipates and I look down the hall and to the door as Liam turns on the faucet.

How pathetic am I? I wrap my arms around my shoulders. He dumped me, and I came over here and let him fuck me. My mouth opens as I realize that's exactly what happened. I cover my face and try to keep myself from crying.

I should just leave before he has a chance to kick me out and give me another it's-not-you-it's-me speech.

Before I can make my move, I hear Liam's hard steps come down the hall. The old wooden floor creaks and he comes back into the foyer with a neatly folded, damp paper towel.

He stops in his tracks as he registers the look on my face. I keep my eyes on the floor. I can't believe how pathetic I am.

"I'm gonna go," I manage to say and take a step toward the door. He reaches out and grabs my waist, stopping me and forcing me to look up at him.

His mouth opens, but he doesn't say anything for a moment. My heart barely beats in my chest. Finally he says, "I have some cocoa," he nods to the kitchen, "if you wanna stay."

I look back at him, not knowing what to say. I only want to stay if he really wants me to. If he really wants me.

As if reading my mind, he takes my hips in his hands,

pulling me closer and puts his nose against mine. “I’m sorry.” He kisses the tip of my nose and I close my eyes. “I’m sorry I texted you that. I want you, Elle.” He brushes the hair out of my face and adds, “Please stay with me tonight.” He kisses my hair. “I don’t want you to leave.”

CHAPTER 13

LIAM

So much for ending it. I look over my shoulder at my Elle. I tried to do the right thing. That's gotta count for something. She should've walked away. Now she's mine. She has no fucking clue what she's gotten herself into. I don't give a shit though. I'm not letting her go now.

Elle takes a deep breath as we sit on the sofa. She's got her mug in both her hands and she brings it up to her chin and blows. She's not looking at me. I know she's still feeling a certain way about me doing that shit. I made her dinner, and we ate in mostly comfortable silence with my arm wrapped around her waist. I don't mind eating with my left hand if that means I can give her some of the comfort she needs. But she's still not quite right. It'll take time, but she'll forgive me for being an ass. I know she will.

"You okay?" I ask as I wrap my arm around her hips and bring her a little closer. I'm careful not to tug her too hard so her cocoa doesn't spill.

She looks up at me with her beautiful eyes and it breaks my heart. "I don't know that I'm going to be okay."

I lean forward and set my cup down on the coffee table. She will be, I'll make sure she will. "I said I'm sorry." I put a hand on her thigh and keep eye contact with her. I wish she'd put her cup down, but she's holding on to it for dear life.

She shakes her head gently and her long dark hair shifts slightly. "I mean…" She clears her throat and puts the cup down before lifting her feet onto the sofa and hugging her knees. I let my hand fall to the sofa. She doesn't look at me. "About my dad."

Her eyes go glassy and I don't know what I should do. That's something I just can't make right. She needs time for that.

"I'm sorry." I kiss her hair and pull her into my lap, shifting my weight on the sofa and leaning back. Thankfully, she leans into me. I gently run my hand up and down her arm. "He loved you so much." I remember how he showed me her picture for the first time. He was so fucking proud.

It was the morning after I spent my first night in this place. I'd walked in with a bottle of scotch, thinking about my own father. I threw the key onto the counter and looked around the place. My old house kinda looked like it. But this place was almost completely empty. All that was here was the old kitchen set, joined by me and the scotch. And memories of my mother and father. Mostly of my dad, lying in that fucking hospital bed. I remember the beeping of the machines, and the lines on the screen that meant he was still alive.

I drank a bit too much and passed out in the living room. I don't even know why I went to his house. I made up some lame excuse. Hungover and looking like shit, he let me in though. First thing he did after making a pot of coffee was show me her picture.

"Why…" She starts to ask something, but then shakes her head and reaches for the cup.

"Why what?" I ask her. I don't care what her question is; at this point, I'll break the damn vow I made to him. She needs closure. And if I can give it to her, I will. "Why did he leave everything to you?" she asks and her voice croaks.

She's quick to add, "It's not about the money. It's not that, it's just..." She pushes away from me and grabs the cup again. She doesn't drink it though, she just takes in a breath and stares straight ahead.

"I know, I know." I pet her back, helping to calm her a little. "You wanna know if you did something wrong. And you didn't. I know you didn't. He…" I trail off, remembering the note on my desk at the office. I wish I'd read it. Maybe he would've made some fucking sense in it. "I don't know why. Maybe he felt like he owed me. He didn't though."

She looks at me for a long moment. "Did you know?" she asks. "Did you know he was dying when you met him?"

I can't lie to her. "Yeah. I knew."

She nearly spills the cup. I take it from her and set it down. "How long?" she asks in a voice cracked with sadness as tears run down her face. "How long did he know?"

"A while," I answer her. I can see her heart breaking right in front of me. "Twelve weeks."

Her shoulders shake with a loud sob and she covers her face with her hands, trying to climb farther into my lap. Like she can't get close enough to me.

"He told you, but not me!" she cries into my chest.

I kiss her hair and shush her. "He didn't want you to see him like that. He was hoping the treatments would work."

She takes in a ragged breath and says, "But I talked to him." Her words are forced, and I can barely make them out. "He could have told me. I wish I'd been there. I would've wanted to be there with him!"

No she doesn't. She doesn't know what it was like those last few days. I hired the nurses to do all that shit, but in the last week and a half, he could barely move. I know what she means, and I still wish he'd given her that choice.

"He just wanted what was best for you." I hold her for a while longer, while she cries it out of her system. After a while she looks up at me, pulling away from my embrace. Her face is red and her cheeks are tearstained. Somehow she looks even more beautiful.

"But why you?" she asks.

"I don't know." I answer her with the truth. "I offered him help. And he accepted."

She takes a few minutes to calm herself down.

"I could've helped him," she whispers. Her eyes close, but she doesn't cry. She reaches for the cocoa and takes a small, cautious sip. "I wish I'd been there for him."

"You were with him. Every day he told me stories about you."

She looks back at me with vulnerability. "Can you tell me?" she asks weakly.

"Tell you the stories?"

"Please," she whispers. I lean forward and take her lips with my own. My heart hurts so much for her.

When I pull away and look down at her, her eyes are still closed and she's leaning into my touch. I rub my thumb along the bare skin of her thigh. I wish I could take all that pain away.

"Of course," I say and tell her every damn story I can remember.

I hold her small body and start with the first one he told me. It's easy to remember that one. And I just keep going. Some of them make her laugh, and a lot of them make her cry. But she lets me hold her the entire time, and just telling her what she meant to him makes the weight lift off my chest.

When I finish the last story and look down at her, she's passed out. Her chest rises and falls with steady breathing and I easily pick her small frame up and carry her to bed.

I hold her close to me while I try to fall asleep, but it's not till she rolls over and grips onto me, resting her face against my chest, that I'm able to drift off into a deep sleep with her.

CHAPTER 14

LIZZIE

I don't know what I should do, I think to myself as I sit down at my computer desk in my bedroom. I haven't checked my school email in days, and I intend to play catch up. But I can't. I keep thinking about Liam.

There's also the dilemma that I have yet to receive any money, and I feel like a whore for even thinking about bringing it up.

One date. He hands over my inheritance. That was the deal, and he told me he talked to the lawyer.

It bugs the shit out of me. I don't know why. I need the money. I have to pay this upcoming semester's tuition, but I don't want to bring it up. I'm so uncomfortable about the entire thing. I love it when I'm with him. I can escape from all this shit. But then when he leaves I have to face the real world. And that world needs money.

Fuck! I don't want to bring it up. I really can't stand the fact that I'm going to have to ask him if he's sending it over soon. It's so awkward.

I have the urge to call Nat and tell her about my problem. At the same time, I don't want to talk to her. She's already told me to relax and to just have fun. I'm going to make myself look insane if I call her back, crying about how wishy-washy I'm feeling. I already know what I'm feeling for him this early is just crazy.

Nevermind looking cray cray, I think to myself. *I'll look more like a whore.* Shit. Thinking about it makes me feel absolutely shitty. But as the saying goes, the truth hurts.

Trying to push my gloomy thoughts away, I log into my email and go through all the unread messages. Then I go about checking my schedule for next semester and looking to see what textbooks I need to order.

I figure if this thing with Liam crashes, I'll be able to return to school and bury myself in my studies. Except I can't even think straight. I'm so damn conflicted. About everything.

Relax, I tell myself. *Breathe.*

I practice a meditation exercise, trying to ease the stress in my body with deep breathing. It doesn't work. Sighing in frustration, I blow the hair out of my eyes and look around the room. I hate this. I hate being here. This big, fucking empty house.

Tears pool in my eyes and I get angry. God damn it! I'm so fucking tired of crying!

I shouldn't be here. I should've gone back already. I need to ask Liam for my money and just leave. That's what I should do. What I feel for him is unhealthy and probably only because of my grief. I don't need a professional to tell me that. It's too soon and too fast.

I don't need him. I don't care how he makes me feel. A couple of months after I'm gone, I won't even remember his name. He's just a crutch. Someone to distract me from my pain. I can survive without him.

Pain stabs me in the chest. I don't know if it's from the thought of leaving Liam, or from the reminder of daddy.

I need to get out of this house, I think to myself. *Do something other than wallow in misery. Like fuck Liam.*

It's horrible. I know it's wrong to be thinking about sex with a man I'm so conflicted by. I just can't help it.

I jump up from my desk and grab my coat. I need to get out of this house. Some time to think, and then I'll decide. I either make a commitment to Liam and get one in return, or I leave him. I can't use him, and I can't let him use me.

And that's exactly what we're doing.

CHAPTER 15

LIAM

I'm gonna fuck this up. Every day I'm waiting for her to tell me she's pissed about something. I fucking love what we have, but I know I'm gonna ruin it. I've never done this before and I'm not the kind of man who knows how to hold onto a woman. I've never tried to, and I don't wanna put myself out there when they can leave me. That's what people do, they leave you. I don't want that. But for her, I feel like I don't have a choice. Everything in me wants to be with her. And I'm just waiting for the moment she up and leaves me.

And it's 'cause of Richard. The reminder of him brings me to the desk in the living room. It's an old flimsy desk, nothing like what I have at work. Richard had asked me to store it here while he was sorting through his things, making preparations for the end. But on top of it is that damn note. I brought it home from the office and I still haven't read it.

I sit down and stare at it. It's just a piece of paper. It's fucking harmless, but it's making my heart beat faster than it should. I take a deep breath and try to calm myself. Why am I being such a little bitch about this?

What if there's something in it for her? That thought has me reaching out and opening the letter. I don't know what his last words to me are, but if they're something she needs, I need to know right now.

The sound of the paper unfolding and soft crinkles as I hold it are the only things I can hear other than the blood rushing in my ears and the thud of my own heartbeat. I shouldn't have worked this up so much in my head, but I have.

Dearest Liam,

Well, the time has come to say goodbye, but I wanted to tell you a few things that I found hard to say in person.

You remind me of myself. I never told you, but my father passed when I was young. I didn't take it very well.

If it wasn't for Elizabeth's mother, I never would have loved in my entire life. I was filled with anger and hate. But worse than that, I just didn't want companionship. I wanted to be alone.

Her mother forced her way in. But it was so much later in life, and she passed away only years after having Elizabeth. I wish I'd met her sooner. I wish I'd had more time with her.

I made a mistake, Liam. I need you to fix it. I know you've done so much for me, but there's one last thing.

I regret it all. You were right. I wish I'd spent my dying days with her. It would have been selfish, because I know it would have hurt her to watch me die. Maybe that makes me an asshole, because I know how hard this was for you. But she isn't going to take this easy. And I can't stand the thought that she's going to live her life with pain and hate.

I need you to help her. I didn't teach her how to want

companionship. I don't want her to live the way I did. I need you there for her.

I'm leaving everything to you. This will help. You'll need all the help you can get. Without something to hang over her head, you'll never get through to her.

If she wants to pound her fists on your chest, please let her.

I can see hurt in you, the same pain I had. Let her heal you, too. You're a good man, and I want her to have a man like you in her life.

I don't want you two to live the life I had. You deserve more. You deserve better.

I hope you'll find that in each other.

Best wishes and blessings for you two,

Richard

I stare at the note for a long time. I try to ignore the way my eyes are glassed over and the way my chest feels like something's wrapped around it, squeezing the air from my lungs.

I finally stand up and let my instincts take over. And they're telling me to go to her. To get lost in her touch. I pick up the phone and dial her number before taking a look outside. The phone rings and rings, but she doesn't answer. Her car's out front. I get her voicemail and decide to wait a minute. Maybe she's busy.

I run my hands through my hair, but all I can think about is that fucking note. I can practically hear him saying those words. My heart clenches, and I grip the cell phone tighter before calling her again. No answer.

I fucking need her right now. I shove shoes on my feet and swing the door open. I don't bother with a coat.

I need to feel her. I need to kiss her. I need her just as much as she needs me.

CHAPTER 16

LIZZIE

I have my nose buried in a book when there's a knock at the door. I stop reading the dark romance, something I've been preoccupying my mind with to keep it off Liam, and get up from the couch. As I walk across the room, I don't even have to guess who's there.

Liam.

My heart begins to pound at the thought of seeing him. And I take a second debating on whether I should open the door, or ignore him for as long as I can.

Relax, I tell myself. *You can do this. I need to have this talk with him. This needs to stop now.*

Still, it takes me several deep breaths to get my pulse to stop racing and for my anxiety to ebb.

A frigid blast of air hits me as soon as I open the door, and I shiver. My mouth goes dry when I see Liam standing there, silhouetted by a sea of white. He's dressed casually, as if it isn't below twenty degrees and snowing. He's just in jeans and a t-shirt.

Good God, I think to myself worriedly. *He's got to be freezing!*

"Liam, what are you doing out in the snow with no coat on? You could catch a cold," I say with concern.

"I'm fine," he replies. He walks past me without asking to come inside.

Anxiety washes over me as I close the door and turn to face him.

Shit. He's looking at me with that intense gaze of his. Trouble is brewing. I don't know if I can do this.

"I've been calling you, but you haven't answered," he says, accusation in his voice.

Ugh. So here it goes. This is going to be rough. "I know. I've just been thinking," I respond slowly.

Anger flashes in his eyes. "Thinking about what?"

"Don't look at me like that," I say, getting angry. This is hard for me. "I think we should stop this."

He clenches his jaw. "You came to me, remember?"

"I'm sorry," is all I can manage. It's the only thing I can say. None of this would've happened if I didn't want it in the first place. I used him. I know that now. And I really do feel like shit about it.

Liam asks quietly, "Sorry for what, Elle?"

Unbidden, tears flow from my eyes and down my cheeks. "I can't do this, Liam," I choke out. "I'm so sorry." It's hard to breathe. It feels like my heart's being ripped out of my chest.

Liam walks over to me and grabs me by the arms, forcing me to look into his eyes. Fuck. It hurts to see the pain reflected there. "And why not? You wanted this as much as I did."

I can't respond. The lump in my throat is too big to swallow. Why does it hurt so fucking much?

Liam looks at me with disbelief. "You really don't wanna be with me? Is that it?"

The pain is crushing me. Any more, and I feel my heart

will shatter. "I don't know," I croak, seconds away from sobbing like a baby.

Liam looks like he's been stabbed in the heart. It's a look I can hardly bear. Surprisingly, he's not giving up. "Well, I don't give a shit. I still want to be with you, Elle. No matter what you say." He looks away and I realize he's trying to keep from crying. "You healed a part of me that I didn't realize was broken." His voice is thick with emotion and it threatens to send me over the brink.

"Please!" I cry. *Please don't do this. Not here. Not now.*

"Please what?" Liam presses.

"I don't know," I sob, shaking my head. "I don't know what I want from you."

Liam pulls me into his arms, holding me close. It feels so good to be enveloped by the warmth of his hard body. "Well, what do you feel? What do you feel in your heart for me? 'Cause I can damn sure feel something in mine for you. And I want to hold onto it."

His words are so powerful. It scares the shit out of me. "But--but it's so soon. We're both grieving...and this is just… it just isn't healthy!"

Liam snorts derisively. "Says who? Who can tell us what's healthy, and what isn't? All I know is I feel for you, Elizabeth Turner. And I don't want it to end."

I can't find the words to reply. I feel for Liam, too. Maybe too much. That's what frightens the fuck out of me. "I'm scared," I say, finally admitting the truth to him.

Liam bends down and kisses the tears on my jaw, then kisses me on the lips. I taste the salt on them. "It's okay to be scared. There's nothing wrong with that. You just have to believe that everything will be alright." He kisses me again and I melt into him. I'm breathless when he pulls away a moment later. "This doesn't have to be anything that you don't want it to be," he says huskily. "We're moving fast right now, but I don't see anything wrong with it. I just need you to stop thinking about tomorrow, and only think about what's here and now."

He's asking a lot from me when I'm so conflicted. So confused. I don't know what I should do. I don't know anything. "I don't know, Liam."

He kisses me again and I feel my defenses crumbling. "Please don't deny me, Elle. I want you." He injects even more feeling into his voice and says, "I need you."

At those words, and the pleading look in his eyes, my defenses are swept away like a leaf in a hurricane. I can no longer deny this man. I am his. Forever.

I melt into him and let him pull me into a strong, lingering kiss.

His lips crash against mine as he pushes me down on the ground and devours me. He pushes his hand up my shirt and lets his hands roam my body. He owns me, and he knows it.

His demanding touch sends shivers over every inch of me. I have to pull away and breathe in the hot air between us. He continues kissing along every inch of my neck with a desperate need.

"Liam," I whimper as he pushes my pants down and cups my pussy.

"Yes!" he says before nipping my earlobe. "I want you screaming my name," he harshly whispers. His words harden my nipples and spike my libido. He pulls my panties down as I take in uneven breaths.

I feel like I'm suffocating. Everything's going so fast. He pulls my shirt over my head and instantly kneads and sucks on my breasts. I'm caged under him. My senses are overwhelmed. His smell. His touch. My body is on fire with desire.

He pushes his thick fingers into my wet pussy, and my

back bows. My neck arches away from him as I scream out his name. “Mine,” he whispers into my neck, continuing his torturous strokes. He doesn’t let up as I try to move away from him. My body is tense and on edge. My release feels heightened and almost like too much as his thumb rubs against my throbbing clit in time with the pumps of his fingers stroking my G-spot.

“Cum for me,” he commands and I obey. Every inch of my skin heats and ignites, and a wave of intense pleasure flows from deep in my belly outward in all directions. My body trembles, and my eyes close as Liam pushes my legs apart and settles between them.

He grabs my ass with both hands and tilts me up so he’s in a better position. I can barely breathe, feeling as though I'm miles away.

My head thrashes wildly as he shoves himself deep into my pussy with one hard thrust. “Fuck!” I scream out.

Liam leans down and bites my shoulder, hard, as he pumps in and out of me.

“My name,” he growls. He picks up his pace as he kisses the bite mark and grips my chin in his hand. I stare into his heated gaze as he continues to ruthlessly fuck me. My body jolts with each hard pump. “Scream my name.”

My body heats as he stares into my eyes and continues to pound into my pussy. I can barely breathe as the extreme pleasure intensifies. Each thrust bringing me closer to an edge that seems too steep.

My eyes start to close and I bite down on my bottom lip as the feeling becomes too much. Liam doesn’t stop, he only pushes in deeper and harder. His pace gets faster and I lose myself to the overwhelming pleasure.

“Liam!” I scream out and he captures my voice with his lips on mine. He kisses me with a passion I’ve never felt. He devours my body as every limb feels heavy with a tingling pleasure. My pussy spasms around him as he thrusts deeper into me, making me grip onto his shoulders and scream into the crook of his neck.

His dick pulses, buried to the hilt and our combined cum leaks down my ass as my breath slowly comes back to me. He braces himself on top of me, whispering my name and leaving a trail of kisses down my neck and up my jaw. My chest rises and falls with deep, calming breaths of hot air. I push my hair out of my face and then take his face in my hands.

My heart swells and I start to tell him the words on the tip of my tongue, but he leans down and kisses me. Taking the words and silencing them.

I love you, Liam.

CHAPTER 17

IAN DRACHO

I fucking hate that prick Liam Axton. He thinks he's so fucking smart. They're coming up with everything they can to destroy my business. Before him, I had it made. These hot shots come in here, thinking they know it all and how they're going to be walking out with their pockets full of my money. I snort a laugh. I'm the only one profiting in the deals I make.

Until Liam fucking Axton. My cell rings on the end table and I mute the game on the television. I need to know what Stephen found out there at Liam's new property. Gino's gone, and I know that fucker's the one who whacked him. I'm gonna make him pay. They'll all pay.

"What'd you find out there?" I answer the phone with the one question that matters. What the fuck is Liam doing with a house out in the suburbs? It came up on his report, and I need to know why.

"Elizabeth Turner," Stephen says, followed by something muffled. He must be outside, judging by the wind blowing against his phone. I can hear the moment he gets back in his car and shuts the door. Everything's more clear. Except who the fuck Elizabeth Turner is.

"Who?" I lean against the back of my sofa and listen to Stephen a little more closely. He's supposed to be checking out the house, not talking about some cunt.

"He's at some broad's house next door."

"Liam is?" I ask. My forehead's pinched with confusion.

"Yeah, I just looked inside," he bellows a laugh. "Got me rock fucking hard."

"If this is just some chick next door that he's banging, I'm gonna be pissed." Something in me is telling me it's not though. Things have been off with that asshole recently. Now's the time to strike. He's weak. And it must be this bitch that's getting to him. "What the fuck is he doing with a house out there anyway?"

"Maybe it's for her?" Stephen sounds a little unsure, but I can't think of any other reason Liam Axton would be out in the suburbs. No fucking way he bought a house to get close to a woman. Unless she means something to him. A sick smile grows across my face.

"Stake it out and find out everything you can about this chick and what she means to him." I wanna know everything. I wanna know how bad it's gonna hurt him when I slit this bitch's throat. I want him to see it. I'll make this asshole pay. "If she's valuable, then we've got a good way in."

"You got it, boss."

CHAPTER 18

LIAM

I can still feel her kiss on my lips as I pull into the parking spot. My chest fills with warmth. It's a long ass drive from her place to work, but it's worth it just to wake up next to her. I've never had this before. It's still new and pure. I'm still afraid I'm going to ruin it, but so far she's happy. It's been almost a month since she's come back and shoved her way into my life. I don't know how I ever lived without her.

Every night we lay in bed and she falls asleep in my arms, I wonder if it's going to be the last night. If she'll wake up and realize she doesn't need me. But then I always wake up to her kissing my shoulder and nuzzling her head into the crook of my neck.

Life's never felt this good. I can't let it end. She's been talking about school and I know she's thinking about what's going to happen when she has to leave. I am too, but neither of us has said anything. We're both walking on eggshells, wondering how long this can possibly last. It's just too good to be true.

As I walk into the elevator a woman in a skimpy black

dress gets on with me, looking more like a hooker than an employee of any of the businesses who rent out these spaces. I keep my eyes off her ass even as she bends over to select her floor. She looks back over her shoulder with a small smile as the doors close. She's looking at me like I'm a piece of meat.

A different time, I would've stopped the elevator and fucked her right here, right now.

Not now. Rather than feeling desire, I'm pissed. It's not her fault. She doesn't know I'm spoken for, but just the fact she's trying to do something that could cause friction between me and Elle makes me tense.

I give her a tight smile and her eyes fall as she straightens her shoulders and pulls her dress lower over her ass. Good. I feel a little bit like an asshole. But I'm glad the message was received.

I'm still feeling tense and off when I get to the top and walk into our space, although I don't know why.

Everything's pristine and in order. But it's quiet. No one's here. I clear my throat and try to get rid of this tension while I unlock my office.

I stop in my tracks as Zac turns in the seat across from my desk and stares at me. I look around the room. Tyler's not here.

"I don't want you to get upset," Zac says as I take deliberate steps to sit down at my desk. A million things are running through my head, but I have no real concrete idea as to what he's talking about.

"Spit it out," I tell him. I don't like not knowing shit. I don't like being tense and on edge, and that's exactly what I am right now.

He slides a photo across the desk. When he pulls his hand away, my blood chills. My heart stops working. It's just a photograph with a hole in the top. Maybe the size of a finishing nail from where it was hung on something.

It's a picture of us. Elle's smiling back at me. Her head's resting on my shoulder and she's looking up at me even though my eyes are on the television that's not in the picture. It's from one of our lazy nights together. In her house, and the picture was obviously taken from a window. Clearly someone's been watching us.

I pick up the photo gently. More carefully than I need to, but I'm afraid my anger is going to make me do something stupid. My entire body slowly heats as my blood fills with adrenaline.

"Tyler's keeping an eye on her now." Zac's words barely do a thing to calm me, but at least he's a step ahead of me.

"Where was it?" I ask Zac. I finally tear my eyes away from the picture. "In the mailbox like the last one?" I remember the threat from before, and my stomach wants to heave. Elle. I need to get to her.

"Yeah," he says easily, although it's completely at odds with how on edge he looks. He looks as though he's going to have to defend himself. He's waiting for me to attack him. But he's not my target. Maybe he's just waiting for me to lose it. Yeah, that's probably more accurate.

"You okay?" he asks. But I ignore him. I flip the picture over, looking for a message. But there's nothing there.

"Anything with it?" I ask him as my thumb rubs over the spot in the picture where her hand's in mine.

"No," he answers in a clear, low voice.

She's so fucking beautiful. That moment was for us. And now it's tainted. I have to put the picture down as my hands fist and I struggle to fight the urge to break everything around me in this fucking room. I need to hold back this rage.

But I also need to do something.

I'm quick to pick up my phone. Zac's eyes go wide and he shakes his head as he says, "That's what he wants, Liam." I ignore my brother's warning. I don't care if I'm giving Ian the reaction he wants.

The phone rings once, twice. *Pick up the phone, you fucking coward.* On the end of the third ring, the phone clicks and I hear his breathing on the end of the phone.

I stand quickly and make my way to the large window in the room. "Leave her out of this," I say simply in a dark voice I don't even recognize.

"You fucked with me, now I fuck with you," Ian says and then the line goes dead.

My body's shaking with rage. She's mine. I finally got a life I want. A life I'm afraid is going to slip through my fingers. He's not going to take that away from me. He's not going to do a damn thing to her. I'll fucking kill him first.

My chest heaves with an angry breath as I look my brother in the eyes and say, "I want him dead."

CHAPTER 19

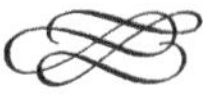

LIZZIE

Crap, I think as I open the fridge and peer inside. *There's nothing to eat.* I have no idea why there's no food in there. Probably because I've been so focused on Liam and forgetting to do normal things, like go grocery shopping. The strange thing is, my appetite is starting to return. What I wouldn't do for some of Nat's delicious sugar cookies right now. Or chocolate. Or wine. Or better yet, all three. I need a real meal though.

My stomach growls as I close the fridge and take a look around the kitchen. It looks different now than it did when I came home. He didn't have half the things I use in the kitchen, so new things have been added to the counter. I threw away a few of the old things he'd kept. A couple I know were my mother's. Like her mixer. I'm keeping that. I'll never throw that away.

I think I'm getting better with dealing with the pain. I find myself no longer thinking of daddy a million times a day, or when I do, I don't instantly burst into tears. Even now, the picture of his face on the fridge only makes my heart hurt a little. I don't want to rip it down and sob inconsolably on the floor.

A feeling of guilt washes over me as I gaze at his portrait. I should still be grieving, shouldn't I? It hasn't even been that long since daddy died, and I'm already forgetting about him.

It just isn't right.

It's Liam, I think to myself. *He's filling that awful void left by daddy.*

If anything, this realization makes it worse. I'm already moving on with my life.

But isn't that what daddy would want? For me to be happy? And with a man he obviously put so much trust in?

I have to believe this, otherwise the guilt is going to eat me alive.

The sound of the front door opening tears me out of my musing. My mood instantly brightens. Liam's here.

"I'm in the kitchen!" I yell, stifling the other emotions and trying to remember what I was doing in the kitchen to begin with.

Oh yeah, movie night. We've been having these little date nights, and I really love them. It's like real life is suspended when I'm with him. I know I have to face reality again at some point, but I don't want to. I just want what we have together.

I'm ignoring all the other responsibilities for as long as I have to. At least I've paid my tuition. The money came through, and everything's taken care of. Liam started the paperwork the day we went on our date. So for days I was worrying over nothing. He says I worry too much and to just trust him. So I have, and I have to admit, life's easier just letting him take care of me. I don't really have any worries, other than my grief over my father passing. But it's getting better. It really is. With Liam helping me, I can keep inching my way toward normalcy.

I'm just trying to live in the moment with Liam and forget that this could be over soon when I have to go back to school. It's better that way. I pull my hair in front of one shoulder and smile thinking about our movie night tonight.

I haven't been to the theatre in so long. I can't wait to go. And have popcorn. I *must* have buttery movie popcorn. It's crazy how much I want it. Just a week ago the thought of having greasy popcorn would make me want to barf. Now I'm craving it like a junkie.

"Liam?" I ask when I hear no response. For a moment, I'm rattled. It's unusual for Liam not to respond. The sound of footsteps grows louder, and my anxiety increases. My heart starts to pound and all sorts of wild scenarios began running through my head when Liam appears in the doorway.

I breathe out a sigh of relief at the sight of him. "Oh thank God, it's you," I say breathlessly, my hand pressed over my heart. "For a moment there, I thought someone had broken in." His eyes flash with worry, but it's gone so quickly I think I just imagined it.

I pause and then add, "You ready to go see Warcraft?"

Instead of responding, Liam just nods. I immediately suspect something's off. My heart twists in my chest. Maybe he's not feeling the same way about me as I am about him. Maybe he's ready to talk about what's going to happen when I go back to school. Fuck, I'm not ready for that.

"Is something wrong?" I ask cautiously.

"Nah." He's lying. I know he is.

"You sure?"

"I'm fine," he replies curtly. Now I really know something is wrong. But I'm not quite sure what to do.

He holds up a DVD. "I wanna stay in tonight." My lips tip down into a frown. It's not that I don't want to stay in. I love it when we do, I was just looking forward to going out. And to getting that popcorn.

It's fine. I shake off all the weird insecurities running through me. Everything's fine. I'll feel better once we're cuddling up. Everything's better when he holds me.

"Well can we at least get some popcorn for the movie?" I ask, trying to change the subject. "I'm really craving some right now."

"We don't need it." My lips part, ready to protest. I can run right out to the convenience store and grab it in like twenty minutes. And I want it.

"But… I really would like to have some." I gesture at the fridge. "I'm hungry, and there's nothing to eat."

Liam sighs. "I don't want to go out, Elle."

Anger surges through me. What the hell is Liam's problem? I was really looking forward to going out and having a good time, and now he's pulling this.

My eyes fall and I struggle to keep my composure. It's gotta be my hormones and insecurities. I close my eyes and almost shake my head. I know it's something else. I can't keep lying to myself. If he's ready for this to end then he can just fucking do it.

Liam senses my anger because suddenly he's in front of me, pulling me into his arms. I use my hands to brace myself on his chest and I was right, just being in his arms soothes something in me.

I still feel vulnerable, until he kisses the tip of my nose. "I'm sorry, Elle," he apologizes. "I've just had a very long day." I close my eyes, letting his touch calm me. "If you really wanna go out, we will."

"Are we okay?" I whisper. I hate that I sound weak, but I can't help feeling like there's tension between us. I don't like it. I want it gone.

"Of course we are," he answers as I look up at him. There's so much sincerity in his gaze that every insecurity vanishes. "I'm sorry, Elle. Of course we can get some popcorn for tonight."

I place a hand on his shoulder and gently rub it. "It's okay. You don't have to apologize. Since you're so worn out, do you want me to drive?"

He kisses me on the nose. "Nah. I'm fine. I'll drive. Where do you want to go?"

CHAPTER 20

LIAM

I should tell her, but I can't do it.

She's gonna be pissed at me. She's going to know what kind of a bastard I am. She's going to question everything. Just knowing all that's going to happen tears me apart. I wanna keep this from her. I need to keep all this shit away from her.

I can't help but feel anxious as I drive down to the convenience store.

"Oh, shit!" My heart stills at Elle's outburst. "I forgot my purse." She sounds so upset. I close my eyes and try to contain my relief.

"No problem." I stop at a red light and dig in my back pocket for my wallet. I have time to pull out a couple of twenties and pass them to her.

"I think one will do," she says in a soft voice. "Thank you," she says, a little uncomfortable. "I'll pay you back."

A smile cracks on my face for the first time since this morning. The light turns green and we move forward as I place my hand on her thigh. "No you won't. You're my girl." I pick her hand up and kiss her wrist, keeping my eyes on the road.

I hear her soft sigh and feel her eyes on me. I take a look from the corner of my eyes and she looks beautiful. It makes my heart hurt.

A small smile is playing on her lips. She's so perfect. I keep rubbing soothing circles as we drive up and I pull in. Right at the front doors, where there's plenty of security and high visibility. I can see everything. I've got my gun in the glove box. We should be fine, but it won't hurt to stay vigilant. I put the car in park and Elle's already moving. Her seat belt's off and she starts to open her door and holds up one finger.

"I'll be in and out real quick." She leans across the console and plants a kiss on my lips. "Promise." Her words echo in my ears as she opens her door.

My heart stops beating as I look past her. One of Ian's men pulls in, and even with his sunglasses on, I recognize him. Stephen.

It's freezing outside, but his window's down and I know why. He's going to shoot. It's a hit. My lungs refuse to fill. My blood spikes with fear as everything plays in slow motion.

Before I can blink, he's pulling his gun out of the window and aiming it right at Elle. I grab her shoulders and pull her down. The bullets fly out with a loud *bang*! One ricochets off the car, I think the hood, and she screams. Another hits the passenger side mirror. She's still screaming, and her hands fly to her head. My heart's pounding in my chest.

"Stay down!" I yell at her, covering her with my body and struggling to close her door. Once I hear the click, I chance a look and peek up. *Bang*! He fires as I duck back down and she shrieks in fear.

Her window shatters as a bullet hits my driver seat. Small shards of glass fall into the car by her feet. She scoots closer to me and I try my damndest to cover her. This is too close.

I stay low. I just need to protect her. I reach up and unlatch the glove compartment to get my gun. I can feel it, but I fumble with it as my heart pounds. Finally, I've got it in my hand. The heavy weight does nothing to relieve my anxiety. She can't be here. I can't let anything happen to her. The car's still running and I put it into reverse, desperate to get out of here. To get her on the other side of me.

Someone runs from the store and ducks behind a car. A few other people are screaming from inside the store as another wild spray of bullets hits the car. Elle's shrill cry pierces my ears as her fingers dig into my leg. She's staying down though and the door is closed. She's as safe as possible for now, but she could still get hit.

I only lift my head up enough to barely see that fucker and quickly shoot my gun, aiming right at his head. He ducks to avoid the first shot and then the second. I don't need to hit him. I just need to get him to stop firing so I can get her out of here. That's what matters. My heart races and my blood pumps with the fear of losing her.

I'm driving in reverse with one hand, my grip tight on the leather steering wheel. My other hand is still holding the gun while pushing down on her back, keeping her down. I hit the gas pedal and turn the wheel as sharp and fast as possible. The back of my car smacks against a lamppost, jolting our bodies. Elle screams again and tries to cover her head, curling into a small ball on the seat.

I put the car into drive and take off. The tires squeal as two more bullets hit the back of the car, each one making her jump and ripping a sob from her throat. She's shaking, and I'm doing everything I can to take care of her and get us out of here.

I look in my rearview expecting him to follow us, but he's turning out of the lot in the other direction. My heart's racing and she's clawing against my arm, trying to get out of my hold and sit up.

I release a breath I didn't know I was holding and let go of her. The light ahead turns yellow and I slam on the gas to get through the intersection. I'm not stopping. I'm taking her to my place in the city until these fuckers are dead. I don't trust going back to her place. I need my guns and my security system. I focus on my breathing; I need to get my shit together. She needs me, now more than ever. My heart's still racing like crazy, but it's starting to calm slightly.

"Oh my God." Tears fall down Elle's face. "Are you okay?" she screeches. Her breathing is frantic and she's looking around, the wind from her open window blows her hair into her face. The glass crunches beneath her feet as she moves slightly and then looks out of the back window like she's expecting to see him. She doesn't even know what she's looking for.

"It's okay, he's gone." I sound cold and devoid of emotion. But this is the most emotion I've ever felt. And it's not one I welcome. Fear. They almost took her from me.

"Did you see him?" Her wide eyes are filled with worry. "We need to call the cops." She searches the floor for her phone and picks it up. I'm quick to snatch it out of her hands, dropping the gun.

"No cops." My words are hard. But I can't let her do that. I'm killing these fuckers. As soon as I can get her safe, they're dead. They've been in hiding, but you can only hide so long. We know where they hang around and now we have their paper work, I know where they live and where their families live. I'm not giving them a chance to run. I'll find those fuckers. "They're all dead."

It's then that Elle sees the gun and puts two and two together. Her eyes widen, and the fear in them changes. She's scared of *me* now. It makes my heart clench in my chest. It fucking hurts, but I knew this would happen. She pushes away from me and leans against the car door. Like she's desperate to get out.

"Why do you have a gun?" she asks; her voice is hollow. I press my lips into a firm line and stare straight ahead. "Why were they shooting at us?" Her voice cracks, and I can see she's shaking again.

"Elle--" I start to speak, but she screams out, "Tell me!"

"'Cause they have a hit out on me." I grip the wheel tighter and add, "On us." Her lips part with disbelief. It fucking hurts me to say that.

"Why?" she asks.

I take in a deep breath before looking at her and answering, "I told you I was a bad man."

"Stay away from me!" she screams. My heart shatters in my chest. I loosen my grip on the wheel and look out of the driver side window.

"That's not an option now." I finally tell her the truth, "I'm sorry, Elle. But you have to come with me."

Her mouth opens, and she struggles to breathe. I wish I could comfort her and that she'd believe me when I say I'll take care of this. But I can tell just from the look in her eyes, everything between us is broken.

CHAPTER 21

LIAM

I open the car door for her and she storms out. She doesn't touch me; she completely avoids me. She's fucking pissed. Her arms are crossed, and she's not speaking. That's fine if she doesn't want to talk right now. I'll wait for her to calm down and figure out how to make this up to her. She's walking the wrong fucking direction though. And that's not going to happen. I'm not letting her leave.

"Elle, get your ass inside!" I yell out as I follow her down the driveway. We're a good distance away from the other houses, but they're within view, and I'm not letting her get close enough to them to cause a scene. My heart's trying to climb out of my throat. I need to get her ass inside. Right. Fucking. Now.

"Elizabeth!" I scream out her name.

She turns on her heels, the crunch of the gravel and my heartbeat the only sounds I can hear as she stares back at my house with anger. "I'm not going anywhere with you," she says with a shaky voice, finally looking at me. Her eyes are glassy. She's a mix of emotions and looks like she's ready to crack

"Elle," I say and put my hands up as though I'm approaching a wounded animal. That's what she is. I hurt her. I fucked up. I know I did. But I'm going to make this right.

She shakes her head and lets out a sarcastic laugh.

"Don't fucking call me that, and don't put your hands on me." She throws her finger out, pointing at me and looking at me with disgust. She walks backward down the driveway with every step I take to get closer to her. The ground's uneven, and I don't need her falling and hurting herself.

"I can't let you go, I'm sorry." I know she's pissed at me. But I'll be damned if I'm going to let her go. I have security here at least. It's something. And now that I know they're coming, she's not leaving my house until they're both dead.

"You can't make me stay here," she says with wide, unbelieving eyes. They're red and swollen from the threat of tears, but she's holding them back. She shakes with anger and sadness, and shouts, "I wanna go home!"

"You're in danger--"

"I can call the police--" she starts to say, cutting me off, but I nip that in the bud.

"No, you can't." I shake my head and take another step closer. She takes one back and her ankle nearly rolls as she kicks out the gravel under her feet. I need her to understand. I don't want to even say this shit out loud. But she needs to know how much danger she's in. "They'll come for you--"

"Because of you!" she shrieks at me, bending at her waist and practically spitting as she yells. I know it had to have hurt her throat. There are a few houses at the end of the drive and then nothing but the woods around the city park. I look over to see if anyone's there. She needs to knock this shit off.

"You need to get inside and stay there." She doesn't answer me. Her skin is bright pink from the freezing air. The wind's blowing harder now, and I know it's gotta be getting to her. Shit, I'm cold, too. "Come inside. And we can talk about this later."

Her eyes whip to mine. "Talk about this?" she asks incredulously, and raises her brows.

"I'll tell you everything you want to know. But right now, you need to go inside."

"What the fuck do you do?" she says and finally looks up at me. She waits for an answer, but I'm not ready to talk.

"You don't need to know right now." I don't want to get into this shit. I need to get her inside and take care of this problem.

She mutters under her breath, "I knew you were no good." It pisses me off to hear her say that. But mostly it fucking hurts.

"Yeah, I'm a real bad man," I admit, "but other bad men are after you."

"It's your fault," she says. And she's right.

"I'm sorry." I can't say anything else. She finally lets me take a step closer to her without moving away from me. "You just have to stay here until I deal with them."

"Kill them?" she asks hysterically.

"It's either you or them, Elle." Her breathing comes in pants, and she glances down the driveway like she's considering running and then looks back up to me.

She glares at me like she hates me. Like she regrets everything, and it makes my stomach churn.

"I trusted you," she says in a small voice.

"I promise I'll take care of you." She shivers and grips

onto her arms, looking defeated but still closed off. I walk behind her as she concedes and slowly makes her way to the door.

"I don't want you to," she says with a coldness I've never heard from her. I swear my heart stops beating and sinks in my hollow chest.

"You don't have a choice."

CHAPTER 22

LIZZIE

What have I gotten myself into?

I stare blankly up at the high ceilings, wondering how I'm going to get out of this mess. It doesn't seem real.

Liam's forced me to stay in his bedroom, a prisoner against my will. The bedroom is comfortable and all, beautiful actually, with a gorgeous view of the skyline and crown molding running along the walls painted a soft shade of cream, but it's still a prison nonetheless.

I shouldn't be here, I think to myself. *I don't belong here, or in this mess. How did I let it come to this?*

It's crazy how close I came to being killed. I was shot at! Never have I been in such fear for my life. Just remembering the bullets whizzing by causes me to hyperventilate. Out of nowhere, I become dizzy and the room begins to spin in front of my eyes. Then my heart starts racing so fast I think I'm having a heart attack.

Jesus, Lizzie, calm down!

It takes a few minutes of calm steady breaths, before I feel like I'm in control although I'm still shaking. After a moment, I sit up and notice I'm covered with sweat, my palms clammy.

I'm not okay. That is the only truth I know. I am not fucking okay.

I knew I never should've gotten involved with Liam, considering the murky details surrounding my inheritance. I should have just sued him and contested the will. No, I had to go fall for him when I should've known better.

Anger burns my cheeks. I'm so mad. Mad at myself.

I gave myself to him! I rage. *I let him eat me out on our first date.* I swallow back the fury in my throat. I feel so humiliated, cheap and worthless. *He so played me for a fool.*

Can my life be any more fucked? My daddy died, leaving me to fall in love with a man he left everything to. I'm so mad at him. I feel guilty for feeling anything but love for my father. But I do. I'm so pissed he died and stuck me with this asshole.

I grind my teeth remembering how I thought Liam practically stole that money from my father. All that anger comes back full force. He's a fucking liar!

I slowly turn my head as I hear the sound of the door opening.

"Elle?" Liam asks with concern.

I ignore him and try to calm my racing heart. I watch from the corner of my eye as he walks towards the bed. I feel the bed dip as Liam sits next to me. Strong arms enclose me, but I push him away. "Don't fucking touch me!"

Liam looks struck by the venom in my voice. In my heart I feel a twinge of pain at the hurt look on his face. I'm mad I even feel that much. He doesn't deserve anything from me but scorn and suspicion.

They were trying to *kill* me. Because of him! He lied to me. How much has he lied? It hurts. Knowing he lied hurts so much. My chest feels like it's collapsing on itself. And what about daddy? I need to know right now. He better tell me everything. Like a slap to my face I realize he could just keep lying. And I'd have no way of knowing if he was telling the truth or not. I don't care though. I need to ask. I need to know what the hell is going on.

"Who were they?" I demand through my cries. After what I've been through, I deserve to know that much. "Who were those people?"

"You don't need to know their names," Liam says firmly, though I can hear the pain in his voice. "It won't change what happened."

I stare at him incredulously. I don't need to know their names? I almost got killed, and I don't need to know their names? What. The. Fuck. "You can't be serious!" I snap. "They tried to kill me because of you!"

Liam stares at me. "Yeah, and trust me, Elle, I'm going to make them fucking pay for it." He searches my grief-stricken face. I can tell he feels uncomfortable, but I don't give a fuck. He's the one that put me in this situation. "But you need to understand, sometimes in my line of business, things get violent. And I'm deeply sorry that you had to witness that today."

"Line of business?" I demand. "You're a restaurant owner!" I yell. "What kind of restaurant owner gets in shootouts with thugs?"

"I'm a bookie," Liam corrects. My eyebrows shoot up in surprise. How many lies has he told me? My breathing comes in faster, and my blood heats with anger and betrayal.

"You're a fucking criminal!" I shout.

Liam swallows and clenches his jaw. I can tell I'm pissing him off. Good. He deserves it for all the shit he's put me through. "I'm not. What I do, it's not really illegal.

There are some situations where I push the boundaries of the law... but it's still legal."

"You know what? Fuck you! You get me involved with all this shit, then you refuse to tell me what the hell is going on." I jump up from the bed and move out into the middle of the floor and start pacing. I don't even want to be near Liam right now. "I trusted you. I gave myself to you, even when I was telling myself that I shouldn't. Turns out, I was right. I shouldn't have given you a chance at all. You no good, lying bastard--"

"Elle. You need to--"

I stop pacing and gesture sharply. "How did you know my dad? Don't try to lie, or tell me I don't need to know." My voice dims, but I stare at Liam with all the rage I can manage. Just the mention of my father has the sadness creeping back in. But I can't let it show. I need to focus on my anger.

Liam holds my furious gaze for a moment, then sighs. "Fine," he says with firm conviction. "I'll tell you."

I hold in a sigh of relief. I'd expected Liam to tell me it was none of my business, just like he has been. "Go on," I command as though I have authority.

"Your dad didn't want me to tell you, but I think you deserve to know." He waits a moment and then breathes in deep. "Your dad needed money, bad," he begins. "He came to me to place a bet--"

"Bullshit!" I interrupt. I'm furiously shaking my head. Lies. More lies. "He wasn't a gambler--"

"Do you want me to tell you how we met or not?" Liam snaps. "I have no reason to lie to you."

We stare at each other. I don't know if I believe him or not. Regardless of what he tells me, I don't know if I'll believe him. "Are you going to listen to me?" he asks.

There's a hint of condescension in his voice, and it pisses me off.

I glower and cross my arms over my chest, but reluctantly nod.

He waits to make sure I have my anger under control, and then he tells me everything. About my father needing the money fast and not being able to sell the house. I listen as he tells me how my father came in and practically forced him to take 22 Wyoming. He tells me how they got close.

I don't know what to believe. I don't want to believe any of it. My head's spinning. He's a liar. That's all I can think. Daddy would never do that. He wouldn't go to a bookie. He couldn't have done something like that. Moreover, why would Liam have gone out of his way to help him?

I shake my head. "I have no reason to believe anything you say. It's all a bunch of lies."

"It's not. He was desperate for money, so I gave it to him."

"Why would you do that?" I ask him. I don't see why he would. He's just trying to make himself look better. He's lying to me again.

"'Cause he reminded me of my own father." I stare at him wordlessly, not believing what he's saying. My armor cracks a bit as I realize I don't know anything about Liam's father. I didn't even know he was dead. He only ever talks about his brother, Zac.

After a moment, Liam adds, "He died when I was younger." My heart sinks and feels heavy. A sadness passes his eyes, and I want to go and comfort him. But I don't know what to believe. I heave in a deep breath. My fingers itch to grab his hand and squeeze. I clasp them together instead. Even though I hurt for him, I can't forget that I have a fucking hitman after me because of him.

"I'm sorry," I manage to say. "About your father. I'm sorry." I wipe under my eyes and shake my head. I look him in the eyes and calm my breathing. "But I don't trust you. And I wish I'd never met you."

Liam goes still. He looks… emotionless. Like he's hiding everything from me. I feel sick. It's not true. What I said isn't true and I want to take it all back. At the same time, he hurt me. And I just hurt him back. I feel like such a fucking bitch. I hold my breath, scared of what he might say next.

But he says nothing, Liam walks out of the room not saying a word. I hear the sound of the door clicking shut and I finally breathe out slowly.

I'm left in silence. Silence so heavy it feels like I'm being suffocated. I clench my fists, wanting to scream at Liam. At the same time, I wish he'd come back so I could hold him and he could hold me. This is so fucked.

I wanna know if it's all true. If he really gave daddy that money to try to save his life. A sob leaves me unexpectedly, and I cover my face with both hands. Did he really do that for him? I take in a ragged breath. I don't know what to believe.

It all feels wrong, and my head is spinning with disbelief.

I wish I could just leave and pretend like this is all fake.

As though I don't love him. I never did.

But as I walk over and lie across the bed and begin bawling my eyes out, deep down in my heart, I know that's a lie.

I love this man. But I don't know if I believe him.

CHAPTER 23

LIAM

It's late and I don't want to leave Elle, but at least one of these fuckers needs to die tonight. And the one I pick is Stephen. The fucker who tried to kill my girl and ruined everything I had with her. His life is over.

Zac's got his home address. Tyler said his wife's there. If she's there, he's gotta be there at some point.

I have to calm myself down, but I'm struggling. I've been on a knife's edge ever since she said those words to me.

I pick up my phone and swallow the lump in my throat. I'll make this right and that starts with killing these fuckers. I've got my gloves; I've got the wire. It's a silent easy kill. I know what to do. My uncle taught me. Tyler's father. When we went to live with him, I learned how to deal with shit the way the mob deals with it.

I shove the gloves and the wire into a small black bag and call my brother. It only rings once.

"You almost here?" I ask him without waiting for a hello.

"Just pulling in now." Perfect fucking timing. I walk to

the foyer and look up the stairs. She's in my bedroom up there, and she's pissed. She deserves to be. But she's going to have to get over it. The doorknob turns and Zac pushes the door open. My brother's silent as he walks in.

"Just stay here and watch her while I go take care of this."

He nods his head. "I know. I've got my phone on me." I look up the stairs one last time and he follows my line of sight.

"She's still pissed?" I don't answer him. I told him what happened; he should know she's pissed. I'd be pissed. My lips are pressed into a straight line. My body heats with anger. This is how she's introduced to the only family I have.

It's fucked up. It's all fucked up, and it's all my fault.

"Tyler's on his way too." I give my brother a nod. I know he is. I almost had both of them stay here with her, but I can't be stupid about this and I need someone with me.

"I'll be back as soon as I can."

My brother's hand falls hard on my shoulder as I open the door wider to leave. I look back at him. "Make it quick and easy," he says.

I keep his gaze and nod. I'd like to draw it out. I'd like to make him suffer. But I need to get back here. I don't like leaving her. Not until both of those assholes are dead.

Ian Dracho and his lackey are fucking dead. Then I can make it up to Elle. She'll forgive me. My heart lurches in my chest as I walk out into the cold. She has to forgive me. She has to.

* * *

I NOD at Tyler as I make my way down to the end of the street. He's in his car and on the lookout in case anything happens or anyone sees what's going on. He could've done this, but I wanted to do it. I want to be the one to put an end to his life.

I sneak through the night, walking a few houses down and hide in the bushes at the back of the house, walking along the brick building. According to Tyler, he comes in this way. He parks in the garage and slips in the back. Like a fucking rat. He's afraid to come in the front door. He should be. He should be fucking terrified.

I peek in the small window above the kitchen sink and see a television on in the living room. I can't hear it, but I can see the back of a woman's head and the edge of the screen. She shouldn't be bothered. He won't see it coming; he won't even have a chance to scream. I resume my position in the cold night and stand behind the bushes next to the door. I'm completely still, dressed entirely in black. My thick leather gloves are on and the wire is wrapped tight over both hands. There's a good seven inches of slack. Enough to go around his throat.

My heartbeat picks up as I see him park his car. The lights shine on the door to the garage before it slowly opens. I can faintly hear the bass beats to whatever song he's listening too.

Time passes slowly and my heart beats even slower as his car disappears into the garage. I have to wait. Tick. Tick. Tick. Time goes slow. So fucking slow. I have to rein in my anger. I have to wait until he's here. So I can choke the fucking life out of the man who shot at Elle. He tried to kill her.

The longer I wait, the angrier I get, the tighter the wire is on my fingers. Finally, I hear a faint beep of the car's alarm. The side door opens and he starts walking along the pavers to get to the back door of his home. The night air is cold and I use it to calm myself. His keys jingle as he reaches for the right one to unlock the door. His head's down. He's not looking. It's fucking perfect.

I jump out and reach my arms up and over his head. His keys fall to the ground with a loud clink, and he tries to scream. But he barely gets any sound out as I pull the wire tight around his neck.

He could've killed her. It's all I think as I pull the wire tighter. My lungs stop working and my muscles scream in agony as I fight against this fucker. He *wanted* to kill her.

I pull the wire harder with everything in me. The thin wire digs into the gloves and feels like it's going to cut my skin, but I know it's not. I lift up as high as I can as he tears at his own flesh, desperate to pry the wire away. He tries to elbow me, tries to kick his leg back. He flails in my grasp, desperate for any escape. Any weakness. But I'm merciless in my pursuit of his death.

I take every hit and respond by pulling the wire tighter. The only sounds are crickets chirping and him struggling to breathe. Finally, he stops moving. I hold still for a long moment, unable to let go.

When I finally do, his body falls to the ground with a dull thud. His lifeless eyes are bloodshot and there are deep cuts on the sides of his throat from the wire.

I stare at him a moment, waiting for any signs of life as my breathing steadies. My head whips to the side and my heartbeat picks up as I hear the clanking of dishes in the kitchen inside. His wife is only a few feet away. She's going to end up finding this fucker out here. A part of me feels sorry for her. The rest of me doesn't give a shit.

I look back down at him and there's only one thing on my mind.

One down. One to go.

CHAPTER 24

LIZZIE

I'm going to make Liam pay for this.

Last night, he left me alone. I heard him come in the house. I heard thc two of them talking, but Liam never came up. Zac's the one who asked me to come down for dinner. I don't even know him. I don't know what to say to him. At one point, I would've been both excited and nervous to meet him. I would've wanted to make a good impression. But not now. I don't trust him either. I didn't eat and I didn't leave the room. I passed out eventually and for the first time in weeks, I woke up alone. I fucking hated it. I hated how I missed him.

He came up once today, and I ignored him. I'm not ready to talk about this. Not that he tried to say anything to me either. It hurt. But I guess that's what I get. And the moment I came downstairs, he left. He announced he was going to go *handle things*. My body chills at the thought of what he's doing. I can't take this shit. But I can't leave.

Liam has instructed his younger brother Zac to watch over me as if I'm some two-year-old. He said it's for my safety, but it's only annoying me. He's keeping me prisoner.

That's what he's doing. I think what bothers me the most is the fact I wouldn't even be in danger if Liam had just been truthful from the beginning.

Like, if he cared so much about my safety, why did he get involved with me, knowing that he was mixed up in criminal activity?

Because he's a selfish bastard that only cares about himself, I tell myself. It hurts to think that though. I rock my leg back and forth; my heel hits the sofa. *Because he loves me* is the answer I want to believe. But that only makes me hate myself.

Lounging in the recliner, Zac stares back at me and then shakes his head. "You shouldn't be so pissed off. This is for your own good."

I roll my eyes. *You probably wouldn't know good if it hit you in the balls,* I think angrily. But I don't bother saying it. "Don't tell me how I should feel!" I hiss. "Do you know what happened to me? I almost got killed... all because of your dirtbag brother."

"Liam's not a dirtbag," Zac protests.

"Oh really? What about a piece of shit then?" I don't know why I'm acting this way. I don't really mean these things I'm saying. I'm just angry beyond belief.

Zac stares at the scowl on my face and then sighs. "Thanks, Liam, for pairing me with this diva."

"Oh fuck off," I snap.

"You're the one with the attitude."

"You're damn right. You spend a minute in my shoes and see if you don't have one after two seconds."

Zac goes silent and stares at me thoughtfully.

"Mind if I put the game on?" Zac asks after a long silence. He's obviously trying to change the subject. For all the good it'll do him, which isn't much.

I shrug. "Do whatever. I don't care. I just wanna leave."

Zac grabs the remote and flicks the TV on, turning it to a football game. "That wouldn't be a good idea. Liam doesn't want you to go anywhere."

I give him a withering look. "He has no right to keep me here... and neither do you!" Fed up, I stand up, intent on leaving.

Zac jumps up and gets in my way. "Where do you think you're going?"

I place my hands on my hips and command, "Get the fuck out of my way."

Zac shakes his head, eyeing me wearily. He's obviously as tired of this as I am. "I can't let you leave, Elle. Sorry." I'm struck by him calling me Elle. I don't like it. That's what Liam calls me. Not him.

"Lizzie," I correct him.

His brow furrows, but then he nods and says, "Lizzie, you need to sit your ass down."

For a moment, I debate on whether to make a run for it, then decide against it. There's no way I'm slipping past him.

I drop my hands to my sides in resignation. "Why are you doing this to me? You don't have to do this on your brother's behalf. I have every right to leave. You're committing a crime by keeping me here."

Zac keeps his eyes on me as if he's expecting me to pull a fast one. "Because you mean something to Liam, and he doesn't want you dead. And as far as committing a crime is concerned, I'd rather commit one than have to explain to my brother that I let you leave."

I scowl. "It's Liam's fucking fault I'm in danger. Not mine."

Zac sighs. "I know he's disappointed you by not being upfront about his business. But Liam is a good man, believe it or not. Dude's got a heart of gold. This is just something that comes with the territory in our line of work."

I snort and let out a wild laugh. "A good man? He's a liar!"

"I'm sure whatever he lied about wasn't to hurt you," Zac tries to reassure me. "Trust me. Liam isn't that type of person."

"The fuck he isn't," I mutter angrily.

Zac ignores me and I see little reason to continue arguing with him about Liam. After all, he's Liam's brother and sees him in a whole different light than I do. Of course he's going to be on Liam's side.

"I need to go to the bathroom," I say suddenly. "I've been holding it for a while."

Zac eyes me with suspicion for a moment. "Alright," he concedes.

I turn and begin walking toward the bathroom, but Zac follows me, practically breathing down my neck.

I turn on him and scowl angrily. "Can a girl use the bathroom without you breathing fire down my neck? Damn."

Zac looks like he's going to refuse, but then he bites his lower lip and says, "You have two minutes."

I walk into the bathroom and slam the door. Then I look around, searching for an escape. *Now how am I going to get out of here?* There's a window above the sink, but it looks like it's too small to get my whole body through.

I sit on the toilet and think. I don't even get a second before Zac's banging on the door.

"Give me a fucking minute!" I yell.

Zac's muffled response comes through the door. "Hurry up!"

Shit. Shit. Shit. I'm looking, but there's no way out.

Unless I can drop ninety pounds in two minutes, I won't be getting out of that window.

"You've got ten seconds to come out of there, or I'm coming in."

Fucking A.

He quickly counts to ten and I don't budge.

"I'm not leaving, so you might as well come out," he growls.

I look around. There's no way out of here. I'm just wasting my time. Letting out a resigned sigh, I get up from the toilet and open the door.

"Feel better now?" Zac asks.

"Fuck off," I say. I brush past him, walk back over to the couch and flop down on it. I cross my arms over my chest and scowl. I'm so fucking pissed off. Why did this shit have to happen to me?

Zac walks over and sits back down in the recliner. He doesn't seem bothered by my nasty attitude in the least, and after studying me for a moment, he resumes watching the football game.

I sit there for about ten minutes, getting madder and madder, until I can take no more. "I'm just going to sleep," I announce, getting up.

Zac doesn't really react. I guess he's had it with my bitchiness. "Fine."

He gets up from his seat and escorts me to my room. I walk inside and am about to close the door when Zac says, "I know you're pissed off and all. And I really can't blame you. I think I would be too if I were in your position. But Liam really cares about you."

I roll my eyes. "Right. You were just calling me a diva. Now you're agreeing with me."

"Seriously," Zac says, ignoring my rudeness. "He

wouldn't be doing all this if you didn't mean anything to him."

I have no response. As much as I want to deny Zac's words, a small part of me wants to believe it's true. A small part of me wants to just give up the resistance and give Liam a chance.

It makes my heart hurt. It would be easy to fall back into his arms.

But I can't, I say to myself. *He's involved in crime... and I can't be with a criminal. He's dangerous.*

I stand there while Zac watches a range of emotions play across my face. He seems to be trying to reach out to me. Too bad I'm too angry and closed off to care. Or at least I'm doing a damn good job at pretending to be. I don't even know what's true anymore.

"Goodnight," Zac finally says softly. He can tell I'm preoccupied with my thoughts and conversation with me is all but useless. "Everything will turn out fine in the end. You'll see."

He gives me a moment to respond, but when I don't, he turns to leave.

Absently, I watch him walk off. And then I slowly shut the door. I look around the room, hellbent on finding a way out of here.

CHAPTER 25

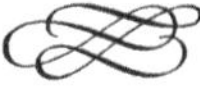

LIZZIE

God, I hope I don't fall and break my neck.

I peer out of the second story window of the bedroom. I've spent an hour debating on whether or not I want to do this. And I've decided that I do. It's a long way down to the sidewalk. But if I want to escape, I'm going to have to take my chances. Bad thing is, there's no real way down I can see other than jumping. I've been eyeing the gutters. I think they can hold my weight, and I can try to climb down.

Taking a deep breath, I climb out of the window, one leg at a time. It's so fucking cold. Outside, I hang on to the side of the window while I look for a way down. I can barely breathe. This is insane. It's fucking crazy, but I need to get away from this mess. I know I can't go home, but I can't stay here.

Holding my breath, I shimmy over to the gutter and grab hold. My fingertips hang on for dear life. My heart races and the chill in the air is actively working against me as it numbs my body. I breathe in deep and scoot over just a few inches, terrified that once I put my full weight on the gutter, it'll snap off. But it holds me. I finally breathe out, but only for a second before looking down. I close my eyes tighter. That was a mistake. It's a few more minutes before I can gather the courage to move in the slightest.

I prep myself to descend when I lose my footing. Shit! I gasp as I come close to plummeting to the ground. Luckily, I have a firm enough hold on the pipe that I save myself. I grip onto the gutter tighter than I have anything else in my entire life. Holy fuck, my heart is slamming in my chest and a cold sweat breaks out over my skin. This was so stupid. I wish I could take it back. I look up and think for a second about going back in there. But then I'm sentencing myself to be a prisoner. And I will not let that happen.

After a moment of deep breathing, I slowly restart my descent down. One inch at a time. That's all I need. I can barely breathe, but I keep moving down. By the time I reach the bottom, my arms are sore and my shoulders are throbbing. But I made it. And that's all that matters. I stand on shaky legs and look up. I can't believe I just did that.

I step away from the pipe and I look at the house, still feeling slightly sick to my stomach. Through the window I can see the foyer and the stairs. The living room is on the other side of the house, so there's no way Zac could see I've escaped. I'm sure he's watching TV with the football game on and Zac reclining in the chair, his eyes glued to the screen.

Take that, Zac! I shout in my mind.

I wonder what Liam is going to say to his brother when he finds out that I escaped under his watch. Fuck, that's not going to be pretty. A feeling of guilt starts to settle low in my stomach. But I shake it off. I shouldn't feel guilty. The danger Liam put me in is unforgivable. I have to repeat that over and over in my head as if I'm trying to convince myself.

I turn away and start walking down the street. There are woods straight ahead. I just need to sneak in there and then I can figure out a plan. I know it'd be stupid to just walk out of the neighborhood. Liam could come home any minute and see me, and then all of this would be a waste.

I can't let him catch me. As I make it up the block, I take out my cell phone. I begin to dial the police, but then stop.

Obviously, those thugs need to go to jail, but if I call the police, there's a real possibility that Liam might, too. He will. Fuck! I know he will. I don't know why this bothers me. Liam's a criminal. He should go to jail. But I can't stomach the thought. I may not be able to stay with him, but I don't want anything bad for him. I don't want to hurt him or get him into trouble. I can't go home though. I'm not safe, and I'm on my own. I'm going to have to call the police. What choice do I have?

I'm vaguely aware of a white car driving toward me. I look up with my heart hammering in my chest, but with a brief glance, I see it's not Liam. I try to stay calm and just keep walking. The woods are past a few houses. I just need to get past them and then I'll be safe. The slam of a door pierces my consciousness and I jump with surprise, dropping my phone. It hits the ground with a loud smack.

I turn around and the car's parked in the middle of the street. I can't tear my eyes away from the man behind me. He's got his eyes pinned on me as he walks away from his car. My heart hammers in my chest and I know something's wrong. His eyes are so dark, nearly black, and the way he's looking at me sends chills down my body. I don't even try to pick up my phone as he takes a single step toward me. I take off running.

I hear him curse under his breath and then the thudding stomps of him chasing me. My eyes widen with shock. Holy fuck! He's coming for me. My mind races with ideas of who this man could be. He could be Liam's guy, parked out here to make sure I didn't get away. But he looks... cruel. He could be the man who shot at us. I want to scream, but my voice won't work. Fear cripples me, but I'm able to run. I can't stop running. Tears stream down my face from the sheer chill of the air battering my eyes as I run. I pump my arms and force myself to run as fast as I can.

My heart jumps up my throat and I bolt to the closest house. My limbs scream with pain as I do everything I can to get away.

Without waiting to see if he's going to stop, I take off into the closest backyard, my heart pounding in my chest like a battering ram. I run faster than I ever have in my life. I can hear him still behind me, but I think I'm gaining ground. His breath is ragged. My own breath is coming in harsh pants. It hurts like a bitch to breathe in the cold air. But I ignore it all, darting into the woods.

I run straight through thin branches that whip across my body like lashings. I don't care though. I keep running through the pain.

After a few more minutes of all-out sprinting, I stop in a copse of trees to catch my breath and look around quickly. I don't see him. I listen for any noise, but I can't hear a thing. I focus on being as quiet as possible and listening. My back is to the tree and I'm too terrified to peek around it. Minutes pass. I don't know how many, before I take a look. No one's here. He's gone.

I sigh with slight relief, although I'm still trembling with fear and my heart is beating mercilessly against my chest. And then I remember. I dropped my phone. Shit. I have nothing. Fuck! I can't go back home, I don't have a car, I don't have my phone. I check my back pocket where I shoved the extra money Liam gave me earlier. At least I have those still. They're hanging out of my pocket though. I check and see I still have them all as my breathing calms down. I lean my back against the tree again, this time for support rather than to hide behind it.

I look back again with paranoia, but no one's there. He was coming for us. No, he could be someone Liam knows or hired. I want to believe that. But I don't think it's true. My mind runs wild with all the possibilities of who he is and what he wants. I don't know, but the idea that he's going to kill one of them makes me want to run back there and warn Zac. Fuck! I can't even call Liam to warn him.

Shit, I don't know what to do. I feel so confused and hopeless. I shake my head and swallow the lump in my throat. I can't go back there. Even if I wanted to. What if he's there waiting for me?

This is Liam's life, and it's a dangerous one. I can't be a part of this. That man is the nail in the coffin. My heart clenches in my chest, but I refuse to give that pain any more attention. I take one more last look over my shoulder and then cautiously move through the woods. I don't have much money on me, but it should be enough for at least one night in some cheap hotel. I can't go back to Liam and I can't go anywhere he could find me. I wish I could go to Nat, but that would only bring trouble to her doorstep. I can't do that to her.

I need to find a hiding place where I can think about what my options are. Although I feel like I don't have a single fucking option, other than calling the police.

CHAPTER 26

LIAM

I know something's wrong the second I walk into the house. I close the door and look up the stairs.

Zac runs down them and his face falls as he slows down and sees it's me that's walked through the door. He's holding onto the railing like it's the only thing keeping him upright.

"What's wrong?" I ask him. He doesn't answer, he just looks at me and then the door. "Zac!" I yell his name to get his eyes on me. "What the fuck is wrong?"

He swallows visibly. "I just went to check on her." My body tenses as he pauses but then continues nervously, "Her window's open."

"She left?" I ask him. I'm surprised by how even my voice is. Inside I feel like a caged animal only barely contained ready to destroy anything it can. But on the surface, I'm still and in control.

"She's," he pauses and takes in an unsteady breath as he registers my anger, "she's gone."

I'm so fucking pissed that he let her go. I storm off into

the next room. I can't deny part of that anger is at her. She's putting herself in danger. It's also a mix of other emotions. *She left me*. My body tenses and the need to take it out on something is strong. Zac is looking like a good fucking option, but I keep my distance so I don't beat the shit out of him. I'll find her ass and drag her back here kicking and screaming if I have to.

I reach for my phone to call her and snort when I see her number calling me. I'm gonna lay into her. She can't fucking run off. She might be mad at me and that's fine if she wants to hate me for a little while, but she's staying with me, whether she likes it or not.

"Where are you?" I get right to the point as soon as I answer.

"I got a call about Stephen this morning. Message received, Liam?" I recognize Ian's voice immediately. Chills prick over my skin. It was her number. My heart beats rapidly, thudding against my chest plate. I know I saw her name.

"Ian," I answer simply, keeping my voice even as a cold sweat breaks out along every inch of my skin.

"We've got your girl here," he says confidently. My heart stops and I lean against the wall as my legs give out. No, not Elle. I swallow the thick lump that's growing in my throat and trying to suffocate me.

"I wanna hear her," I push the words out. Zac comes into the room and gives me a confused look. I feel sick to my stomach. I can't look at him. This can't be true.

"Sorry, but I can't; her mouth's full right now," he says and gives a disgusting laugh. I pound my fist against the wall in anger. Rage and adrenaline course through my blood. "How's this, we'll send a finger every hour until you fucks pay me the money you stole from me and shut down your business."

"Don't you fucking touch her!" Zac's face goes white as he takes in what's going on. I'm so fucking angry, my body's shaking.

"Come to Thirty-Five Lakeview," he says, and I try to hold in my rage so I can hear what he's saying. I know the place well; it's where they do their meets. "No weapons. We'll do a trade. You for her."

I can't hear a damn thing after the click, it's all white noise.

I look down at my cell again, it was definitely her number. They got her. They have my girl. I try to breathe, but it's hard. All at once, I snap out of it and the only thing on my mind is that I know I need to save her. I have to go to her. I have no other choice.

"Where's Tyler?" I barely recognize my own voice. Both of us were out looking for that asshole this morning. After Stephen shows up dead and Ian being left all on his own, I figured he would be planning his leave. I was wrong. I was so fucking wrong. And it cost me the one thing I care about. I can hardly breathe.

"He's still upstate." Fuck! I grip my head in my hands. He's hours away, searching out Dracho's family homes. He's fucking useless to me now. I don't have time to wait for him to drive back down here.

"I'm sorry, Liam," Zac says but he can't even look me in the eyes. He tries to and his voice cracks as he continues, "I didn't--"

"It's not your fault." My blood won't heat. My lungs won't work. My body's failing me. He has her. I can't let him hurt her. Before I can even think about what I'm doing, my body's moving.

"Don't go, Liam! It's obviously a setup." Zac's talking, but I brush past him and keep moving. "He hasn't showed proof of life; she could already be dead. You think he's going to leave witnesses?" Zac grabs my arm and tries to hold me back. But I rip it out of his grasp and move quickly to the front door.

I don't even listen to his words. I don't care if he's right. They have her. They have my girl. I won't let them touch her. I won't let her die for my sins.

Zac's screaming at me, trying to talk sense into me. But I don't even register a single word coming out of his mouth. He grabs my chest, wrapping his arms around me to keep me back. He's smaller than me though. There's no way he can stop me.

"You can't keep me from her, Zac." I'll trade my life for hers; it's done.

I snatch my keys off the front entry table and turn around, punching my brother square in the jaw. It's hard enough that he's knocked to the ground as his head slams against the floor.

He slowly comes to and cups his chin in his hand on the floor. He starts to get up, reaching for me. He's gonna do everything he can to keep me from going.

I take off before he gets up. I slam my car door shut as he comes barreling out the house, screaming for me to stop.

As the tires squeal and the car propels me forward, I see my brother racing to get to me in my rearview, screaming not to go. Screaming that he's sorry.

I drive faster than he can run and ignore the pain in my chest of leaving him this way.

I hate that I drove off without saying goodbye, but he'd never let me leave. I hate that he blames himself. He may always carry this with him. It's not his fault though. I don't blame him. All of this is my fault. I have to go to her. I have to save her.

CHAPTER 27

LIZZIE

What do I do?

I'm sitting in my new hiding place, a rat-infested Motel 6 in a rundown part of town, wondering how to plan my next move. For the past thirty minutes I've been mulling over whether I should call the cops or not. It should be an easy thing to do, but my feelings for Liam are getting in the way.

There's gotta be a way to get rid of these guys without involving Liam, I think. But I can't think of any. I need to look out for me. I'm the one person I need to worry about. I can't stay here. I can't hide forever. But damn it, every time I press the buttons into the phone I feel like I'm literally stabbing Liam in the back. It's bad enough that I left him.

If only I didn't care about him. Then it would all be so easy. I'd dial up 911 without even thinking.

Maybe I should call him, I think to myself, *tell him it's over and explain that I have to call the police. I need protection, and I don't want it from him.*

I pick up the hotel's landline and dial Liam's cell. It rings for several seconds and then his voicemail picks up.

You've reached Liam. I'm busy right now, but if you leave your name and message I'll get back to you as soon as possible. Beep.

I sit there with the phone pressed to my ear for a moment and then hang up. God. Just hearing his deep voice again makes me feel weak. After a moment, I decide to try his house phone.

I get his voicemail again. When the beep comes, I've summoned the courage for a message.

"Liam," I say heavily over the huge lump in my throat. "I'm sorry. I didn't want to leave, but I just can't deal with what's going on. I can't be with... someone like you." I feel like a bitch for saying that. I close my eyes and hate myself. "I'm so sorry, Liam," I sob. "I really did love you, but this shit you're involved in... I can't. Goodbye." Feeling like my heart is going to burst, I hang up the phone.

I'm about to break down when the phone rings. I stare at it, wondering what I should do. It has to be Liam calling back. I'm conflicted about answering it. I'm supposed to be breaking it off with him and figuring out how to keep myself safe, not making it harder.

Screw it. I have to hear him out. I can already feel myself crawling back to him.

Taking a deep breath, I snatch up the phone. "Hello?" I say as my voice wavers.

"Lizzie!" My heart drops into my stomach. It's Zac.

"What do you want, Zac?" I ask flatly, pushing all the conflicting emotions away.

"Lizzie, are you alright?" Zac asks concernedly. I'm surprised by the worry in his voice. Apparently he's not pissed about me escaping right under his nose. "They don't have you, do they? Liam's going there now." His voice rises, "It's a setup; they're going to kill him."

Fear cripples me and my body chills. "What the hell are you talking about?"

My heart skips a beat. What the hell is going on? Liam's in danger? My body inches forward on its own. I grip the cord in my hand and wait with bated breath. "Where is he?" I cry, panicking. I rise from the bed as anxiety runs through me.

Zac quickly tells me what's happened, and I feel absolutely sick to my stomach. I listen to him anxiously until he's finished.

"We have to the call the police." I should've called already. If I'd called them, maybe this wouldn't be happening. This is all my fault. I never should've left. I cover my mouth with my hand, feeling like I'm going to throw up. If I hadn't left, he wouldn't be driving to his execution right now.

"No! Lizzie, don't--" Zac sounds frantic. I feel overwhelmed with heat and anxiety and not knowing what I should do, but knowing I need to do something. And I need to do it fast.

I'm about to hang up on Zac and call the cops when I realize that Liam's location is close by. Only a few blocks away. "I'll get to him; I'll stop him," I say as I begin to hang up the phone.

"Lizzie?" Zac sounds panicked. "Lizzie, what are you doing? Lizzie I need you to stay put--"

I hang up the phone, my mind and heart racing, and run my fingers through my hair. I'm shaking. My entire body is laced with anxiety.

I can't let Liam die. He's so close, and he's in danger all because of me.

Really though, what can I do? I'm an unarmed woman

who's frightened out of her mind. I would be of no use to Liam in a gunfight. I'd probably only end up getting myself killed. I don't even have a gun.

But I can't let Liam die for me. Not after all we've been through. I don't care about anything other than saving him. I have to do something. I love him. It would kill me if he died. I can't let it happen.

I quickly grab my coat and put it on as I walk as fast as possible to the lobby. I nearly trip on the stairs; my feet just won't move fast enough. I need a taxi or something. I don't know. I need help. He needs help!

I walk out into the parking lot, where the bitter cold smacks me in the face. I search the street for a taxi or a street sign at least so I know which way to run when I see a car idling. Someone left it there to warm up. The keys are right there. I bite down on my lip and silently send a prayer of thanks.

My heart sputters. I wait half a second before I commit the first crime in my entire life and hop into the driver's seat. I slam the door shut and hit the gas. I don't look in the rearview mirror, I just drive, tires squealing as I turn out of the parking lot and onto the snow-dusted road. The back tires slip, and my breath catches in my throat. I struggle to put on the seat belt and keep the car going at the same time.

I can't fucking get into an accident. I swallow thickly and try to calm down and think of a plan.

I need to go to him. I need to save him.

I can't let him die.

CHAPTER 28

LIAM

My heart's pounding in my chest. But it's so slow. Everything is slow. It's like I'm seeing everything differently now.

Ian's a piece of shit and I know he wants me dead. I know there's a possibility that he's gonna kill me as soon as I get there. But if he's got my girl, I have to try to save her. I'm not positive that he'll let her go. But I have no other options. If I don't go, she's dead. And I can't let that happen.

I can't let her die because of me. I'll never forgive myself. I look at the gun in the passenger seat as I slow down at the red light. I'm almost there. Maybe ten minutes, just a few blocks away. I'm resisting the urge to drive over the curb and push the pedal to the floor. But I can't get on a cop's radar. If I get pulled over, or worse, taken in, she's dead.

My hands are sweaty and I have to rub them off on my jeans before gripping the steering wheel again. The gun is the only thing on my mind. If I go in there with it, they'll probably find it and take it from me. If I were them, I'd check me. I wanna be protected, in case he goes back on his word, but they may see it and kill her. He said no weapons.

I slowly push the pedal down and the car moves. I'm driving to my death. But it's for her. I have to. I breathe out deeply. If there's a way to save us both, I'll do it. But if not, I'll die for her. I'll happily give my life to keep her safe.

My phone starts buzzing in my pocket. I only look to see if it's Ian. It's not her number. My brother keeps calling, but I can't answer. I know he's not on board with this plan. He'll hate me for leaving him like this. He doesn't understand. But when he finds someone he loves, he'll get it. He'll forgive me one day. And he promised to take care of her, that's what matters. My heart shatters in my chest. My phone won't stop going off. It's vibrating on my lap, and this time when I look it's my brother, but calling from my landline at 22 Wyoming. I bet he's trying different numbers, and I can't blame him. He just wants to convince me not to go. But it's not happening.

"I'm sorry," I say to no one as the phone stops ringing. I'm only a few blocks away. My resolve is firm.

I loved her before I even met her. I can't let her die.

This was all meant to happen. I couldn't save my father or Richard, but I can save her.

It'll be the one good thing I've ever done with my life.

CHAPTER 29

LIZZIE

I put the pedal to the metal, running red lights and turning right on left turns and doing all sorts of crazy shit on my way to intercept Liam. I'm risking being stopped by the police, but I don't give a damn. I can't let anything happen to Liam. I can't afford to lose another person I love.

If I don't get there fast enough, I think worriedly, *they'll kill him. Why else would they tell him they have me? He has to know it's a setup.*

My heart pounds as I speed around a right corner, and my mind races through gruesome scenarios. I'm scared of what I might find when I find Liam. Will they have already gotten to him?

If they do, it will be all my fault. Fuck, I can't stand the thought. I feel so sick. I should've just listened to him.

It's hard to keep myself together and drive at the same time, but I'm doing it. I'm barely holding on, but I am.

I reach an intersection close to where Liam's supposed to be going. I know I'm going the right way. I know what road Zac said, and I'm close. I'm so close.

I have to slam on my brakes and stop at a red light because there's too much traffic. The tires slip on the slick road, but I manage to maintain control and avoid a collision. I slam my fist on the dash, hating that I have to waste even a second. Then I look all around, making sure I'm not missing anything.

Suddenly, I see Liam's car speeding up from the side road. Liam! Hope rises in my chest. He's alive. He's right there! "Liam!" I scream out even though there's no way he could hear me. I bang on the horn, over and over. I lay all my weight on it. Staring at him. Begging him to look at me.

But he doesn't. Everyone around me is watching. They don't know. He's about to drive to his death, and I'm stuck watching him, unable to do anything about it. No! I honk again and again as he gets closer to the intersection. But he's not seeing me. He's not looking anywhere but straight ahead.

With how fast he's going I'm sure he won't see me. I can't let him pass.

With only seconds to react, I floor the gas pedal and smack into the car ahead of me. I push down hard, shoving the car out of my way as my own car jolts forward. I hear the screams and honking from the other drivers gathered at the red light. They're yelling and pissed, but I don't care. Faster! I have to go faster. He's so close. He's almost at the intersection in front of me. I slam on the gas and head out into the middle of the intersection just as Liam comes speeding through the center.

I know the meet is right there. If I don't do this, I won't be able to get to him in time. We're both going too fast. I speed my car ahead and close my eyes, knowing he's going to hit my car on the passenger side. But it's the only way I can stop him. I lay on the horn and speed my car right in front of his and I prepare my body for the blow.

The screech of metal and shattering glass is deafening as he broadsides me, spinning my car out of control. My body's forced to the right with a stinging pain from the seat belt. My head's violently whipped to the side as the car comes to a halt and I slam my head on the driver's window with a loud crack.

Fuck! That hurt. As the car comes to a sudden stop, I wince and slowly lift my hand to my head. I look down at my fingers and see blood.

My body aches all over, and there's a sharp, stabbing pain in my side. A pounding sensation throbs inside of my skull, causing black spots in front of my vision.

I feel like absolute shit.

"Liam," I call weakly. He's the only thing I care about. I'm so dizzy and can barely see anything, but I can't think about anything other than Liam.

"Liam," I repeat in a half-choke, half-cry. *Please don't be dead.* My heart beats faster as I try looking out my shattered windshield.

Groaning, I fumble with my seat belt, trying my best to undo it, but it's stuck. I have to get out of here. Now. But I feel so fucking weak.

For a moment I fear I'll get stuck in the car and get burned alive. In a panic, I start rattling my seat belt, hoping it will just loosen. It doesn't unsnap. Fuck.

Suddenly, my door is being ripped open and a deep, familiar voice asks, "Elle?" His voice is full of worry, but also disbelief.

Relief floods my body at the sight of Liam. He looks bruised and battered with a few cuts on his face and arms, but other than that, I've never seen him look so damned good in my life.

"Liam, don't go!" I yell at him, shaking my head.

"You're here," he says as he looks at me with utter disbelief before looking down at where I'm trying desperately to get the buckle undone. I need to get out of this fucking car and hold him. He's really okay.

Without hesitation, Liam bends into the car and rips my seat belt off. Then he pulls me out and into his arms. I hold on to him even though my body is screaming in pain. I just need to hold him.

He squeezes me gently. I feel like I can finally breathe. I grip on to him tighter, refusing to let go as he kisses me over and over again. "I'm so sorry," I whisper against his chest.

Liam hugs me close again. "Jesus, Elle." He pulls back to look at me. "Are you okay?"

I shake my head. "You were going to die." I hold him closer and just try to breathe. "You were going to die for me?" I pull back to look at him. His fingers gently touch the gash on my scalp.

Liam peers at me with disbelief. "I would do anything for you. I love you, Elle."

My eyes prick with tears at the admission. "I love you so much."

Hot tears begin streaming down my face like a waterfall and the words start gushing out. "Oh my God, I'm so sorry that I left you. I wasn't thinking. I was just so... so scared." The words tumble out of my mouth. I shake my head, wishing none of it were true. If I'd just listened to him, none of this would have happened.

Liam kisses me on the forehead, pulling me close. "It's okay. You're okay, that's all that matters."

I look up at him, my heart clenched tight, needing his forgiveness. I know this is all my fault. "Please forgive me."

Liam gently caresses my tearstained cheeks and shakes

his head. "I can't forgive you, Elle." My breath catches in my throat, and I feel tears welling up again in my eyes. I've ruined things between us. It's too late.

"I can't forgive you, because you haven't done anything wrong." He kisses me then, a deep, long lingering kiss that leaves me wanting for more. When he pulls away I'm breathless, and in pain. The car crash has banged me up pretty good.

"We need to go before the cops show up," he says urgently.

I look around, and people are stopped at street corners staring at us and taking pictures with their cell phones. Some are even on their phones, talking while surveying the devastation. Cars are starting to pile up as they try to maneuver past the wreck.

"Shit! Get down!" Liam suddenly yells, yanking me to the ground just as I was starting to stand, and pulling us close to the open driver's door. I get a quick glimpse and see the man from before, the man with the cold, dark eyes. My heart hammers in my chest. My body feels paralyzed.

The crack of gunfire splits the air and I let out a piercing scream as another whizzes by us and hits Liam's car behind me. Immediately, Liam pushes me against the car and covers me with his hard body, sandwiching me between hard metal and his protection. So many people are screaming and running. I close my eyes tightly as my heart leaps in my chest.

Oh my God, I think, frozen with terror. *We're going to die.* My fingers dig into him, holding on as tight as I can as my body tries to curl into a ball. The cold wind travels beneath the open door. We hardly have any cover.

Another gunshot fires off and I can't help that my body jolts with the loud bang of the bullets plastering the car. Liam continues to shield me and I wish I could protect him. I can't bear the thought of him being hit. Each second that passes seems like an eternity, but finally the gunfire ceases.

Liam immediately goes into action. He rolls off of me, staying crouched down.

"Get in your car and drive!" Liam orders, keeping his eyes focused ahead, looking for the target.

I hesitate, worrying about what's going to happen to him.

Liam gestures sharply, his face twisting in anger at my hesitation. "Go! I'll cover for you. You need to get out of here!"

"You can't stay here!" I protest just as three more gunshots go off. I wince and duck down out of instinct. My heart can't take this. I'm so fucking scared, I'm shaking.

Liam peeks over the hood of the car. "Don't worry about me. I'll be fine." When I don't budge, he reaches into his pocket and brings out his cell. He taps the screen, speed-dialing someone.

"Zac, where are you?" Liam asks. "Yeah. We're on South Street. Yeah. Bring heat." He takes the phone from his ear and looks at me. "I'm going to be fine, Zac." He cups my face in his hands. "You don't have to worry about me."

I stare into his eyes and all I see there is love. I can't leave him. I won't! "Please, I can't do this right now," I croak. "I need you."

Liam shakes his head angrily. "Get in the car! Now."

"No!" I yell, shaking. "I'm not leaving without you." *If something happens to you, I won't be able to live with myself.*

"Fuck," Liam growls. He brings the phone back to his ear and says, "Zac, don't come. I'm leaving with Elle... Yeah, I have to get it. I'm not gonna leave without trying to take him out." He hangs up and pockets the phone.

"Stay here and don't move," he says sternly and quickly crouches down and goes to his car that's just behind mine.

"No!" I yell out and try to reach for him, but he's gone before I can get to him. He's completely unprotected for the briefest of moments, but I can't stand that he's putting himself in danger. I think about losing the cover of the door and trying to follow him, but I feel his body slam against the back of the car, before I can move.

He comes back with a gun and cocks it. "Get in."

I'm so fucking scared, but I do as he says. Keeping low, I climb in and crawl to the passenger seat. Another bullet hits the car and I stifle my scream.

"Keep your head down," Liam orders, starting the car while keeping his head low. As if in response to his order, several bullets come flying through the windshield, raining glass on my head.

I cry out, my heart beating so fast it feels like it's going to explode. Small shards of glass cover the seat and my body. I pull the sleeves of my sweater over my hands for protection. The sounds of sirens wail in the distance and I feel a moment of relief. The cops are coming.

"I won't let him live." Liam say, making my body chill. He responds to the gunshots with a few shots of his own. *Bang*! *Bang*! *Bang*! I hear someone yell something, but I can't make out what it is. It's so quiet now. All I can hear is my own breathing. I steal a glance over at Liam; he looks so intense; he doesn't even look like he's breathing. I jump when he fires off two more shots. I hear a short cry and then nothing.

Liam finally sits up and looks behind us as he puts the car into reverse and hits the gas. We hit his car and then he puts the car in drive and takes off.

A few precious moments of silence pass as the car takes

off. I'm still low and Liam's still tense. “Did you get him?” I finally ask, my heart still racing.

Liam looks at me, dropping the gun in his lap.

“Yeah,” Liam replies, “I got him.” He puts his hand down for me to grab, still keeping his eyes on the road. I slowly rise and look around as Liam pulls off into a neighborhood. “It was only him. It's done.” My body eases slightly. “It's over.” He says with finality.

I struggle to believe it's true and to know what to say. We drive in silence. *It's over.*

“We gotta ditch this car.” He looks at me with sympathy in his eyes.

I can hardly breathe. This doesn't feel real.

“Hey,” Liam says, holding my hand. “It's okay now.”

It doesn't feel okay though. I'm still shaking.

The car slows a few blocks down, and Liam shuts down the engine. He looks over at me, his jaw clenched. “Promise me.” He pauses a moment to take in a deep breath. “Promise me that you'll never do something so stupid again.” His voice is hard, cold, nothing like what I expect from the heated look in his eyes.

Tears pool in my eyes. He seemed okay when we were getting shot at, now he's acting like he's pissed at me. “I told you why I did--”

“You left me,” he growls. “You left me when you knew you were in danger.”

“But,” I begin to protest, but I can't think of any words. I'm so overwhelmed, and I know at the time it had felt like the right thing to do.

“I don't want to hear it,” he says sharply. “Tell me right now that you'll never do that again. Ever.” I'm shocked by the anger in Liam's voice, and I stare at him with my mouth open. Then it slowly dawns on me; he's scared. He's so scared he was going to lose me. He's literally shaking.

He reaches across and strokes my injured face. "You don't know how much you mean to me, Elle," he tells me. "If something had happened to you..." His voice trails off, and on his face is a pained expression.

I swallow the lump that forms in my throat. "I'm sorry, Liam. I promise you. I'll never do that again."

He leans across the console and kisses me. I easily part my lips and kiss him back with the same passion he has for me.

He pulls away from me and looks into my eyes. My heart's racing, and everything feels like it's too much to handle.

"This--" Liam begins to say, as he must sense the worries I have. "This will never happen again. This isn't okay, and this isn't normal."

I search his eyes. "I've never lied to you, Elle." I part my lips to protest that bullshit, but he puts his finger up to my lips and continues, "I've kept the truth from you, but I've never lied. And I promise you this. I fucking love you, and I will never let anything like this happen again."

I don't know what to think, or what to say. All I know is what I feel. And right now all I feel for him is love. I don't trust it though. I feel stupid for even being with a man like him.

"I'm done with this shit. I'm completely done. All I want is you. I will do anything and everything to have you and to keep you safe." Something shifts inside of me. As if those were the words I was waiting for.

"Just stay with me." He says as his thumb brushes over my lips. "I'll always protect you, and I know with everything in me that I love you. Just stay with me and let me be there for you."

It's so easy to give in, and I want to. I lean into his hand

and close my eyes as I nod my head. I can be with this man. I know it in my heart. He was going to die for me. If that's not true love, I don't know what is.

"I will." I open my eyes and see nothing but devotion in his. "I love you too, Liam."

CHAPTER 30

LIAM

She's barely said a word since I've brought her back. I expected her to demand I take her back to her place, but instead she keeps looking over at me with worry in her eyes. Like she can't believe we're really safe.

"You still mad at me?" Zac asks her. The three of us are in my living room. I know the cops are going to show up at some point. They'll probably have a warrant too since my car was at the scene of the crime, and there's probably witnesses who saw me. It's alright though. My uncle's still got contacts, and I'm sure I'll get off without a hitch. Until they get here though, I'm going to be on edge.

"I'm not mad at you," Elle finally answers. Her voice is small and lacking the bite she usually has. She hasn't eaten anything. I know she's still rattled from everything that happened. I wish I could take it all back.

"Then play some cards with me," Zac offers, holding up a deck. We were playing earlier to pass the time and help Elle get out of her funk. She's not used to this, but she doesn't ever need to get used to it. I swear I'll never let this kind of thing ever happen again.

Elle narrows her eyes at Zac before responding, "You're a filthy cheater." Zac laughs and I let out a chuckle, pulling her closer to me on the sofa.

"You're a poor loser," Zac says, setting the cards down on the table.

We've got the news on, but other than a little snippet earlier, there's nothing about what happened. Ian Dracho is dead. I already knew he was, but seeing it on the television made Elle relax somewhat. I shot that fucker right between his eyes and then his throat. I've never felt so much relief in my entire life. I remember how tense I was, waiting with slow and steady breaths. I just needed him to come up so I could take another shot. Although it was only seconds, the time passed so damn slow waiting for my target to show himself.

I shake off the tension creeping up on me and look down at Elle. I have to tell her everything. I promised her I would. I know she's not going to like it, because it's not pretty, but hopefully it'll earn her trust.

"You okay?" I ask Elle quietly as Zac gets up and leaves the room.

"I'm scared, Liam," she whispers back, and I kiss the tip of her nose and push the hair out of her face.

"There's no reason to be scared." I give her a small smile. "I know it's gonna take a little while before all that shit gets out of your system, but I swear to you, it's all over. Everything's okay."

She searches my face for something, and whatever it is, I hope she finds it. She settles into my lap and puts her cheek against my chest.

"You belong here, Elle." I kiss the top of her head. "You belong with me."

She huffs a small laugh and gives me the faintest of smiles. "Yeah, I do."

"You know I love you, right? And that I'm really sorry." I say the words with every ounce of sincerity I have. I hope she knows it's true. I can't do anything but keep telling her and showing her until she believes me.

"I know," she says as she leans up and plants a kiss on my lips. "I love you, too."

* * *

Two weeks later

ELLE'S FINALLY COMING AROUND. At first she was hardly talking to me. But she wouldn't let go of me. She wouldn't let me out of her sight. Everything was cleared with the cops; I got off easy, no charges. My uncle came through with his connections. I told my brother and my cousin that I was out and they agreed it was for the best. Even after all that, she still looked at me like I was gonna be killed any second.

I'll earn her trust again. And to do that, I'm starting with this move. I'll live an honest life with her. I know she loves me and I love her, so the rest will come with time.

I'm moving in with her. Technically it's to a new place, but it was her choice, a place close to her school. Just for five months until she's done, then her ass is coming home. I may not be working with my family anymore, but I want to be by them. And so does she.

She wants to work in a school, so there's plenty of jobs for her when we move back here. And she wants to come back. Which makes me happy. She doesn't have any family, but I do and I don't want to leave them.

Not now.

I want as much family around us as we can get. And as soon as she's ready and trusts me again, I'm gonna do right by her and put a ring on her finger. I don't care if this is fast and it's only been a couple of months. What we've been through is hard, but we did it together. I need her, and she needs me. That's all that matters.

I look around my bedroom and make sure I've got everything packed.

I do, everything's all set. Except for the letter. I've held onto it. But I haven't been able to give it to her. I take a deep breath and slip it out of the envelope. We're moving forward with our lives and I want her to see for herself what her old man was thinking. She should know.

I take deliberate steps to where Elle's standing in the kitchen.

"Hey Elle," I say and lean in to kiss her cheek. "You ready to read it?" I ask.

She looks at the note and a flash of sadness crosses her eyes as she registers what it is. She gives me a small nod. "You said he reminded you of your dad?" she asks as she walks toward me. The reminder makes my heart pang.

"Yeah, a little," I admit.

"I'm sorry." She cups my face in her hands and plants a kiss on my lips. "I'm sorry, Liam." She holds my gaze and I look back at her, not knowing what to say. It was so long ago, but it does hurt from time to time still. I kiss her on the lips and pull her closer to me. I just wanna hold her. That makes everything feel better. Having her to love makes the pain go away somehow.

I sit at the small table in the kitchen and wait for her to take a seat on my lap. I kiss her cheek, but it doesn't help. She still gets a little sad whenever her old man comes up. I can't blame her. It's gonna take time.

Her hand rests on my shoulder and she leans in, resting her cheek against my chest.

I shake the letter out and hold it so she can easily read it, too. I know this is gonna be hard for her. But I'm here. We'll get through this together.

CHAPTER 31

LIZZIE

"I can't believe how well business is doing!" Nat cries as she sets out another fresh batch of her infamous sugar cookies.

Since it's the day before I leave, I figured I'd come spend time with Nat before I say goodbye. I feel like myself again, most of the time. When I'm with Nat, it's easier. She brings out the old me.

Only when I arrived, I found Nat swamped with customers. I offered to help Nat keep up with the demand. Unfortunately, it took just a few minutes of being bossed around before I wanted to strangle her.

Luckily for me, Nat's two new hires came in to help, April and Haley, and they're busy running the cash register and filling the orders, allowing us a moment to chat in the back and catch up on each other's lives.

"I can," I say, fighting back the urge to snatch one of the fresh cookies off the tray. They smell damn delicious and it's hard to keep my eyes off of them. Seriously, I could eat the entire batch by myself right now! Ever since making up with Liam, my appetite has returned in full force. I think

I've put on a good ten pounds and even have my voluptuous figure back. "Have you tasted your cookies lately? They're out of this world amazing!"

Nat grins at me as she gently prods one of the cookies to test its softness. "You're such a suck-up, you know that?"

I wink at her. "Why wouldn't I be? After all, you're like the town's queen of baking."

Nat pokes another one of her cookies and snorts. "Goddess of baking is more like it. Hell, I should have my own show on the Food Network with all the work I put in."

I raise an eyebrow. "My my, modest, aren't we?"

Nat laughs. "I'm just playing. You know I don't have a big head like that."

I nod, my stomach growling. I can't stop eyeing those delicious cookies. A second longer, and I'm going to need handcuffs. "Mmmhmm. Sure. Anything you say. Just wait until you expand and open up your next bakery. Then you'll probably fall over from the weight of your head."

Nat laughs. Then she groans. "Ugh. Don't tell me about it. I was already looking at my balance sheet the other day and realizing I'll have this paid off by the end of the year, which will give me room to expand if I want." She sighs. "I've already started stressing out, staking out prime locations for a new shop in the town over."

"Take it slow," I advise, still staring at those damn cookies. "Don't worry about that until it gets here. You have all the time in the world to enjoy the success you're having now." Screw it! I can't take it anymore. I take one of Nat's cookies and pop it in my mouth. The rich, delicious sweetness invades my taste buds, and my eyes roll back in my head at the taste. God, so good.

Nat glowers at my theft, but deep down I know she loves that I can't keep my hands off her cookies. It's the hallmark of a grandmaster baker. "You know what? You're right. Speaking of which, how are things with you and Liam?"

I pause, my heart fluttering in my chest at the thought of Liam. He's been the best lately, renting out the perfect place for us while I'm going to school, and doing what he can to make my life easier. It warms my heart, because it means he cares, and he's trying to make up for everything that went down. Still, I feel guilty about him paying for everything, but he insists not to worry about it. He says I'd do the same for him if I were in his position. And I would.

I can hardly contain the smile on my face as I finish off the delicious morsel. "They're good." *More than good.* I told Nat about Liam the other day. A little more than I should have, I think. I even included Liam's dad dying, him staying with his uncle and how he's a bookie. I probably shouldn't have said anything about the business. But Liam keeps saying it's legal. And he's quitting. For me. That's the only reason I told her. I pop another delicious cookie in my mouth to keep in all the other details that have been dying to come out. She doesn't need to know about everything that happened. No one does. I want to forget it all and pretend like those few nights never existed.

Nat's eyes flash dangerously at my bold theft, and I hold in a laugh. "I don't know Liz, isn't this rather fast to be doing all this?" she asks, watching me gobble down the cookie. "After what happened, I'm kind of worried about you."

"Don't be," I say. "I know it's only been two months, but Liam and I… We've really gotten to know each other." It's hard to put into words what I feel. I feel like he's my soul mate. Nat would have to find her own to understand.

Nat doesn't look totally reassured as she says, "I hope so."

Then she asks, "But what's he going to do while you're at school?"

"A lot!" I say excitedly, momentarily forgetting the tray of cookies. I've been dying to tell her of Liam's plans to build up his investments.

"Well, he's got enough cash flow to invest in a few companies." He told me he loved the restaurant, but he didn't want another. Something about numbers and return on investments. I didn't quite keep up with what he was saying, but he was excited to tell me about the other companies.

Nat makes a surprised face when I'm done. "That's odd."

"What?" I ask.

"With how hot Liam is, I'd thought he'd have shit for brains. This guy sounds smart as hell."

"That's not nice," I protest. She shrugs.

"Sorry. But it's the truth. Guy like him could make millions on his looks alone, instead he chooses to use his brain. I know if I could model and make megabucks, I sure in the hell wouldn't be breaking my back doing this." Nat shakes her head sorrowfully.

I chuckle. "He totally looks like he'd be some vapid model instead of head of his own empire--"

Nat suddenly motions with her hands as if to warn me to shut up. "Speak of the devil."

Strong arms enclose me, and a deep voice murmurs in my ear, "Speaking of what devil?"

My heart does several backflips. "Liam!"

I turn in his arms to be greeted with a deep, smoldering kiss that has me wanting to strip naked and fuck right then and there in the back of Nat's bakery. In front of Nat.

We're both so lost in the kiss that it takes Nat to break us out of it.

"Get a room! Jesus!"

I pull away from Liam, my face burning. "Sorry!"

Nat is unconvinced. "I'm sure."

Liam chuckles, totally unashamed by our hot and heavy display of affection and wipes his lips. I'm sure I taste like sugar cookies, but Liam probably likes it. "Hey Nat."

Nat does a little wave. "Hey Liam. How's it hanging?"

Liam grins and I know he's thinking something dirty. "Alright. How's the bakery going?"

"Absolutely fantastic," she says, gesturing to the front of the shop. "Can't you tell by the line outside?"

Liam shakes his head. "I snuck in the back."

"Figures." Nat scowls at me. "I wonder who left the door open."

I look innocent. "Surely not me."

Nat scowls harder, threatening to send me off into gales of laughter.

Liam stares at Nat's fresh batch of cookies. "So are these the famous cookies I've been hearing so much about around town?"

"Yes they are," I'm quick to say. I gesture at the tray. "You should try one." *Heaven knows, I could eat five more.*

"I think he already has," Nat growls, staring pointedly at the five empty spots on the tray. "Sugar lips."

Liam laughs as he realizes why I tasted like a sugar cookie. "Well, if that's the case, I guess I have to have one. 'Cause Elle here tasted sweeter than usual." He walks over to the tray and looks at Nat for permission.

Nat waves him on. "Go ahead, you certainly can't do any more damage than your girlfriend did."

"I resent that," I say.

"Bite me."

"Don't tempt me."

Liam isn't paying attention to our bickering. He takes a

cookie and pops it in his mouth. His eyes widen a moment later. "Shit. These are really good," he says.

Nat beams with pride. I can tell she takes his compliment to heart since he's someone that knows good food. "Thank you."

Liam shakes his head, grabbing another cookie. "No. Thank you. Seriously, I could totally see you going on TV and winning one of those baking contests and then ending up with your own reality show."

Natalie looks at me with an 'I told you so" look. "See, Lizzie? What'd I tell you?"

"Careful, Liam," I warn. "You give her too many compliments, her head might explode."

"Better than my stomach exploding from eating too many cookies," she retorts. I giggle at her insult.

"If you're looking for a business partner, I could certainly help you out in the investment." I'm surprised by Liam's offer and judging by the look on Nat's face, so is she.

"I'll..." she starts to say and then purses her lips. "I'll have to think about it," she says confidently and then nods with a smile. "But thank you. If I need a partner, I'll keep you in mind."

"Fair enough," Liam says with a smile. "You ready to go, Elle?" His eyes are hooded with lust as he looks at me, and a shiver of anticipation shoots up my spine.

"Yes," I say huskily. "Just let me say bye to Nat and then we can go."

He pulls me into a light kiss that makes me weak in the knees. "Don't keep me waiting long." He gives Nat a nod goodbye, and she does the same in return as he walks out the back door.

"I'm gonna miss you," I say with a pout.

She gives me a pout back and embraces me in a hug.

"We'll be back in a few months." We already talked about it. I wanna stay close to home, and he wants to be with his family. I have two semesters left and then we'll be moving back here.

"Bye Nat." I give her another embrace and turn to leave but stop to say, "Don't you ever stop baking."

Nat gives me a look. "Are you crazy? I'll never stop doing that. Who else is going to make your wedding cake?"

* * *

As we drive down the road, the orange glow of the sunset basks us in its radiance. We pass familiar places on the way out of town, and I'm almost overwhelmed by the feelings. I'm going to miss this place. Nat, the bakery, daddy's house. Everything. Even if it's only a few semesters. Thinking of the house makes tears prick in my eyes. I don't wanna leave. Emotions creep up on me out of nowhere. I've been doing so good lately.

Seeming to sense my sadness, Liam looks over at me just as we hit the highway. "It's going to be okay, Elle."

I smile at him and stroke his arm. "Thank you," I say simply.

"No, thank you. For sticking by me through all the bullshit I put you through."

I stare at him, love filling my heart until I feel like it's going to burst. He didn't have to thank me. I'd die for him at this point. I was so terrified of losing him. It was all I could think about. Now I realize there's no way I'm letting him go. No matter what happens.

"I love you, Liam," I breathe, meaning it with all my heart.

Liam looks over at me, his eyes filled with love. "I love you too, Elle."

EPILOGUE

LIAM - TWO YEARS LATER

I can't stop looking at his little feet. He spreads his toes and squeals as Elle tries to latch him on again. They're so tiny. Everything about him is tiny. We took his little footprints and put them with the rest of the valuable things that are priceless to us. My father's silver pen, her father's note, and our little man's footprints. We've gotta find the perfect place to put them, but until then they're in my office, proudly on display within a shadowbox Elle bought just for them.

I look up at Elle and she looks so tired, but also worried. He's lost eight percent of his weight and I keep telling her it's normal. So do the doctors, but she's scared.

She takes in a steady breath and repositions our little man. I watch as he shakes his little head back and forth, and finally the squeals stop and I can faintly hear suckling.

Elle smiles slightly, and her body sags in relief. She's doing such a good job. She's so critical of herself, and she doesn't even realize what a wonderful mother she is already. Everyone from her work agrees. She's a counselor at the high school and she loves it there. I love that she has the entire summer off for our little one. Last year it was for our honeymoon. I look down and smile at the platinum band on my ring finger. After our big wedding, we took two months off to unwind. Planning that shit really stressed her out, but it was all worth it though. She was a beautiful bride, and now she's an even more beautiful wife and mother.

She doesn't have to work though. Not with all the investments we have. She wants to, and that's fine with me, as long as she's happy.

"He's perfect," I say just above a murmur. Her eyes meet mine and they shine with love.

"He looks like you," she says as she looks back down at our son, Michael Richard Axton. We named him after both of our fathers. "I think his eyes are going to stay blue, too."

He's not even a week old yet, but he's so loved.

I settle back on the new sofa. Elle didn't want to take any of the furniture from her stepfather's. It's all been donated. All except for his leather recliner. That's still in the house. It's mostly empty, and we have cleaners coming and a crew to fix it up some. But we aren't selling it. The house next door is being rented out, and her family home may be rented out too someday. But for now, it's for storage until Elle says otherwise. She needs time still. We both do. Losing someone you love is never easy. Grief is a journey. I don't think it ever really ends.

I take in a deep breath and look around our new place. We've still got boxes of things that need to be put away, and bottle nipples and pacifiers to sterilize. Our little man came five weeks early and gave us a scare. So the new place is a mess. Elle didn't even get a real baby shower.

Nat's throwing her a surprise one next week. She said it's more of a sip and see, whatever the hell that means.

Either way, little man has been showered with love and so has Elle.

I can't even tell her how I feel. There are no words.

Little man sighs and pops off Elle's nipple. I look into her eyes and see a flash of worry until he settles against her breast and nuzzles down to go to sleep.

She sighs with content and gently pats his back.

I lean in to kiss her cheek, but she turns her head and takes my lips with hers. I smile against her lips and brush the tip of my nose against hers. My heart swells in my chest.

I say the only thing I know that's absolutely true, "I love you, Elle. I love you two so damn much."

She reaches her hand out to take mine and squeezes. "I love you too, Liam."

MR. CEO

From USA Today bestselling authors, Willow Winters and Lauren Landish, comes a seductive office romance.

I'm used to dominating the boardroom and getting what I want.

But I've never wanted anyone like her.

Even though I have the world at my beck and call, it no longer excites me.

Nothing does.

. . .

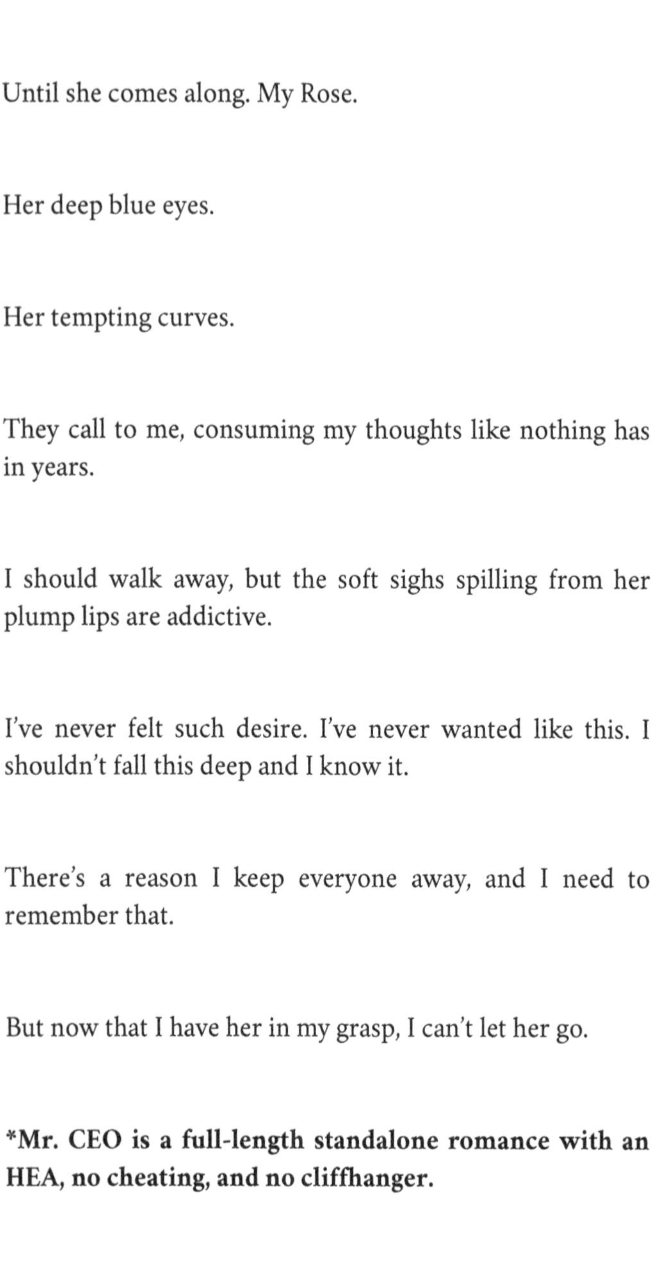

Until she comes along. My Rose.

Her deep blue eyes.

Her tempting curves.

They call to me, consuming my thoughts like nothing has in years.

I should walk away, but the soft sighs spilling from her plump lips are addictive.

I've never felt such desire. I've never wanted like this. I shouldn't fall this deep and I know it.

There's a reason I keep everyone away, and I need to remember that.

But now that I have her in my grasp, I can't let her go.

***Mr. CEO is a full-length standalone romance with an HEA, no cheating, and no cliffhanger.**

PROLOGUE

LOGAN

She thinks I don't know what she's been doing.

My Rose.

She's been teasing me. Taunting me with those swaying hips and short skirts. Making my dick so hard it fucking hurts.

"Bend over." I give her the simple command and hold her heated gaze. She's a rebel at heart. She has no reason to obey me unless she wants to. And I fucking know she wants to. She wants *me,* just as much as I want her.

Her lips pull into a sexy smirk as her hands slowly fall onto the desk and she spreads her legs slightly before bending over. My dick instantly hardens in my pants. She looks over her shoulder at me with nothing but lust on her face.

"Like this?" she asks in a soft sweet voice, feigning innocence. She's not innocent at all. She practically begged for this.

Her skirt's slipped up past her upper thighs, and I can see her garter belt and the beautiful curve of her ass. I lower myself to the floor behind her. That's what she does to me. She makes me fall to my knees.

"Just like that," I murmur as I gentle my hands on her thighs.

I inch my fingers up, playing with the thin black straps. The tips of my fingers trace along her creamy thighs, leaving goosebumps in their path.

I lightly brush my hands along her panty line and I'm rewarded with a soft moan spilling from her plump lips. "You like that, Rose?" I ask her as I hook my fingers into the waistband of her lace thong.

I keep my eyes on hers as I slowly pull the skimpy lace thong down to the floor. Her mouth parts slightly and her eyes widen, but she doesn't stop me. I know I shouldn't be doing this. I shouldn't give in to the temptation and make this more complicated. But I'm a selfish man, and I want her.

I repress a groan as she slowly steps out of her thong and widens her stance for me.

"Yes, sir," she breathes out in a voice laced with desire, "I do." I can't help the asymmetric grin that pulls at my lips. I splay my hand on her lower back, just above those cute little dimples and push her down.

She's spread and fully bared to me, glistening with arousal.

"I wanna taste you," I say against her hot pussy before taking a languid lick. Her legs tremble in her high-as-fuck black leather heels and for a second I worry she won't be able to maintain her balance in them. But I wanna fuck her in them. Just like this, this is exactly how I want her. I've dreamed of this every day since the first day I laid eyes on her.

I need to get her good and ready for me.

I take my time forcing those sounds of pleasure from

her lips. I lick my lips and groan at her sweet taste before flicking my tongue against her throbbing clit. Her back tries to arch off the desk, but I hold her down.

She's going to give me every fantasy I've ever dreamed of. I can't tell her the truth about me, and I know I shouldn't bring her into this, but her taste on my tongue and the soft sounds that spill from her gorgeous lips make me weak.

She moans my name, and it's my undoing.

I can't take it anymore. I stand and quickly unbutton my pants, shoving them down as quickly as I can. She turns her head to watch as she waits patiently, remaining in the position I left her in.

I kick my pants off carelessly with my eyes on hers and stand behind her with my hands gripping her hips. Her eyes are clouded with lust. Not the fear that used to be there. She trusts me. She wants me, and nothing's holding her back now. If only she knew the truth. I can never give her what she needs.

I know I'm selfish, but I'm taking her.

CHAPTER 1

LOGAN

The ice in the cognac glass clinks as the bartender sets it in front of me on the small white cocktail napkin. I give him a small nod and return my attention to the tablet in my hand. I'm not going to drink the whiskey I ordered. I'm not going to talk to anyone in here, although I'm sure a few business men will approach me. I'm simply waiting for my associate, Trent Morgan.

He's much more… sociable than I am. I prefer solitude. I do my best work in my office. And if it were any other day, that's where we'd be. On the top floor of the high-rise that encompasses the success of my company, Parker-Moore Enterprise. From the outside, the sixty-four story building looks as though it's one sheet of mirrored glass with symmetrical beveled lines that separate the floors.

I inherited the business, but the building is all mine. The idea and the structure. I get the credit for that. The massive influx of clients and profits, they're all me, too.

And I didn't get there by holding meetings at a bar in the Madison Hotel.

Dozens of men and women are lingering around me.

Some at the high top tables near the large floor-to-ceiling windows that look over the edge and onto the crystal clear harbor below. It's breathtaking, and at one point in my life I may have enjoyed this room, but right now I'm irritated.

I look back to my tablet, to the one thing I have a vested interest in, my work, and ignore the hum of small talk and the faint sounds of laughter from the other side of the room. There are two companies I'm interested in. They're the reason I'm sitting here. On paper, they're nearly identical. I want to see the *people*. They'll tell me which of the two is worth investing in. People run a business, and if I can't have faith in the men and women heading the company, then I have no interest in investing.

I glance up as a small, delicate hand gently brushes my forearm. Her thin fingers and glossy red nail polish make her hand look extra dainty resting easily on my dark grey custom-tailored Armani suit. I clear my throat and turn my head slightly to look at the woman who takes a graceful seat on the barstool next to me.

It takes great effort not to stare at the cleavage she's obviously put on display. Her form-fitting black dress has a plunging neckline, with a sharp "V" that travels too far down to be professional.

She practically purrs, "I was hoping you'd buy me a drink."

I huff a small laugh and smirk at her. That's a cheeky come-on I wasn't expecting and I can appreciate her charm; the drinks are free for the conference. And I can tell from the soft blush across her cheeks and the sweet grin on her lips that she already knows that.

She's beautiful and refined. Her confidence is alluring, but it does nothing for me.

"I'm waiting on a colleague." I'm short in my response for a reason. I don't want to open doors for discussion.

If we'd met in this scenario three years ago, things would be different. I'd have taken her upstairs to my bed in the penthouse suite and given her what she's looking for. I wouldn't have thought twice about it. I would've satisfied the both of us and moved on to the next sweet little thing looking to sink her claws into a wealthy man.

Things change. People change.

I have no room in my life for complications anymore. I don't mix business with pleasure. I lead a private life for good reason. And if my parents' failed marriage and brutal divorce taught me anything, it's that I should never trust anyone. And I can't afford to let anyone in. Not now. Not ever.

The little minx gives me a tight smile and gathers her clutch in a white-knuckled fist before sliding off the barstool. I don't mind her disgruntled departure. I'm used to it, and I prefer it that way. I could apologize for being blunt and to the point, but I'm not sorry. And I don't make apologies.

There are only two people in this world I'm close to. My father, and the man who just walked into the room, Trent Morgan. He cocks a brow and watches the woman pull her dress down a bit more as she gives me the cold shoulder and stalks off without a word.

A sly grin forms on his cleanly shaven face as he takes her seat and looks at me. "Already pissing people off. You couldn't wait for me to start the party, could you?"

I let out a deep rough chuckle. I've always liked Trent. He's nearly a decade older than me as he approaches forty, but we've gotten along since day one. Which isn't the case for most Parker-Moore executives.

I've always taken this business seriously. After seeing my mother shred my father after his stroke and try to steal the business out from under him, I knew anyone and everyone who thought they could try to take it from me would. And I was ready for them.

I'm not sure if Trent liked the fact that I was ruthless in business and didn't trust anyone even at such a young age, or if he was just relieved that his new twenty-two-year-old boss wasn't some spoiled brat who didn't give a fuck about the business he'd just inherited.

But seven years later, he's my closest ally. He's my *only* ally.

He signals to the bartender for a drink before looking down the bar at mine. "I'll take care of that for you," he says as he picks up the glass. The napkin sticks to the bottom as he brings it to his lips and downs the drink in a single swig.

"Stressed?" I ask him with a cocky grin.

"I am," he answers without looking at me. I know why he's anxious, I'm just waiting for him to say it. He smiles at the bartender as he orders another Jack on ice. I got him hooked on my drink of choice. He turns to face me before he says, "We need to choose, and neither of them look like they can handle our influx."

He has a right to be upset. We bit off more than we can chew. We have the manufacturing capabilities, but the sales just aren't there. Hiring out isn't paying off like it should. "Our profits are shit for the retail division," Trent says, accepting his drink and taking a modest sip.

"I'm aware," I say and nod, rapping my knuckles on the bar, "and that's a fixable problem."

He looks at me from the corner of his eye. "You're more laidback about this than you should be."

I shrug. I may be a little less stressed than normal over this, but it's because this has happened before. "For every problem, there's a solution," I say easily.

"I imagine that means you got good news on Thursday?" he asks. My body tenses, and I don't answer. Instead

I face the bartender and wait for him to make eye contact with me.

I'm vaguely aware of Trent apologizing to me as I'm distracted, hearing a small feminine voice to my left. It catches me off guard for some reason, and I turn and see a beautiful short woman with sun-kissed skin and gorgeous blonde hair talking to the bartender.

She gives the the man a small smile, but it's merely to be polite. Her brilliant blue eyes are dimmed by something. In a room full of people, she stands out. She's like me in that she doesn't belong here. But I'm not sure why.

I watch her body language and see how closed off she is. She's uncomfortable. A small sigh leaves her plush lips as she sits back at the bar with her eyes closed. The sight makes my dick instantly harden. She looks vulnerable and beautiful. She looks tempting in so many ways.

The sound of her giving in, that soft sigh--I want that. I want to hear it again and again. Even more than that though, I want to force those sounds from her lips myself.

CHAPTER 2

CHARLOTTE

Your shit better be gone by the time I'm back!

My last words to my ex run through my mind as I step into the Madison Hotel bar. I stop for a moment to address my outfit, a black pencil skirt with a shiny belt wrapped around my waist, giving my figure a shapely appearance, and a pearly white blouse. I scan the room, noting it's filled to the brim with business people, and wonder if I should head back out into the lobby to collect myself. This is a business convention and I need to be on my A game. But I didn't come down to the bar for business.

I'm supposed to be focused on this presentation and making contacts, but all I can think about is what happened. What *they* did to me.

Even now the pain is razor sharp, cutting me deep.

I turn to leave the bar, but then stop.

I can't go back, I tell myself. *I refuse to go back to crying over people who aren't worth an ounce of my time.*

It's easy to tell myself this, but harder to put it in action.

The betrayal has been a difficult thing to swallow. Especially considering the source of my agony.

Sarah was once a good friend to me, a co-worker and confidante that I thought had my best interests at heart. Turns out her only interest was getting my boyfriend's cock out of his boxers and into her lying mouth.

Ian's infidelity had been bad enough, but Sarah's disloyalty was deeply personal. I'd trusted her, and with everything. The way she played up to me all that time, giving me advice on everything from my hair, makeup, outfits and my relationship with Ian, only to stab me in the back when the first opportunity arrived--makes my blood fucking boil.

Screw her, I think to myself angrily. *And screw him. They both deserve each other. I'm here now, and it's time to move on with my life.* The wounds are only a little over a week old, but I'm tired of wallowing in grief. It's useless. And I can't let anything ruin this job for me. I couldn't stand being near that bitch so I left in the heat of the moment. Not the smartest thing I've ever done. But I still managed to get a good recommendation and land this job quickly. Thankfully.

Deciding it's time to drink my worries away, I head over to the bar. The clicking of my heels from the hallway is muted by the thin carpet in the lounge area. I grab an end seat in a leather wingback chair, loving the open yet cozy vibe of the room and signal the bartender, a young blond man dressed in a black tux; he's quick to make his way over.

"What will you have, sweetie?" His voice has a high-pitched note to it.

I give him a friendly smile in return. He's handsome and all, but definitely batting for the other team. "Apple martini, please," I reply.

He winks at me. "You got it."

I watch as he leaves me.

Everything's going to be fine. Just watch.

I'm just starting to feel more relaxed when I feel eyes boring into the back of my neck. I look around, and then my breath catches in my throat.

Holy hell, I think to myself, my eyes widening slightly.

A man seated at the bar just a few feet away is blatantly staring at me. Not just any man. The perfect mix of CEO and sex god. I can see he's wearing a crisp white dress shirt with only the top button undone under his suit, and his dark hair is slightly messy on top. He looks like he'd pin your legs back and take what he wanted from you.

My breath catches in my throat. He's so fucking handsome. There's no way he was looking at me. No way in hell. He's way out of my league. His suit looks high dollar, and he's groomed to perfection. Even the air around him is too expensive for me.

The bartender startles me as he comes back with my drink, and I break my eye contact with the mystery man. I give the bartender a nervous smile and wiggle the thin cocktail pick with a bit of apple on it around in the glass, my heart pounding in my chest. *Jesus.* I feel like I'm having hot flashes. I have to wonder though, if that guy can do this to me with just a look, what could he do with a single touch?

I can't help myself. I have to look back over. I chance a quick peek. *Shit.* He's still looking right at me. I jerk my eyes away with my breath stilling in my lungs. Holy shit. He *is* looking at me. His light blue eyes pierce into me this time, holding my gaze. My lips part slightly as the feeling of being trapped washes over me. My body tenses. He's intense. *Too intense.* Luckily a man to his right taps his shoulder and Mr. CEO turns to face him with a look of annoyance.

I take that as my cue to get the hell out of here while I can. *He* is a bad idea. And I need to stay far away.

I abandon my drink, nearly spilling it on the bar as I set it down as quickly as I can along with a twenty from my purse. I grab my black leather Coach hobo with both hands, my eyes focused on the open entryway. My skin flushes as I pass him, making my exit a little too quickly to go unnoticed.

I don't even breathe until I'm on the elevator and the doors are closing. I stand there feeling overwhelmed and not even realizing that I need to hit the button to get this thing moving.

I need to get a grip. I push the button for my floor and lean back against the wall of the empty car. A waist-high bar is behind me and I hold it to steady myself. What the hell was that about? I replay the scene in my head, but there's no way I'm remembering it right.

The way he looked at me triggered something deep inside me; something I've never felt before. A mix of fear and lust.

It was like he owned me.

CHAPTER 3

LOGAN

The curtains are open in the penthouse suite, but the soft glow from the harbor outside does nothing to brighten the darkness in the room. It doesn't matter. The dim light from my laptop is all I need. I'm used to it. I'm most productive at night.

This is the ideal atmosphere for me, but I can't focus. I've been staring at the same portfolio since I came up here and took my seat at the corner desk in my hotel room. My fingers tap against the smooth surface of the hard maple desk in a soothing beat.

I can't calm down though. I'm nothing but tense and anxious.

I want something I can't have, and that's a rarity.

She's someone I shouldn't pursue. I already know this, yet I'm toying with the idea of making her mine. There's a difference between finding a quick fuck to ease my appetite and taking with the intention of keeping her.

And I already know once won't be enough.

What's worse is that I know keeping her entails a sort of relationship. One I'm not inclined to have. A fuck buddy is an impossibility for me. I've learned that the hard way. Women lie. I don't know whether they're lying to themselves or just to me, but when they say they're happy with only being my fucktoy, they're lying. Even if I'm paying them. They always want more.

I don't know what came over me downstairs and even now. I can't get her out of my thoughts. I shouldn't even be considering this knowing what she'll be getting in return, or should I say what she won't be getting.

I want her though, and I haven't ever wanted someone like this before. I wish she were here now, and I keep picturing it over and over. I want her straddling me, with her shapely legs draped on either side of mine and her arms wrapped around my neck.

My cock hardens in my pants. I can hear those soft moans as I fist her hair at the nape of her neck and thrust my dick over and over into her hot, tight cunt. I lean back in my seat and sigh as I try to erase the image from my head.

I've sworn off companionship. I don't need it. But something about her is drawing me in. Insta-lust at its finest. I haven't fallen victim to that in quite a while.

I don't need anyone. And it's best I don't get attached. More so for them than for me.

I'm a selfish man, but I'm not so selfish that I'd bring another person into my life. There's a reason I keep them away.

I need to remember that.

I can't have her; I'm firm in that decision. But even as I come to that conclusion, I find myself looking through the convention's website. I just need to know her name. With a little digging I'm certain I'll lose interest in her. I'm sure it's the fact that she left before I could talk to her, leaving me wanting, that has the image of her branded in my consciousness. At least that's what I tell myself to justify looking through the list of presenters with their square pictures and short biographies.

I fucking want her.

As the thought hits me, her picture appears on the screen. My fingers stop on the touchpad as I take in the soft curves of her face. Her beautiful smile puts my memory to shame.

Charlotte Rose Harrison.

I focus on her middle name Rose, which is also the color of her lips, and the delicate features fit her perfectly. She was meant to be a Rose.

Keynote speaker for Armcorp and former executive of sales for Steamens Marketing.

Education: Graduated from North State University (2013) with master's degrees in business, marketing and economics.

I've seen resumes like this before. Although I have to admit her progression in a mere three years is impressive. I'm not concerned with her work habits though. I should be, but in this very moment, I don't give a fuck about any of that. I want to know about *her.*

I open a new browser tab and type in her name.

Specifically, I want to know who she's fucking. That's the only thing on my mind.

Before I can press enter, I shut the laptop with more force than what's needed and slowly rise from my seat, shaking my head.

Now's not the time or place for this shit. This is business. And she could be an employee of mine if we settle on her company. It's one of the two we're considering.

I stalk across the room in darkness and head to the large windows.

The idea of buying Armcorp just to be close to her eases the part of me that's panicking to act now before she slips through my fingers. If she's close, I can keep tabs on her until my interest wanes. And I'm sure it will.

I run my hand through my hair and then lean against the window. It feels cool against the palms of my hands.

It's an easy enough decision to make. A shit reason to make a business decision, but I don't need anyone's approval. I own my business, and I can do whatever the fuck I want to do with it.

I close my eyes and lean my forehead against the cold glass. It's late and I can't be rash in this decision. My hands ball into fists as I push off the large window and move to the king-size bed in the room.

Tomorrow I'll decide. Either I'm taking her, or I'll leave her and this fantasy alone. As I close my eyes my dick begins hardening with the thoughts of what I want to do with her and I already know what my decision will be.

Charlotte *Rose* is *mine.*

CHAPTER 4

CHARLOTTE

The pressure is real.

Convention hall. Game face on.

I'm sitting in the audience filled with my peers, coworkers and powerful business executives, trying to calm my rising anxiety. A lot is riding on this presentation. It could literally be the difference between having a job, or being on the street. Armcorp just hired me, and if I don't ace this I know they'll be wondering if I'm worth it.

To make matters worse, my boss is sitting right behind me and he'll see everything. I'm doing my best to stay still and not appear nervous. I hold my head upright and do my best to project confidence, even though I'm drowning with anxiety inside. I hope he can't sense that I'm nearly having a panic attack right beneath his nose.

I can do this, I tell myself. *I'm strong, smart and confident. I have this presentation memorized. This is what I do, and I'm damn good at it.*

I keep repeating these words in my mind, letting it become a powerful mantra that drives back the anxiety that threatens to send me running from the room a nervous wreck.

I will succeed. There's nothing I can't do. They hired me because they were impressed by my resume and experience. I have absolutely nothing to worry about.

I obsessively click on my phone and look at the time. Each presentation is fifteen minutes long and I'm up next. Two minutes left. *Shit.* My heart won't stop racing. I dim my cell's screen and put my phone away.

I don't know what I'm going to do when I'm called up on that stage. I'm practically shaking like a leaf.

A soft voice interrupts my anxious thoughts.

"You're going to do fine," Eva White, a coworker who's sitting right next to me, says. I look over and she's staring at me with empathy, her large brown eyes looking at me reassuringly. For a moment, I feel my anxiety ease and I'm grateful that she's sitting next to me.

Like me, she's dressed to impress, in a sleek black pantsuit with her dark red hair pulled back into a professional ponytail.

I smile back at her, unease twisting my stomach, and mouth, *thank you*.

"You're welcome." She gently pats me on the leg to comfort me and I'm reminded of her nickname. *Sweet Eva*. I'm so lucky to call her a friend. In the corporate world, there's no shortage of people who will backstab you in the blink of an eye to climb the ladder, but not Eva. She's a team player, and it's one of the reasons I trust her already. When we're together, shit gets done.

The announcer walks back up on stage to the podium as the previous presenter leaves, and despite my mental pep talk and Eva's reassurance, my heart begins doing backflips and sweat slicks my palms.

"And now," he says into the microphone, "I'd like to

introduce the keynote speaker presenting Armcorp's quarterly report, Miss Charlotte Rose Harrison."

Oh my God. I'm so fucked.

Polite applause floods my senses and I climb to my feet with a tight smile on my face.

You'll do fine, Eva mouths to me.

I give her a thankful smile despite the butterflies fluttering in my stomach.

I make my way to the front of the room as quickly as I can without falling on my face in these heels, my heart beating wildly with every step. I'm careful not to trip as I climb the steps to the stage and walk over to the podium. The announcer hands me a small clicker to control the projector behind me. I glance up and see the powerpoint I prepared. My heart races as I square my shoulders and straighten my back.

Alright, Charlotte. You can't fuck this up.

For a moment I'm blinded by the bright lights on the stage making me the center of attention in the darkened room. I can't view the sea of executives in the audience or anything for a moment. It's just me and the stage with the projector behind me.

Slowly, everyone comes back into focus. I can see them all. Faces I know, some that I don't. They're all waiting for me. Staring. I swear I'm starting to sweat in places I didn't think I could. The pressure is immense.

Get on with it, girl! I can do this.

I swallow, and then take a deep breath. The lights are shining on me, waiting. My voice is caught in my throat, suffocated by nerves. But I take another deep breath and begin what I've rehearsed. It's almost like white noise in my ears as I rattle off the background and current state of Armcorp's hold on the market. I know these lines by heart.

I turn to the projected slides and click the small button

to move forward. Everyone's watching. My blood heats and my heart races, but I know this. I quickly hit through all my notes and bullet points with an ease in my voice that doesn't reflect my nerves, and the more I talk, the more my confidence grows. This is how it is every time. I can barely handle the pressure, and it's huge, but I'm damn good at pushing through and maintaining the professional presentation that's expected.

"So as you can see, the company's market share is growing by seventeen percent and it's on an upward trend," I say, turning around to face the room of corporate executives. They're all watching and judging me. And they should be; this is business, after all. "By reaching out to the other markets depicted in table five of this slide we anticipate a growth-" I pause as my eyes lock with the handsome stranger from the bar last night, my ability to speak momentarily stolen. The lines I've rehearsed seem to vanish and not a word can pass the lump in my throat.

He's sitting in the back of the room, watching me with an intense gaze that makes me feel like I'm sitting in a 120 degree sauna.

Jesus. Focus, Charlie!

I clear my throat and open my mouth to continue. But nothing comes out. My mind's blank. I stand there for several moments, my heart pounding. I need to get myself together. The corner of Mr. CEO's lips rise in an asymmetric grin as he stares at me. He's affecting me, and he knows it. Suddenly, I'm pissed. My nerves shift and anger replaces them. Nothing's going to stop me from acing this and proving to everyone that I'm damn good at what I do and that I'm worth it.

I tear my eyes away from him, trying to unscramble my thoughts. A few attendees shift in their seats. They're probably thinking I've suddenly gone brain-dead.

I turn my back on the room and face the drawing board, pointing with the tiny light in the clicker at the projection screen. Even with my body breaking out into a cold sweat, I push forward, quickly thinking on my toes until I'm able to remember my presentation. "And so what we have here…" As I point my wand at the graph, my hands start to tremble.

"Is room for exponential growth," I continue on smoothly with my presentation as if nothing happened, even though it feels like my heart is climbing up my throat. I get through the next few minutes, presenting data clearly and easily. By the time I'm done, I'm covered with a sheen of sweat. But I'm sure I've done a competent job.

"And we will grow our profit margin by nearly ninety percent," I say, turning to face the room in conclusion. I smile brightly and signal to the announcer that I'm done. Looking at the large clock on the far back wall, I see I've hit the fifteen minute mark right on the dot. *Perfect*. "Thank you for having me." The room bursts into a scattering of light applause. I beam with relief although I'm still hot as hell with anxiety. Both from the presentation and from *him*.

My nerves are still high, but I feel a slight sense of relief. I did it. It's over, and other than that hiccup it went just as I planned. No thanks to Mr. CEO. I start to look his way but then stop. I'm not going to give him the satisfaction. He almost ruined my presentation.

I make my way back to my seat as the announcer walks up to introduce the next speaker, being careful again not to trip in my heels. That would be embarrassing as fuck.

I wiggle my way through the row and back to my seat next to Eva. She's looking at me with admiration as I sit down.

"See, what did I tell you?" she squeals in a hushed voice, pulling me into a soft embrace. "You did fantastic!"

"Thank you," I whisper back. "I couldn't have done it without you."

Eva waves her hand as she releases me from our hug. "Nonsense. You had that in the bag before you even stepped foot on the stage. Hell, I wish I could speak like that in front of a large crowd. You're a natural."

"Job well done, Charlotte," my new boss, Charles Hastings, chips in from behind me. I turn to face him with a grateful smile as he places a hand on my shoulder. Charles's an older man in his forties with dark hair, greying at the temples, and a chiseled jawline that is beginning to lose its strength. He's the type of man I'd be attracted to if I were into older guys. Or if I was about five years older, he definitely could get it. Except he doesn't hold a candle to...

I try to push Mr. CEO out of my thoughts, but it doesn't work. All I can see is his handsome face in my mind's eye, his piercing gaze, his crisp suit and his full lips. All I can think about is how much I want to kiss them. Good God.

"Thank you, sir," I say, trying to shake the man from my mind.

"No, thank you, Charlotte," Charles tells me, patting me on the shoulder. "That was a wonderful presentation. You made our company look good."

Seeing as how I was about to pass out from anxiety before taking the stage, I should be overjoyed that I'm getting such praise from my boss. But I can't fight the urge to look over for the stranger.

My heart does a little jolt. His seat is empty. He's gone.

I settle back in my seat feeling a pang of disappointment.

I try to focus on the next speaker as the slides change on the screen in front of us. But I can't concentrate. I can't shake the hold he has over me. And why? Why does he have such a strong effect on me?

I can't tame the urge to look back over my shoulder. He's not there. I swallow thickly and try to ignore all thoughts of him. I don't even know his name.

But I want to. I'm woman enough to admit that I'm at least curious.

CHAPTER 5

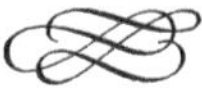

LOGAN

"Why this one?" Trent asks me again. He's been eyeing me since we sat down in the meeting room.

I settle back in the seat although it's extremely uncomfortable and try to relax. I can't wait to get out of here and take this damn jacket off. I feel restless now that I've made my decision. I have to wait and that's something I'm not fond of. Patience has never been my strong suit. And I need this deal. I never *need* anything, but right now I do. Armcorp had better take my offer.

"It's the best choice," I answer simply, not giving anything away. He gives me a look laced with suspicion but closes his mouth and looks back down at the papers in front of him.

I take a long look around the plain hotel meeting room with distaste as I wait for the heads of Armcorp to arrive.

This room is small and the large table that nearly takes up the entire space and the chairs surrounding it are cheap. It's nothing like the suite upstairs or my office back at Parker-Moore. I practically live there and I made sure it had every amenity I'd need. But this small square room… it's lacking. The walls are a stark white and the thin carpet on the floors makes it feel even more inferior. I'm ready to go back to the comfort of my own building and business, and I've decided I'm taking my Rose as a parting gift.

"Armcorp looks like a ton of work. We should give them a year or two to see how well their new outreach performs." Trent's right, and I can't deny that. But I'm not waiting. I've made up my mind.

Watching her on stage created more conflict than I needed. She's graceful and intelligent. But when we locked eyes and I felt the intensity of the spark between us, I knew I had to give in. She sealed her fate when her lips parted and she got lost in my trance. It's one thing for me to be affected, but knowing I do the same for her makes this decision easy.

"We should wait, Logan. The board will-" I don't care what argument he has. In fact, I know there are good reasons to wait or to go with their competitor. But I don't give a damn. I'm not waiting anymore. I fucking want her, and I'm not going to deny myself. I don't give a damn if I'm selfish. I'm taking her. And this is the first step.

"No, I want it now." My voice is hard and the trace of annoyance causes Trent to flinch. I clench my jaw, wishing I could control myself. I need to. I pride myself on discipline, but when it comes to her, I feel like I'm losing it. Once I have her under my thumb, it will be easier.

Trent doesn't say anything in return. He leans back in his seat and nods his head. Although I consider him a friend and I'm grateful for his advice when it comes to running this company, I'm the CEO and sole proprietor; what I want, I get.

As the thought registers, the door to the meeting room opens and we rise to stand from the cheap seats. I button my suit jacket and wait at the head of the table for Armcorp's CEO, Scott Nathaniel Murphy. He's accompanied by the head executive of sales, Mr. Hastings, and another man I don't recognize; he has a pad of paper and a pen in his hand so I'm assuming he's a secretary.

"Good morning, gentlemen," Murphy addresses us with a firm handshake. He places his other hand on top of mine as our hands clasp and looks me in the eyes. He's an older man and set in traditional ways. I admire that, at times. I give him a tight smile and take the head seat. I'm the first to sit, but the other men quickly follow suit.

"Thank you for attending this meeting on such short notice, gentlemen," I say and clear my throat and prepare for a hopefully quick and agreeable contract.

"The pleasure is ours, Mr. Parker." Murphy angles his seat slightly and says, "I was surprised to hear your offer is for silent partnership?" He says it as though it's a question. I'm not interested in dismantling the business. I merely want control over it so I can use their sales division for my own benefits.

I nod my head slightly and reply, "It would certainly benefit us both... immensely."

All the men nod their heads slightly in response, with the exception of Trent. There's no hint of his usual smile on his face. The sight makes the corner of my lips itch to turn up into a smile, but I resist. This is business.

I clear my throat and begin to say, "Let's get to the point and make this as easy a transaction as possible-"

Before I can finish, Murphy interrupts me by saying, "You'll need to come up in price then." I'm not used to being cut off, and I don't fucking like it. But I'm more than willing to get right to the point. I'm also not surprised. In the proposal, I put in an extremely low bid, not so much that it would be insulting, but low enough that I have plenty of room to make a guaranteed profit. I'm the only buyer, so I can offer whatever the fuck I want.

"We had almost four million in revenue last year, and that's only increasing." I hold Murphy's gaze as he does his best to give me a hard sell. I don't care about this shit. I know his company inside and out, what I want is his counter offer.

"Revenue isn't profit," Trent says, speaking up for the first time. And it's a very good point, but again, I couldn't care less.

"Our return on investment last year was nearly two hundred percent," Hastings says as he sits forward in his seat. His suit already looks wrinkled from his posture. He steeples his fingers and continues, "The evaluation of the company two years ago didn't account for our growing sectors. We've outgrown expectations while maintaining our cash flow."

"That's an excellent indication of budgeting, but that's not what we're discussing," Trent says with a hard voice.

"Our profit margin is-"

"Minimal," Trent interjects. He barely says the word, but it's enough to stop Murphy in his sales pitch.

I keep my shoulders squared and stare straight ahead, unaffected by the tense air between Trent and Murphy. I will say it's a nice change of pace for Trent to be the one heading the negotiation. Usually I'm the one who comes out looking like an asshole. Not that I matter much. It's business. Always. I never take it personal, even if they do.

"A price?" I ask. It's all I want. And frankly, I'm so anxious to ensure I have my Rose under my thumb that I need to be careful and not agree to the first number he spits out.

Murphy straightens his tie and shifts slightly in his seat. Finally, he gives me the answer I've been waiting for and says, "The board won't settle for anything less than sixty million."

They don't even know their own worth. This is going better than I could've hoped.

Trent sits back in his seat and then looks at me. I can feel his gaze on me, but I ignore it. It's the *we've won* look. I can practically hear him screaming, *Take the deal!*

"We'll settle on fifty-five and your entire operations will relocate immediately. There's a floor that's prepared to accommodate your current staff and needs although it will need to be outfitted as the two of you see fit."

I know the offer is lower than what he asked, but not by much. It's a shit ton lower than what I anticipated paying. I could give him the sixty mil he asked for, but the old man is bluffing. No one in this business gives a bottom line price on the first offer. No one.

"And the cost of the outfitting?" Murphy asks with a raised brow. I resist the pull at the corner of my lips to smile. I know I've got him.

"Company expenses--of course, *my* company expenses." He purses his lips and looks at Hastings.

"Do we have a deal?" I ask in an even tone. My face is neutral. I keep it that way for a reason. No emotions in business.

Murphy gives me a broad smile as he says, "We have a deal, Mr. Parker." He reaches his hand out and I easily give him a firm handshake with my other hand on top of his. I finally allow the grin to show. *She's mine.*

"You'll have the files faxed to you in the morning, and I'll see you on Monday." I finally give him a nod as I rise from the table.

"Pleasure doing business with you Mr. Parker," he says, releasing me from the firm handshake.

I force the smile to stay put and reply, "The pleasure is all mine."

Trent follows my lead as I make for the door, leaving everyone else to do whatever the hell they want.

A sense of ease settles through me at the thought of Rose and knowing she'll be in my building in only a few short days. That's too long to wait, but it's the best I can do in terms of business. For now, I'll need to be patient and that may be a challenge. If anything, I can find her here and buy her a drink. I remember the way she looked the first night at the bar, the way she bolted.

A smile slips into place as I realize she won't be able to do that now. I've got her now.

Trent gives me a hard smack on the back as we walk out of the room.

"You're a shark, Logan," he says with a smile. I huff a small laugh and try to push down the anxiety and unsettling feelings that are threatening to consume me. If only he knew my real reason. That would wipe the smile off his face.

CHAPTER 6

CHARLOTTE

"I'm gonna fuck five hot guys tonight," Hannah, one of my new coworkers, announces as she grins and leans back in the seat. She's tipsy and happy and just joking around. And it's infectious. She laughs as she fixes the straps of her black clubbing dress. I swear her D-cup boobs are about to pop out. But maybe that's what she wants. "It's five or bust!"

We're driving in a corporate stretch limo up the Las Vegas strip. The girls--Eva, Hannah and Cary Ann--want to hit a couple of casinos and a few clubs before returning to our hotel rooms to retire for the night. I'm not sure I want to be a part of the excursion, but Eva convinced me to join in on the fun to keep up with appearances.

As the new girl, she didn't want me to seem like a Debbie Downer to the others.

I wasn't sure what to expect when we all piled into the limo, but I found myself quickly relaxing when I realized the other girls had quite the sense of humor. All of them seem down to earth and don't take themselves seriously, which is a good thing. It makes fitting in with them easier.

Cary Ann, a petite blonde with platinum highlights, frowns. She's seated across from me and is wearing a purple dress that is far too short, the hem rising so far up her legs that I think I can almost see her uterus. Cary jokes, "Only five? Why not make it ten?"

"Yeah," adds Eva. She's sitting next to me and she's looking pretty hot in her red-hot halter dress and her dark red hair pulled into a sleek ponytail, if I say so myself. Her makeup is flawless and her eyes, which are framed by dark mascara and liner, look bigger than usual. "It's Vegas, chica. Go big or go home."

Hannah bites her lower lip, twisting her face into a serious expression. "I don't know, guys. I'd definitely do ten guys if I could... but…" She trails off and shakes her head morosely.

"But what?" Cary Ann demands, leaning forward as the limo goes over a speed bump and we all jolt to the side.

Hannah pauses for a long moment before breaking out into a wide grin and howls, "I don't know if I have enough holes!"

The girls scream with laughter. Even I have to join in. I really need a good laugh and a fun time after all the stress I've been through these last two weeks. The fucking breakup. The pressure from the presentation. The feeling of dread I feel about returning home and finding my boyfriend hasn't moved out yet. Or worse, finding him shacked up in bed with Sarah.

I really need to just unwind and relax so I don't have a nervous breakdown.

Despite Hannah's rowdy boast, I know this group isn't serious about hooking up with anyone tonight. Most likely, we'll all have a couple drinks, flirt a little, *maybe,* and return to our rooms tipsy a few dollars richer or poorer.

I know I won't be getting any action, I tell myself. *That's for damn sure.*

"There'll be none of that over here," Eva says, doing a swirling motion with her hand around her lady bits.

Hannah frowns, messing with her bra. I swear her right boob almost popped out. I have to put my hand between my legs to keep from reaching over and pulling up the neckline of her dress. "Why's that?"

Eva raises her head and says haughtily, "Because I have a loving boyfriend who can't wait for me to get back home."

Cary Ann snorts and drunkenly blurts out, "Please, he's probably at home banging his side chick in your bed right now!"

"Okay!" Hannah reaches across her seat to high five Cary Ann, nearly popping out of her dress in the process, and the two girls burst into giggles. "You know what they say; a man is only as faithful as his options!"

Eva grimaces and glances over at me. I know what she's thinking. And she's right. The joke makes me feel like shit.

Cary Ann pauses when she sees we aren't laughing. "Did I say something wrong?"

I can't respond. My throat is tight with emotion.

Eva comes to my rescue. "Charlotte's going through a breakup," she says quietly. Fuck, I hate this. I feel so damn uncomfortable.

Cary Ann's face crumples into a frown and she reaches across the limo to place a consolatory hand on mine. "Oh honey, I'm sorry. I didn't mean to upset you."

Tears burn my eyes and I swallow the lump in my throat. "It's okay."

"You sure?" asks Hannah. "I hate to think that we upset you."

"I'm fine," I lie, putting on a fake smile. "Really, you guys don't have to walk on eggshells around me." I wave it off.

"Okay, sorry," Cary Ann repeats. I can tell she's really mortified that she's caused me unintentional pain.

"Don't sweat it." I look around and ask, "So what are you guys having to drink when we get to the club?" I want to change the subject and get the focus off me. As soon as fucking possible.

Hannah claps her hands together, causing her boobs to jiggle. "A bahama mama! 'Cause I'm a big, hot mama."

"The walking dead!" Cary Ann squeals. "'Cause it's my favorite show!"

"A blue Hawaii," says Eva, "my favorite."

There's a moment of silence and the girls look at me expectantly.

"Bloody Mary," I say, thinking quickly on my feet. *Because I want to fucking murder Ian.*

"Let's hit Surrender first," Cary suggests as the limo slows and we climb out. "I hear it's awesome."

"Hell yeah," says Hannah. "I'm game."

We make our way inside and I'm immediately enveloped by a pleasant tropical smell and the sounds of slots machine. It's so bright, I have to blink a couple of times to adjust.

The noises, the lights, the flood of people, it's all overwhelming. Sin City. This definitely looks like a place made for sin. I walk behind the ladies as they stride confidently to wherever they're taking me. They've been here before and they're acting like they own the place. I do my best to do the same and look like I belong.

I take my seat next to Eva and put my clutch on the bartop, taking another look around. This place is overwhelming.

I start to ask Eva how many times she's been here, but

before I can even get a word out, she's holding her finger up and reaching in her purse for her buzzing phone.

She snatches it out and taps the screen. "Hold on a min," she says, turning her back and typing out a text. Damn. She's acting like whatever she's typing is top secret, her fingers flying across the touch screen like a roadrunner.

I used to do that, I think sadly and a surge of loneliness washes over me. *When Ian used to text me, I acted like it was the most important thing in the world to text back immediately.*

"It's Kevin," Eva says when she's done, confirming my suspicion.

I nod and force a smile as I watch Eva slip her phone back into her purse without a worry. "How's he doing?"

"Alright," Eva replies, "but he misses me." My heart clenches in my chest, but I keep the smile plastered on my face. "He hates when I'm away on business trips."

I nod and say a silent prayer of thanks as the bartender comes over and interrupts us. I order a long island iced tea in place of that Bloody Mary so I can get trashed. I'm not messing around tonight. At this point I need something strong.

Eva joins in with the other girls who are gossiping about someone who works for another company now. Someone I don't know.

I nurse my drink and try to keep up and chime in, but I have no clue who and what they're talking about. After a few minutes, their conversation seems to turn to white noise and I find myself staring into my drink, moving the ice around with the straw and wondering why I'm in such a horrible fucking mood.

Hannah and Cary Ann get up, causing me to snap out of it, and announce they're going to go *dance their tits off.* I have to cover my mouth as the guy at the end of the bar looks over at the two of them with a raised brow.

My smile instantly falls as Eva grabs me by the hand and pulls me off my barstool. I resist a little and say, "Seriously, no one wants to see me dance." I haven't had nearly enough alcohol to embarrass myself that much.

"Come on!" She tugs a little harder and I actually have to take a step forward to keep my balance.

"I really don't want to." I shake my head and hold my breath. I know I'm being a downer, but this isn't my thing. At all.

Luckily for me, her phone rings. She instantly drops my hand to take out her phone and begins typing like a mad woman again. I use the moment to plant my ass on the barstool and take out my own cell phone. As if it would possibly have a message waiting for me.

She's texting Kevin again. I really don't see a point in being here. Hannah and Cary Ann are over on the dance floor having the time of their lives, while I'm standing by watching Eva text her boyfriend.

It goes without saying--this night totally blows.

Screw this. I pull my cell out of my clutch and click over to the messages screen. I quickly locate Ian's name.

Your shit better be gone by the time I'm back.

There it is. The same text I sent several days ago. My stomach twists into an angry knot. The message is marked as read, but Ian hasn't even bothered to reply.

No sorry. No begging for me to take him back.

He simply doesn't care.

He's probably shacked up with her right now, fucking her brains out, I tell myself. *In my bed.*

The thought enrages me and before I know it, my fingers are flying across the screen of my cell.

You're a real piece of fucking work, you know that?

I hit send before I can stop myself. Shit. I shouldn't have

done that. I close my eyes, feeling pissed off at myself and at how poorly I'm handling all this shit.

I stuff my phone back in my clutch and turn to Eva. "Hey, I think I'm gonna go," I tell her over the bass of the music.

Eva looks up from her phone and sees the expression of misery on my face. She taps out something quickly and then puts her phone away. "I'll go with you," she offers. I can tell that she's worried about me now, but I don't want her to be.

"Are you sure?" I ask. "You don't have to. We just got here and it looks like Hannah and Cary Ann are having the time of their lives." I gesture toward the other end of the bar where our two coworkers are entertaining a group of young guys. One guy has his face almost resting on Hannah's chest, practically motorboating her tits.

Eva waves away my worry. "Nonsense. I can tell you're not in the mood to be here. Besides, Kevin won't quit texting me. I should go somewhere a little less busy so I can talk to him."

I start to refuse, but then I think better of it. I can tell Eva doesn't want to be here any more than I do. "Okay," I agree. "Thanks."

We go outside, where it's still bustling with tourists, and flag down a cab. Within minutes we're making our way back down the strip to our hotel. At the first stoplight, Eva breaks the silence and asks, "So how do you like it here? And the girls? I know they can be a little crazy, but I think you really fit in well."

"I like them, they seem pretty cool."

Eva looks at me closely, her big eyes concerned. "You're still not bothered by the cheating joke, are you?"

"No. It's cool." Yes I am. But my anger isn't for them.

Eva looks unconvinced. "You sure?"

"You know what I don't understand?" I'm forced to say.

"What?" she asks.

"How Ian couldn't even be bothered enough to tell me sorry for what he did."

"The guy's a scumbag. What would you expect from someone who was having an affair with your friend?" She snorts. "If you can even call her that. I sure as hell wouldn't. A friend wouldn't have slept with my boyfriend the first chance she got."

Her words hit me in the gut. It's true. Why would I expect a selfish jerk to be repentant? "You're right," I say and nod my head. "Ian's trash. I don't know why I expect anything from him. And Sarah? She's a bitch."

"Just forget them, like yesterday's news. Let me be the first one to tell you that you're smart, beautiful, intelligent and going places. And you certainly deserve much better than a cheating asshole." She rubs my arm affectionately.

"Thank you." I bite down on the inside of my cheek before answering, "I really do like it here. Everyone's really nice."

She leans across the seat and gives me a hug as the cab slows to a stop. It's a bit awkward, but I accept it. I'm done with this. I'm done with letting Ian ruin my nights. Fuck him, and fuck Sarah.

"Come on," she says, releasing me and popping her door open. She forces it open wider with her heel and pulls me out.

A young man in a tailored black suit holds the large glass door open for us. He gives me a warm smile and I have to smile back. Inside it's so cool and calm compared to the busy and noisy streets. Our heels click on the marble floors as I walk her to the elevator, right across from the bar.

I could use a drink. That long island didn't do a damn

thing and I don't want to go back to the room feeling so emotionally raw.

"You're not coming up?" Eva asks me as the elevator doors open.

I shake my head. "I want a real drink before I go pass out."

Eva bites her lower lip as she studies me. I can tell she's worried about me. Bless her heart. "Okay," she says finally, pulling me in for a brief hug. "But please don't overdo it." She disappears into the elevator and I make my way inside the hotel's bar.

As I walk in, I remember how I left last time. I remember the gorgeous man in the suit. My body shivers as I remember the way he looked at me, the way his looks make me feel. I could really use one of those looks right now. It made me feel... sexy. Wanted.

I take the closest seat to the exit at thc bar, signaling the waitress for a drink. As I wait for it, I pull out my phone and check the status of the last messages I sent Ian. They haven't been read. God. He's not even reading my texts now. I don't know why, but this makes me feel even more alone and angry.

It's not like there's anything wrong with being alone, I just didn't think I'd wind up single at this age. I smile while placing my order, although it doesn't at all reflect what I feel.

I thought for sure I'd have a couple of babies with Ian by now, I think to myself sadly. I shake off the depressing thought and promise myself that I won't dwell on it anymore. As far as I'm concerned, I dodged a bullet.

The waitress comes back with my glass of cabernet. He gives me a sexy grin as he sets it down. He's a cute brunette and all, sexy even, but I'm just not feeling him. He's not my type.

My stomach twists with desire as I remember Mr. CEO again. There's just something about him. His raw sex appeal and obvious power; the way he wears his suits--like he fucking owns his dominance. It's funny, because in my life of business I'm surrounded by men in suits, but none of them look anywhere near as good as he does in them.

I smile as I bring the glass to my lips.

The bartender must think I'm smiling at him because he winks and says, "It's on the house, sweetheart," when I try to pass him a tip. He gives me a cocky smile as I watch him walk off to serve another patron. I get the feeling he's going to come back over when he's done and try to see if he'll get something for his free drink.

He'll be sorely disappointed if he does. I'm not that cheap.

I'm taking another sip of my cabernet when I suddenly feel a large hand on my waist. I nearly spit my wine out onto my blouse as thick fingers dig into my skin and I turn to push whoever it is away.

"What in the-" I turn to see a man who's gotta be in his late thirties leering at me with his bloodshot eyes. His hair's short, cut in military style and he has a serious case of dimples.

"Hey, sugar. What are you drinking tonight?" asks the man, his breath carrying the strong smell of whiskey.

My first reaction is to tell the man to get the hell away from me. But I glance around the bar and notice the upscale patrons and business people that are probably from the convention. I really don't want to cause a scene and have it get back to my boss.

"Just a glass of wine *by myself* tonight," I say politely, putting emphasis on 'by myself'.

The drunk guy fails to get the message. He tugs on his plaid tie that's already loose around his neck and wobbles as he takes the barstool next to me. Eventually, he manages to mount it and then he turns to me, practically staring at my breasts.

Okay, now I'm seriously uncomfortable.

"You've got a nice outfit on," he says in a low, gravelly voice. He leans in close, invading my personal space, so close that the smell of his breath becomes overpowering. "I think it'd look better on the floor though."

Oh hell. I need to get out of here now.

Just as I'm about to get up and leave Mr. Drunk to hump my empty barstool, I see movement out of the corner of my eye. I turn and my breath catches in my throat at the sight before me. It's Mr. CEO, walking through the bar like he owns the place, and his eyes are focused on me.

CHAPTER 7

LOGAN

I've held many business meetings at restaurants or bars just like this one. The back booth in the Madison Hotel bar is perfect for this meeting. I don't usually like it, but it does have advantages. It makes it easier to slip out and leave the company with a round of drinks on me. But tonight I chose this bar hoping to see my Rose again. And she didn't disappoint.

I noticed her the second she walked in. There's an air around her that commands my attention. Stevens was in the middle of a counterpoint on international resources when she walked through the open doors and walked to the same seat she was in before, directly across from the booth I chose.

I've barely listened to a word from Trent or Stevens. The meeting's done as far as I'm concerned. We're not pushing it through until we meet agreeable terms. Stevens can insist that the cut in costs makes it worth it, but I know better. It's best not to cut corners, especially when quality and timing are concerned.

Her shapely legs are crossed and it pulls her black skirt

up a little farther. She's wearing a loose slightly see-through blouse and even with the dim lighting in the room, I can easily make out her curves. Her tall heels hook onto the leg of the barstool and she sighs heavily before leaning her forearms against the bar and waiting patiently for the bartender.

She came in alone and I can't help but wonder why. My heart slows as I watch her baby blues skim the bar. She's not looking for anyone in particular. She brushes her hair out of her face and leans in slightly to order a drink. I can't hear her, not with all the other noise in this place, but her lips mesmerize me. They're a darker shade of red tonight than I've seen on her before. The deep red makes her beautiful eyes shine brighter, but that look is still there though. That sadness that's haunting her. I don't know what's causing it, but I want to find out.

"Are you going to drink that or not, Parker?" Stevens asks me from across the booth, bringing my attention back to him.

"Not," I answer and push the cold glass with the back of my hand toward Trent.

I stand tall with my shoulders squared, ready to make a move on Rose. I may appear confident, but my nerves are getting the best of me. She could say no; she may not be interested in me in the least. Or worse, she may be taken already, though my research on her didn't turn up any partners. But I'm not going to take no for an answer.

Nothing extreme, I'm just going to offer to buy her a drink. She can't deny me such a small request. I slip off my jacket and loosen my tie.

Trent eyes me suspiciously. "Where are you headed?" he asks with a bit of suspicion in his voice. I never stay for drinks, and I never stay for anything other than business. As my right-hand man, he knows my habits.

Stevens looks past me and right at Rose. His thin lips pull into a smirk and then wider as he realizes my intentions.

"You've got a date, haven't you?" he says, raising his glass of scotch. The ice clinks as Trent leans forward and looks past me to look at Rose as well.

I stand for a moment and let a waitress pass. She gives me a heated look and blushes as she walks by. I keep my eyes straight ahead on my prize and undo the top button of my dress shirt. I don't get nervous about first impressions. I have no one to impress. My track record and bank account are enough to give me a presence in the boardroom.

"A date?" Trent asks with disbelief and then shakes his head. "She has a date, but it's not with Logan." He sits back in the booth, causing the slight shifting of the black leather seat, content with the fact that Stevens must be wrong. It's irritating that he's so sure she's not waiting for me. It shouldn't be annoyed since I shouldn't even be pursuing her, and he knows that. Still, it pisses me off. Maybe more so because she isn't waiting for me. He brings his jack and coke to his mouth as I turn to face my Rose.

And some fucker who's pawing at her.

Anger rises slowly inside me. Anger and jealousy. It's not a good look and I don't let it show, but it's there. It's heating my blood and forcing my limbs to move. His hands are on her as though she belongs to him.

My anger is relieved slightly when I take in her body language. She's not interested. She tries to push him away, but it's not happening. And that's my cue.

I leave, not bothering to look back at either of them. I know they're going to be watching; I don't give a damn what they think.

It only takes six long strides, turning my body ever so slightly between two small tables, until I'm beside her.

I lean forward, laying my jacket down and bracing my hand on the bar between my Rose and this fucker.

"I leave you alone for one night and you're already replacing me?" I look into Rose's widened eyes and wait for her to respond. Her breath hitches, and that sexual tension I've felt the last two times between us rises to a nearly unbearable level. My back is to the asshole who's still not taking the hint. I completely ignore him.

Before she can answer me, I hear the prick clear his throat. "Hey-" His weak tone comes to a halt as I stand and turn to face him. I'm a full inch taller than him. He's got a little muscle to him and could probably get in a good hit if he wanted, but he's got nothing on me. I make it a habit to keep my body in shape. I have to. The thought makes my hands ball into fists until my knuckles turn white, but I release them just as fast.

"Yes?" I ask in a low, threatening voice, daring him to utter a response. I narrow my eyes and wait for him to make his move. He's drunk, but he's not stupid. The intimidation he's feeling is clear on his face, and he struggles to respond. He opens and closes his mouth without saying anything. His forehead's pinched and I can tell he's debating on how to handle it without looking like any more of an ass. I can feel eyes on us and the bar's noticeably quieter. We're all waiting to see what this asshole's going to do.

But he doesn't get a chance to do anything; instead, my eyes are drawn to Charlotte's small hand gripping the front of my shirt. Her other hand comes around my other side to rest just above my hip. She presses her front to my back and I stifle my groan at the feel of her breasts pressed against my lower shoulders.

I look down at her as she peeks her head around my arm to look at me. Her voice is soft but strong, and on the verge of being casual. "You wanna go?"

I look back at the asshole and he takes the chance to turn on his heel and walk off without a word. Smart move on his part. When I look back at my Rose, her eyes are on him as he leaves, and she visibly relaxes, releasing her grip on me.

I miss her touch instantly. I want it back.

As soon as I turn to face her, everything changes. A spark ignites between us and she takes a hesitant step back, suddenly realizing how close she is to me for the first time. The stool behind her scratches against the floor and her hands fall behind her to grip onto it. As though it can protect her from me.

A heated moment passes as her eyes wander down my body. I let a smirk kick up my lips and enjoy the fact that she obviously likes what she sees. The same is true on my part. Up close, she's even more beautiful. Her skin is sun-kissed, but also flushed. She has yet to disappoint me.

I wait for her eyes to find mine again. There's a blush on her cheeks, but the confident woman that took command of the stage is staring back.

"Thank you…" she says, eyeing me warily. "For that."

I hold her gaze. "No need to thank me, Rose."

"It's Charlotte-"

"Charlotte Rose… yes, I know."

"How do you know my name?" she asks suspiciously. Her breathing picks up, making her chest rise and fall a bit faster and I find my eyes drawn to her gorgeous curves. I quickly lift my gaze back to her eyes, but I know she saw.

"I saw your presentation," I answer simply and pull the stool out for her to take a seat.

"I saw." A knowing look crosses her face as she slowly sits down. She parts her lips as if to say more, but the bartender brings a drink and sets it down in front of her. He looks at me and starts to ask if I want a drink, but I wave him off.

She sees and purses her lips. There's an air of distrust around her and I can tell she's debating on getting up and walking away. But I can't let that happen.

Before she can come up with an excuse, I say teasingly, "I think you owe me at least one drink." I set my hands on the bar as I say, "I'm Logan, by the way."

"But you aren't drinking," she says, still eyeing me with caution.

"I'm not," I say easily, although the fact that it makes her suspicious pisses me off. "I'm done drinking for the night." She rests the tip of her finger on the rim of the glass as if debating if she should drink it.

"Your presentation went well," I say to change the subject. "Have you worked for that company very long?" I already know the answer, but I want to get her talking.

"I actually just started," she says a bit peppier, but her body language doesn't match the false tone in her voice. She seems angry, pissed off at me. I don't know why, but fuck, it turns me on.

"What'd you do before this?" I ask her easily before signaling the bartender. I was bred into this lifestyle, so if there's one thing my father taught me well, it's how to charm women. I haven't needed it… ever. But I know I can win her over.

"Let's see..." she pauses and straightens a little as the bartender stops in front of us.

"Could we see the dessert menu, please?" I ask. I'm going to guess she's a chocolate cake kind of woman. "You were saying?" I ask as the bartender sets down a menu and

I slide it over to her. I tap on the picture of the lava cake and raise a brow.

She gives a small shake of her head. "No thanks," she says, eyeing the cake. "I don't want anything."

I grin at her refusal. I'm going to have her eating cake right out of my hand.

I wait for the bartender as she rattles off her past employer, giving me details I'd find on a resume and nothing more. When the bartender catches my eye, I hold up the menu. "The lava cake," I order and then look back at Charlotte.

"And why did you leave?" I ask with genuine curiosity. I have no idea why she left, but I'm grateful she did. Steamens Marketing never attends conferences, so I doubt I would have met her if she hadn't left.

"Because my ex is a cheating prick and my *former* best friend is a whore." The second the last word leaves her lips, she grips the stem of the glass tighter. I imagine her hands gripping my cock with the same force, and my pants grow a little tighter. "I'm sorry," she says a moment later, though it's clear she's not. I love how anger colors her voice. Makes it deeper. Sexier. "I didn't mean for it to come out like that."

My Rose has thorns.

"Nothing to be sorry about," I tell her. "I take it you worked with them?"

"Yes, that's why I left."

I nod my head and say, "So that means you're single."

She pauses for a moment, taken off guard. "I am," she says finally, her voice on edge.

"Well that's a win for me," I say as the bartender sets the cake down on the bar. Two spoons. He's a good man. Charlotte's eyeing me with a look that turns me on; half suspicion, half defiance.

"Would you like a bite?" I ask before I take a bite myself and offer her the other spoon.

She stares at the spoon for a moment. "I don't think so…"

"I insist," I say, swallowing down the cake. It's rich and velvety.

"Well, if you're going to twist my arm," she says, taking the utensil and scooping up a healthy portion. I watch as she closes her eyes and moans around the small bite of cake. My dick hardens as I picture her on her knees wrapping those lush lips around my cock.

She looks back at me with an innocent wide-eyed look. Fuck. I can't tell if she's doing it on purpose to turn me on, or if she's genuinely enjoying it.

"It's delicious," she says, wiping the bit of chocolate from the corner of her mouth and slipping her finger in quickly. "I don't usually eat dessert," she says as she takes another spoonful. "I'm always full by the time I'm done with dinner."

She continues taking small bites, savoring the cake and making my cock rock hard. All the while making casual small talk about the marketing business. She's bright and knowledgeable. My admiration for her grows, as does my sexual appetite.I have to force myself to look away and take another bite. I don't taste a damn thing though, I'm just doing it to get her to take another bite.

Each small bite seems to open her up more and more, until it's all gone and she's scraping the plate for crumbs. That forces a rough chuckle up my chest.

I lean in and whisper, my lips barely touching the shell of her ear, "You're beautiful, Rose." Her head leans back and her lips part. It takes everything in me not to take them with my own. I pull back slightly, fighting the need to restrain myself and when I do, she looks back at me with nothing but lust.

"It's Char-" she starts to respond, then stops as a chair scrapes loudly across the floor behind us.

A group of men rise and make a noisy exit. My eyes flash quickly to them and then back to my Rose who's turned to watch them leave. Her hair is on her opposite shoulder, leaving her slender neck bare. My dick twitches in my pants with the thought of leaning down and leaving an open-mouthed kiss along her neck and down to her shoulder.

"I better get going," she says suddenly. She doesn't move though.

"You don't have to; I'm enjoying your company."

"I have to be up early. The conference is early tomorrow." She looks to the doors of the bar, but again makes no move to leave. "I don't want to give my boss a reason to fire me."

"Let him. I'd hire you in an instant." I'm quick and hard with my words, and I let them resonate with her.

"I'm flattered, really. But I don't think that would be wise," she says flatly. "At all."

She's resisting. I like that. "And why's that?"

"Because... you're…" her voice trails off and she bites her lower lip. Fuck. So sexy.

"I'm what?"

Her voice is heavy when she responds. "Bad."

I chuckle. "Is that so?"

"You almost ruined my presentation, you know that?" she growls angrily, changing the subject. She's grasping at straws here. Trying to find a reason to push me away. How… cute.

So this is why she's a touch on the pissed side. "I did?"

Maybe I shouldn't have made it so obvious that it pleased me when I threw her off her game.

She glares at me, only turning me on more. "Don't play coy. I lost my train of thought because of you." There's a small smile to her lips, letting me know she's not truly angry.

I grin and say, "It's not my fault that you're attracted to me."

"I think you're getting a little ahead of yourself. I said you made me lose my train of thought, not that I wanted to sleep with you." Her eyes stay fixed on the back of the bar.

My grin grows wider. "So now we're talking about sleeping with each other?"

A bright blush colors her cheeks and she doesn't respond for a moment.

I wait for her to look at me. "Tell me why," I say and stare into her eyes. She's defensive and that's fine, but she's also turned on and right now that's all I need her to be.

"Why what?" she asks without moving an inch. That guard of hers is about to crumble around her.

"Why you lost your train of thought when you saw me."

She tries to look away again, but I place my finger on her jaw and tilt her head to face me. "You did the same for me. It's only fair that I affect you just as much."

Her lips part and her eyes heat with lust at the knowledge I've given her, but she still doesn't respond. "Tell me why, my Rose."

"I don't know," she finally answers me.

"I can tell you why," I say. "You want me." She purses her lips and goes silent, clenching her thighs and licking her bottom lip. She fucking wants me. And just as much as I want her.

I lean forward. "You know what I think? I think you

would love to get to know me, that you could learn to love me being your boss."

Her breathing is coming in heavier.

"Tell me," I say and my command brings her eyes back to mine. I want to hear it directly from those beautiful lips of hers.

"I think I'd get in trouble if you were my boss," she says and her breathy words make my dick hard as fucking steel.

"Is that so?" I ask her calmly, moving my hand to her thigh and brushing my thumb back and forth against her bare skin. I lean forward and whisper into the crook of her neck, "I think I'd like that. In fact," I say and pull away to look at her face. Her head's tilted back and her eyes are half-lidded, but then she slowly tilts her head forward and looks me in the eyes. "I'd fucking love it," I conclude.

"We shouldn't do this," she whispers, but I can tell her defenses are nonexistent. She's inches away from being mine.

"We should be doing *exactly* this. I want you." I brush the pad of my thumb along her bottom lip and add, "Tonight."

CHAPTER 8

CHARLOTTE

Although I'm walking with confidence behind him, I'm a ball of nerves on the inside. I shouldn't be doing this. It's reckless. Stupid, even. But my primal needs are winning the battle with common sense. I'm so messed up over Ian, I feel like I need this. I *need* Logan.

His hand splays across my back as I stand next to him at the elevator. I peek over my shoulder toward the entryway. I don't want anyone to see. This will look bad. My panic rises, but then Logan leans into me, so close I can feel his hot breath on my neck, sending shivers down my back.

"Relax," Logan says to me, his voice deep and sexy, the sound causing prickles to go up all along my arms. God, I could just melt into him. What's worse is that I can't think of a reason not to. As my eyes close with lust, the doors open with a loud *ping,* knocking me out of my trance.

He pulls me into the elevator, pressing me up against the wall.

A feeling of panic surges through me, telling me to get the hell out before the door closes. But I fight the need to run as the doors close slowly and his large body cages me in.

What's so bad about giving into my desires?

It's just one night.

A night in Vegas.

What happens here, stays here. Right?

There's nothing for me to worry about.

The thought gives me the courage to reach up and spear my fingers through his hair as he leans in for a passionate kiss and the elevator climbs the floors. I open my mouth wider and let him in, arching my body and moaning into his mouth.

His hands roam up my side, causing me to lean into him. I want him to take me. Right here, right now.

The elevator reaches his floor as I'm clawing at the buttons on his shirt. I pull away from him, breathless and nearly gasping, and he leads me down a long, ornate hallway to a large door.

He's hasty with getting the key into the door, his other hand holding mine, and when he opens it my breath catches in my throat. It's a penthouse suite, with floor-to-ceiling windows, a vast open floor plan, and stunning contemporary furniture.

Holy shit, I think to myself. *This place is incredible.* Luxury. It oozes luxury the way he oozes power.

I don't get time to admire the stunning view, because suddenly Logan is pressed against me, sending my body temperature soaring and his lips pressing hungrily against mine. His hands find my ass cheeks, gripping them tightly before lifting me into the air and my legs wrap around his waist instinctively.

He pulls away from me for a moment, keeping me perfectly balanced. Below, I can feel his big, throbbing cock pressing against my pussy, demanding entry. Fuck! God,

I'm so wet for him. I suck in a heavy breath, my chest heaving with desire.

He carries me up the stairs to the loft, holding me firm every step of the way and kissing along my neck. I struggle not to squirm in his embrace as my nails dig into his crisp white dress shirt. He kicks the door shut and throws me on a king-size bed in the center of the room. I bounce on the bed with a gasp and I look up at him as he stands above me, his huge cock pressed against his slacks, my breathing a series of desperate pants.

For a moment, I'm filled with fear at what's about to take place, but burning desire sweeps it aside as Logan slowly takes off his tie and then his shirt. My legs scissor on the bed as I sit up and take in the sight of him. His muscles flex as he tosses his shirt to the floor. My pussy clenches around nothing. I push the hair off my neck, feeling hotter. I feel like I'm on fire.

It's just one night.

It feels so wrong, having a one-night stand. But I'm dying to have one with a man like him. Especially knowing he wants me as much as I want him. And no one will know. My fingers reach for the buttons on my blouse and I slowly undo them with trembling hands.

His eyes stay focused on mine. His heated gaze is a trance pinning me to the bed to do his bidding. He won't let me go.

As the silky fabric slips off my shoulders and the blouse falls into a pool around me, he makes a move to come closer for the first time. He unbuttons his pants and shoves them down as his lips attack my neck. He ravages me while he rips my bra down and sucks a nipple into his mouth.

My head falls back and soft moans spill from my lips, along with whispers and pleas for him to do what he wants to me. To take me. I don't recognize my own voice. I don't recognize the woman I am, caught in the heat of the moment and desperate for him.

My clit's throbbing as he pushes me farther up the bed and pulls my skirt down over my ass and off of me. I'm so hot for him. So wet. He groans as he cups my pussy, the thin lace the only thing separating us.

I expect him to rip them with the way he's handled me so far. But he doesn't. He sits back on his heels, and that's when I realize he's completely naked. I can barely breathe as his fingers slide gently up my thighs, leaving goosebumps and shivers up my body,

He gently pulls the lace down my ass and I have to lift up slightly for him to pull them off. His eyes stay on mine. My chest rises and falls harder with each passing second. I can't believe I'm doing this. He reaches over to the nightstand and I can't quite see what he's doing, but the sound of a wrapper makes it obvious.

Shit, I didn't even think about asking. What am I doing? As my body heats with anxiety, he pushes my legs farther apart.

I start to prop myself up on my elbows and think about backing out. It's all too fast, too soon, but his lips crash against mine and his large hand grips my hip, holding me down.

My body melds to his as he lowers his chest to mine. He nips my bottom lip as he pushes the head of his cock just slightly into my pussy. My body begs me to move, to take him in deeper, but his grip on me is relentless.

His large body cages mine in and the look in his eyes takes my breath away.

"Tell me again," he says and his deep voice vibrates up his chest. His eyes are the brightest I've ever seen as he stares at me, willing me to obey him. It takes a second for me to realize what he wants to hear.

"I want you," I say, and as the last word slips past my lips, he slams into me. His large cock fills me almost to the brink of pain. My back bows and I let out a strangled cry of pleasure. So full, so hot. He stays buried deep inside of me, letting my walls adjust to his size before pushing farther in. My legs squeeze around his hips and my toes curl. It's too much. I whimper as he pulls out slightly and then pushes forcefully back in.

He groans in the crook of my neck, "I knew you'd feel like this." I wish I could respond. I try, but nothing comes out. My neck arches, forcing my head to dig into the mattress as he fucks me at a merciless pace.

He kisses my neck as my head thrashes and he thrusts over and over into me.

My nails dig into his back as I grip onto him as though he can save me from the overwhelming sensations threatening to consume me.

His pace picks up and forces a scream from me. My body heats in intense waves as my nerve endings ignite all at once.

He rides through my orgasm, thrusting his hips at an angle that brushes against my throbbing clit each time. Pushing my orgasm higher and stronger, and dangerously close to too much.

"Logan!" I scream out his name as another release crashes through me.

My breathing is frantic at the feeling of him pushing in me to the hilt and I feel his thick cock pulsing against my tight walls.

He gently kisses my neck and my shoulder as my body trembles beneath his.

His large frame moves away from mine, leaving the cool air to kiss my skin. He plants a single kiss against my lips and I easily return it. It's a tender touch, one I wasn't expecting.

As the highs of my orgasm come crashing down and slowly leave me in waves, I realize what I've done. I pull up the covers a little higher and wonder if I should leave.

I can hear the muted padding of his footsteps against the tiled floor as he turns on the light to the bathroom and faint light floods the room. I see my clothes on the floor. And suddenly I feel cheapened.

I knew what I was doing.

I try to calm myself as he comes back into the bedroom. His corded muscles ripple as he walks to the edge of the bed. It dips with his weight as he peels the covers back. His eyes are on my face as he does it, as though he's expecting me to protest, and a part of me wants to.

He runs a damp cloth between my legs and kisses my neck as I wince. I'm already a bit sore. I already feel regret working its way into my consciousness.

My body stiffens as he gets off the bed and leaves me with my thoughts.

I need to get out of here the moment I get the chance. And forget this ever happened.

CHAPTER 9

LOGAN

My Rose shifts in my arms. She hasn't been still since I crawled into bed next to her. Something's off. Everything was exactly how I imagined it'd be. Until it was over.

I keep my breathing steady and eyes closed. I pretend like I'm asleep. I'm not though, and I haven't been. I don't sleep well at all, let alone with someone next to me.

I know she's going to bolt. She's a runner. That's easy to tell. I don't mind, because I know she won't be running far. Come Monday, she'll be in my building and I'll have more control of the situation. Right now I'm limited.

The comforter moves slowly down my body as she slips out of the bed and lets a gentle chill in. There's a soft creak from the bed and she stills. Her breathing is the loudest sound in the room. After a moment, she finally moves. I can hear everything she does. I can practically picture her slipping her clothes into place as the sounds fill my ears.

She's sneaking out. I have to force myself not to smile at the thought. If only she knew.

I open my eyes to peek at her as I hear her walk over to my desk. What the fuck is she doing?

Everything I have is password-protected, so that doesn't matter, but if she's snooping then I have a much larger problem on my hands. Although, that could work to my benefit, but that wasn't the kind of relationship I had in mind.

My heart squeezes slightly in my chest as I hear her pick up her clutch off the nightstand. She's leaving. It's amusing in some ways, but disappointing in others. I wonder for a moment if she thinks this is what I want, or if it's her preference to leave.

I suppose it doesn't matter though. This will be the first and last time she slips out on me.

I wait a minute as I hear the door open and close with a faint click, leaving me in silence. She left. I'm not completely surprised, but it does cause a stir of emotions that I'm not fond of. There's a reason I stopped forming any attachments. People are good at leaving.

Once I'm sure she's not coming back, I move from the bed and walk straight to the desk to see what the hell she touched. A sticky note is affixed to the top of my laptop.

Sorry I slipped out, I had to go. Thank you for last night.

I huff a humorless laugh and run my finger along the feminine script. She's a runner, but I already knew that. I wasn't expecting this; it doesn't change anything though.

A wicked smile turns my lips up. She's going to be shocked on Monday. More than that, pissed.

I'm looking forward to the fight though. I know there will be one, and the thought makes my dick twitch. I look back to the empty bed and rumpled sheets. If she were here now, I'd take her again.

I'd make sure her sweet cunt was so fucking raw tomorrow she thought of me every time she sat down. It's a tight fit with her, so hopefully I left her so fucking sore it lasts until Monday.

My smile fades, and I toss the note to the desk. She's not here, and she's not mine yet.

But she will be.

I walk to the bathroom, stretching and remembering how good she felt beneath me. She was everything I wanted. I flick the light on and dig in the travel case on the counter.

It's only a matter of time before I have her again. Next time, she won't slip out in the middle of the night.

I look down at the pill case as I pop a tab open, revealing the brightly colored pills and hate that I have to take them. I hate it all. I hate myself more.

I've set the pieces in play for her downfall. All because I selfishly want her.

I take three pills and swallow them, not bothering with water to wash it down.

I toss the case on the bathroom counter and walk to my briefs on the floor of the bedroom, carelessly putting them on before sitting back at the desk in the room and opening my laptop.

It's nearly 4 a.m., but there's work to do, and I know I won't be sleeping tonight. I'm sure there are at least a few dozen emails that require my immediate attention. My assistant will have a list for me in only two hours. I should finalize the other business deal I came here for, although I'm not sure I'm interested if they don't come down in price and agree to the last two terms.

I sigh heavily and run my hands through my hair. It's just another day. They'll bend to what I want, or I'll simply walk away. That's how it works in my line of business. And they know it.

As soon as the screen comes to life, her picture stares

back at me. I never should have touched her. I'm a bastard for what I'm doing.

My heart clenches slightly, a feeling I'm not used to. I start to feel regret, but she loved every second of it. I made her come alive beneath me. I saw how she became paralyzed with pleasure under me. I can give her that. I can give her the escape she desperately needs.

She's running away from her past more than she's running toward me. This will help her.

Even as I try to justify it, I know there's no good reason I should continue this. I know this is wrong. I don't give a fuck though.

I still want her. And I'm not going to take no for an answer. Nothing is going to keep me from having her.

CHAPTER 10

CHARLOTTE

I wince as I set my suitcase down in the living room of my apartment.

I'm still hurting from Logan. It's such a good hurt though. One I've never felt before.

My sore pussy clenches with desire at the thought of the previous night. The way Logan fucked me has me going through all sorts of unwanted emotions all morning. I crave the feeling of my body aching, but it was a one-time thing. Seriously, he's a master in bed--a fucking sex god. I can't help that I want more. Ian has never been that hungry for my body, nor attentive to my needs.

Selfish bastard. Neither has anyone else I've ever been with.

As I stand up straight, a feeling of guilt washes over me. I've been running from the feeling all morning, but now it's finally caught up with me.

Logan gave me the best sex of my life, I tell myself, *and I repaid him by leaving him with just a note.*

I'm not sure why I care so much. I feel horrible. Like I've committed some awful crime. Logan most likely doesn't give a shit. After all, it was just a one-night stand. And I'm sure he gets more pussy than a cat catcher. We'll never see each other again, anyway.

I set my coat down and begin unpacking when I notice a box sitting beside the couch. It's Ian's, and it's sitting exactly where it was when I left. I glare at it, anger knotting my stomach.

"I told him his shit better be gone when I got back," I mutter angrily. "Figures it's still here."

I feel like going over and kicking it, and then stomping it with all the rage I have pent up inside. I resist the urge. It won't do me any good. What I need to find out is if he's been here or not. He could just be fucking with me, trying to piss me off.

I walk into the kitchen and see that his work keys are gone. They were here when I left, so it means he came and got them, but left his box of shit.

I'm quick to grab my cell and send him a text.

You left a box of your shit here. Can you come get it, please?

I want to add on 'asshole' at the end of the message, but I exercise immense restraint and just press send. I stare at the screen and wait for a response before adding:

If you don't come get it, I'm going to donate it to the Salvation Army.

He's had plenty of time, and I've been more than reasonable. I wait for a reply, but after it becomes clear he's not going to respond, I let out a sigh and set my cell on the table. Staring at it and resisting the urge to smash it with a hammer, just because it reminds me of him.

"I need a cup of coffee," I mutter, walking over to the Keurig machine, starting it, and then sitting down in a kitchen chair. I bought this dining set right before he moved in. My first meal at this table was with him. I cooked something special, I don't remember what. I let out a long exhale and try to ignore the painful reminder that I once loved him. I gave him everything I had.

Sighing, I place my head in my hands and try to calm my racing thoughts.

I focus on work. That's always a good outlet. It's productive and motivating. But even after acing my presentation at the convention, I feel stressed. There's a meeting on Monday and I have to be prepared, but with thoughts of Logan and the prospect of dealing with Ian on my mind, it's going to be a struggle.

I'm on edge and afraid of losing my job. I was hired as a temp, so I'm essentially on a probationary period. All signs point to me being just fine, but I'm feeling so damn insecure. Even though after how good I did with my presentation, I should be more than fine. I guess I'm worried because after losing Ian, my job is the only thing I have left.

At this point, I need my job just to stay sane, I tell myself as I pick at the loose thread on the tablecloth. I need a new one. I need a new everything.

Definitely a new man… like Logan. I wish I were back in Logan's bed, being devoured, feeling wanted. No man has ever made me feel like that before. I felt... powerful sleeping with a man of his stature.

I shake off the desire and the guilt from leaving.

It's best that I left the way I did and nipped that in the bud. A relationship between us would've ended badly anyway. I could easily see myself getting attached to him and then being discarded like yesterday's news. I don't need a man right now. I run my hands down my face and get up as I hear the coffee machine spurting out the last few drops.

I don't need anyone. I pour a ton of sugar in my mug and then stir it up before sitting back down.

Monday morning will be here before I know it. Then I can stop all this worrying and just focus on work.

I take a nice, relaxing sip of coffee and already feel a little better, so I check my phone. Still no message from the asshole even though it's marked as read. Fucking hell. I slam it down on the table and grip my coffee cup.

"Whatever," I mutter, resisting the urge to send him a particularly nasty text. I am a better person than this, and I do not need to lower myself to his level.

I get up from the table and walk into the living room and take my anger out on Ian's box instead, delivering several sharp kicks to it. My coffee's in my hand and the first kick sends a little spilling over the side of the box. I don't care. I use the inside of my foot so it doesn't hurt. Or maybe I'm just not kicking hard enough since there's only a small pathetic dent in the side of the cardboard. Whatever. I feel better. Sort of.

Not nearly as good as I felt last night.

If being with Logan taught me anything, it's that Ian didn't know a goddamn thing about putting it down in the bedroom. Just thinking about it causes my pussy to throb with need and pain, a reminder of how hard Logan fucked me. Shivers tingle down my spine and send goosebumps over my body.

Shit, I need to go upstairs and work until I pass out and get him out of my head. It's the best thing for me.

Pushing Logan from my mind, I check all the messages on my landline and make sure the doors are locked before turning in for a long night of work. As I climb the stairs to my room, I realize getting Logan, his powerful body, and his massive cock out of my mind will not be an easy task.

It's definitely going to be a long weekend till Monday.

CHAPTER 11

CHARLOTTE

Thank fuck it's Monday. Getting Logan off my mind… well, it didn't happen. I got a ton of work done and even forgot about my asshole ex. But every time I fell asleep, I dreamed of Logan's touch. That's not a good sign. And waking up horny and lonely is not a good combination.

As I climb out of the car and head to the building, I know I need to immerse myself in work and forget about both Ian and Logan.

I walk into the office building, shoving the door open with my forearm as I carry my daily morning coffee in one hand, and a paper bag with a tempting donut I couldn't resist in the other, and do a double take.

What the fuck? I think in panic. There are boxes everywhere. Literally, everything in the front room is packed away. Feeling weak in the knees, I lean against the doorjamb, my breathing coming in shallow gasps, my heart pounding.

Oh my God! I yell in my mind. *The company sold out.*

There were rumors last week of a buyout, but I thought they were just rumors. Fuck!

As I try to calm my racing heart, I think of every other place close by that I can apply to. I need a job as soon as fucking possible. But there's literally nowhere else. I know. I fucking applied practically everywhere two weeks ago!

"Are you okay?" asks a familiar voice near my ear.

I jump and let out a little cry of surprise as I drop the bag with my donut. "Jesus, Eva!" I complain, turning to face her with my hand over my heart.

She looks beautiful today in her black pantsuit and dark glossy heels, her hair pulled back in a businesslike ponytail. More than that, she looks fine. Calm, even. "You scared the shit out of me," I say admonishingly. I gesture nervously at all the boxes. "What the fuck is going on?" I ask in a hushed voice as I bend to pick up my bag.

Eva looks at me with apprehension and then lets out a laugh. "Someone's bought the company. But don't worry, it's a silent partnership." She sounds all peppy and happy. I don't know if she's got inside information that's making her feel secure, or if she's just naive. "We have a board meeting about it in like five minutes." She leans in close and whispers, "You didn't read your email on Friday, did you?"

"Shit." I just breathe the word. I don't remember an email, but my head has been so lost in thought.

Eva shakes her head. "It's fine," she says as she waves it off and walks with me to the meeting room in the back corner of the building. "From what I can gather, the company was forbidden to talk about the sale while it was under contract. That's why I'm guessing we never heard about it." She places a comforting hand on my shoulder, seeing the worry etched across my face. "Don't worry,

Charlotte. We've been assured that our jobs aren't in any danger."

"How can we trust that?" I ask. "You know how those corporate heads at the top think. They don't give a crap what happens to us down at the bottom." Anxiety is coursing in my blood. I wish I could trust her, but I can't.

"Because it's under the terms and conditions in the agreement of the sale. They can't fire any current employees for several years."

"Are you absolutely sure?"

"Positive."

I let out a small sigh of relief I relax slightly, bringing my coffee to my lips. I make a promise to myself not to freak out until I have a real reason to.

"But there's a catch," Eva adds, and I hold back a groan. "Part of the agreement involves relocating, hence all the boxes."

Behind Eva, I watch as several people walk into the boardroom. I can handle this change. Sometimes change is good.

I shift the bag to hold it in one hand along with my coffee so I can scratch at the back of my neck as we walk into the room and take our seats. "Where's the new building?" I ask her quietly. Everyone around us is engaged in quiet small talk, too.

"Parker-Moore on the city skyline," Eva replies. "About a half hour from here?"

I nod, but I'm not really happy. "That sucks." I vaguely recognize the company name. I almost applied with them, but I didn't. The skyline is a far drive. This place is nearly half an hour-long commute for me. So now I'm looking at an hour-long drive, and that's without traffic.

"Yeah, it does." Eva nods in agreement. "But it could be worse. We could all be looking at pink slips right now and a shitty severance that barely covers a month's worth of living expenses."

I sigh. "I guess you're right."

Mr. Hastings walks into the room, waving his hands to quiet the room of gossiping employees. "I know some of you are concerned with the buyout, but please rest assured that none of your jobs are in jeopardy. I'll kindly ask you all to go with the flow for now, as this is just another normal day working here, and help with packing things up."

"For those of you who have long commutes to get here already, temporary housing will be available for you if you need it. If you don't want, or are unable to pack your items yourself, please label them and move them against the far wall."

Hannah stands next to Hastings with a stack of large booklets in her hand. Mr. Hastings gives her a tight smile and then gestures at the bundle she's holding. "Hannah here has all the packets of information you'll need about the new company and housing. All of you are expected to have moved and completed the transfer by the end of the workday, and will be required to attend tomorrow at the new work site. If you can't move your items to your new office, simply label the boxes and put them against the far wall. The movers will handle the transfer for you and they'll be waiting for you in the new building tomorrow."

I barely pay attention to the questions everyone asks and the vague answers Hastings has as I accept my packet of information from Hannah, and try to stop worrying about the long drive that I'm going to have now. At least I have a job. I keep telling myself that throughout the meeting. That's what matters.

The meeting's finally adjourned, and I return to my office without a word. There are moving supplies lined up against the far wall and I grab a roll of packing tape and a few boxes. I think I'll only need two.

Eva's gabbing with the other girls, but I just want to get this going and begin sifting through my things, making sure everything's in order. I can talk to them later, when I'm calm and less on edge. My hands tremble as I organize my things, a feeling of anxiety overtaking my body.

I hate this shit. I don't want to have to relocate. I tape up the bottom of one box and cringe at the sound of the tape pulling from the roll. I grit my teeth as I pick up the things from my desk and easily set everything in the box. It's like deja vu. I just did this. I close my eyes and cringe. I just fucking did this.

Eva comes in when I'm almost finished taping up the last of my boxes and I try to keep a positive vibe around me. I don't want my negativity rubbing off on her.

"You know, this could turn out to be pretty good," she tells me as she steps into my small office. It's really small and with her in the doorway, it already feels cramped.

She has a stack of papers in her hand and a smile on her face. "I heard we're going to be getting raises, and the new company is going to be bringing in an influx of clients." She leans against the wall, making herself comfortable. "Hastings is so excited about this. He told me there's going to be *huge* opportunities for us."

"I'll believe it when it happens," I say skeptically.

"Pessimist," Eva teases. She begins to walk out of the room, but then stops. "Hey, you know what? I just looked up our new boss on my phone. He's fucking crazy hot. Like seriously, I don't even know how he's a CEO of a company and not out modeling somewhere."

Probably not as hot as Logan, I think to myself.

"Let me see," I say. I almost want to tell her about

Logan… I wanna brag, but I shouldn't. A one-night stand doesn't color anyone in a pretty light.

"You're gonna totally flip," Eva warns me. She walks over to my desk and sets her papers down and then pulls her cell out the pocket of her chic-as-fuck pantsuit. I eye it with a hint of jealousy as she brings up the picture. "Say hello to our new boss. Or as I'd like to say, BILF." She takes out her phone and brandishes it my face, grinning with absolutely glee. "See? Isn't he the hottest fucking thing you've ever seen?"

My heart nearly stops at the grinning face staring back at me. Eva stares at me, waiting for me to react, but I can't speak. Not a single. Fucking. Word.

Oh my God. It's him.

CHAPTER 12

LOGAN

I lean back on the bench. It's nearly six thirty and I need to leave. I'm anxious to leave, in fact. I haven't been this damn excited for work in years.

The crisp morning air whips across my freshly shaven face. It feels refreshing as I take a deep inhale and listen to the wind. The soft, relaxing sounds are interrupted by my father's low, gruff voice. Bringing me back to the present.

"How was the conference?" he asks me. His voice is a bit muffled. It's not the strong tone I grew up with. His stroke left him paralyzed down his entire left side.

I lean forward with my elbows on my knees and look up at him. He's on the opposite bench. I'm facing the the stone wall of the back of the nursing home and he's overlooking the woods behind me. "Productive. I knew it would be."

He nods his head and looks behind me. The daylight is just rising through the trees behind the nursing home. It's private and the gardens are comforting for my father. Or so he says.

"So you settled on which of the two?" he asks. Although

the stroke left him physically impaired, he's mentally the same man he's always been, and I do my best to include him. Although I don't have to. But it gives him something to do that's useful. His life used to revolve around work. It was all he had. Growing up, I barely ever saw him and when I did, he made sure I knew I was being groomed to take over the business.

We didn't have father-son time. We had business training. At times I resented him. I hated watching my mother lose interest in the two of us. She looked at me as though it was my fault that he spent every waking moment in his office. I don't remember a time that she looked at me with love. She hated that I was just like him. Even though I had no choice, that didn't matter to her.

"Armcorp."

His brow furrows and he pats his right hand against his leg. I can tell he's not happy with the decision.

"Fairmont would have been better," he says simply. He hasn't been happy with many of my decisions over the last seven years. Each year I've branched further and further away from his counsel.

"I wanted this one." I tell him the truth, which is more than I gave Trent. I won't admit to anyone that I made a business decision because of a woman.

His eyes flash to mine. "Wanted?"

"Yes," I say simply. I wanted it, so I took it. I wanted *her*. There's no discussion on this matter. I'm the CEO, this was my decision, and as selfish as it was, it's done. I'm not turning back on my word.

My father must sense that I've come to terms with this choice. He doesn't push me for more. As I stare back at him and his eyes move to the forest behind me, I see him for who he is in this moment. Once a strong man of power, now weak and reliant on others. I grit my teeth, hating that this is the way it works. I'll be him one day. In many ways, I already am.

"How are the treatments going?" he asks after a long quiet moment.

"Everything's fine." I look him in the eyes as I answer.

He breaks eye contact and the corners of his lips turn down into a scornful frown. "That's what your mother used to say."

I don't hide my scowl. I hate it when he brings her up. I hate thinking about her in general. My father may have raised me to be a cold ruthless fuck incapable of real attachments and emotion, but at least he tried to be there for me.

My mother is a money hungry bitch. She took my father for everything he had and moved on to the next rich man she could spread her legs for. I was a hindrance for her. I haven't spoken to her in at least three years, maybe more. I don't need this today.

I give my father a tight smile. "I need to get going."

He eyes me, but nods slightly.

"Come back tomorrow," he says without looking at me.

I don't know why I even come here anymore. Some false sense of obligation to a man who never knew me, I guess. He gave me this life. He raised me to be the man I am. I should be grateful. Men would kill to be in my position, but I want something more. I don't want to end up like him.

I nod, unsure of whether or not he sees and walk quickly through the path at the front of the nursing home. My Aston Martin's out front, waiting for me. I usually have Andrew drive me so I can get work done in the limo during the drive. But not today. Today is different.

I try to remember the easy feeling I had this morning. The excitement of seeing her reaction as I settle into my seat and look at the phone sitting on top of my suit jacket. I'll be in the office in twenty minutes, but I want to know now if she's already there.

Charlotte. I did this for her. She could quit though. I imagine the thought has crossed her mind more than once since she found out.

As I go through the list of signatures, I spot her feminine writing.

I lean back easily as I start my car. It rumbles with a soft purr of satisfaction that mirrors what I'm feeling.

At least I have my Rose waiting for me.

CHAPTER 13

CHARLOTTE

"Can you believe how amazing this is?" I ask Eva, staring up at the tall Parker-Moore skyscraper. We're both preparing to go inside for our first day of work, starting with the board meeting, but have to stop to admire the workmanship of Parker-Moore. This building has to be the tallest and finest corporate building in all of downtown.

Eva shades her eyes, squinting up into the sky. "It sure beats Armcorp's, that's for sure. Makes it look like a hut."

"I guess we *are* about to get a pay raise," I predict, stifling a yawn that creeps up regardless of the fact I'm an emotional wreck. Last night I was unable to sleep because my thoughts were consumed by Logan and what this all meant. I feel awful that I'm this exhausted on my first day at my new job, and I'm almost convinced I'm going to mess something major up and end up out on the street. At least Eva's company during our carpool kept my mind off of Logan. And the fact that he's now my boss. Thinking about it causes anxiety to wash through me, but I shove it down, gripping my purse as if it can save me. "There's no way we won't," I say with as much confidence as I can manage.

Eva tears her eyes away from the tall building and growls, "You're damn right we will."

Our heels click across the polished marble floors as we enter the lobby, and my jaw nearly drops. It's even more beautiful on the inside than it is the outside. The walls are painted a muted shade of taupe, and they're adorned with gorgeous antique paintings that must've cost a fucking ton. Complementing everything is upscale, contemporary furniture. Seriously, some of this stuff I wish I could steal and take home to put in my living room.

On top of that, in the middle of the room sits a beautiful marble fountain with a naked Greek statue at its center, filling the giant lobby with the soothing sounds of running water. Meanwhile, classical music plays softly over a speaker system giving the atmospheric vibe a very relaxing feel.

It feels so high class in here.

"I feel like a high-class whore now," Eva whispers to me as we watch employees making their way to whatever departments they're headed to.

"I know, right?" I say, swallowing back another yawn.

We share a nervous smile and then continue on to the hallway and enter an elevator. Thankfully, no one else gets on, and it's just the two of us. Eva presses the button for the top floor, and the door slides close.

As we rise to the top floor, I start feeling even sicker with anxiety. This is a big day for me, and I don't want to fuck it up somehow. I keep feeling like something bad is going to happen and I'm going to end up without a job, even though I should be confident in my abilities. It's because of Logan. I have no clue what he's going to say or do when I see him.

By the time we reach the top floor, I feel like I'm going to hurl.

Seeing my worry, Eva gives me a pat on the back before we leave the elevator. "It's gonna be okay," she assures me. She has no fucking clue.

I'm a ball of nerves as we enter the new boardroom. I literally feel like I'm trembling all over. For a moment, I want to run away and flee the building.

You have to stop this, I tell myself, steeling my resolve. *You are in control. There is nothing you can't do.*

As we make our way to two empty seats around the large mahogany meeting table, my heart skips a beat.

Logan's sitting at the head of the table, looking sharp as a tack in his grey, crisp business suit, his hair gelled and slicked to the side. God, he's so fucking handsome. He looks like he owns the entire room, like corporate royalty. I can feel his eyes on me, boring into me with an intensity that causes my skin to prickle.

I'm forced to look away, my cheeks burning, my mind filled with images of our night of hot sex.

I don't know how I'm going to get through this, I think as I lower myself in my seat and place my briefcase on the floor next to my chair, doing my best to avoid his gaze. Honestly, I feel like Logan can make me cum by just looking at me. Lord knows how fucking horny I am, having thought about his hot body and massive cock all night. I couldn't help it. I almost didn't come. But I need this job. If I didn't, I would have quit the second I found out he was my new boss.

Unconsciously I bring my thighs close together and my pussy clenches with need. Shit, my panties are wet. I'm annoyed by this, but I can't help it. I'm practically burning up with a desire that's almost painful.

In fact, if I were a guy, I'd have a case of blue balls right about now. The funny thought does nothing to ease the tension running through my body.

Noticing my obvious discomfort, Eva glances over at me. "You alright?" she asks softly.

"Yeah," I say, my voice strained. "Just a little nervous."

She smirks and nods toward Logan while leaning in and whispering, "He's absolutely gorgeous, isn't he?"

You have no fucking idea.

"Fucking fabulous," I mutter, keeping my eyes carefully in the safe zone.

Luckily for me, the meeting officially begins and several speakers get up to talk about the merger, going over the finer details of the contract. A lot of it was already told to us by Hastings and is outlined in the pamphlets we received the day prior.

I concentrate on keeping my eyes on the speakers, until the last one sits.

Logan rises to his feet and speaks for the first time. His rough baritone voice sends shivers through my body. He stands tall and commanding. It's obvious that he's the one in charge, and he should be.

I try to ignore the effect he has on me and when that doesn't work, I try to ignore him entirely, concentrating on the table, the blank projection screen behind him. The beautiful wallpaper in the room. Anything and everything except for him.

He begins announcing job positions of his new employees. I listen intently, half marveling at how sexy and deep his voice sounds, and half wanting to get up and run from the room. I don't expect Logan's going to call my name for anything important, and if he does, I'm convinced he's going to regulate me to an intern position just to put me in my place for slighting him. The thought makes my stomach twist with anxiety. I fucking hope not. I don't know if I'll be able to handle myself if he does. Thoughts of trying not to call him out and making a fool of myself run rampant in my mind.

When he says my name, however, I almost need to be picked up off the floor.

"Miss Harrison is the new head of the sales department," Logan announces, turning to look at me with a mischievous smile, his eyes sparkling with mirth.

Almost immediately, Eva gives me a congratulatory pat on the back followed by a thumb up, her eyes sparkling with pride. "Congrats, girl!" she whispers fiercely. "You deserve it." I feel all eyes in the room on me and several of my coworkers start whispering amongst themselves. And I can't blame them, I had only just stared at Armcorp's a few weeks ago.

Meanwhile, I'm unable to react, frozen with disbelief. Seriously, I'm fucking floored and feel absolutely sick to my stomach. I mean, what is Logan thinking? After the night we shared, this has to be a huge fucking conflict of interest.

And it's the reason why he did it, I say to myself, noticing the way Logan is getting a kick out of this. He did this on purpose. I wonder how long he'll play up this charade. I've never had a position like this before. Head of Sales. I don't know if I can handle it.

Maybe that's why he assigned it to me. I don't know what to think. I don't know how I should feel either. I don't know if I should be angry, but I damn sure am shocked.

Looking like he's firm and confident in his decision, Logan outlines my role and duties in great detail. I'm to be in charge of twelve new clients, all of whom are from his company and have no marketing strategy, and we launch in four weeks.

"You can create your own team," Logan says when he's finished outlining what I need to do, "but you will be solely responsible for each of the launches."

I sit there, simmering with disbelief and worry. Being new, I have practically no resources at my disposal to make things happen so quickly.

"Mr. Parker," Hastings politely interrupts. He's sitting near the head of the table, next to Logan's seat. "I think you're asking a bit much of Charlotte. She's new here." Nausea threatens to humiliate me. Even my boss who had all the praise in the world for me doesn't think I can handle it.

Logan turns to survey Hastings with a grim expression. "There's a reason Armcorp hired her and then made her the keynote speaker. I was there for the presentation. And I plan to take full advantage of Miss Harrison."

CHAPTER 14

LOGAN

"Miss Harrison?" I raise my voice so Rose can hear me as everyone starts filing out of the room. She was the first to stand when the meeting was concluded, and it's obvious she's making a run for it. She wants to get away from me, but I'm not done with her yet.

She turns slowly to face me, pulling at the sleeve of her blouse as she says, "Yes, Mr. Parker?" Hearing her soft, sweet voice makes me want her even more. It was difficult enough to restrain myself throughout the hour-long meeting. Now that it's over, I'm ready to face my Rose. I'm anxious to see her reaction. She's obviously affected, but the lack of an outward reaction has me on edge.

"Stay for a moment, please. I'd like to have a word."

Trent speaks in a low voice as he stands to leave, "Let's meet at three to go over these last two files."

I nod although I'm not quite paying attention. It can wait.

A woman next to Charlotte, obviously a friend, asks quietly if she wants her to stay behind. I narrow my eyes and wait for her to respond. I can barely hear her over the sounds of everyone else leaving and quietly talking to one another. I don't hear what Charlotte says, but I see her shake her head no. It soothes the beast inside of me pacing with the need to be alone with Rose. Good girl. She may have conflicting feelings, but she's playing along for now.

I can feel Hastings looking back at me as he exits, waiting to catch my eye, but I ignore him and gesture to the chair in front of me while making eye contact with Rose instead. I wait a moment, watching her hesitantly stand at her chair while the rest of the company files out around her.

"I'd like to talk to you afterward, Charlotte," Hastings says to her loud enough for me to hear. I resist the urge to smirk at him. He can feel however he wants about her being head of sales. They picked her to do that presentation for a reason. She's damn good at what she does. We need to impress clients, and she knows how to do that. I don't give a fuck if it's a lot of pressure on her, she'll learn to adjust.

It's a new department, and I can appoint whoever the hell I want to that position. And I'm choosing her. Whether he likes it or not.

Charlotte makes her way over to me and takes a seat, putting her hands in her lap and looking everywhere but at me. She's nervous. I fucking love it. I love that I'm getting to her.

Everyone files out and as Trent exits, I call out to him, "Please close the door behind you, Trent." He's the last one to leave.

His eyes dart from me to Charlotte with a slight unspoken question, but he doesn't object.

The door closes with a loud click, leaving us alone.

I'm sure the only thing on her mind is our night together and the way she left me.

I imagine she's rethinking that decision to sneak out and leave me with only a sticky note. If she thought she could get away that easily, she knows better now.

I shift forward in my seat so I can take off my suit jacket and ask her, "I need to know when you'll have a sales pitch ready."

She blinks a few times with her lips parted in shock.

I resist the urge to show her how much I'm enjoying this and instead set my jacket gently on the table. I rest my elbow on the table and place my head in my hand, looking at her beautiful blue eyes and waiting for a response.

After a moment she clears her throat. "I'll need a few days to go through all of the products and the ideal placements." Her voice is strained, and she shifts uncomfortably in her seat.

She hesitantly parts those lush lips and I know she wants to ask about that night, but she doesn't. Her cheeks burn a bright red as I stare at her with a blank face waiting for more. Her breathing picks up a bit and she refuses to look me in the eyes. A sadness crosses her face that has me questioning this game I'm playing. Maybe she thinks I don't remember.

There's no way that I could ever forget that night. But she doesn't know that.

"Sorry," she says and pulls at the hem of her skirt, not looking at me, "I'm just a little..."

She breathes in deep.

I sit upright and lean forward, close enough to touch her, but I don't. "A little what, Rose?" A knowing look flashes in her eyes at my pet name for her. I arch a brow and wait, but she just stares at me like a deer in headlights.

"I asked you a question; when will you have the sales pitch?"

She clears her throat and squares her shoulders,

seeming to right herself. All trace of emotion gone, now that she knows what I'm doing.

"I'll need at least this workweek. I can have something to you by Monday for the first one, but nothing will be finalized until I can arrange meetings with our business partners." For the first time today, a smile grows on my face.

"Your presentation skills are excellent." I look past her, remembering her presentation at the conference. She's amazing at what she does. And she's youthful, and a beautiful woman at that. It's going to be hard for them to tell her no. "You were meant to lead the sales department. Don't let anyone tell you differently."

A small, sweet smile plays at her lips although it doesn't get rid of the apprehension in her expression. "Thank you, Mr. Parker," she answers respectfully and looks to the door.

"Thank you, Miss Harrison, that's all."

She looks flushed and parts her lips, but doesn't say anything.

"Are you alright?" I ask her.

She gives me a smile and nods, holding the folders she came in with close to her chest.

"I'm fine, thank you." Her response is short and expected.

"I'll see you on Friday at the next meeting." She purses her lips and looks at the door and then back at me. My heart pounds in my chest. I can tell she's debating on saying something. She doesn't though. She opens her mouth once, but slams it shut and stands up, smoothing her skirt quickly and then takes a single step to move around me.

I make my move then. My hand reaches out and brushes against her thigh, skimming up her skirt slightly.

She gasps slightly and wavers on her heels.

"One more thing," I say as I turn her to face me, putting my other hand on the back of her knee.

"The note you left… I'm choosing to ignore it." Her breath hitches, and her sweet lips part for a moment before she moves out of my grasp and takes a step back.

"I don't think we should do this," she says slowly, her eyes staying trained on mine. She sounds unsure, because she is.

"I think we should," I say as I stand in front of her.

Her breathing comes in heavy pants. I stand and take a step toward her as she takes a small step back. "I still want you."

I splay my hand on her back and walk her to the door, but I don't open it. She moves to leave, but I put my hand on the door and stand behind her.

"I thought it was over in Vegas," she says softly. She looks at the door and then at me. "I can't-"

"You can." I cut her off. "This is just me and you."

Her eyes search my face as I speak. "There's work, and then there's this." I lean in and plant a soft kiss on her lips. Hers are hard at first, but they quickly mold to mine. Yes! My hardened dick strains against my zipper. I should take her against the wall right now. But I can't. Not yet. She's hesitant, and I can't push just yet.

I kiss her deeply and with a passion that echoes what we had that night together. Her back arches slowly and her hands slowly slip up my shirt, letting her fingers trail along my hard chest.

I pull her hips toward me so she can feel how hard I am for her. I want her, and I need her to know that. She lets out a small moan. I lean forward, breaking our kiss and whisper in the crook of her neck, "My sweet Rose, it's not over until I say it's over."

CHAPTER 15

CHARLOTTE

"I'm worried about you, Charlotte," Hastings tells me in a hushed voice. He takes off his reading glasses and sets them on his desk, looking at me as though he feels sorry for me.

I knew this was coming when I walked in here this morning. He was too busy to meet with me yesterday by the time I left the *meeting* with Logan. So now I'm sitting in his office trying hard not to be offended, while also trying to project the confidence that I can do this. "I think that Logan is doing you a disservice, putting that much on your plate so soon."

"I'll be okay," I say confidently, flashing an easy smile. Though I'm trying to seem upbeat, I'm not at all. If the shock and self-consciousness about all this shit with the buyout and Logan weren't enough, I got into a nasty fight with Ian last night. He showed up without warning on my doorstep, demanding that I let him in. I shoved his box out there for him to take, but that's not what he wanted. He was looking to actually stay over.

I told him that he no longer lived with me, but he wasn't taking no for an answer. He tried to push his way in, but I slammed the door in his face. He has a key, which sucks. But I had a bolt. So he was fucked. Last night, anyway, since today's a different story and in the pit of my stomach I know this is going to be an issue. I called the landlord and asked him to change the locks. I'm just praying they get it done in time before that asshole locks me out.

I spent the rest of the night laying in bed, hating Ian and this shit position I'm in. The only other thing I could concentrate on was how Logan wanted me yesterday. All I could do was think about how hot Logan looked in the boardroom, how sexy he made me feel. I am shocked at the sudden turn of events with him taking over the company and naming me head sales rep, but I'm convinced he's up to something.

He's the cat, and I'm the mouse.

I don't care what Logan's plans are, I think to myself angrily. *I'll show him that I'm not some toy to be played with on a whim.* Yesterday I was caught off guard and shocked. Today's a new day.

Thinking about the way Logan looked at me yesterday in the boardroom causes my blood to heat with desire. It pisses me off that I'm turned on by a man who's toying with me. What's worse is that my job is at stake. My heart clenches, but rather than be worried and upset, I hold onto the anger. Without realizing it, I find myself scowling at Hastings in irritation.

Hastings frowns at me, his bushy eyebrows drawing together. "You're glaring at me, Charlotte, did I offend you?"

"Oh, no, Mr. Hastings," I say, quickly morphing my scowl into a smile. "I'm just thinking about how I'm going to go about preparing for a successful launch with the resources I have at my disposal."

Goddamnit, Logan.

Before Hastings can respond, there's a knock at the door. I turn to see Eva poking her head in the doorway. She looks the consummate professional today with her hair in an elegant French twist and dressed in a crisp white pantsuit that makes me want to go shopping. "Is it alright if I come in?" she asks sweetly.

Hastings nods, "I think we're done here?" he says although he's asking me. I nod with a tight smile.

Eva walks in with a bright smile. "Good morning, Mr. Hastings. You're looking mighty handsome today."

Mr. Hastings chuckles, his cheeks turning a rosy red, and waves his hand dismissively. "Oh stop it, Eva. How are you enjoying the merger?"

"It's going better than I expected," Eva replies, giving me a smile. "It doesn't hurt when you have such an awesome boss to help smooth things out with the new one." She bats her eyelashes, and Mr. Hastings turns redder.

I shake my head. Eva must want something from Hastings, and knowing her, she's most likely going to get it.

The two talk about business matters for a moment. Specifically, the new building, commuting, and Hastings gives her a bullet list of things to do to get everything up and running smoothly. Meanwhile, all I can think about is how I'm going to handle Logan. I have no fucking clue. As I come to that conclusion, Eva turns her gaze on me. "Ready for lunch?"

* * *

"WHAT'S ON YOUR MIND, GIRLIE?" Eva asks as she dips a salty french fry in a pile of ketchup. "I can tell something's been bothering you."

For lunch, we've settled on an upscale cafe down the street from our new workplace. We're seated in the middle of the cafe in a small two-person booth. Between the two of us we're enjoying two big burgers, fries, a vanilla shake and a diet Coke. It's a pretty swanky restaurant, with gleaming marble floors, gold-plated trim and crown molding. I love the burgundy and white color scheme, and the ambience is relaxed.

Too bad I'm a swirling canopy of emotions and can't calm down and enjoy it.

Should I tell her? I wonder. *And would she even believe me?*

I grip onto my diet Coke with both hands, debating inwardly. It could look very bad if I told Eva that I slept with Logan in a moment of weakness. I like to think that she'd understand, but I'm not sure I want to risk it.

Don't, I decide finally. *No matter how much I trust her, there's no telling what could happen if word got out that I slept with the boss.*

When it comes down to it, I don't want Eva to think less of me. She's been a good friend, my only friend really, and I would hate to lose her at a time where I'm going through so much in my life.

"Nothing," I say with a sigh, "it's just this merger is proving to be stressful. The extra commute time, being handed all this responsibility right off the bat. And my breakup with Ian."

Eva frowns at me and washes down her fry with a slurp of her vanilla milkshake. "I'm sorry, Charlotte. I don't know why Logan is putting so much pressure on you." She pauses to dip another fry in ketchup. "Did Ian come get his stuff?"

I nod and then scowl at my untouched burger. I'm such a bundle of nerves that I can't even think about eating. "Ummm," I say, "we kind of got into a fight."

"Kind of?" Eva sits back against the booth. "You're broken up; what's there to fight about?"

"Yeah. He wanted back in, but I wouldn't let him. I mean, can you believe this guy? He thinks he should be able to stay in our apartment after what he did? I ended up throwing all his stuff outside. We started yelling at each other, cursing each other out. Girl, it was awful."

"Well, at least you got to tell that douche how you really felt."

"That's the thing. I'm mad that I did it. It didn't change anything. He's not going to say sorry or beg me to take him back. All it did was show how much I still cared."

Just thinking about the previous night makes me angrier. I still can't believe Ian hasn't had the decency to tell me sorry or begged for my forgiveness. After he got caught cheating, his personality took a 180 degree turn. Like Dr. Jekyll and Mr. Hyde, I'd been sleeping with a stranger the whole time I was with him. And to think that he should be allowed to sleep under the same roof with me after what he did? The nerve of that prick!

Eva reaches across the table and puts a hand on my arm concernedly. "Charlotte, don't be so hard on yourself. You're only human. It's only natural to have those emotions."

I sniffle, staring at my burger. "You're right, Eva. I need to stop thinking about it. I wish he'd just move the fuck on so I can let him go live his happily ever after with Sarah."

I give them two months, I think to myself, *before they're at each others throats and Ian is cheating on her with a new whore.* The nasty thought only makes me want to cry. What if it was really me, and not him? What if they do get their happily ever after? I shove down the thought and stuff another fry into my mouth before I cry any more over that asshole.

Eva smiles at me and takes a sip of her vanilla shake. "That's the spirit. Fuck Ian! You'll find your own happily ever after with some sex god that's better in bed than Ian. You'll see."

I almost choke on how ironic her words are, though I think a fairytale ending with Logan has zero chance of happening. "I wish."

Eva sets down her shake and fans herself with both hands. "Oh, oh! Speaking of happily ever afters and sex gods, did you see how hot Logan looked in the boardroom yesterday? My God, that man is pure sex on legs!"

"He's alright," I lie, trying to keep my thoughts G-rated. Eva needs to stop bringing up how hot Logan is, especially when it's hard enough to get the man out of my mind. "Nothing you can't see in any GQ magazine."

Eva gives me a look. "What? You're crazy. On a scale of one to ten, that man is a hundred! Shit, if I weren't in a relationship with Kevin..." Eva makes a sound and shakes her head.

I don't know how I feel with Eva going crazy over Logan. On one hand, she's in a happy relationship and I know that she's just joking around, but on the other, I want to tell her about my predicament so she'll stop bringing him up. I know it's not like he's mine or anything, but I don't like her talking about him like that.

When I don't reply right away, Eva frowns. "Look, if you're so worried about commuting, why don't you sign up for the temporary housing the company's offered? It'll help until you can find a place nearby to move to."

I pick up a fry and take a small bite. It's extra salty, like how I feel inside. After a few halfhearted nibbles, I put it down. It's all my stomach can handle right now. "I thought about it, but I don't know," I say. If I take the housing offer it'll only be one more thing that Logan has over me, and I don't know if I can abide by that.

Eva takes another sip of her shake, this time nearly draining it to the bottom. "Well you better decide before you end up knee-deep in work and don't have time to get it done. You can't fail your startup because you're overworked and tired from working long hours and then having to commute long distances."

I have to agree with Eva, and it makes me more upset at Logan.

This is a game for him. I don't want to play a game.

This is my life. I start to get choked up, and I try to ignore it. I wish I wasn't so emotional. I wish I could just be rational about all this, but how can I be?

I'm worried this could all be a play on his part so he can humiliate me for leaving him in Vegas. His endgame could be to set me up to fail, so he can fire me and make sure I never work in sales again.

At the thought, anger and desperation mix and churn in my stomach, and a surge of anxiety rolls through me. I need to stop being scared and confront him like an adult. If Logan's plan is to humiliate me, there's nothing I can do about it but prove to him that I can handle whatever the fuck he throws my way. Just because he's my boss now doesn't mean I have to let him treat me this way.

Well, I think to myself as I signal the waiter for a to-go box so I can put my untouched food away for later, *if he wants me to play games, fuck it. I'll play.*

CHAPTER 16

LOGAN

"Mr. Parker?" Charlotte asks with an even voice and the door cracked. "You wanted to see me?" She doesn't leave the doorway though, and it forces my lips into a straight line.

I tap my knuckles on the desk and stare pointedly at the door. "Close it." My voice is low and she stares back at me with her chest rising and falling.

My command seems to trigger something in her. There's an obvious shift in her demeanor. Her eyes narrow at me but she closes it, kicking it shut with her heel and making her way toward me.

"Logan," she says in a harsh voice. She looks pissed as hell and for some reason it turns me the fuck on. My cock twitches in my two thousand dollar slacks, and my heart races in my chest. This isn't why I called her in here. I don't know what's gotten into her, but I need to fix this.

"If I'm going to lose my job over this, so be it, but I am not some office slut." She spits out the last part with venom. Is that what she thinks? Fuck! This was supposed to be enjoyable for her, and just as much as it is for me. I feel like an asshole. I should have explained things better to her.

"I am not some-"

I look her in the eyes and cut her off. "If you don't want me, there's nothing left to discuss. You still have your job, you earned it. You deserve that position."

Her forehead pinches and she opens and closes her mouth taking deep angry breaths as though she's ready to lay into me, but she's lost her steam. She wasn't expecting me to bow out of this argument so easily.

This is something she made up in her head. It's my fault for toying with her, but I didn't expect this reaction.

"If you don't want to fuck me, then don't," I say easily. "It's been two days since our discussion, and I couldn't wait another hour to see you at the meeting." I stand and walk my way around the desk to her. She eyes me warily as I lean back, both hands gripping the edge of the desk.

"You aren't an office slut, and I don't see you like that at all." My eyes roam her body as I speak. "But I wanna fuck you like one," I confess to her.

Her eyes widen and she takes a half step back.

I turn to face her and take a full step forward so I'm close enough to pull her toward me, but I resist.

"I want you, Rose. I want you in my company making me proud, and I want you bent over my desk cumming on my dick."

A small pant slips past her lips. Her thighs clench, and knowing that I'm exciting her makes my dick stiffen. I reach up and slowly run my finger along her bottom lip. I can see her on her knees, sucking me off under my desk. I want that. I desperately want that.

"You're striking; it's only natural that I want you."

Her eyes stay on mine and she speaks in a low voice,

"I'm not a fucktoy." There's no fight in her words though. I can see she's just as turned on as I am.

"You're not, but I think it'd be fun to treat you like one, for both of us. It doesn't have to be degrading…" I trail off and watch as her eyes fall to the floor before continuing, "unless you want it to be."

Her beautiful blue eyes snap up to mine and I can see she still wants to fight the sexual tension between us. She doesn't want to give in to the primal needs that she has.

"Today for instance," I start to say, turning away from her and walking back to my desk. If she wants this, she's going to have to prove it to me.

I sit easily in my chair as she stands defensively across the desk.

"Today I wanted you to play my secretary. I dreamed of fucking you on my desk." I put my hand out in front of me. "Right here," I say as I pat the desk and maintain eye contact with her. "It's a fantasy I've had before, but I've never fulfilled."

She scoffs at me. "I don't believe that for one second." Her defenses go up and her eyes light with a passion to prove me wrong. It pisses me off. I'm not a liar, and I've never given her any reason to think I would lie.

Before this day is over, I want her on her knees, begging me to forgive her and choking on my cock.

"I've never and I never will lie to you," I say with a lowered voice.

She stays mute, refusing to believe me but not offering me a rebuttal.

"I thought you enjoyed me fucking you." Her small hands ball into fists. "It certainly seemed that way when you were screaming my name."

"Fuck you." She practically hisses.

"Yes, please do," I say back to her with a small smile.

It's quiet for a moment, the two of us at odds. Pointless really, we both want each other. She just needs to let go and give in. I can give her pleasure while she fulfills my needs.

"This isn't a game to me," she finally says. She's not angry though, which is what I expected. She sounds sincere, and genuinely upset. "This is my life."

I grind my teeth, hating that I'm unsure of what to do. I want her. And I'll have her. But not yet. She needs something from me before she's going to give in. It's a challenge that I readily accept.

I clear my throat and sit up straight in my seat. "Is there anything else you wanted to talk about?"

She stares at me in an attempt to calm herself down. I want to walk over and pull her into my embrace, to soothe her worries and tell her everything is going to be alright. But right now she's hostile. It would only make matters worse.

"I'll see you in forty minutes then, Miss Harrison." She nods quickly and turns on her heels.

"Rose," I call out her name and she stops with her hand on the doorknob, but she doesn't turn around. "My door is always open for you. If you decide you need anything." I hear her take in a deep breath. I'm not sure, but I think she may be crying. It fucking shreds me. "There's a bathroom to your right, if you need it before leaving my office."

She shakes her head and mutters, "I'm fine."

But she's not fine, she's so far from it.

CHAPTER 17

CHARLOTTE

God, he's driving me insane.

I walk into the bathroom around the corner from Logan's office and grab a handful of toilet paper from the first stall to blow my nose, feeling a cauldron of emotions bubbling inside. Anger, shock, lust and sadness. I don't know what to make of Logan. At first I thought he made me the head sales rep just to humiliate me. Now I'm having doubts.

What's worse is that I want to take back these last few days and play along with his game. I just want him to take me and fuck me like his office slut. How fucked up is that?

I feel ashamed thinking this way, but when he started talking dirty to me in his office, it was all I could do to hold my ground. I wanted to give into him right then and there, get on my knees and let the image he described come to life.

This is wrong. I shouldn't be entertaining these feelings. I'm so confused by what's happened. But some things are very clear. Logan is my boss now. A relationship between us would be inappropriate.

I wrap my arms around myself, squeezing tight and trying to clear my head.

Why do I have to resist? No one has to know about our relationship. It could be our little secret. A giddy grin comes over my face at the thought. *Don't I deserve this after what Ian did to me? Why can't I use Logan for pleasure just like how he wants to use me?*

... 'cause then I'll feel like a whore.

"Damn him," I growl, blowing my nose and throwing the paper towel in the wastebasket. I'm torn and conflicted. I don't know if I can trust what Logan's offering, and I don't know what to do. I sure as hell know what my body wants though. That I can't deny.

I blow out a deep breath. For right now, I need to get myself cleaned up. I can't miss this meeting.

* * *

THE BOARD MEETING IS STUFFY, and I'm finding it hard to focus while an intern named Harold gives a presentation about a new method of advertising online. I should be paying attention to what he says, but all I can think about is Logan.

The way he looked at me in his office, with a hunger that was almost palpable and how much he wanted me, is doing crazy things to my body. The way he said, "fucktoy." The memory sends shivers down my body.

Unconsciously, my gaze is drawn over in his direction. My breath catches in my throat. He's staring back at me with a ravenous hunger in his eyes. My clit throbs in response and a prickly sensation goes up all over my arms. Not here. My heart beats rapidly. Not with everyone else watching. My eyes dart around the room, but everyone's looking at Harold.

Doesn't he know that you shouldn't mix business with pleasure?

Oh, he knows, I tell myself, *but he doesn't give a fuck. He's a man that wants what he wants, and everything else be damned.*

Logan continues to stare at me, his eyes boring into me like I'm the only person in the room. I shift in my seat, my core heating from his gaze alone. Good God, I'm not sure how I'm going to get through this.

"So how much will this new tactic cost us?" Logan asks, his eyes still on me.

It takes a second for me to realize that he's talking to Harold, and I feel a small twinge of disappointment.

Harold, a pudgy younger man with a balding head, beams happily, pleased to have caught the interest of his new boss. "Practically nothing at all, sir," he says. "It's a pop-up, and it won't cost more than the small yearly fee of an ad."

My ears perk up, and I tear my eyes away from Logan. "That's not true," I argue. "Using this method will result in a huge loss of revenue. Studies have shown that buyers are less likely to buy and checkout when a pop-up occurs." I turn my gaze back on Logan. "It pisses them off, and they get turned off by it."

Harold goes red in the face. I can tell that I've embarrassed him, and I cringe internally, but I can't help it.

I'm not going to let someone propose an idea that would be bad for the company. I could have eased into it, but it had to be said.

"That's not true," Harold objects, shaking his head. "Layman Corp uses this very same method, and they've seen profits grow by two hundred and fifty percent."

I open my mouth to set him straight, but then stop. I'm not sure if this *debate* with a coworker in front of a room of executives would be a good look. But I know what Harold is saying isn't factual and could prove disastrous for our sales department.

Logan catches my eye and gives me an imperceptible nod.

"But were pop-up ads all they did to increase revenue?" I ask, my voice picking up confidence as I speak. "Or is there a bigger picture that you're not looking at?"

Harold stands there, glaring at me angrily.

"You do realize Layman Corp utilizes various tactics for their ads, one of which is testing ad methods that are proven to be bad for business to see if they can improve them, right? They released a study just last month that backs up my claim that they are dismal for business and through testing pop-up ads they came up with a more effective ad campaign, and *that* is what caused their profits to grow by two hundred and fifty percent."

I take in a breath, hating that I feel like I'm arguing. I don't want to. He can read the study, and this conversation would be null and void.

"Charlotte's right," Cary Ann pipes up from at the end of the table, brandishing her work tablet and drawing Logan's gaze. It's been several days since I last saw her, but she looks like she's had a long night, judging by the bags under her eyes. Her red cashmere sweater and white dress pants look nice on her, though. "There have been several studies done that show pop-up ads only piss off users, and some have actually resulted in lawsuits."

Logan swivels back around to appraise Harold who's looking like he's about to blow steam out of his ears, his face red as a tomato. I feel sorry for the poor guy. And I didn't mean to embarrass him, but I know I'm right in this.

"Is there anything else you would like to add, Harold?" Logan asks easily, seemingly unaffected.

For a moment, it looks like Harold's going to start

yelling at me and branding me the demon bitch from hell, but instead he shakes his head and says, "Thank you for listening, sir." And he returns to his seat.

Close by, Eva gives me a thumbs up. She thinks I've done a good job, but I feel horrible. I didn't want to step on anyone's toes, and I'm pretty sure I've just made a new enemy. Great.

For the rest of the meeting, several people get up to speak and I do a better job at paying attention, but I catch Logan gazing at me every time I look at him. I spend awhile thinking about what just happened before the meeting and what it all means. A part of me wants to apologize to Logan for how I treated him, and how quick I was to accuse him of being an asshole. Another part of me wants to just quit this job and run away from this stress.

When Logan dismisses the meeting, I grab my briefcase and get up to leave, intending on putting everything behind me, but I freeze when Logan issues a command. "I need a moment to speak with you, Miss Harrison."

Holy hell. Not again.

Slowly, I lower myself back in my seat, anxiety twisting my stomach. I'm not sure what Logan could want with me, but whatever it is, it can't be good. Not with what happened earlier.

I sit there, my pulse picking up speed as everyone slowly files out of the room. Eva is one of the last to go and she sends me a flirty wink as if to say, 'he has the hots for you, girl' and then she leaves the room and I'm all alone with Logan.

God. If only she knew.

CHAPTER 18

LOGAN

I can feel her eyes back on me. She's back to being lost in thought as the meeting wraps up. She's so beautiful and intelligent with a poise I admire. Yet I've damaged that. That's what I do, it's what I'm good at.

I'm not used to giving a fuck. But I brought her close, and I know damn well I'm responsible for that hurt look and distant stare. She doesn't realize how fucking obvious it is.

Hastings is watching her like a hawk.

They're going to think I yelled at her or did some fucked up thing to her. And I did.

I didn't realize it though.

I shouldn't be pushing this; I should show some fucking restraint. But she's all worked up and feeling insecure because of me. Not about what's between us, but over her job. I don't fucking like that. I didn't even consider that it would be an issue.

I never considered it because it's simply not a matter I've ever had to worry about.

It's been bugging the shit out of me since she left my office. I feel like a fucking prick.

This isn't a good look for me. I really don't give a fuck about the office, but for a woman I've slept with… I don't like her thinking I was going to hurt her. It makes me uneasy. I need to make this right.

Harold Geist wraps up his presentation. He's completely deflated now that Charlotte's corrected him. She didn't mean to shut him down. She's right though. It would have been a horrible move. I was at least going to wait for his talk to be done to tell him no. But Charlotte stepping up and telling him outright how his decision would negatively affect sales only proves to me more that I made the right decision.

I don't want to lose her.

My heart twists in my hollow chest and I'm not sure that I like how strongly I feel toward her. "That's all for today." I end the meeting abruptly. "We'll reassess next week."

Charlotte's quick to stand, and I know she's going to bolt. I'm an asshole for taking advantage of my position, but I call out, "I need a moment to speak with you, Miss Harrison."

At least this time it's for her benefit, not mine. I still can't look her in the eyes. I can feel the gaze of several people in the room, but I ignore them.

I couldn't care less about them and what they think about me.

I finally look at where she was seated, half expecting her to have just left, but she's still there, staring at the pen in her hand as she taps it lightly on the table. The rest of the group files out, most people not paying much attention to either of us.

The second the door shuts, she looks up at me with a glare. "I told you, I didn't want to do this."

I hold her gaze and watch as several emotions flit across her face. But the one most evident is insecurity. She still doesn't know what to think.

What she needs is a good fuck. She needs a release, and so do I.

She's making this so damn difficult. Part of me wants to bend her over this table and take care of her like I want to. She'd feel better then. She'd be happier.

My dick hardens just thinking about it. Charlotte clears her throat and starts going on about how she wants the same respect as everyone else. Something or other that I don't really pay attention to. After all, I respect her more than most of them. Whether she wants to believe it or not.

It doesn't stop me from picturing her plump lips parted as she pants and moans in time with me leaving a bright red mark on her ass and fucking her.

Soon… if I play my cards right.

Right now she can yell at me all she wants. She can fight this and pretend she doesn't want it. I have the time.

The thought makes my eyes drop to the floor and my fists clench. It's only when I stop hearing her sweet voice that I look up.

"You weren't even listening!" she says with exasperation.

Fuck! I didn't mean that. How fucking deep am I going to dig this damn hole I'm in?

I hold my hands up in surrender as she breathes deeply and starts to lay into me again, "I don't know what you expect from me when you won't even listen to me!" Her voice is getting louder and I'm sure they're going to hear her if she yells anymore. I should probably wait to approach her again, but I'm an impatient man.

I keep my hands raised in surrender, "I'm sorry. I do apologize."

She looks at my hands and shifts uncomfortably in her seat. She grips the pen and then looks back at me. She swallows thickly and asks, "What do you want, Logan?"

"I want to take you to dinner," I say simply.

The words come out without my consent. I hadn't anticipated it. I didn't even know what I wanted to tell her when I called out her name. I just couldn't let her leave with the way we left things.

She looks at me completely bewildered, as though she doesn't believe what I said. Her mouth opens and closes, with nothing coming out.

I only want to give her pleasure. I can see how easily it would work. She'd benefit as much as I would. But it was never meant to leave the office. It can't be… more.

This is dangerous. More for her than me. It's one thing to take her as a fuck buddy for mutual enjoyment and keeping things limited to the office. That's what I had in mind when I saw her in Vegas. Nothing more than that. But I didn't anticipate feeling… guilty.

I hurt her, and I want to make it right. I think she just needs to see me in a different light. She has me built up as the enemy. I don't want that.

I can take her out this one time. Just once. Just to smooth things over and get her naked on my desk tomorrow morning.

"No strings. No commitments. Just dinner."

"That's why you asked me to stay?" she asks with slight disbelief.

"Yes." My heart hammers in my chest as I tell her again. "I just want to take you to dinner."

CHAPTER 19

CHARLOTTE

Just dinner. That's what he says. A part of me wants to believe him, but I get the feeling that he wants more. It makes me feel uneasy, but a part of me wants more, too. I crave what happened in Vegas between us, it was the first time that I've felt anything since breaking up with Ian.

I feel like I should be telling him no and staying away. This whole relationship is wrong, and it won't end well. I just know it. But I can't resist him. He's too tempting. And I'm addicted to him like a junkie that needs her next fix.

What if he holds it over my head if I turn him down? I wonder. *This is liable to get out of hand.*

Somehow, I doubt it. But even if he doesn't, I feel like another hookup will only cause extreme tension in the boardroom and I don't know if I can handle any more of that. Yet at the same time, it's all I can think about.

I look out the tinted window of his Aston Martin as we ride through downtown, my mind racing with all sorts of thoughts. A call comes through his car speaker, the third since we started the drive, and we've only been driving for less than five minutes.

I see him watching me out of the side of his eye as he hits the hang up button on the touchscreen of the vehicle's console. The sounds of soft, classical music fills the car once again. *Beethoven.*

I'm not usually one for this type of music, but I do find that i's easing the anxiety I feel in my stomach.

"You know," I say, turning to look at him, "you can take the calls if you have to. I don't mind."

He glances over at me, and his lips quirk up into a smile. "I do. They can wait."

My heart does a backflip. Logan is choosing me over what could be important business calls. It makes me feel special, but at the same time wary. I open my mouth to say something, and then pause. I'm not sure what I should say.

How about we stop this car and you fuck me right now? I think lustfully. I feel ashamed, but not as much as I did earlier. Not when he's treating me like this. This makes things different. It makes them easier.

"Why didn't you want to see me again?" Logan asks, breaking the silence.

"I never said I didn't. It's just that I was worried about my job and-"

"I'm talking about the note... In Vegas." His voice is heavy, and I can almost feel his emotion. Pain laces my chest, and I cringe inwardly.

"Well you know what they say, what happens in Vegas..." I say, trying to make light of it, even though I feel guilty.

Logan chuckles, although it doesn't seem genuine. "Indeed. Except, I didn't stay in Vegas."

He's right about that.

The car slows at a red light and Logan looks out of the

window, contemplating something. This car drives so damn smooth, it makes my Nissan Altima seem like a damn clunker. "So I was just a one-night stand?" he asks, turning to look at me.

I duck my head, wanting to hide in the backseat. "Yeah... something like that."

Silence reigns between us for a moment and then he asks, "What about an office affair? Is that a fantasy of yours?"

Oh boy, I think to myself. *I have a lot of fantasies, and I know you could fulfill every last one of them.*

I want to say yes and tell him I'll be his office slut, his whore, his... whatever he wants me to be, but I can't find the strength to voice the words. Shit. I feel so damn conflicted about all this.

"It isn't anything more than sex, Rose," he tells me softly.

I suck in a breath filled with emotion. I love the way he calls me Rose. It makes me feel… special. But it couldn't just be sex for me. Not now. I feel too... I'm scared to admit.

The light turns green and he drives up several blocks before turning into a recently paved restaurant parking lot. It's a large, modern-looking building and looks like it cost a pretty penny to build.

This is probably where all the rich folk go, I think to myself. A small thrill goes through me. I've never had a man spend more than a couple of hundred bucks on me and I'm sure Logan is about to drop that much on one meal like it's nothing. After everything, I would think I'd feel guilty about this, but I don't. I'm excited to be taken to dinner. Especially somewhere so nice. I try not to analyze it too much, looking out of the window at all the beautiful details on the building. It's late and dark, but the uplighting is exquisite.

"Don't think about it now," he tells me as he pulls into a parking space. "Let's get dinner first and then we'll talk about it."

I open my door before he has a chance to walk around and open it. Which is exactly what he was going to do, judging by the look on his face.

I'm not going to be good at this. I'm not going to meet his expectations. My insecurities grow as he takes my hand and walks me into the restaurant. I try to shake it off, but every click of my heels against the pavement brings us closer to the obvious conclusion. I wasn't bred for this like he was.

As we approach the door, he leans down and kisses my cheek, giving my hand a squeeze, "It's just dinner," he whispers. I'm caught off guard by the open display, but he seems unaffected and easily releases me, as though it wasn't unnatural at all. I'm overthinking everything. I breathe in deep as we walk through the door.

The opulence of the decor in the is breathtaking. The restaurant is sectioned off in several areas, but all the materials used in the architecture are top-notch. Crown molding lines the ceilings, the floor is paved with gleaming marble and the tables are dressed with fancy tablecloths and gold-plated silverware.

An older man dressed in an expensive suit and greying hair greets us at the door. He must know Logan well, because he greets him with a wide and genuine smile along with a handshake.

"Mr. Parker, how are you this evening?" he asks in a rough voice that shows his age.

"Very well, Jacob. And you?"

He smiles kindly, causing wrinkles to form around his

eyes and says, "Just fine, sir. Let me lead you to your table." I admire the dining room as we walk through to a private room lit with dim lighting cast by a few candles that Jacob lights as we slip into opposite sides of our booth.

The candles give off a sweet, smoky scent that fills me with warmth. It's simply gorgeous.

I hesitantly smooth out my skirt, trying my best to take it all in as Jacob asks what to start us off with to drink.

Logan answers, "Waters please, plus a large wine glass, and Cabernet?" he asks me and the two of them look at me for an answer. I nod slightly and feel like an idiot. All he did was ask if I want wine, and yet I can hardly answer. I breathe out slowly and relax. It's just dinner.

"Right away sir," Jacob says before disappearing from the room. I'm fidgeting in my seat, fiddling with my salad fork and trying my best to adapt. I can feel Logan's eyes on me, but I'm not ready to look him in the eyes.

"You're overwhelmed." Logan speaks clearly although it's formed as a question.

I answer honestly, "Yes, this is overwhelming. All of this is overwhelming."

"If you would just relax, you would be enjoying yourself." I believe what he's saying, but it just simply isn't that easy.

I bite the inside of my cheek. "It's my job, and you're my boss." I try to think of a way to explain it, but he interrupts my train of scattered thoughts.

"And we both have needs. I know you feel the tension that I feel. You want me, and I want you."

"We shouldn't though." I shake my head, my eyes pleading with him to understand.

He takes in a breath to speak, but then looks over my shoulder. I hear the door softly close and then a young waiter is at our table.

He pours a bit of wine for Logan, who doesn't drink it but nods at him to continue. I say a soft thank you and take my glass as the young man goes over the menu.

"May I order for you?" Logan asks. I'm quick to nod yes, although I'm not sure I'll be able to stomach any food. I'm full of nerves and apprehension. I take a sip of the wine and listen as he orders a stuffed chicken, beef tenderloin and salmon. I think they were three separate dishes, but maybe one is a combo. I'm not sure.

I give the waiter a polite smile before he leaves, my fingers running along the rim of the wine glass. "This is uncomfortable, Logan," I finally admit to him.

"Why's that? This is meant to make you feel more at ease."

I struggle to explain it. "I didn't know this was going to happen. I'm not used to this, and I don't understand what you really want from me." A weight feels like it's lifted off my chest as I finally say words that make sense.

Logan takes a moment to assess the words. He's giving me his full attention and looking as though he's bartering a deal. Which, in a way, he is. Finally he says, "You need to stop worrying and just enjoy yourself."

I take another sip of my wine, practically a gulp this time. I don't think he could possibly understand. I set the glass on the table and Logan's hand reaches out for mine.

"Give me tonight." His thumb brushes over my wrist in soothing circles. "One night to show you what it could be like." I stare into his eyes and want to give in. I want to feel like I did that night we spent together. I want this tension between us to disappear and be replaced with the fire I long for.

I nod my head as I hear the door open behind me and resist the urge to turn and look over my shoulder. Delicious smells flood my senses and I wait patiently for the waiter to set the plates in front of us. Beef tenderloin and salmon for him, and a stuffed chicken for me.

"Is there anything else I can get for you?" the waiter asks.

"That's all, thank you." Logan lays his napkin across his lap and then asks me, "Which would you like?"

I look between the plates, they all look tempting. "Whichever you don't want is fine with me."

He leans forward with a smile on his lips. "I want them all." He picks my hand up and kisses my knuckles. "We can have it all, Rose. Let me show you."

I utter a yes, caught in his trance, and give myself over to him.

Just for tonight.

CHAPTER 20

LOGAN

I open the door and gently place my hand on her lower back, leading her into my home. Up until now, I've been a gentleman. I've shown restraint so I can ease her into this.

As soon as I get her into bed, *she's mine.*

"Oh..." she says and trails off with obvious appreciation as she takes in a view of the house. It's an open floor plan and modern. I hired a designer to make it feel like a real home. In some ways it does. I've lived here for five years now, but in many ways it's more a place to sleep and shower when I'm not in the office. There aren't many personal things. Anything of real value to me is in my office. I have a room attached with everything I need to stay late there. At first that spare room felt like a hotel. But it quickly reversed. Now this house is the rarity and feels new and cold when I come here. And the spare room in the office is where I spend most nights. It's where I'm comfortable.

I take a look at Rose as she appraises the modern space,

but I don't give her much time to look around. There's only one room I'm interested in her getting acquainted with.

I close the heavy front door and lock it, tossing my keys on the front table.

I wrap my arms around her small waist and pull her curvy body into mine. I breathe in her scent and whisper into her hair, "Wait till you see the bedroom."

She laughs a little at my joke and easily tilts her head as I kiss along her jaw and then down her neck. Her hands grip onto my arms, her blunt nails digging into my skin as I move lower, rocking her gently and taking full advantage of this view of her breasts.

"Logan," she moans, and it's the last straw. I pick her small body up and carry her up the stairs, taking them two at a time.

She holds onto my neck tightly and gasps at first, but then her eyes focus on the dip in my throat and she kisses me right there and then up my throat. Each kiss makes my dick harder and harder. Her passion is addicting.

I'm desperate for her by the time I place her gently onto my bed.

"I want you naked," I breathe as I unbutton the top button of my shirt and then rip it off and over my head. She's quick to undress as well. It's tit for tat until we're both naked and breathing heavily. Her eyes are clouded with desire as she takes in my naked body. They widen as she sees my dick, hard as a fucking stone and just for her. No condom this time. I have her medical records and I know she's on the shot.

I climb on the bed and it groans with my weight. She backs up slightly and gets onto her knees. She licks her lips, her eyes focused on one part of me. I don't waste a second to grab a fistful of her hair at the base of her skull and guide her lips to my cock.

She doesn't hesitate to take it into her greedy mouth. As she swallows my cock down her throat my head falls back. Fuck, she feels so good. She tries to take in more of me, hollowing her cheeks. I look down with my eyes half-lidded as she bobs up and down my length.

I could watch her all fucking day, but I want her pussy. I wanna hear her moaning my name and prove to her that this is worth it. That she didn't make a mistake by giving in to me.

I pull her off of my cock and she looks up at me with a heated gaze as she wipes her mouth. She has no shame. I fucking love it.

"Knees." I release her and she only hesitates for a moment. I can see she's debating on whether or not she's going to give me control. But she makes the right decision, spreading her legs slightly with her ass in the air. She's bared to me and glistening with desire.

I run my fingers down her spine and farther down to her wet pussy. "So fucking wet," I say as she softly moans into the sheet. Her hands move to either side of her head and she grips onto the sheets as I push my thick fingers into her. Fuck, so tight, too.

I pump my fingers in and out of her as her back arches and her head falls against the mattress. She bites down on the sheets to muffle her sweet moans. But I don't want moans, I want *screams* of pleasure. I want her to call out my name like she fucking needs me. Like I'm her everything.

I slowly pull my fingers out of her and bring them to my lips to clean them off. I practically moan as I taste her on my tongue. So fucking sweet.

I grip my dick and stroke it once as she looks back at me with a passionate gaze. She whimpers in need, but I have every intention of giving her what she needs. I push the head of my cock easily through her pussy lips and slowly move forward. Watching as her pussy takes in more and more of me. I'm slow and deliberate. My eyes move from her cunt to her face. Her lips part wider and wider, and her forehead pinches as I push deeper and deeper into her greedy pussy.

She writhes under me as I near the last few inches of my thick cock and her head thrashes side to side. She starts to move under me, but I hold her hips still.

"You can take me, Rose." She moans with a mix of pain and pleasure as I push all of myself into her. Her hand grips her breast and she bites down on her lip. I gently still deep inside her, letting her adjust before pulling out slowly and then thrusting back in to the hilt.

She lets out a loud moan and looks back at me with a mix of fear and desire.

I do it again and this time there's only pleasure. She rocks her hips with arousal leaking from her pussy onto my thighs. I move my hands to her hips and steady her as I pull almost all the way out and then thrust into her. I keep this up over and over in a steady rhythm.

"Fuck!" she screams out as I pound her tight pussy. Her body jolts with each thrust and she struggles to stay still and take it, but she does.

I keep up the relentless pace until she's trembling beneath me and whimpering with her impending orgasm. Her walls tighten around my cock, and I know she's close.

I angle my hips so I hit her clit with my balls each time, giving her more and more pleasure and enough to take her over.

I groan in utter rapture as I rut between her legs. Her pussy spasms on my dick as she screams out her release.

Fuck, yes. She feels so fucking good. I can't stop as I ride through her orgasm.

Her body goes limp and her pants get louder as I continue to fuck her like I own her body. Like she's mine.

I thrust into her warmth as a tingling sensation starts at the bottom of my spine and flows through me in every direction. My toes curl and I know I'm going to cum as my balls draw up, but I don't want to. I want more of her. I almost slow down, but the threat of losing the high makes me pick up my pace.

I strum her throbbing clit with a desperate need for her to cum with me. The hardened nub is soaked. So are her thighs, and each pump of my hips is accompanied by a wet smacking noise. I fucking love it.

"Again," I growl into her ear, my voice so harsh I hardly recognize it.

In an instant she obeys. And the feel of her pleasure pushes my own over a steep cliff. I thrust myself all the way to the hilt, feeling her tight walls pulsing around every inch of my cock. Thick bursts of cum leave me in heavy waves. My back arches as she screams out my name and I give her everything I have.

As the waves dim and she lowers herself to the mattress, her chest rising and falling frantically, I pull out slowly and quickly climb off the bed and head to the bathroom to clean up.

I take my time and watch her from the corner of my eye through the ensuite's doorframe. She lays still on the bed, looking completely spent.

I'm quick to clean her up and then I toss the cloth into the hamper in the bathroom.

I walk back into the room ready to pass the fuck out. It's late, and I'm exhausted. I stop short when I see her reaching for her clothes on the floor, with the blanket held close to her chest.

"I think you'd sleep better in a tee shirt," I say and look to my dresser, knowing she could easily wear one of my undershirts. "Although I'd rather you were naked." I let my eyes fall to the bit of her cleavage still exposed. "I *much* prefer you slept naked."

"I think maybe I should go," Rose says quietly. My body goes cold for a moment. It's late. Very fucking late. And a part of me was looking forward to having her available to me in the morning.

"Do you *want* to leave?" I ask her as I walk slowly to the bed and stand next to her. She looks at the bra in her hand and doesn't respond. I cup her chin in my hand and force her to look at me. "Or do you think I want you to go?"

Her lips part slightly, and her eyes tell me everything I need to know.

"I want you to stay," I whisper against her lips and then kiss her gently. "I want you here naked in my bed, and I want you to use me for your needs. And I want to do the same to you." It's the truth. Every word.

She blushes and gives me a soft smile, pulling out of my hold. "Well, I wasn't sure how needy you were," she says playfully. It brings a smile to my lips.

She looks good in my bed, but this is an exception. The reminder makes me question if I should bring that detail up now. I imagine it won't go over well. This... *relationship* needs to stay at the office. We can't get close, this is just sex, and limiting the arrangement is the best way to ensure it doesn't get out of hand.

As I climb into bed and debate on telling her just that, she beats me to it.

"Don't expect me to be at your beck and call. I don't think sleepovers are the best thing for this..." She doesn't finish her statement, and I simply nod as she motions between us.

Although I was going to tell her the same damn thing, I don't like hearing it. And I sure as fuck don't like that she said it first.

I should be happy about it. But I'm not. And that could be a problem.

CHAPTER 21

CHARLOTTE

What the hell have I gotten myself into?

I look out the window of Logan's stretch limo as it rolls through the downtown streets back to my apartment, thinking about the night before and trying not to bite my fingernails. The whole morning I've been struggling with the feeling of regret. For having an affair with my boss. It sounds stupid for even thinking of it that way, but it's his power of authority over me that makes this so uncomfortable.

Our little tryst was definitely mutually beneficial. I'm just not sure if it's a mistake.

At least I get to drive home in luxury. Although it's one of the reasons I feel cheapened. I can't even make eye contact with the driver. I'm sure he's not thinking the best things of me right now.

I need to make a choice. Either accept this lifestyle and our arrangements, or cut it off. I swallow the lump in my throat. The lines are drawn and I have a better understanding of everything. But I'm still unsure. It won't be just sex for me. I can't imagine this ending well.

My eyes meet the driver's as we slow in front of my apartment.

"Here we are Miss Harrison," he says easily.

I give him a warm smile and say, "Thank you." I wish I could remember his name, but I don't. I climb out and wince. I'm sore and aching, all thanks to Logan. My smile grows. It's a good feeling, being deliciously used. I shut the door and give the driver a polite wave.

As I walk up to my apartment, I slowly feel better. I think it was just the drive maybe? The idea that it was a walk of shame of sorts. But being back here and knowing it was my choice makes me feel more at ease with the decision. The keys clink in my hands as I unlock the door.

I freeze when I open the door, nearly passing out onto the floor.

Ian and Sarah are sitting on the living room couch, practically making out. Sarah, who's dressed in the skankiest outfit I've ever seen, has her hands on Ian's crotch, rubbing it like it's a pot of gold and Ian is running his hands all over her body.

What the fuck?

They stop when they see me standing in the doorway, glaring at them with a mix of hatred and shock. My gut reaction is to scream at them and tell them to get the fuck out, but I know better. Ian isn't going anywhere, especially with Sarah here, and he's more liable to throw me out than to sit there and listen to me badmouth him.

"Do you mind?" Sarah snaps nastily, her hand still on Ian's crotch. Tears prick my eyes. She was my friend for so long. My grip on the doorknob tightens as Ian grins at Sarah, kissing her on the forehead as if she's done a good job snapping at me.

I grit my teeth and then bite my tongue, chanting internally to myself to stay calm, cool and collected. Ignore the pain and be the bigger person. I need to call the fucking landlord again, too. I swear to God if he put his name on the lease at some point when we were together I'll loose it, but I can't imagine there's any other reason that he'd be in here right now.

Fuck this. I don't have time for this. I need to get to work.

It takes everything in me, but I manage to tear my eyes away from them and I continue on to my room. Behind me, I hear them say something about me and laugh. I just ignore it and go about getting ready for work.

I take a quick shower, scrubbing my skin harder than I should and am dressed in my business attire within fifteen minutes. My hair's damp, but I just throw it into a bun. I have an hour-long drive anyway, so it can dry on the way.

I stare at myself in the mirror, not wanting to go back out there. I don't want to have to deal with this. When I finally decide I have to get the hell out and walk down the hall, I hear banging sounds coming from the second bedroom and Sarah moaning at the top of her lungs as if she wants the entire world to hear.

I ball my hands into fists, anger threatening to overwhelm me. My jaw clenches, and I'm overwhelmed by all the emotions consuming me. I'm not going to cry. I refuse to cry and scream and give them the reaction they're hoping for. I'm not going to give them the satisfaction and engage them with their bullshit.

In fact, I'm over this. I take confident strides to the front door and I don't look back. Fuck them. I'm moving on with my life. They can have each other.

Grabbing my briefcase, I walk out of the apartment, Sarah's pleasured cries trailing me, with one thought on my mind.

I guess I'll be applying for that temporary housing after all.

* * *

I DRIVE to work and I'm pissed the entire drive, my mood dark and gloomy. I hate the fact that they got to me. I'd be a liar if I said I was unaffected, but I plan to remedy that very soon. The first chance I get, I'm putting in for temporary housing.

The image of them going at it will haunt me for some time, so I'm going to have to busy myself to forget it. I refuse to let those two assholes fuck up my day and distract me from my job.

Wearing a scowl on my face, I walk inside Parker-Moore and make my way up to my office. There's a stack of papers waiting on my desk when I walk in and I feel like it's just what I need. Bury myself in work, and at the same time bury Ian and Sarah. A win-win.

I set my coat and purse down and go get coffee from the break room before returning to look through contracts and emails.

Over the next half hour, I find myself immersed in work and I lose track of the time. I'm just finishing up working data into a sales graph on my laptop when my cell rings.

"Just when things were starting to get good," I grumble in annoyance. Busying myself in work has made me feel much better and it reminds me of how much I love my job. It's been the perfect antidote to forget about Ian.

For a moment, I debate ignoring the call. It can't be anyone important, but curiosity gets the best of me. I pull it out and glance at the caller ID. Anger surges through my chest. It's fucking Ian.

Why the hell is he calling me?

It annoys me that he's back in my mind after I'd just

managed to get him out of it. Scowling, I tap the ignore button on my phone and toss it to the side. I don't know what Ian wants, but I really don't care. I'm done with him.

I try to get back to work, but now I can't focus. I'm too irritated. Ian had no business calling me, and it's brought back that dark feeling that was finally starting to go away. I find myself wishing I had something or someone to make me forget my awful morning.

Logan.

The thought of Mr. CEO fills me with desire and pushes Ian out of my mind. The session we had the night before was mind-blowing, and I can't help but wonder what he's doing right this second. Is he working, busy running his company? Or is he up in his office, thinking of me?

I hope he is, I think to myself, feeling my core heat, *and I hope he's hard as a fucking rock.*

The thought elicits a soft moan from my lips and I squeeze my legs together. This is why this relationship with my boss is bad news. Next thing you know, I'll be bringing a vibrator to work.

I should go see him, I tell myself. But I'm not sure of what I'd even say. We've already crossed the line, mixing business with pleasure, and I'm not sure what's going to happen. Maybe I should let it go and just let him make the next move.

The ring of my cell breaks me out of my thoughts. I pick it up and check the screen. Ian. Again.

"Fuck off," I growl, tossing the phone back down. I don't know why I just don't block his number.

I spend the next few minutes trying to get back into the groove of studying sales data, but I give up and start going through my emails instead. Responding to them takes less focus, and at least I'll be able to get something done.

As I'm finishing up answering the last one, I receive a visitor.

"Hey chica, what's shaking?" Eva chirps, sticking her head in the doorway. As usual, she looks sharp in a pearly blouse and black slacks, a glossy belt wrapped around her trim waist. Her hair is down today and is styled with voluminous curls. It looks good on her and makes her big eyes seem absolutely huge. On top of that, she's sporting a huge smile on her face that says she's happy-as-fuck about something.

"Nothing," I mutter, sitting aside my work laptop. "What's got you so chipper today?"

Eva steps into the room and begins wringing her hands excitedly. "You know that deal I've been working on?"

"Yeah?"

She does a little victory jump. "Well, I got it!"

I get up from my seat and go over to give her a big hug. "Congratulations Eva, I'm so happy for you!" I really am. She's been working her ass off over this. I give her a tight squeeze.

"Thank you!" Eva grins at me as we pull back from each other. "We've gotta go out and celebrate!"

For the first time in hours, I smile a genuine happy smile. I am definitely getting drinks with Eva and letting loose.

My desk phone rings before I can answer, and I hold up a finger to Eva. I need to take the call in case it's a client.

"Why the fuck are you ignoring me?" Ian snarls. "Couldn't handle seeing me happy, huh?"

Anger burns in my chest and I grip the phone so tightly I fear it might crack. It's hard keeping my emotions in check, but I somehow manage. This gives me comfort. I feel like I'm in control now. I take a deep breath and calmly say, "Just leave me alone, Ian. Please. I'd appreciate it if you just forgot my number. I don't want to ever see or hear from you again."

"You act so pissed, like I did something so horrible to you." Ian argues. "When it's obvious you bear some responsibility for what happened, hell, you brought all this on yourself."

Again I feel a surge of anger, but it's weaker than the last time. This man, if I can even call him that, is someone I never really knew. Why should I let anything he does or say bother me? His words are designed to bait me into a screaming fit, and he knows what he's saying is utter bullshit. I'm not going to play into it. He's not fucking worth it. Not anymore.

I look at the doorway and mouth an apology to Eva. Her eyes are full of pity, and I hate it. I shake my head and close my eyes. I am at last done with Ian. Forever.

"You never loved me, did you?" I say to him. "You were just using me this whole time, pretending to be something you weren't." I don't know why, but saying the words out loud shatters my last defense. I feel raw and vulnerable, but in a way, stronger for admitting the truth. I open my eyes as Ian goes off about how I wasn't there for him, saying things that are mostly falsehoods designed to get me worked up. But I'm no longer listening.

Bye, Ian.

Tiredly, I drop the phone from my ear and lean over to hang it up.

At that moment, I hear a small sound near the doorway and I look over. My heart skips a beat. It's Logan, standing behind Eva... and he's staring at me with a pissed off expression.

Oh shit. I don't know what all he heard me say, but this isn't what it looks like. My heart beats frantically, and I try to think of how to explain it. But it's too late.

Before I can think of what to say, Logan turns and walks off.

CHAPTER 22

LOGAN

I know my driver, Andrew, is waiting out front of the building. I stare out of the large windows and look down. I need to go. There's more work I can do here. There's always more work, more deals and emails and business ties. But I want to leave and get the fuck out of here. I'm pissed.

She told me she was single, and I believed her.

I clench my jaw and try to relax my fists.

The way she was talking to him didn't fucking sound like things were over between them. I don't like it.

I don't like that I feel lied to. More than that, I don't like my reaction. I wanted to pin her down and fuck her while he could hear her on the phone. I wanted to show her who she belonged to. And that's dangerous.

She doesn't belong to me. That's not what this is supposed to be. I can't deny what I'm feeling though. And I fucking hate it.

I haven't gotten one productive thing done since I walked in on that phone call.

I breathe heavily and turn away from the window. I feel like a caged animal in this office. I need to find a release.

I look back at my computer screen and feel a small pang of guilt.

It's a record of her phone calls and texts. It wasn't quite legal to do, but it was easy. And I needed to know.

My father used to do this shit to my mother. I don't want to be like him. I hate falling into his old habits.

When he looked at her messages though, he found plenty. All I'm seeing is evidence that they're over.

It doesn't make me any less angry. I don't like her getting worked up over him. I want all of her passion. Every last bit. That fucker doesn't deserve an ounce of it. If she wants someone to yell at, I'd rather it be me.

I've been obsessing over that thought since I've realized it's true. I shouldn't want it.

It's well past five and this floor of the building is silent. Everyone's gone home, so I'm certain Charlotte has already left. I may drop by her office.

I crack my neck and ignore the pings from my computer and the direct messages on my screen. I have a heavy duty punching bag in my basement. It's for moments just like this.

I've never thought of myself as a selfish man. Cold at times and distant, sure. I have flaws. Not selfish though.

But I am when it comes to her.

As if my thoughts brought her to me, a timid knock sounds at the door and then it slowly opens to reveal my Rose. I stand behind my desk and wait for her to enter. The air is thick with tension as she slowly shuts the door and finally looks up at me with those sweet blue eyes.

"Hey," she says and her voice is soft and she's twisting the bit of hair hanging along her shoulders from her ponytail around her finger. I've never seen her look so insecure in my life. Her eyes dart around the room as she stands in the doorway.

"I-" she clears her throat and then looks me in the eye. "I just wanted to clear up what that conversation was about down there."

My body's tense and I feel on edge. I'm not giving her anything. I want to hear what she has to say. "Go on," I say simply as I walk to the door and lock it.

"I... Ian and I," she starts and takes an unsteady seat on the leather sofa in my office. It makes a soft sound as she settles into it. She clears her throat and sets her purse on the floor.

She looks uneasy. It makes me feel off balance. I like knowing how things are going to play out. I set the terms, I decide how it ends. This little prick is making me have doubts. Ian is going to pay for that.

"Your ex?" I ask, as if I don't know who she's talking about. I now know everything about that fuckface. I resist the urge to take out my anger on her and instead I slip my jacket off and lay it neatly on the desk.

"Yes. Ex." She emphasizes the word and it's the first time since she's been in here that she's had any confidence in her voice. Good. The anger turns to a low simmer and I turn away to unbutton the cuffs of my shirt.

"I am completely over him." She throws her hands to the side and continues to talk with her eyes focused on the desk. "I swear, there's nothing there whatsoever." She pauses and a flash of sadness crosses her eyes. "He just... won't leave." There's a hint of desperation in her voice and her eyes gloss over with unshed tears. She fights them back and continues, "Him and my friend--ex-friend, they were there this morning and-"

I turn and face her and press, "Won't leave?"

"Yes," she says with conviction. "It's *my* apartment. It

may be shitty, but it's mine. I had it before he moved in, and now he's refusing to leave."

I walk quickly back around my desk and hit the spacebar to bring the computer back to life. Ian Rutherford's information is still there.

Charlotte goes quiet. And after a moment she reaches for her purse. Her voice is tight as she says, "Anyway, I just wanted to clear that up." She sounds defeated as she stands.

"What are you doing?" I ask her.

"I'm gonna head out," she says listlessly.

"The fuck you are. You're going to go back to him?"

For a moment she's shocked, but then the anger sets in. She takes harsh steps toward me with her heels clicking loudly on the floor.

She points her finger at me and parts those gorgeous lips of hers to snap at me, but I'm quicker.

"How badly do you want to fuck him over?" I ask in a low voice.

Her hand slowly lowers and the hard lines in her face soften. She waits a moment to answer, "I just want him gone."

Yes. That's what I want to hear. No anger. Nothing for him, not even anything negative. Empathy is far worse than anger.

"You can simply end the lease."

"I-" she stops herself and goes back to being uncertain. "I need to wait on the housing."

I pick up the phone and call Trent. It's a little after five now, but he should still be here. The phone rings and rings. Finally, he answers.

"I didn't expect to hear from you after our meeting today," he answers.

I huff into the phone. The meeting didn't go so well. It's rare that we disagree, but that's exactly what happened.

"Did you call to tell me I'm right?" he asks.

I let out a small humorless grunt and choose not to answer him. I don't have the time or energy to get into that shit with him again. "I need a favor."

"What's that?" he asks. I can hear Charlotte moving in the office. She has her purse in her hands as she walks over to the wall of meaningless awards displayed in place of family photos that don't exist for me.

"I need one of the housing units."

"For Armcorp?" he asks. I bring up his email along with all the details he needs. And then I start typing everything in, including Charlotte's current address.

"Yes," I answer as Rose turns back to face me. Part of me expects her to object. She's not one to hand over control so easily. But she doesn't.

"I have an employee that needs to be moved in by tomorrow morning. I want a moving truck there now, her lease ended, and everything in place by tomorrow."

"I'll need her-"

"Sent," I answer, hitting the enter button and sending him all her information.

Charlotte walks over to my side of the desk and I'm quick to shut off the screen and turn to her in my chair.

"Can do, anything else?" Trent asks. My Rose sets her purse on my desk and sits easily on my lap.

"That's all."

"You're going to tell me I was right and you were wrong one of these days, Logan." I smile into the phone.

"I wouldn't hold your breath if I was you." I wrap my arm around Charlotte's waist and pull her in closer. "I have to go."

"Good night, Logan," I hear him say as I slowly set the phone back down on the hook.

Charlotte leans closer to me, her lips close to mine.

"Thank you," she barely whispers. "You didn't have to do that."

"I don't have to do a lot of things; I do them because I want to."

She closes her eyes and presses her lips to mine in a sweet kiss. "Thank you." She pulls away and looks down at her purse. "Are you doing anything tonight?" she asks, a little uncertain.

"What do you want to do?" I ask her, leaning back to take a good look at her. "Because right now I wanna take you home and fuck you until you don't remember him." The words slip out so easily, I don't want to take them back. They're true.

"I don't want to wait until we get home," she says, her voice full of lust.

She leans in for a kiss, but I put my finger up and press it against her lips.

She blinks twice, and her breath falls short.

A slow grin slips into place. "I want you naked first." She smiles, the perfect picture of sweet sin, and nods.

"Yes, sir," she answers, moving her delicate fingers to the buttons on her blouse. My cock responds instantly, hardening at her delight in my request.

I slowly push the blouse off her shoulders. The thin material falls into a puddle on the floor and she shivers as my fingers trail down her arms and then back up.

"Stand up, Rose." She slowly slips off my lap and waits expectantly. I love this submissive side of her. She's exactly what I crave.

"Strip." She obeys, with confidence in every move. Her lace bra falls to the floor revealing her small rose petal nipples, already hardened. Followed quickly by her skirt and thong. My breathing comes in heavy as I watch her slowly reveal every inch of her gorgeous curves to me. She steps out of the skirt and intends to pull off her heels, but I stop her and pull her hips toward me.

"Leave them on." I lean forward and suck her pebbled nipple into my mouth. My fingers dig into the flesh at her hips and her head falls back as she moans softly. I twirl my tongue around her hardened nub and pull back slightly with suction, my teeth grazing her skin. I release her with a pop and grin at the red mark I caused before doing the same to the other side. Her hands tangle in my hair and she pulls slightly, causing a hint of pain that makes my dick that much harder.

When I'm done I take her breast in my hand and rub my thumb along her sensitive nipple. She moans my name with desperation and puts her hands on my shoulders.

"You're so beautiful," I say with a hint of awe. I reach down and cup her pussy. Her heat and arousal make me groan. "And fucking soaking for me."

I stand quickly, the chair rolling backward as I unzip my pants and pull my dick out. I can't take my eyes off my Rose. She bites down on her lip as she sees my cock come out on full display. "Bend over," I say, giving her the simple command. She's quick to turn as if I'll change my mind if she doesn't obey fast enough. She's eager for this. Thank fuck, 'cause so am I. Her upper half lays easily along the desk with her hands at the sides of her face.

I stroke my dick once and line up my cock at her pussy. I could go gentle, but I want her to feel this for as long as possible.

I slam into her and she lets out a cry, her hands shoot forward and she pushes a stack of papers off the desk. They flutter in the air and fall to the floor as I quickly pound into her pussy again and again and again. Her fingers grip the other side of the desk. My own grip both her hip and the nape of her neck. I can barely breathe as

I mercilessly thrust into her slick heat over and over again.

She screams out with every thrust, although she's trying desperately to silence them. I fucking love it. I want everyone to hear it.

I've wanted this since I laid eyes on her. Me fucking her over my desk. I'm still fully clothed, but she's bared for me. I slam into her harder, wanting more from her. Needing to hear her scream my name.

Her nails scrape along the desk, trying to hold on and her head thrashes to the side.

Her hips crash across the desk and refuse to give her any escape.

Her body stills and trembles as she sucks in a breath and I know she's close. I pick up my pace and give her everything I have. Needing to cum with her. I need it as much as she does.

Her lips part as she screams out my name. Her pussy spasms around my length. My breath comes in quick pants as I pump into her again and again, loving how tight her cunt is as her orgasm rips through her. Finally my toes curl and waves of pleasure rocks through me. My head falls back as thick streams of cum leave me. I push in short shallow thrusts until the final wave has passed and I feel like I can breathe again.

Her eyes close and her head falls limp to the desk with her heavy breathing. I love seeing her spent like that. I want it again. And again.

I quickly tuck myself back in and grab a tissue off the desk, wiping up the cum from her sweet cunt and tossing it into a bin.

I kiss the small of her back and then playfully nip her earlobe. She shudders and gives me a soft smile. She's sated and exhausted, still lying how she was while I took her. "I want you tonight. I want you available and ready whenever I want you." I'm still hard. I should take her again now. The thought of having her in the back of my limo stops me. She finally props herself up slightly and looks back at me over her slender shoulder. "Tonight?"

I nod a yes and say, "You can stay at my place tonight."

So much for keeping things separate.

CHAPTER 23

CHARLOTTE

What the hell am I doing? I ask myself.

I'm sitting at the bar in Logan's kitchen, engaged in thought, while he readies the dinner table. Our hot lovemaking session worked up a hunger and Logan ordered Chinese takeout on our way over. Yet with how my anxiety is growing, I'm not sure I'll be able to eat by the time it arrives.

I feel like I'm losing control. This whole thing with Logan is supposed to be mutually beneficial, friends with benefits, but I'm starting to think that it's more than that. At least to me. I can see it growing to that already. And that scares me. It terrifies me that I think I'm falling for him. Especially when I feel like this is still a game to him.

I wrap my arms around my torso, squeezing myself tightly, feeling a range of emotions. I'm not sure agreeing to stay at his place for the night is a good idea. Not when I can't trust my feelings. I should tell Logan that this is starting to be a problem, but I feel anxious about how he might take it.

He says this is just sex, just for our enjoyment and

nothing else. And God, am I enjoying it. But I'm starting to feel that it's more than that. Much more. And I'm afraid if I tell Logan, I might drive him away. As much as I feel like a relationship with him is a bad idea, I don't think I'm ready to lose what we have. I don't want to lose *him*.

And maybe I'll never be ready.

"What are you thinking, Rose?" Logan asks me as he finishes setting the table.

I snap out of my pensive thoughts, focusing my eyes on his gorgeous face. He's studying me with a look that's intense and at the same time brooding.

"I was just thinking about how absolutely gorgeous your kitchen is," I lie. Though I'm trying to hide my emotion, I do have to admit it does look like a grandmaster chef's paradise with gleaming quartz countertops, stainless steel appliances, and tons of space to whip up gourmet meals.

I give him a weak smile and add, "I get the sense that you don't cook very often, though." I'm choosing to just ignore everything that happened in the office about Ian. I think it's better this way. It actually brought out a side of Logan that makes me feel comfortable and secure. But that's what's causing this new insecurity. I'm just moving from one problem to the other. For a moment I feel pathetic. But then I look up at Logan. It's because of these men.

Logan shakes his head. It takes me a moment to realize he's answering my question about cooking.

Of course he doesn't cook, I say to myself. *The man could hire a score of personal chefs to cook for him. Why would he go through all the trouble?*

"Seems crazy to order takeout when you have all," I gesture expansively at the grand kitchen, "this."

Logan, walks over to me and I feel the beginnings of

desire stir, along with a dull ache from where I'm sore. He's just so irresistibly sexy. I never stood a chance. "Would you rather cook for me then?" He nods back at his huge, state of the art, stainless steel refrigerator. The damn thing even comes equipped with a touchscreen and WiFi. "I'm sure there's something in there to make..."

"Me?" I snort. "Sure... if you want to end up dead on your kitchen floor."

Logan lets out a dry chuckle. "I bet you're being too hard on yourself." He leans against the island's granite top. "Your cooking can't be all that bad."

"Trust me, one taste of my cooking and you'd be changing your mind in a heartbeat."

Logan laughs again and the rough sound combined with the sight of him so at ease and happy stirs an emotion in my chest. I suddenly feel a wave of apprehension as the feelings I've been struggling with threaten to overwhelm me. I try to push it all away, but it stays with me.

I tap my fingers on the counter and try to ignore them. The soft *click, click, click* of my nails aren't soothing though. For the past few hours, things have been better that way, with me ignoring the constant insecurities and red flags going off in my head. Yet I feel like if I don't get what I'm feeling off my chest, things are only going to get worse.

Just tell him, if he gets spooked by how I feel, then this wasn't meant to be.

The notion that he'd cut me off as soon as I tell him that I might be feeling more for him than the sex fills me with dread. But I'm burning with the need to put this out there. I want to get a feel of where we're at. And it's not going to happen if I keep pretending like this is all just hot sex.

Summoning my courage, I say seriously, "Logan."

Logan's expression is solemn as he looks at me, and I

get the sense that he already knows what I'm going to say. "Yes?"

I hesitate. This is it. This is where I tell him how I feel, and it'll be our last night together. "I'm… scared," I say finally. There. I said it. If he pushes me away after this, so be it.

Logan doesn't seem at all surprised by this admission. In fact, it seems like he's been expecting it. "About what?"

My heart pounding, I gesture at the space between us. "About this. About us. I feel like this could… become more than just sex for me."

Logan walks over and climbs onto the stool next to me, taking my hand and kissing it softly, sending tingles up along my arm. Then he looks me straight in the eye. "I appreciate you being honest."

Searching his face, I wait for him to say more, to tell me that this is becoming more to him as well. But he doesn't say it, and instead he looks like he's calculating what he wants to tell me, like he wants to be very careful of what he says next.

This fills me with wariness, and it's just another red flag that I'm better off leaving, yet I remain glued to my seat.

After a moment, Logan offers, "How about this. Let's just enjoy each other for as long as we can, and if everything goes well, we can reassess later?"

It's not the words I want to hear. I'm telling him how I feel now, and if I'm already feeling like I'm too invested, what's it going to be like later? Will he just keep stringing me along as I slowly fall in love with him, using me as his sex toy until he wants to discard me?

It's an unsettling thought and not one I want to believe he's capable of doing. But the fact that he isn't starting to feel the same is yet another warning sign. I shouldn't be here. And I need to get out before I'm in too deep. I just don't know how.

"I don't know if I want to do that," I say. "I don't know if I can handle another..." my voice trails off. *Ian.*

Logan stares at me and I feel like he wants to say something, but is holding it back.

My lips part to ask him what it is that he's not telling me, but the sound of the doorbell interrupts the moment. Our food is here. Planting another kiss on my hand, Logan gets up from the bar and goes to pay for our meal. I take a deep breath as he leaves the room and try to shake out my nerves. On top of being sore from our fuck session, I'm tense all over.

This is going to end up not working, I tell myself. *I'm going to end up heartbroken and all alone, my faith in men shattered.*

I don't want to believe this. I want there to be something between me and Logan, as there's so much more to him than sex. But there's a reason why he doesn't want to become more involved, and I need to just accept that.

I need to just tell him that after tonight, this is over. There's no reason to string this along if it's never going to turn into anything. I'll just end up a messed up basket case.

"What can I do to ease your mind?" he asks me as he sets the bags down on the counter and takes out one white takeout box at a time. The smell fills the room and although my mouth is watering, I don't have an appetite. He takes my hand in his and I feel like just melting in his arms and telling him, *Tell me that you feel the same way.* Without that, I'm not sure I can, or should, move forward.

But I can't say the words, because I know I'm just setting myself up for disappointment. Logan knows how I feel and if he wanted to put me at ease, he could just simply say that he feels the same as me, even if only to get me to shut up. The fact that he hasn't shows that this is as far as he wants it to go.

"Outside of assuring me that you won't leave me for feeling like I want more out of this relationship," I say over the lump in my throat, "nothing."

I wait for him to tell me that he won't abandon me if I get too attached, but he sits there silently with that apprehensive look again. It's like he's afraid, but of what? I'm the one with more to lose here while he's a goddamn billionaire that can have any woman he wants and I'm just his little fuckdoll that he can choose when and where to have.

Anger burns my sides and I snatch my hands out of his. Why the fuck am I still sitting here? He's all but telling me that this won't ever be anything more than just sex, and I'm just being stupid by thinking it will ever be anything but.

"I think I should go," I say and swallow the lump in my throat and slip off the stool to my feet to leave, but Logan holds me in place.

"Don't go," Logan says simply.

"Why? I mean nothing to you." I'm surprised by the hurt in my voice. He *shouldn't* care about me. This was just supposed to be fun and games. No strings attached. It's not his fault that I've reneged on the contract and am wanting more out of this.

Logan looks like he's about to say something, something that he's been badly wanting to say, but he swallows it back. "That's not true at all, Rose."

"Then why?" I ask. "Why can't you... say that... that this is going somewhere?"

Logan stares at me for a long time and I wait with bated breath. "We just need to give it time," he says finally. "I just don't think you fully know what you're getting into."

What the hell is that supposed to mean?

"What do you mean by that?" I ask warily. "I know

exactly what we're doing. And I know where it's headed. Or in your case, *not* headed."

Logan looks at me, and I see pain in his eyes. "I understand," he says finally in a grave voice.

It shatters my heart that he can't give an inch. Especially when I just opened up to him like that.

He takes my hand and pulls me close, and I'm enveloped by the heat of his hot body. I don't want to move away. I want the comfort. I need it.

"You just need to relax, and live in the moment. I want you. I don't want you to leave. Not yet." The pained look in his eyes is replaced by a desire that's hard to resist.

"But what-" I begin to protest, but he kisses me on the lips to smother it.

"Just give in, Rose," he whispers, slowly bringing his lips down to my neck and nibbling softly.

Every cell in my body is telling me to push him off me and demand that he tell me why he'd rather pretend this situation is going to get any better, but I'm overcome by his advance. I tilt my head back and my lips part into a soft groan as his hands move up my thigh.

"We don't need tomorrow," he murmurs, delivering another scorching hot kiss to my neck while undoing my skirt, "just tonight."

CHAPTER 24

LOGAN

I take another look at my phone as the driver pulls up to Charlotte's new place, the temporary housing I arranged for her. It's been nearly two weeks. And more than half the time, she's stayed at my place. She's staying here tonight. Her decision, not mine. I'm glad she's the one who brought it up. She can't come back with me tonight, but luckily I didn't have to tell her.

She's typing away on her laptop as we drive to her place. Busy with her new ventures in the marketing research department. She's doing well. I glance up at her as the faint sound of her tapping on the keys stops. She leans back and reads whatever it is she wrote out, or maybe something else, I'm not sure.

She looks so beautiful though. Her hair is down from the ponytail it was in and it flows in soft curls over her shoulder. There's still a faint blush to her cheeks from our earlier adventure in the office. She's becoming a bad habit of mine. Although Trent seems to think I'm more amicable now that *something's changed.* He obviously knows judging by the way he smiles when she knocks on my door.

I look back at my phone. There are other people who know, too.

I should tell her about the photo and the message. There's nothing in the photo that's scandalous, nothing that's harmful. Just a picture of the two of us leaving Parker-Moore. She's walking beside me as we approach the limo out front. Anger rises within me. I don't like her being watched. I don't like her having a target on her back.

She deserves to know. But I don't want to give her a reason to stay away. She's right to be cautious. But not for this reason. Not for some asshole who thinks I'm *screwing the secretary*. She's not a secretary and her position here has nothing to do with this.

It's an innocent enough photo, but the message is what pisses me off. And the fact that someone thinks they can fuck with me. I just don't know who. I will though. Maybe then I'll tell her.

She seems to only just now notice that the limo has stopped. She shuts her laptop and slips it into her bag, unbuckling her seat belt and getting ready to leave me.

As she double checks that she has everything, including a dry cleaning bag of three of her outfits she's left at my place, she gives me a small smile and grips everything in her hands.

"I'll go with you," I offer.

"No, don't," she says stubbornly, "I've got this." She leans forward and plants a kiss on my lips and pulls back slowly. At the same time my phone beeps and vibrates in my hand with a text.

It catches me off guard. Maybe it's my nerves. She seems to realize I'm off a little, but before she can think on it, I pull her closer to me, one hand on her lower back, the other on the back of her head and slip my tongue along the seam of her lips until she parts for me. The dry cleaner bags ruffle as she drops them to run her hand through my hair. Andrew starts to roll up the partition and I let out a small chuckle.

Charlotte backs away and leans down to grab her bags.

"I'll see you first thing tomorrow." She nods and slips out of the limo. It's not until she's in her building that I tell Andrew to head home.

"Thank you for that, Andrew." His eyes catch mine in the rearview mirror and he smiles.

"No problem, sir."

My home is only fifteen minutes away and I spend the time looking out of the window and watching the people walking along the busy streets of downtown. Couples holding hands and laughing, a few men and women in power suits and brightly colored pencil skirts talking on their cell phones and walking at a quick pace and brushing past the slower walkers.

The world keeps moving. No matter what happens, it's merely small ripples for the most part.

I don't even realize we've traveled up the hillside to my house on the cliff of the city, until Andrew clears his throat.

"We're here, sir," he says, looking back at me in the mirror.

"Thank you, Andrew." I quickly grab my briefcase and make my way inside. Before I push the large maple door open, I turn to my right and see the doctor's car parked in the circle driveway.

My heart sinks. I have these visits. I grit my teeth and try to forget everything else. This must be done.

Marilyn greets me at the entrance. The front entrance has a fresh citrus scent and there are fresh flowers in the vase on the entryway table. Signs of her work.

"Hello and goodbye, Mr. Parker," she says with a small smile.

"Good night, Mrs. Doubet." I leave the door open for her.

She says in a quieter voice, "The doctor is in the great room, waiting for you."

I give her a tight smile and nod. I answer, "Thank you."

She doesn't respond, instead she ducks out and leaves to go back to her family or maybe somewhere else. I watch her leave and then close the door behind her, leaving my briefcase on the table.

I take off my suit jacket and unbutton my shirt as I walk straight to the great room.

It's my favorite room in this house. It's why I bought it. The back wall is lined with floor-to-ceiling bookshelves. The dark wood shelves and chair legs are freshly polished, shining from across the room and the faint of smell of citrus fills my lungs. There are two large tufted sofas and a grand fireplace made of slate. The thick red curtains covering the large windowpanes are always drawn back, giving the room a more open feel.

I haven't lit the fireplace in God knows how long. As I walk across the room to the leather chair that the doctor's pulled out for me, I realize I haven't been in here since the last time he came for a visit. Two months.

It's my favorite room, but on these days I hate this fucking room.

"Doctor Wallace," I greet as he hears me walk into the room and turns to face me. He's an old man with a slight hunch to his back and thick glasses that cover his pale blue eyes. He doesn't look quite like a doctor in slacks and a red polo that looks like it should be worn by a younger man.

I take the seat and slip my shirt off, tossing it onto a nearby end table.

He gives me a small smile and nods. I'm not one for small talk. He's used to getting this over with quickly.

"Anything new since we last met?" he asks me as he puts the stethoscope to my back and then tells me to take in a deep breath.

"No changes." I say the words, but internally I feel like a liar. She's new. My Rose.

My fingers touch my lips and I remember the faint sounds of her moaning in my mouth.

It would be nice to have her home with me. But not tonight. She can't be here for my appointments.

At the thought I take my phone out of my pocket, remembering the beep from the text earlier. It's Trent. Doctor Wallace pulls away, giving me space to look at it.

My heart stills as I read through the message.

That fucking bastard. I stand instantly with barely contained rage.

Chadwick Patterson. That fucking prick. Trent traced the message, or had someone else do it for all I know. But he's certain the message is from him.

He's going to fucking regret it.

I think for a moment about how I can get back at him. This isn't the first time that he's tried to fuck with me. He's pissed the division of Parker-Moore went to us. The Parkers. He was an heir to it in his head. As Moore's bastard. But when that old man died, it was all left to my father. The business anyway. Patterson was given a chunk of inheritance, but not a damn bit of the business. So he quit. Made a fucking scene on his way out, too. He wasn't happy with a job, he just wanted a stake in the business. He's a fool and I've never paid much attention to his antics. But it's one thing to fuck with me, and it's another thing entirely to bring my Rose into this.

"Mr. Parker?" Doctor Wallace asks as I pace in front of the open windows.

I shake my head. "I need a moment."

I see him take a seat from the corner of my eye. I pay him well. Damn good money. He can wait a moment longer.

He needs to have some sort of consequence happen to make it damn clear that he needs to back off. I'll look over his businesses. I know there's going to be a soft spot somewhere. I need to find it. I need to find a way to hit him where it hurts. As I scroll through the businesses listed on his company directory on my phone, I try to remember the conference and which talks he attended, who he was trying to negotiate with.

A smile creeps to my lips. I know he settled on a new business with Arrivol. Their manufacturing plant is in horrible condition and he placed a bid on the old Chrysler plant. I put two and two together and know exactly how to fuck him over. Worth a few billion at least.

I dial up Trent, knowing exactly what to do.

"You got my message," he answers on the second ring.

"I did. And I want to fuck that bastard over where it hurts."

"Calm down, Log-"

I cut him off, I don't need to calm down. "I want the plant on Levington." I stop walking and stand in front of the far window. It overlooks protected woods that are a part of the city park. It's peaceful, elegant even. It's everything I'm not.

"We can use that in the-"

"I don't care what we use it for. Patterson *needs* it."

"I'm sure it's a silent bid," Trent says after a long moment.

"I don't care how much it's going to cost to win that bid. If you have to overspend, do it."

"By how much?" he asks.

I snort into the phone. "I don't give a fuck if you spend another four million on the property. Patterson needs it or he's fucked, so fuck him. Make sure he doesn't get it. Is that clear?"

"Understood," Trent starts to say something else, but I'm done talking. My blood is pumping with adrenaline and I can feel anger boiling beneath the surface.

I hang up the phone breathing heavily and squeezing the phone with rage.

"Mr. Parker," Doctor Wallace says, snapping me back to the present.

I clear my throat and nod, setting the phone down and walking back over to the chair in the middle of the room.

"You should take it easy; stress isn't-"

"I'm fine." I cut him off and try to calm my racing heart.

"You're not fine," he says, walking over to the large bag he placed on the table. He looks back at me through his spectacles. "You need to keep that in mind, Mr. Parker."

I take in a slow breath and nod.

For nearly three years it's been on my mind every minute that I'm not working. I've never been able to ignore it. My heartbeat slows and I retake my seat.

Until her.

My Rose. Such a beautiful distraction.

CHAPTER 25

CHARLOTTE

I stride confidently down the hall to Logan's office, my heels clicking against the gleaming hardwood floors. I'm dressed in a white blouse and a tight black skirt that shows off my curves; I want to look good for my boss. For the past few weeks, this has become a regular thing for me, and I no longer feel anxious about meeting Logan without an appointment.

I look forward to it even though I still question our relationship. I know it's stupid, falling for a man that doesn't want to commit, but I can't help myself. He makes me feel good. Valued. Even when I do get pissed off with him being evasive about us being together, he's always able to deflect my ire with passionate kisses and a good hard fuck.

If I was smart, I'd leave him. But it's too late. I'm addicted to him, mind, body and soul. And worst yet, I think I'm falling for him. Hard.

As I pass his receptionist's desk, I nod at his secretary, Eleanor. She's an old lady, probably in her mid-seventies with stark white hair that she always wears in a severe bun.

She returns an imperceptible nod. She's so used to seeing me show up unannounced that she doesn't even bother greeting me anymore.

I'm sure she's wondering what's going on between me and Logan, and why I have special access to him, but most of the time, I don't give a fuck. Logan is a man that gets what he wants, and he wants me. Still, I'm uneasy about being so bold about our relationship, even if it's only his secretary who suspects something is going on. It's only a matter of time before the whole building knows, and I'm not sure how they're going to react when they find out.

When I get to the oakwood double doors of Logan's office, I pause, my heart racing.

Why do I keep doing this? I know this isn't going to end well. He's all but admitted he wants to continue to take this one step at a time and won't guarantee I won't end up with a broken heart.

It's a pointless question, because I can't help myself. I *have* to see Logan. He's become a necessity, like food or water. And there are no guarantees in life.

He's told me not to knock, but I don't like just busting in on him at a moment's notice. I think a little heads-up is the polite thing to do. Taking a deep breath, I gently rap on the doors.

"Come in," I hear Logan's muffled command.

I open the doors and walk in, but nearly trip before I do, closing them behind me. Logan's on the phone, but goddamn he looks sexy as fuck. My heart beats faster and I unconsciously lick my lips. He's sitting in his tufted leather office chair, wearing a black dress shirt, his red tie loosened at the collar, his shirt open at the chest. His hair, which is usually gelled and slicked, is kind of messy, like he just woke up.

My core heats with desire at the sight of him.

He looks up at me as soon as I enter. "Hold, please" he

tells whoever it is on the other end of the line. He drops the phone to the desk without waiting for a response presses the hold button.

He always makes them wait… just for me.

This is why I can't leave him, I tell myself. *He makes me feel more important than any man I've ever been with.*

"Rose," he says, standing from his desk and stalking toward me as I make my way to him. His eyes are narrowed and heated, staring at me as though I'm his prey. But I walk straight to him, and let him devour me.

He's quick to wrap his arms around my waist, pulling me toward him and making my back arch as he kisses me with a heated passion I can't deny.

I lose myself in his embrace as our tongues intertwine, massaging against each other with intense need. I fall back against his desk, my skirt rising up my thighs. Fuck. He can take me right here. Right fucking now.

Before I can shove his shirt off of him and reach for the buckle of his belt like I so desperately want to, Logan pulls away from me and I gasp, my chest heaving. Slightly embarrassed, I straighten up and pull my skirt back down, my thighs trembling.

"We can't," Logan says quietly, smoothing his slacks. I can see his large hand pressing against his dick and readjusting it, and my mouth waters at the sight. "And I think I'm going to have the worst fucking case of blue balls when the day hasn't even started yet."

"Sorry," I say breathlessly, straightening my outfit.

"I'm good," Logan says. His voice lacks his usual fervor. "I'll make sure you make it better later."

The way he looks at me tugs at my heartstrings, and for a moment, I want to bring up our situation again, tell him how much my feelings have grown even after several weeks. But I realize this is not the time, nor the place. It can wait till later.

"Can we do lunch?" I ask instead. I've been having a hell of a time being wined and dined at all the expensive restaurants on Logan's dime. I've almost forgotten what it's like to go through a drive-thru. "Maybe fast food for once?"

Spearing his fingers through his messy hair, Logan takes a moment in responding and I feel a twinge of concern. "I have to take a raincheck," he says. His eyes have a worried look in them and he glances at the phone, something he never does. Usually he'll leave them on hold so long they hang up.

"Of course," I say, doing my best to hide my disappointment. I feel slighted, but I shouldn't. Logan has literally made time for me at all hours of the day. I can't expect him to keep doing this forever. It would be selfish of me.

Still, I can't help but wonder, *Is he getting tired of me? Is this the reason why he didn't want to commit, because he knew that this day would come?* I clear my throat and try to ignore my quickened pulse and the feeling of dread washing over me.

It makes sense. Now that Logan's had his fill, maybe he was ready to move on. The idea frightens me more than I'd like to admit.

Logan dampens my worry with a soft kiss on the lips, but his demeanor remains solemn, almost sullen. "Thank you. I promise I'll make it up to you."

As excited as I was to walk into Logan's office, I'm starting to feel tense. This muted welcome is worrying. "I'm going to hold you to that promise."

"I have absolutely no problem with that." He pauses and looks at me, noting my subdued mood. "You sure you're going to be alright having lunch by yourself?"

I flash a weak smile. Something is definitely off with Logan, and I don't know what it is. "Yeah. Actually, Eva's probably looking for company, so I'll just hit her up." I need to talk to Eva anyway, I've been putting her off since getting closer to Logan and we have a project we're working on. I take out my phone and send her a quick text.

Me: Hey chica, lunch?

I look up to talk to Logan, but he moves around to his desk and shakes his mouse to look at the computer screen. My phone pings.

Eva: Yup, where at?

Me: At the Blue Cafe on the corner.

Eva: See ya there.

I put my phone away. "I'm gonna meet her at the Blue Cafe."

Logan relaxes. "Good. Do you want to use my limo?"

I shake my head, though I'm pleased by the offer. It'll raise Eva's eyebrows if I showed up in a limo to a cafe that was just two blocks from the building. She probably already knows what's going on. I get the sense that a lot of people do. Still, lately I'm feeling different about keeping my relationship with Logan a secret. If it weren't for his reluctance to have a real relationship, I'd want the world to know.

But the way he's acting now has me wondering.

"No, I'll walk." I step forward and give him a quick peck. "Thanks for offering though."

"And thank you for being so understanding," Logan says before picking up his phone and taking it off of hold. "Are you there? ...Alright." Logan gives me a distracted wave as I leave, and I can't shake the feeling that something is wrong as I walk out of his office.

Outside it feels good, a cool breeze sweeping up the

street. The sky is clear, and the deep blue color would take my breath away if I wasn't in such a sour mood.

If this is the beginning of the end, then it will be no less than I deserve. I knew I shouldn't have gotten involved with him.

I make it halfway down the block, lost in my thoughts and hardly watching where I'm going, when I feel a prickling sensation on my neck. Someone's watching me. I turn around, scanning behind me. There are a couple of people walking on either side of the street, entering businesses, and cars driving by, but no one stands out.

For a minute, I continue to scan, my eyes darting everywhere, but I eventually give up.

After a moment, I turn and continue on, thinking, *Relax, Charlotte. You're just being paranoid.*

* * *

"DID you see what happened with that celebrity guy in the news?" Eva asks me as she takes a bite out of her blueberry bagel that's covered with cream cheese. We're sitting in the Blue Cafe in the corner. It's secluded and private which is nice. It's been awhile since I've eaten in a place that has a dollar menu, but I'm happy to see Eva and catch up on corporate gossip and talk about the project we're working on together.

As usual, Eva's dressed sharp as a tack in a red pantsuit and matching lipstick, her hair pulled back into an elegant ponytail. I need her to be my stylist.

I pause, peeling the plastic wrap from around my banana nut muffin. I'm trying to be cheerful with Eva, but I just have a bad feeling. I don't like how distant Logan was with me in his office. "What guy?"

"It was what's his face," Eva snaps her fingers together multiple times trying to jog her memory, "the hot young guy that plays a president on that one show and he cheats on his wife with an intern." She motions at me as if I'm supposed to be a psychic and give her the answer. "You know, *that* guy."

Actually, I have no idea who *that* guy is. I'm drawing a blank. Since starting the new job, I don't watch much TV, and the only hot guy in my life is Logan. "I don't know who you're talking about-"

"Jake Goldwater!" Eva yells and slaps her hand on the table. "That's it!"

I vaguely know who she's talking about, I think I've watched a few movies he's been in. I don't think he's anything special. "What about him?"

"Well supposedly, in real life he also heads his own company, Goldwater Productions." She taps a finger against her chin thoughtfully. "I think he even owns a building several blocks from here. Anyway, he got caught banging one of his secretaries... on video."

"Damn," I mutter, shaking my head. "I'd hate to be that girl. She'll be humiliated for the rest of her life."

Eva gives a short laugh. "You'd be one of the only ones. There's probably scores of women who'd sleep with him on camera."

"Good for them," I mutter darkly.

Eva bringing up Jake's scandal hits close to home. The parallels are freaky. I'm not Logan's secretary, but I am sleeping with him. It makes me feel ashamed that I just don't come out and tell Eva. I almost feel like a fraud.

It would be nice to have someone to confide in, someone I can tell my doubts about Logan to. Someone who can tell me that I'm insane for staying with a guy, even if he is rich, that won't commit.

Eva peers at me with concern. "Something wrong?"

"No," I lie. "I just feel overwhelmed with all this work."

And worried about the direction my relationship with Logan is going.

"Aren't we all." Eva pauses and she looks like she's debating on whether bringing up a topic.

"Speaking of hot bosses, there's a rumor going around about Logan..."

"Eva," I say, cutting her off. Here's my chance to come clean with Eva. At this point, it'll be a relief. With all my doubts about our relationship, I don't see a reason to hold back anymore. I just hope Eva doesn't judge me too harshly.

She shakes her head, setting aside her bagel, her face twisting with shock. "Oh no, don't tell me..."

"I've been sleeping with Logan," I say super fast. There. I was right. I feel so much better already.

Eva's mouth opens wide with shock. "Jesus, Charlotte, how long has this been going on?"

I tell Eva everything, about Vegas, about sleeping with Logan and then leaving him. I hold nothing back, and when I'm done, I feel even more liberated. "After Ian, it was so easy to just fall in bed with him. He was just so charming and... sexy. I couldn't help myself. But now I'm worried that we're..." *Finished.* I feel a lump form in my throat at the thought.

Maybe I'm just overreacting and it's all in my head.

That's what I want to believe, but deep down inside, I know otherwise. That Logan's hiding something from me, I'm certain, I've just been doing a decent job in deluding myself that things will get better.

Eva's shaking her head in disbelief and doesn't seem to notice my last sentence. "No wonder he gave you the head sales position."

"So you think that's the only reason I got the sales job?" I ask irritably. I thought Eva would be giving me relationship advice, not questioning my position in the company.

"Don't you dare," Eva says defensively, seeing that I've taken her words the wrong way. "You know I would never think so lowly of you. You're a beast at what you do, and everyone knows it. That's why Logan hired you." The passion and sincerity in Eva's voice make me feel ashamed for jumping to conclusions.

Eva shakes her head. "What I *meant* is that Logan wanted you, and seeing how good a sales rep you were, he made sure you'd work closely with him."

"I'm sorry, Eva," I say softly. "I didn't mean to snap at you."

Eva waves away my worry. "It's no problem. I woulda got pissed too and thought the same thing if I was in your shoes."

She pauses and then gives me a look. "So is everything okay with Logan? You sounded like you're having some serious issues… despite the good sex."

I let out a sigh. "He won't commit. He just tells me we should live in the moment. But I don't know what to do... I think I'm falling in... falling for him. And I'm afraid that I'm going to end up..." My heart clenches and I take a deep breath. It's so hard to admit.

Eva grimaces. "That's… not good."

"Yeah, and I'm not sure how much more time I should devote to something that's never going to work out. Even if the sex is good. I don't want a repeat of Ian, you know?"

Eva nods and makes a face. "Yeah, but ugh. It sucks because you're at a disadvantage in this relationship. Like, he can totally get rid of you if you suddenly decide you've had enough and want to break it off with him."

Eva isn't saying anything I haven't already considered, and it's depressing. I'd like to think that Logan would never do such a thing to me even if we did break up, but then I remember Ian. I thought I knew him, thought I'd marry him and have his children even, and he turned out to be a totally different person than who I thought I'd fallen in love with.

When it comes down to it, I don't really know Logan either.

"So what are you gonna do?" Eva asks, her expression deeply concerned. "I'm afraid to give you advice on this because I don't see a clear answer." She leans forward and takes my hand in hers and gently adds, "I just don't want to see you hurt."

The answer should be easy. Stop wasting time. Leave Logan no matter the cost. But when I think about leaving him, I feel overwhelmed. I don't want it to have to end. Yet I hate being in this state of limbo.

"Charlotte?" Eva asks when I don't answer right away.

I sigh and squeeze her hand before letting go. I take a bite out of my muffin, shake my head, and reply, "I don't know, Eva. I really wish I knew."

CHAPTER 26

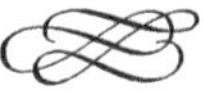

LOGAN

My eyes are drawn from my computer to the large doors of my office at the sound of a loud knock.

"Come in," I call out. I half expect it to be Rose even though it's a quarter to five and I doubt she'll be done with work this early. I want it to be her. But it's not, it's Trent.

As he closes the door, I stretch my arms above my head and sigh heavily. It's been a long fucking day.

"Did we get it?" I ask as he slumps into the sofa and leans forward, his elbows on his knees with his chin resting in his hands.

He nods and says, "It cost us forty-three million. But we won the bid."

I finally let a grin slip into place.

"We overspent, but it's still usable," he says.

I huff out a breath, the smile unmoving. It feels good knowing how badly I fucked over Patterson. And he's going to know. There's not a damn good reason for me to have bought it otherwise.

"Logan," he says and waits for me to look at him.

I raise my eyebrows as he makes me wait in silence.

"Yes?" I ask him, finally leaning forward and giving him my attention.

"Are you alright?"

He hasn't asked me that in quite a long time.

"I am." I clear my throat and look at the clock and then back to him. "I'm fine." I'm not fine. But I'm not as bad as I once was. I know that's why he asks. I can run this company. He's the only one who knows about my condition beyond my father. If it got worse, I'd tell him. I wouldn't let the company fall.

"That's not what I mean."

I look back at him with my forehead pinched in confusion.

"It's about Miss Harrison."

"Charlotte Rose." I feel my hands grip the arms of the chair. My blunt nails dig into the leather. "What about her?" I ask, my voice on edge.

"Is she-" he stops to look away and then back at me. "Is this serious?" he asks.

I wait a moment to answer. I know the truth though. It is. I've never been more serious about anything in my life. I want her. I need her to be mine.

"Yes," I answer and hold my breath, waiting for him to tell me all the reasons we shouldn't be together. Instead a smile grows on his face.

"I'm very happy for you, Logan." He leans back and says, "I'd like to meet her; maybe outside of the office?"

I scoff a laugh and finally relax. I nod my head, looking back at the clock. "I think she'd like that. Maybe a corporate lunch."

He lets out a laugh. "To think you have a life outside of work."

I bring my fingers to my lips. It's certainly something different. *She's* something different.

"Does she know?" he asks. My breath catches in my throat as I maintain eye contact. I don't want to answer. I can't admit to him what a selfish prick I've been.

I'm saved from responding by a small, timid knock on the door. It opens before I can respond, and Charlotte appears.

She's in a simple shirtdress that flatters her curves, and I can't help letting my eyes roam her body as she hesitantly walks in. "Are you in the middle of a meeting?" she asks in a hushed voice, gripping the edge of the door.

Trent has a wide smile on his face and answers for me. I'm caught in a trance at the sight of her. As if telling Trent she was mine somehow made it more real. More tangible. Something I can actually have.

"Not anymore, we've just wrapped up." He slaps his hands on his thigh and stands.

"I'm not sure we've met officially," he says and holds a hand out to her and I finally rise to walk over and help introduce them.

She accepts his hand. "Trent Morgan." She says his name with confidence and with her back straight. Her purse jostles as she shakes his hand. "It's nice to officially meet you; Logan has said nothing but nice things about you."

Trent laughs and pats the back of her hand before releasing her and says, "He must not have said much then." A small chuckle rises through my chest at his joke as I wrap an arm around her waist. It's the first time I've ever held her in front of anyone. A small gasp leaves her lips and she looks at me, nervously tucking her hair behind her ear. Her eyes flash with surprise.

"I'm glad you've met her, now get the fuck out." I say

the words easily with a grin and he nods, picking up his jacket off the sofa.

"You two have a nice night," he says as he opens the door.

"You too," my Rose says in a slightly high-pitched voice.

She watches the door until it closes. And then she looks up at me and asks, "We're an item now?" Although there's skepticism in her eyes, her voice is laced with a hope I've never heard from her.

I simply nod. I don't like that she's questioning it, that she's doubting me.

I understand, but I don't fucking like it.

"Like..." She pauses and takes in a short breath before pulling away slightly and then looking back at me. I keep my feet bolted to the ground and wait for whatever the hell she's thinking to come out. "Like people can know?"

I huff a small laugh and walk over to her, she refuses to believe me. "Yes. The world can know you're mine."

"Do you mean it?" she asks in a soft voice that displays her vulnerability. I hate that I ever made her feel so insecure.

I nod and whisper back, "Yes." Her body relaxes somewhat, but she doesn't respond.

"Do you want me, Rose?" I ask her, turning her in my arms and pulling her soft body into mine. "Because I sure as fuck want you."

She braces herself with her small hands on my chest as she looks up at me with wide eyes. She nods, and breathlessly says, "Yes. I want you."

I crash my lips against hers in a bruising kiss. The need to claim her has my dick hard as a fucking rock.

I pull away and tear at the sash around her dress, desperate to get it off. Her nimble fingers unbutton her dress fast enough to save it from being destroyed.

I pull back to look at her. Her tempting body in nothing but heels, a black bra and matching panties. Her chest rises heavily with quick breaths, and her face is flushed with desire.

Fucking gorgeous.

She quickly unbuttons my shirt, not waiting for me to act. I reach around, undoing her bra as she kneels on the floor, unbuckling and unzipping my pants with a desperate need. She tugs them down and releases my cock. My hands fist in her hair as she quickly takes the head of my dick into her mouth.

I groan, but I don't let her take any more. I pull her off and step out of my pants. She waits on the floor, watching me, but not for long.

I reach down and pick her up in my arms. Her lips press against mine and she parts for me. My tongue massages along hers and the air turns hot between us.

My fingers curl around the flimsy lace and I easily shred them and toss them carelessly to the floor, not breaking our kiss.

I push her back against the wall for leverage so I can move one hand off her lush ass and down between us.

I slide my dick between her folds and then roughly push into her hot pussy.

She moans loudly, slamming her head against the wall. I leave open-mouthed kisses along her slender neck as I thrust up and into her welcoming heat.

"Mine," I groan in the crook of her neck. She whimpers my name as I quicken my pace.

One of her heels falls to the ground with a loud bang as her feet dig into my ass, her legs wrapped tightly around my hips.

"Say it," I command her.

"I'm yours!" she cries out with her head arched to the side. "I'm yours, Logan!"

Yes! I slam into her over and over. Each time the wall shakes, threatening to knock the frames off the wall.

I look to my left, to the large windows covered by blinds. I grab her ass with both hands and move us to them, opening the blinds and continuing to fuck her as her back hits the cold glass.

"Logan!" she cries out, her breasts pressed against my chest as I continue my relentless pace.

I pull out of her and turn her around, pushing her beautiful frame against the glass. We're so high up I can barely make out the people below. But I want this.

"What are you doing?" she whispers, her voice laced with desire. I reach my hand around to her front and rub my fingers against her clit. She moans and tries to move away slightly. I slam my dick back into her and continue mercilessly stimulating her throbbing clit.

"I'm gonna make you mine, and the whole world's gonna see it," I growl.

"Oh, fuck," she moans out, her hot breath leaving fog on the cold glass as her cunt clamps down on my dick.

Her eyes go half-lidded and her body tenses.

"Yes," I breathe onto her neck, my lips just touching the shell of her ear. "Cum with me, my Rose," and on my command her head falls back against my shoulder and I lose it. Everything in me comes undone as my orgasm races through my blood. I kiss her lips as my dick pulses deep inside of her.

We stay just like that for a long moment after, both of us trying to calm from the intensity of our orgasms.

I finally let her go and turn to grab a few tissues, cleaning her first and then my cock, which is still hard.

She walks to the corner and sags slightly, her legs still trembling as I gather our clothes.

I can't stop watching her as I dress myself. Picking up the now-wrinkled shirt and slipping it on as my breathing tries to steady itself. We could stay here in the office, but I want to bring her home.

"Logan," she says with great effort, finally picking up her bra and dress and slipping them on.

I smile down at her as she tries to speak. I walk over and hold her small body to mine. "Are you alright?" I ask. She leans into me and nods her head. I kiss her hair. "What did you need?" I ask.

She finally stands on her own, pushing me away slightly and pulling her hair out of her face. "Nothing," she says with a small smile, shaking her head.

She picks up her heels and slips them on, giving me a sweet smile over her shoulder. I eye her, but leave it at that. I pick up my tie off the floor and shove it into my pocket.

She picks up the lace scrap on the floor and looks at me as though I've committed an awful crime.

"I'll get you more."

"But what am I going to wear out of here?" she asks in a hushed voice.

I walk over to her and take the torn thong, tossing it into the trash bin under my desk. I lean into her, with both hands on her ass and squeeze as I kiss her, silencing her sweet squeal of surprise.

I pull back with a grin. Her face is flushed and her breathing heavy.

"Nothing," I finally answer her.

She looks at the trash bin and then up to me with a devilish smile before nodding and pulling her dress down over her ass. She grabs her purse and opens the door, waiting for me.

That's my Rose.

There's a faint sound of my secretary, Eleanor, tapping on the keyboard from the entryway of the office, but not any other sounds.

I look up at Rose as I lock the door behind us and lead the way. She's not showing any sign that she's affected, so next time I'll have to up the ante.

"Have a good night," I say and nod at my secretary, the only person left on the floor, and keep walking with the sound of Charlotte's heels accompanying us.

"Should I go home tonight?" she asks as we walk side by side to the elevators.

I'm not sure if it's because all the blood in me is still in my dick, or because I've already made decisions about our relationship that she hasn't come to realize yet, but it takes me a moment to realize that she means her temporary apartment. But I want her in my bed tonight. I'm finding that I sleep much better with her there.

"No. I want you in my bed tonight."

She looks up at me with apprehension, but nods as the elevator dings and the doors open. It's empty and quiet as I press the button for the main floor.

She purses her lips. "And my car?"

"Can stay here," I answer easily. I watch her, waiting for some sign that we're on the same page. She nods and grips her purse with both hands. She's tense.

"We can take things slow," I say, staring straight ahead.

She lets out a small laugh of disbelief.

I cock an eyebrow and smirk at her.

She smiles and leans into me, giving me a chaste kiss on the lips. "If you say so, Mr. CEO."

CHAPTER 27

CHARLOTTE

I'm completely immersed in going over contracts when the phone rings and disrupts me. The ID says it's a call from Hastings. I don't want to stop what I'm doing, so I ignore the chimes of my ringtone, but he doesn't give up, immediately calling again. Damn it. I sigh with slight irritation. I'm exhausted and I don't have time for interruptions, but this must be something important.

"This better be good," I grumble before picking up the phone and subtly clearing my throat. "Hello?" I answer in a professional tone.

"Charlotte, you finally answered," he says, voice low and carrying a tone of urgency. "I need to see you in my office. Now."

I glance at the pile of contracts sitting in front of me. "Is this something that can wait? I really need to get these last few things done…" I feel bad being so forward. "A lot is riding on this," I add.

"No," Hastings says firmly. "I want to see you this instant." My eyes widen and my heart skips a beat in my chest. Something's wrong, and I can't help that a sickness stirs in the pit of my stomach.

I'm silent for a moment, and it's long enough that he adds--

"Now, Charlotte... You need to hear about this in person."

"I'll be right there," I answer quickly and hang up. I can't shake a bit of dread.

I sigh and smooth down my chiffon dress as I walk down the hall. I feel a prick of distress as I think everyone seems to be turning to look at me as I make my way over to Hasting's office, but I brush it off due to the fact of what I'm wearing, a brightly colored dress. Still, I feel a little uneasy. The stares aren't normal.

I knock lightly on Hasting's door, my heart beating a little faster and my palms a bit sweaty before stepping in into his office. I freeze when I see who else is there. Eva. It looks like she's distressed, her large eyes filled with worry as they fall on me.

A feeling of dread runs through me and numbs my body.

Hastings nods at me, his lined face drawn and serious. "Close the door, Charlotte," he orders.

The intense feelings grow stronger and my chest starts feeling tight.

With my heart racing, I do as he commands. The door closes with a loud click and I walk over in a daze and sit down next to Eva. She takes my hand in hers, squeezing it lightly, causing me to shake like a leaf in the wind. I don't make eye contact with her even though her eyes are boring into me.

Hastings leans forward across his desk, clasping his hands together. "We have a problem," he tells me.

I nod my head rather than speak around the lump

growing in my throat. My heart's racing so fast it's about to beat out of my chest. There's no doubt in my mind that this is bad. *Very bad.*

I'm about to pass out, and I haven't even heard the news yet. *I'm fired,* I think to myself. *This must be it. I've just lost my job.* My mind is racing at light speed with a number of dark scenarios.

Hastings sucks in a deep breath and my eyes dart back to his, waiting anxiously. "I don't know how to tell you this Charlotte, but we… were emailed photos of you this morning."

Hastings lowers his head as if he's almost ashamed. "Of you and Logan Parker… together." His last words leave no doubt about what he means by 'together'. My face heats and my blood goes cold. I try to speak, but I can't.

Hastings turns his monitor and Eva pulls her hand away, leaving me feeling alone, but I reach out and grab onto her. She's quick to lean forward and hold my hand. I need her. I'm thankful she's here.

My heart jolts in my chest when I see a picture on the screen and I immediately start to hyperventilate. It's hard to look at and tears prick my eyes, but I don't let them fall.

Eva gives my hand another squeeze and rubs my back, but it doesn't help. I'm shocked, angry and hurt beyond belief. I can hardly breathe.

Seeing the shock and anger on my face, Hastings raises his hands out to me. "Now now, Charlotte, I want to assure you that no one here thinks any less of you." He nods at the envelope. "Do you want to see them? I know it's a horrible thing to ask, but you should know what was sent to us. Take all the time you need before you look."

I stare at the desk for a moment, feeling a mountain of shame pressing down on my chest, and then burst into tears, sobbing uncontrollably.

Immediately, Eva pulls me into her arms, whispering comforting words in my ears that I don't hear.

"We're going to help you get through this, Charlotte," Hastings tells me firmly. "I promise. Whoever is responsible for this vile act will be held accountable. I've already contacted the authorities."

His words barely register, and they do little to comfort me. The damage has already been done. I'm ruined. I'll never be able to come to work again without feeling like a cheap whore.

Shame drives me from Eva's embrace and out of my seat. I have to see Logan and tell him what's going on.

Alarmed by my behavior, Hastings rises out of his seat and reaches for me as I storm toward the door. "Charlotte, wait!"

I ignore his command and I hear Eva say something to him, but I don't catch what it is. I'm too consumed by my emotions to care. On the way up to Logan's office, I ignore the dubious stares I get. When I hit the top floor, I march past Eleanor's desk without a word.

I burst into Logan's office, swinging the double doors open wide, feeling the last bit of control I have slip away at the sight of him. Logan, who's sitting in his chair and on the phone, looks up with surprise.

"It's over," I say and my voice cracks, barely able to keep myself from collapsing.

"I'll call you back," Logan says quickly into the phone, hanging up. He jumps out of his seat and makes his way over to me. "What's going on, Rose?" he asks, pulling me into his arms. I collapse against him, a blubbering mess.

I try to tell him what's going on, but my words come out all garbled as I cry and sob. I'm a mess. I can't help it. I'm practically shaking.

He shakes me gently, trying to get me to stop sobbing. "Rose, I need you to calm down."

How can he begin to tell me to calm down? There were pictures of us screwing being circulated around everywhere. I bite back my anger, he doesn't know.

"They have pictures of us," I manage to push out the words as I pull away from him, tears streaming down my face.

"Pictures of what?"

"Pictures of us screwing!" I yell.

Logan's face turns hard as he pushes me to the side and takes large strides to the door. Several people are looking in, making my heart still as he slams it shut and turns to look at me with a deadly expression I've never seen.

CHAPTER 28

LOGAN

I close the door and lock it. Charlotte's hysterically crying on the sofa with her phone in her lap. She's practically shaking and I need to comfort her, but first I need to end the web conference. I quickly stride to the other side of my desk and type in a message that the meeting is canceled. Voices from the executives fill the speakers, but I shut off the microphone and the monitor, my heart racing in my chest. I doubt they heard. Even if they did, I wouldn't give a fuck.

She's hurt though.

Photographs.

Of us fucking… so *new* photographs. My heart hammers in my chest as the anger rises, threatening to consume me. I'll fucking kill him. I'll destroy him and everything he's ever touched.

I walk slowly to the sofa and kneel on the floor.

I pet her hair as she wipes her eyes and looks up at me. "Everyone," she says as her voice cracks and she wipes under her eyes angrily. Her mouth stays open, but nothing else comes out.

"It's going to be okay," I say as calmly as I can.

She pushes my arm away. "It's not! How can you say that?" She looks up at me with a pained expression. "Everyone saw me…" Her face falls, and she can't finish. She manages to look away from me and the anger courses through her. Her hands ball into fists as she looks up and past my desk.

"Right fucking there," she says and points to the window. "No one will ever respect me."

She heaves in a breath and continues, "They're going to think I only got this job because-"

"Stop it." I stand up, cutting her off. "What they think doesn't matter," I say and my voice is hard and full of venom. "This will be dealt with."

"Dealt with?" she asks incredulously. "My job is ruined."

"It's-"

"I rely on presentations, I can't hide behind a computer ignoring everyone. Everyone I ever meet will have seen them."

She reaches for her phone, and my heart slows as I realizes she's bringing them up. Her shoulders rise and fall heavily as the shock and sadness leave her and anger takes the forefront. She finally passes me the phone, angrily wiping the tears from her reddened cheeks.

I look down with the intention of it being a glance, but I focus on it. She looks beautiful, in complete rapture. Every inch of her on display. My grip tightens on the phone.

She's for me and me only.

I don't want anyone else to see that look on her face. It's for me. Anger consumes me as I throw her phone onto the sofa and push my hands through my hair. It's my fault.

"It's my fault," I can barely breathe out.

"No." She brushes her tears away, shaking her head.

"This was a mistake," she says in a small voice and doesn't look me in the eyes.

Mistake.

My heart slows, and my blood turns to ice.

"Whoever did this," I start to say although I already know who. Patterson. I'll confirm it and then he's done. "I'll make sure they pay."

She rises from her seat and slowly grabs her cell phone as she heads for the door with a look of defeat and despair.

"Rose," I call to her, but she ignores me, intent on leaving. No. I stare at her, my heart thudding painfully in my chest. No. "Rose!"

"I'm sorry, Logan," she says in a pained voice, reaching for the door.

I slam my hand against the door above her head before she can open it. "Where are you going?" I ask her as calmly as I can, although I'm not anywhere near that emotion.

"I knew I should've never gotten involved with you," she says in a soft voice that cripples me.

She tugs on the doorknob, but I lean my weight against the door and cage her body in. "Rose, don't leave."

"I have to, Logan." She stares straight ahead and closes her eyes as I lean forward and kiss her neck.

"Don't." Her voice cracks and tears slip down her cheeks. "Please, just let me go." She wipes the tears away and swallows thickly. "I need to go."

"You don't."

"I do," she says the hard words with conviction. Shaking her head, she says, "I can't stay here. This was wrong. I knew it; I'm sorry."

I can make this right. I can calm her down and make her understand that everything will be fine. But as I try to think of a way to ease her pain and have this blow over, I can't think of anything. I'm paralyzed with the fear of her leaving me. My heart slams against my chest, willing me to do something, to say something.

But I have nothing. For the first time in my life, I feel true panic and it cripples me. I'm failing her, and I know it.

"I'm sorry, Logan," she says with her eyes still closed.

"Nothing to be sorry for." I'm quick to say the words, shaking my head, completely aware that I'm in denial. She's not leaving me. She can't.

"It's over," she says as she covers her face with her hands, finally releasing the doorknob.

Her shoulders shake and I pull her closer to me, but she pushes me away, shaking her head.

She turns to look up at me with tear-stained cheeks and puffy eyes as she says, "Just let me leave."

The words resonate with me. I've heard them before. My mother told my father that I don't know how many times. I do what my father never did, and back away from her. I stare at the wall of frames and try to ignore the sound of the door opening and then closing. Leaving me alone as I struggle to breathe.

This was going to happen. It's the way these things work. I try to convince myself I'm telling the truth, but it doesn't stop the pain. I brace myself against the wall, in complete shock and disbelief. It hurts. The crippling pain brings me to my knees. I lean my back against the door, not wanting this to be real.

I finally had something I never thought I would. And I let her slip through my fingers. It's my fault. It's all my fault.

I stay in that position for I don't know how long. Letting the scene play out again and again. I finally move, but I feel as though I'm not really here.

At least she's away from me now.

I walk out of the office, and it all falls into a hush. A few phones are ringing and some people are typing, but the sounds of keys clicking dims as I lock my office door.

I don't make eye contact with anyone, although I can feel them all staring at me. This is what she went through. I fucking hate them all. I clench my hands into fists and ignore my secretary as she stands and says something. I don't hear it, it's all white noise.

I take the elevator to the parking garage. I don't even know if my car is here. I've been using the limo so I can spend quality time with my Rose.

I don't know if her car was here. I call her as I head to my car. I need to make sure she's okay.

It rings and rings. She doesn't answer.

My car's there, parked in my spot.

I get in and sit there for a moment. And then I finally put the keys in the ignition. I don't turn it on though. I keep hearing her words play in my head. It's over.

She's sorry. She knew she shouldn't have.

My head falls back against the headrest and I stare at the cement brick wall ahead of me.

I don't know what to say to convince her otherwise. I shouldn't. I shouldn't try to convince her otherwise. But what we had felt so good. So right. It felt *real*.

The sound of a car's horn from outside the garage wakes me back to the present. I finally turn the car on and drive home.

A long time passes with no sound, and I don't even realize it. I debate on turning up the volume, but I don't want to. I wouldn't listen to it anyway.

When I walk inside, my house feels colder and emptier than usual as the keys clank against the table.

Charlotte's dry cleaning is on the entry table. It's there to greet me.

I walk past it and straight to my bedroom.

I lay on the bed fully clothed and look at the ceiling. My chest hurts. My body hurts. I can hardly stand the pain. The cell phone's right there. I know where she lives. I need her in this moment. I know she's what I need.

I pick up my phone to call her, but can't press send. It's my fault he did that to her, and I can't take it back. There's no fix to this. I deserve this pain. I knew I was no good for her.

I close my eyes, hating that my actions caused her pain. That I *ruined* her.

I never thought this would happen though. Anger simmers beneath the pain. I grip onto it. Needing it and feeling alive again with it.

I'll ruin Patterson. I'll make sure he pays for what he did to her.

CHAPTER 29

CHARLOTTE

I *wish I could afford to tender my resignation,* I think to myself as I set my glass of hot tea down on my desk and peck out a response to an email. *Then I'd be gone like the wind.*

I lean back against my headboard in my PJs, working on my laptop, sitting cross-legged in bed. I'm trying to focus on getting work done, but all I can think about are the events of the past few weeks that led up to this. The pain, the humiliation. These emotions haunt me daily and makes it hard for me to focus on important tasks. I wish I could just leave. But quitting means giving up this apartment and my paycheck. I have no savings. I have to keep working. I applied to nearly sixty jobs yesterday, none of them in my field. I'll take the pay cut and start at the bottom. I never wanna go back. I take in a shuddering breath. I have to until I have something else though. At least Hastings is letting me work from home.

But he can't save me from everything; I have a press conference coming up on Tuesday, and I desperately don't want to go. I don't think I can bear it, seeing Logan, seeing all those accusatory eyes on me, knowing what they're thinking.

She's a whore, an office slut. I can just hear it now. I lean back and close my eyes.

For days now I've been weighing my options. I could quit, but there was no telling if I'd be able to find another job. By now, word of my sexcapade with Logan has spread throughout the entire sales industry. No self-respecting corporation that cared about their public image would ever hire me, and I'd probably be laughed out of interview rooms across town.

I just have to face it--I'm stuck. And a part of me blames Logan.

It hurts just thinking his name. I feel horrible for leaving him the way I did. I was just emotional and feeling alone. I've waited all week for him to call. He hasn't, and it hurts. I thought what we had together meant something to him.

I was a fool to stick around when he told me to my face that he wouldn't commit. I deserve this.

The pain almost overwhelms me and tears burn my eyes. I climb off the bed and grab a tissue from the box on my desk to blow my nose, then toss it into the wastebasket with a hundred others. I knew I shouldn't have gotten involved. I feared ending up like this, becoming a sorry, broken mess.

He should've called me, I think to myself, *even if he doesn't think I want to talk to him, to prove me wrong. To show that he really does care about me. At the same time, I should have called him.*

Even Hastings has called me, though he's kept everything professional and hasn't once mentioned the photos. I think he feels sorry for me and wants to keep an eye out, make sure I don't go try to go jump off a building somewhere.

If I can get through these next few months, I'll look for another place... in another city, I tell myself.

The thought makes me miserable and I slog through the mass of emails feeling like shit. I'm just through responding to my last email when I get a call from Eva.

"Hello?" I answer the same way I always have.

"Charlotte!" Eva cries, her voice joyful. "I'm so happy to hear your voice!"

I hold in a groan. I know she's trying to be cheerful because she knows that I'm in a dark place, but it's not going to help. Despite what she says, it's hard not to think that she thinks less of me after she saw the photos of Logan and I screwing. "Thanks," I say. "How are things going?"

There's a pause on the other end of the line and then I hear Eva suck in a breath. "Alright. Things have been going great with the project." She's not mentioning anything about the photos. Good, because I don't want to hear it. Although she did leave a message on my voicemail about it on the day after it happened and the first day I stayed home from work. I never returned that call. I suppose she got the memo.

There's another pause and then she blurts, "Hannah, Cary Ann and I are doing a ladies' night tonight. Wanna come?"

Not really, is my initial thought. I shift on the bed, pushing the laptop away and trying to get comfortable. I don't want to go, but I feel somewhat obligated because of how supportive Eva is trying to be. I know she only wants me to get out of the house and out of this depression. Yet there's no way I'm going to go and deal with the stares... the looks. I haven't talked to Hannah and Cary Ann since it happened, and I'm sure they're going to have questions for me. I can't handle that tonight. It's just too much. "I'm sorry, Eva," I say finally, "but I really don't want to."

"Please," Eva implores. "I'm just worried about you. Getting out for some fresh air and a relaxing drink would be good for you."

"I... just can't." It's obvious that we handle things differently, and she's only trying to help. But I know I won't be alright. I'm not ready to put myself out there like that.

Before Eva can reply, there's a knock at the door. "I gotta go, Eva. Sorry." I hang up the phone and crawl out of my bed, quickly jogging to the front door so they don't leave. When I get there, it's a different story. For a moment, I debate on even opening the door. There's no one I wanna talk to... other than Logan.

Instead I peek through the peephole. I see an old man dressed in black standing outside. I watch as he raises his hand and knocks again. I wait, hoping he'll go away, but he stands there and knocks several more times.

I finally answer the knock with a raised voice, "I'm not presentable right now, so I would prefer you leave and come back at a decent time."

I can barely hear him through the door, but my ears perk up when he says, "It's about Logan."

The chain lock clinks as I unlock it and I swing the door open. "What about Logan?" I ask breathlessly.

The old man doesn't answer right away, taking in my PJs and disheveled appearance.

"Miss Harrison?" he asks.

I grip the door and answer, "Yes. I would really like to get straight to the point." Even in my PJs I'm attempting to command a sense of professionalism. It's laughable, but I don't have the energy for small talk.

He nods politely. "What happened between you two," he explains, clasping his hands in front of him. "Logan's done this before. He destroyed a woman's career, and it was extremely unfortunate to watch."

I cross my arms, suddenly feeling extremely exposed and try not to let the tears pricking my eyes come. I hate how everyone knows. Worse than that, the implication this man is making. Logan wouldn't do that. I shake my head slightly, but the man continues.

"You should sue him," the old man continues. "Make him pay for what he did to you. It'll be hard for you to get a job if you suddenly find yourself unemployed, no? If you take him to court, you won't have to worry about that." I can't believe this man has the audacity to make such an accusation. As if reading my mind, he holds up his hands in defense. "I knew her well. And she was never able to recover, so that's why I'm reaching out to you. For your benefit and hers." His voice is soft and soothing. It's genuine. My heart crumples in my chest. I can't breathe. Logan… set me up?

"But why?" I barely breathe the words out.

"He has a history of hurting others for sport." I cover my mouth with my hand as my blood turns to ice and my stomach churns. No, I can't believe that. "Mr. Parker has deep pockets. I'd bet he'd settle out of court to avoid the negative press it would bring his company. And you wouldn't suffer over the damages he caused you."

When I don't reply, the man says, "I just wanted to let you know your options." He hands out a gold-plated business card to me that reads, *Johnny Black & Associates.*

"Here's my card. If you decide you want to take action against Logan, call me."

He turns and walks off, leaving me standing there running my finger along the edge of his business card and struggling to understand and accept why I fall for men who only want to hurt me.

CHAPTER 30

LOGAN

I look over the email from the lawyer once more. It's on my phone as I sit in the car outside of Charlotte's apartment. I'm pissed. I can't stand waiting on the law for judges to sign off on warrants. I already have all the information they need. Although, it wasn't obtained legally and for now I need to wait. Patterson is guilty, and I'll spend whatever it cost to ensure he does jail time. I won't settle on anything less.

But for now, I need to keep my head down and talk to public relations, according to the lawyer, Joseph Casings. I sigh heavily and sit back in my seat.

I grit my teeth. I don't fucking like waiting. I can't sit back and do nothing. Which is precisely what PR told me to do as well. To carry on as though nothing has happened. And as for Charlotte, she's to do the same. Although I haven't had a moment to speak with her. She hasn't come to work, and I haven't called her without knowing how to make this right. But I know now, I have something to offer her. I only hope it's enough.

My body tenses and my heart slows as I think about how she must feel. I don't know what else to do.

I fucked up though. Although Patterson would have found a way to use her against me, it's still my fault that *this* is what happened. My ego gave him an opportunity that destroyed her, and no matter how much I'd like to deny it, it will affect her career. For awhile at least.

I sent out an email and made an announcement this morning. If anyone utters a word about those pictures, they'll be fired. No questions or excuses. The legal department has to handle the rest, but it won't be enough. Nothing can make it go away.

And now I'm sitting outside of her apartment like a lovesick puppy debating on crawling back to her and begging for her forgiveness. Debating on *how,* really. Not if I will… just the best way to go about it.

She needs to know that I'm sorry, and that I'm going to make it up to her as best as I can.

My heart hammers in my chest as I finally get out of the car and make my way up to her apartment, and again I feel that pain rip through me. I pause on the stairs and lean against the wall, waiting for it to pass. It doesn't seem right. The pain radiates in my leg. Awareness races through me. My heartbeat slows with fear. But the pain seems to dim. I hold my breath, ignoring it and willing it to leave me the fuck alone. Something's off, but it can wait. It has to wait until I've at least talked to her. I need to tell her. The pain lessens to a tolerable level, and I continue climbing the stairs with shortened breath. At the top, I consider calling Doctor Wallace. In the past two years, I've only called him once. My jaw clenches and with the pain nearly gone, I decide to let it go.

It'll be fine. I'm fine.

I walk to her door, a gold 22 on the plate on her door,

and I knock three times. I take in a steady breath and nervously straighten my jacket as I wait. I can just barely hear shuffling noises from inside her apartment and then a click of the lock.

It takes a long moment of waiting with bated breath before she opens the door slowly, only a few inches at first, and then a bit more.

My Rose.

The dark circles under her eyes make my heart sink. She looks tired and unhappy. Her lips are paler than usual, and her eyes are red and slightly swollen. My poor Rose.

"Rose," I say and start to reach out to her, but she pulls away quickly and the soft lines of her face harden.

"Logan," she says, leaning her body slightly forward and making it obvious that she's not going to let me in. I'm caught off guard. I know she left me, but this seems... uncharacteristic.

"I just want to talk," I tell her.

The expression on her face changes slightly, showing her sadness, but only for a second. A split second so fast it makes me think I imagined it.

"Talk then," she says in a clipped voice.

I swallow thickly. I didn't anticipate discussing this in the hallway. I didn't think she'd be so defensive either. I debate on asking her why, but then I think better of it. Whatever she's comfortable with will work for me. "Public relations' suggestion is to carry on and essentially pretend this never happened." Her eyes pierce into me as though they're daggers. I clear my throat and stand a little straighter.

"The lawyers are going to make sure that he pays for doing this to you." Her eyes narrow, but she doesn't respond. She's sizing me up and I can see she's going to snap at me. She's just waiting for a chance. I welcome it though. I need something from her. I'd take anything right now, but she's giving me nothing.

"I'm going to handle this, Charlotte." She stands in her doorway, pulling the door closer to her. "He won't get away with it." I'm doing my best to convey that I've done everything I can do. "I promise you." I put as much emotion as I can in my voice, but her body language is still tense. My heart squeezes in my chest.

She looks at me with complete distrust, and I don't understand it. I don't know where this animosity is coming from.

"Please forgive me, Rose," I whisper and put my hand up to push her hair out of her face, but she flinches and moves away, leaving me to let my hand fall.

I clear my throat and let the silence pass between us. She looks past me, and doesn't say anything.

"I'll keep you updated on the legal matters." Her eyes dart to mine. "We can sue him for harassment at least. I'll bury him financially. Taking away his social circle, bankrupting him, it won't be enough." My heart beats frantically as the adrenaline pumps through my veins. I will make him pay for what he did. I stare into Charlotte's baby blue eyes, but she gives me nothing in return. Cold as ice.

"I'm sure Patterson will have his legal team try to shut down the case, but my legal team is far better than anything Johnny Black can throw at me."

"Who?" she asks, with her forehead pinching, her demeanor changing slightly.

I nod my head, realizing I jumped into this without explaining much. Fuck. I wish she'd just let me in so I can talk to her without this awkwardness between us. "His name is Chadwick Patterson. He's the one who sent the emails, it was his IP address and it's not the first-"

"No, Black. Johnny Black." She says his name with a

harsh edge and a bit of distaste. It's odd, he has a reputation, but I'm surprised she'd know anything about him or his shady legal tactics.

"Yes, Patterson uses Black for his legal defense and I'm sure he has him on retainer."

She looks me dead in the eye as her breathing picks up. Her grip tightens on the door as her face reddens and her bottom lip trembles with a mix of anger and sadness.

"I'm so tired of being lied to and not knowing what to think." She spits out her words with venom. She's practically shaking, and I'm not sure what to make of the situation. I put my hands up in surrender.

"Rose," I say and try to keep my voice gentle and calming, "I'm not lying to you. I've *never* lied to you."

She throws the door open and turns her back on me. The doorknob hits the wall, sending the door flying back at me. I put my hand out to keep it from shutting and cautiously take a step forward. She's not okay and she needs me, but I'm not sure what the hell is wrong with her.

No fucking way am I walking into her apartment. Not without knowing what the fuck she's doing, and whether or not I'm even welcomed.

"Rose?" I call out to her as she practically stomps to the kitchen island and snatches something off the counter.

She walks back to me with a deadly look. "This Johnny Black?" she asks, her voice accusatory, with a raised voice, shoving the card in my face.

I take her wrist in my hand and lower it, keeping my eyes on hers as a warning. She's upset, but I don't fucking like the way she's talking to me.

Her breathing is still frantic, but she seems to calm slightly. As she looks at the floor, I take a look at the card.

"Yes," I say and her eyes reach mine and they flash with a knowing look. "Where did you get this?" I ask. My voice is low and threatening, but not toward her. I'm fucking pissed that she had any contact with that snake at all.

"I've been online, I've been searching and searching for the name of the woman you did this to before, but I couldn't find anything."

"What the fuck are you talking about?" Anger makes me push the door open and slam it shut behind me. She takes a step back into her foyer and keeps eye contact.

"He told me you'd done this before." She motions to the card. "You don't know how much it hurt me," she says and her voice cracks and her eyes glass over. The strong suit of armor crumbles into dust and the pain I know she's feeling comes through as her shoulders hunch and her arms wrap around herself. "I couldn't believe you'd do this to me," she says in almost a whisper before wiping the tears from her eyes.

"Never," I say just above a murmur, taking another step forward and slowly pulling her into my chest. "I would never. I have never done that. I would never do anything to hurt you," I whisper into her hair. Her body is tense and stiff, but after a moment, she relaxes against me.

"He lied to me," she says softly, letting her cheek rest against my hard chest. Although anger is coursing through my blood, holding her in my arms is taming the beast that's pacing inside of me. I'll save my anger for them.

Right now she needs me.

"I don't know what to believe." She speaks so low, I barely hear her. She pulls away slightly, and it cracks a barrier that's kept me from taking her. Her words trigger something in me. A need to prove to her that she's mine. That I would never hurt her.

I take a step forward and then another. Her eyes widen and stare back at me as her back hits the wall of her small apartment foyer.

"I didn't do that to you." There's a hint of anger in my voice. I'm angry that she doesn't trust me. "I didn't set you up and I *will* make him pay for hurting you."

She still seems slightly uncertain and I hate it. "I'll destroy him for what he did to you. He tried to hurt me. Not you. You got caught in the crossfires."

She looks wounded and raw, so full of emotion and I'm not sure which is winning out.

I take her shoulders in my hands to steady her and lower my lips so they're almost touching hers. "You need to trust me, Rose."

Her eyes search my face and her breathing picks up. Her plump lips part and she sinks her teeth into her bottom lip with her eyes on my lips.

It's all I can take.

I crash my lips against hers and cage her small body in.

She instantly melts into me.

"Rose," I say her name reverently and then push her back against the wall, crushing my lips to hers. My dick hardens and presses into her stomach. I'm angry and frustrated, but mostly relieved. I need her. I need her to feel what she means to me.

I pull back, and look down at her.

"I'm sorry, Logan," she says in a hushed voice, staring at me through her thick lashes, willing me to believe her. "I didn't-"

I cut her off, pressing my mouth to hers, my tongue diving into her mouth. My fingers spear through her hair as I kiss her with every bit of passion I have. She pulls away, breathing heavily.

"Please, Logan. You have to know. I'm so sorry. I-"

"Stop." I close my eyes and rest my forehead against hers. "I-" I stop myself before I say words I shouldn't. My chest pangs with pain and I ignore it. I ignore everything and whisper into the hot air between us, "Just let me hold you."

She leans up and presses her body to mine. "I need more," she whispers. My hands roam down to her waist and ass, until I finally pick her up and carry her to her sofa.

I lay her down and kiss the crook of her neck as she frantically unbuttons my shirt.

"I need you, Logan," she says with shortened breath. "I lo-" I crash my lips to hers and move between her legs, intent on making everything up to her the best way I know how.

I give her all of me. Everything I have.

Even though I know it won't be enough.

CHAPTER 31

CHARLOTTE

P*lease give me the strength to get through this,* I think to myself as I step out of the Parker-Moore building with Eva.

We're on our way to a press meeting involving the quarterly report of Parker-Moore.

Unfortunately, I've been assigned to answer questions about the new direction of Parker-Moore sales department. Despite not wanting to go, I'm required to be there. It's going to be awful, I just know it. My stomach has been fluttering with butterflies all morning.

Still, not all things have been bad. Yesterday was my first day back at work and no one said anything about the photos, thank God. But people kept coming up and talking to me, making small talk. I knew they were just trying to fish out how I was doing, so it didn't bother me. It did get old after awhile, however.

I hope they'll stop it there, I tell myself as Eva and I climb into the stretch limo that's waiting for us. *Because the constant hovering makes me feel uncomfortable.*

"Are you alright?" Eva asks me as I settle down into the

plush leather seats. She's dressed sharper than usual today in a crisp black suit, her hair done up into a single braid down her back, and her makeup is flawless.

I nod my head and say, "Yes, why?"

"You're scowling."

I relax my face muscles. I hadn't even realized that I was doing it. "I just don't want to go to this press meeting. And I think you know why."

Eva gives me a sympathetic look. "I do, but everything will be okay. You have me here. If anyone says *anything* to you about you-know-what, I'll knock them out."

I snort a laugh and she grins at the ridiculousness of what she's said. Eva's not gonna do shit. "Right."

It's silent on the drive over there. Logan's there already. I pick at the hem of my skirt. I wish he was with me now. It's different when he's next to me. It's when I'm alone that the dread and regret and anxiety start to consume me.

"How's things with Logan?" she asks a moment later.

My heart does a flip at his name. I'm honestly kind of angry with him for wanting to take over the plot to destroy Patterson's company. I'd rather confront the bastard myself and take matters into my own hands. But Logan isn't having it. He wants me to trust him to handle everything. I've agreed... as long as I can stay in contact with the lawyer.

"Good," I answer, letting out an easy breath. "Better than I thought it could be."

Eva smiles and leans over to take my hand. "That's good. I'm happy for you."

And I know that she means it.

Walking into the press room, I'm a ball of nerves. I know people are watching me, judging me. It makes me feel sick to my stomach. Seriously, I'm about to hurl all over Eva's high-dollar suit if I don't get my anxiety under control.

Logan's already on stage taking questions from reporters. I can't get over how professional he looks in his business suit, his hair slicked back. For the first time, he actually looks like who he is. The Boss.

The CEO.

Before I can take my assigned seat on the platform behind the podium, a reporter, a man who looks like he's in his mid-thirties in khaki pants and a plaid shirt, asks, "Mr. Parker, can you tell us how long the affair was with Miss Harrison?"

Anger grips my throat and it's hard to keep a straight face. I knew questions like this would come up, but it's still hard not to react. Eva grips my hand tighter and I walk straight ahead, not looking at the audience and slowly falling into my seat.

I watch as Logan clenches his jaw and I can tell he's trying to keep from blowing a gasket. "I'm not going to answer that question," he responds, his voice tight. "I keep my personal and business life separate, and this press conference is strictly for business."

The man doesn't give up. "But can't you see that what you engaged in is alarming for your company and the stockholders? As head of your company, you should--"

"I said I'm not here to talk about personal matters," Logan says and lowers his voice. "If you don't like it, you can leave." He scans his gaze over the reporters in the room and says, "I will only entertain questions that pertains to Parker-Moore's business dealings."

"But what happened has hurt your company's image,"

the reporter argues, ignoring Logan's request. "You need to address this issue unless you want to create further damage to your brand."

Logan clenches and unclenches his jaw, anger evident as the veins stand out on his neck. I don't think I ever seen him so angry.

Logan stands there for several moments before saying through gritted teeth, "I'm only going to address this once." Flashes of photos being taken seem to pick up as Logan responds. My heart beats frantically and I try desperately just to stay in my place, remembering the advice from public relations. "The photos that have been circulated involving myself and Miss Harrison were taken with the intent to hurt myself personally as well as Parker-Moore." He huffs, "A rival of sorts. They can try to slander my name all they want, but what they did was wrong and charges are being pressed. And that's all I'm going to say on this issue."

I hear a mocking laugh in the audience and I scan the crowd to see who it is. I do a double take. It's Patterson. I've seen his picture over and over now that I know who it was that destroyed me without a second thought. He has an evil fucking smirk on his face that makes me want to punch him. "You better watch those accusations, Logan, before you have a lawsuit on your hands. We all know who the 'rival' is that you're talking about, and as far as I know, you have no proof of any wrongdoing on my part."

Logan stands at the podium radiating anger, and the intensity is enough to still my breathing. He stares down Patterson but says nothing. He looks deadly, but Patterson ignores the warning.

"You got caught banging your secretary, and now you're trying to blame me for it... It's obvious you only gave her the job so you could bang her."

I rise from my seat without my own conscious consent

and try to dive for Logan as he climbs off the stage and into the crowd of reporters. He's furious, and he's snapped. Adrenaline pumps through my blood and my body heats. No! The entire room lets out a collective gasp. His face going white, Patterson tries to scramble over several people to get away from the raging Logan, but he's too slow. Logan climbs over two people and the metal chairs are tossed out of the way as the crowd disperses, moving away from Logan's target. He grabs Patterson by the collar, yanking him close. I can't see everything, but I can see the first punch. Logan has him on the ground. Fuck! The room erupts into chaos, and the crowd surrounds the two men, shouting and yelling and snapping pictures. I can barely breathe as I push through the crowd.

"Logan!" I yell, my heart beating within my chest like a war drum. There's no way Logan is leaving this room without handcuffs. And even worse, this is going to cause more damage to Parker-Moore than the erotic photos of us ever will. I try to reach him, but I keep getting shoved back. I can't let him do this. I have to stop him.

I'm pushed back against a tide of bodies and am nearly trampled as I stumble off balance. Logan could end up killing Patterson, but all these vultures care about is getting their precious photos to sell to the highest bidder.

"Logan! Stop!" I scream, regaining my balance and trying to push my way through to him. I'm not sure if he heard me, but the crowd parts behind the fight, and I stand as tall as I can to see why.

Bloody and covered in sweat, he begins pushing his way through the crowd of shouting reporters. He's silent and heaving in his breaths. Ignoring everyone and heading toward the exit.

Not wasting any time, I chase after him, shoving and pushing my way through anyone that gets in the way.

When I make it outside, there are a crowd of reporters crowding Logan, snapping pictures left and right.

"Logan!" I yell, running in my heels and trying to get his attention. But he doesn't see me, and he doesn't hear me; he's too busy rushing toward the sidewalk where his limo awaits. I watch as Andrew gets out of the vehicle and rushes around to the passenger side, opening the door and holding it open for Logan.

I run as fast as my legs can carry me to the sidewalk, shoving shouting reporters out of the way. I look up, frantically breathing and our eyes meet. Logan gets out and walks straight toward me, pulling me into the limo with him and slamming the door shut. Andrew's already pulling away with screeching tires by the time I'm able to catch my breath and sit up.

"Why did you do that?" I shake my head, practically screaming at him with tears in my eyes. My heart's still pounding. This is bad, it's so fucking bad.

"No one's going to talk to you like that." His voice is weak.

"This isn't good," I say and take in a slow breath, closing my eyes, trying to calm down.

When Logan doesn't respond, I open my eyes and lean forward, peering at him with concern. It's the first time that I really take a good look at him. His knuckles are bruised and cut, and there's dried blood from his hands up to his arm. It's all over his shirt. I finally reach his face, and my heart stops beating. His eyes seem distant, something... something's wrong. "Logan?"

It takes him a moment to register that I'm talking to him. Logan tries to say something, but his words are unintelligible to my ears and his body sways.

"Logan?" I ask again, panicked now and gripping his shoulders and then head, trying to get him to look at me.

His eyes rolling into the back of his head, Logan collapses against the seat. *Oh my God. No!* "Logan!" I scream, shaking him and refusing to believe this is real. He's unresponsive. I press my hand against his throat.

"What's going on?" Andrew asks with concern.

I scream, "He needs a hospital! Now!"

CHAPTER 32

LOGAN

The constant *beep, beep, beep* from the machine is giving me a fucking headache. I stare at it. The blue and red lines are moving rhythmically across the screen. My back is stiff from being in this fucking hospital bed. The sheets they have are thin and scratchy. My shirt's ripped down the front. They couldn't fucking unbutton it fast enough.

I'm pissed. I don't want to be here.

I'm not ready.

"Mr. Parker?" Doctor Wallace says. I take a deep breath and turn to face him on my right. I school my expression so I don't take the anger out on him. It's not his fault.

It's no one's fault. It just is what it is.

"We need to move this to radiation. It's now stage four non-Hodgkin lymphoma."

I smile weakly and let my head fall to the side.

"The intravenous didn't work then, I take it?" I've been getting intravenous chemotherapy with rituximab every other month for almost two years. At first it was just the pills. Then oral chemo and steroids to reduce the swelling in my spleen and prepare my body for chemotherapy.

I was hoping intravenous every other month would be enough. After all, money can buy the best doctors and good health. Can't it? Apparently not.

"I'm sorry Logan, it's time that we move to the next step. The scan shows that it's moving from the bone, which can be painful."

I huff a humorless laugh. Painful doesn't begin to describe what I felt on that stage. It was like someone stabbing me in my calf, straight to the bone over and over again.

The anger was just barely enough to keep me from acting on the pain. Chadwick Patterson is going to go down for what he did to my Rose. He had the fucking audacity to show up to the conference. That motherfucker. Smashing in his face isn't anywhere close to justice.

I look down at my hand for the first time since I woke up. An IV is sticking out from the back of it, with a thick piece of tape holding it in place.

As I flex my hand it moves slightly, and it's irritating as fuck. There are small cuts on my knuckles that are raw and bruised. Good. I hope his face looks even worse.

"The radiation is only for twenty-one days and it's user-friendly, so to speak." I look back up to the good doctor and feel slightly sympathetic that I've been ignoring him.

"You'll remain relatively pain free, just tired constantly, and you shouldn't lose your hair," he continues.

"Do I have a choice?" I ask. I don't want radiation. My grandfather died the day they started radiation. He was fine up until then. The slight pain in his chest was the only indication that anything was wrong. I see it as a sign. I don't want it.

"If you want to kill it and live," he says and I look him in the eyes while he gives me a grave expression, "then no, you don't."

I nod my head solemnly, giving in to the inevitable.

A small knock at the door takes the doctor's attention.

He opens it and reveals Charlotte, my Rose. So fragile and beautiful. Yet something I shouldn't hold.

Guilt presses against my chest as I stare into her glassy eyes. Her cheeks are red and tearstained.

Doctor Wallace turns to face me, standing in the doorway to prevent her from coming in farther. "Mr. Park-"

"Yes, let her in." I won't deny her.

She lets out a small sob as she walks into the room.

"Logan," she says and her voice cracks.

"I'm sorry, Rose." She puts a small hand over mine. "I should have told you."

In this moment I hate myself. I know I never had a right to make her feel anything for me. I was selfish. I'm so fucking undeserving of her.

She shakes her head and doesn't answer me. Instead she grips onto me tighter and tries to calm herself down.

"I still have faith that you'll get through this, Logan," Doctor Wallace says as he opens the door, "I need you to agree to do the radiation though. You have to stop working and work on yourself."

Rose watches as he shuts the door, leaving us alone in the small room.

"I'm sor-" I start to speak, but she interrupts me.

"I talked to the nurses," she says as she goes to the corner of the room and drags a chair across the floor and brings it closer to the bed. She flinches and mouths, *sorry* when the leg of the chair scraping along the floor causes a loud scratching sound.

She clears her throat and picks my hand back up. "They said it's curable."

Her eyes move from where our hands are clasped to my eyes. "They said the odds are in your," her voice breaks and she lets go of my hand to cover her face.

Fuck. It breaks my heart to see her like this.

She takes in a ragged but steadying breath and angrily wipes under her eyes.

"Rose, my Rose. I'm so-"

"I'll stay with you." She interrupts me again and takes my hand with both of hers. My lips part and my heart swells. I want so badly to be a selfish prick and not push her away.

But she deserves more.

"I might not make it through this..." A small sob is ripped through her throat again as I press on and say, "You deserve so much more."

She shakes her head and refuses to look at me. She needs to let go. She should just move on with her life. I should've left her alone. This is my fault. "I never should have done this to you." She's quiet for a long moment. My heart is shredded. I don't know how I let this get so out of hand. "You have to go, Charlotte." Her eyes snap up at me at the use of her first name. I have to send her away, it's the right thing to do.

"I won't go, Logan Parker, and you can't make me." She's angry. Furious even. I didn't expect this reaction. I take in a sharp breath and remember the woman I first met. The one who came into my office and was ready to bite my head off for toying with her. "I mean it," she says and her voice takes on a hard edge. "You will not throw me out, Logan."

"It's what's best for you." I try to reason with her.

"I am a grown-ass woman and if I want to stay with you, I'm going to."

My head falls back against the hospital bed. My heart aching and the desire to keep her to myself clouding my judgment. I can't look at her as I say, "Rose-"

"I love you," she says harshly. "I love you, Logan and I'm not going anywhere." My heart does a flip in my chest and I have to stare at her in shock for a moment. I try to comprehend how she could forgive me so easily. She shouldn't. She shouldn't love me either. Not after what I've done to her.

She cups my face and like the selfish man that I am, I lean into her warmth. I open my eyes and stare into hers. There's nothing but love reflecting back at me.

"I'm sorry," I whisper. She kisses me deeply and I reach up to cup the back of her head to deepen it. "I don't deserve you," I say and I know I've never said truer words.

"You don't see yourself clearly." She tells me the words I told her months ago.

I tell her something that's equally true in return. "I love you, my Rose."

CHAPTER 33

CHARLOTTE

"You need to take it easy," I scold Logan, standing over him like a worried hen, my hands on my hips.

It's the second week of Logan's radiation treatments, something that usually leaves him drained and tired, but today he seems to have energy.

The first week was really hard on him, and it seems to be getting better each day. But I can't get over how difficult the first week was. *Today's a new day,* I think, closing my eyes and breathing in deep.

He hasn't needed my help with getting out of bed nor with putting his clothes on. He's even lifted a few things, despite me telling him not to, and hasn't seemed to exhaust himself doing it. Still, I think he should be in bed resting like Doctor Wallace ordered, but he doesn't follow the rules no matter how hard I try to enforce them.

Logan gets what Logan wants. Everything else be damned.

Such thoughts would've turned me on in the past, but now I'm constantly worried. This is his health at stake. He needs to conserve every ounce of energy so he can fight the battle that lies ahead, not use it on work that will be there whenever he's ready to come back to it.

For the past hour I've been trying to get him to get some much needed rest, but he's refused, opting to answer business emails and go over contracts on his laptop instead.

"The company is running fine without you, trust me," I assure him. *If only Logan would relax,* I think to myself, *it would make my job so much easier.*

Since Logan's left the hospital I've become his unofficial nurse, checking up on him and handling all of his immediate needs. It hasn't been easy with his constant desire to keep tabs on Parker-Moore, and it makes me frustrated. His health is more important.

"I'm fine," Logan assures me, tearing his eyes from his laptop screen and looking up at me with a handsome grin. Surprisingly, he looks well rested today and he's sitting in his office chair in just red boxer briefs and no shirt. I must admit, he's a sight for sore eyes, but I'm more concerned with his recovery; it's all I'm concerned about. I let out a heavy sigh and push my hair over my shoulders. My heart feels so heavy.

I'm still having a hard time getting over the shock at finding out he has cancer. He looked so healthy, I never would have suspected he was sick. Just knowing that he's been secretly dealing with this pain all this time makes me want to break down into tears. "I'm just answering these emails and going over some contracts."

I open my lips to argue, but then close them. I know Logan isn't going to listen to me, no matter how much I bitch at him.

Good thing Trent is running the company, I think to myself. *Otherwise, Mr. CEO here would kill himself to make sure everything was working right.*

After he found out the news, Trent offered to take over as CEO until Logan is well enough to work again. To ensure that Logan doesn't try to overwork himself, he's refused to give Logan updates about the company's status and he won't take his calls.

It's pissed Logan off, but it's for his own good.

As far as anyone at the company knows, Logan is on a three-week vacation. There was some gossip back at the company about Logan going to jail, but after Patterson was arrested and plead guilty to the charges after seeing the evidence against him, that all stopped.

"You need to stop worrying about me," Logan scolds me, seeing my concerned expression. "You're only going to stress yourself out. And I don't want that."

"Well that's not happening," I tell him firmly. I hate how casual he is about brushing off my concerns. I think he does it to hide his worry and put me at ease, but he doesn't have to. I don't want him to either. I'm here for him. All of him. I wish he would confide in me more. "I'm going to worry whether you like it or not, thank you very much."

Logan cocks an eyebrow and sits back in his chair. Desire stirs within me, seeing his six-pack abs that seem even more well-defined these days. He's lost some weight from being sick in the hospital, maybe five pounds, but he still looks the same, still devastatingly handsome. And the sight of him brings the part of me that needs his comforting touch to the forefront. "Oh yeah?" he asks.

"Yeah."

"Come here," he says and pats his lap, scooting the chair out from his desk. I hesitate for a moment, wondering if it's prudent to sit on him, but I can't deny the urge. For a full week, sex and even the idea of sex have been nonexistent. Worry and fear were a constant, but things are different now. And I love it when he holds me. Right now,

I need him to soothe my pain. Even if that makes me selfish.

Wrapping my arms around his neck, I nestle into his lap as he spears his fingers through my hair. He looks up at me with an intensity that makes shivers run down my neck and arms. "You're so fucking beautiful, you know that?"

My cheeks heat at his praise and warmth flows through my chest at his words. "Stop it."

Logan shakes his head. "No," he begins and there's strength in his words I don't expect, "the day I met you was the luckiest day of my life." He gently rubs his nose against mine and says, "You saved me."

Tears prick my eyes and begin rolling down my face. "I love you," I whisper, my heart aching. I tell him that as often as I can. If nothing else, I need him to know how much I truly love him. I wipe the tears from my eyes and try to stop being so emotional.

"And I love you too, my beautiful Rose." He pulls me down against him, pressing his lips against mine. I kiss him back with all the passion I have, pushing myself into him. His hands roam down my body and I groan at the sensation. It feels amazing to be touched by him again. Beneath me, I can feel his hard cock against my ass, pulsating and throbbing. I want him, and I moan into his kiss at the thought. I *need* him. Now.

We shouldn't be doing this, I tell myself, but I don't push him away. I gasp as he pinches my nipple, which sends a throbbing need to my clit. He groans into my mouth as his hand travels up my shirt. *Logan should be resting and recovering.* But it feels so right. And I want him just as much as he wants me.

He's in the process of undoing my bra when there's a knock at the door. Startled and breathless, I jump out of his lap and start smoothing out my outfit.

Shit. I forgot Doctor Wallace was stopping by. I try to smooth out my hair and calm myself down as Logan smirks at me and rises out of the chair. I watch as he repositions himself inside his boxers to make his erection less obvious before he goes over to answer the door.

The lust I was feeling moments ago floods out of me as Doctor Wallace walks into the room carrying a large black bag, and I'm filled with anxiety.

"Good afternoon," the doctor greets me with a smile that makes me even more nervous.

"Good afternoon, Doctor Wallace," I barely say above a murmur as I respectfully give him a wide berth, taking a seat in the corner of the room.

The doctor gives me a tight smile and says, "Just checking in on Mr. Parker here." He sets his bag down on Logan's desk, and I stare at it numbly, hating it. Hating that Logan has to go through this, hating that he's sick at all. I clench my fists with anger thinking about it.

I need to think happy thoughts and stay positive. But it's hard. Logan's outlook looks bleak. Stage four. Who beats that? My heart squeezes in my chest and I have to close my eyes to keep the tears from sliding out. I just want him healthy.

Doctor Wallace begins his physical examination that I've seen a few times now, checking Logan's vital signs, shining a light into his eyes and performing an oral examination. All the questions are the same. This isn't the first time I've seen the examination, but I listen just as closely, and my heart slows all the same. Every second feels like a lifetime. I just need him to be okay.

"Everything seems to be as expected, Mr. Parker," Doctor Wallace says when he's done with his diagnostics. "Well, you're doing better than I expected you would at this stage." He sits back with a nod and says, "That's a good sign."

The doctor's words are soothing, but it's still hard to have hope. Just because Logan appears to be doing okay, doesn't mean anything if the cancer is still there.

I pray that it only gets better from here. It has to. It better. "It does?" Logan lets out a deep breath and says, "Good."

Doctor Wallace nods. "It does indeed." He looks around and scratches his nose. "Actually, I thought you'd be in bed like I told you."

Logan grins over at me. "It's hard to lie there and sleep when I have such a beautiful woman to keep me company."

The doctor chuckles, and a fierce blush comes over my cheeks. It's cute, but I know Logan is worried just as much as I am deep down. I want to laugh and pretend that everything is okay, but I can't. This cuts too deep.

"What happens after this?" I ask concernedly.

Doctor Wallace turns to look at me. "We continue the treatments everyday so long as Logan feels well enough, until it's gone." He looks back at Logan and pats him on the shoulder. "If it gets to be too much, we can take a break and see how you recover." His voice is somber, and it makes my heart clench.

I suck in a painful breath, my heart feeling like it's being crushed. I wish there were something I could do to cure Logan, to take his pain away.

Fuck cancer, I think to myself angrily, fighting back the sea of tears. *Logan doesn't deserve this shit.*

"I'll see you tomorrow, Logan," Doctor Wallace replies, rising to his feet and gathering his instruments into his black bag. Tomorrow's another day of radiation. At least the weekends he has off. But knowing tomorrow is going to be difficult... it hurts.

Bidding us farewell, Doctor Wallace turns to leave the room, but before he can walk out, I stop him at the door.

"Is he really going to be alright?" I ask him quietly. I hate asking him this, and I feel somewhat confrontational, but I can't let him leave me with a sense of false hope. I don't want to think Logan is going to be okay if he's not. "Please, don't sugarcoat it. I want the one hundred percent truth."

Doctor Wallace gives me a sad smile and places a firm hand on my shoulder. "As much as I would love to be able to ease your worries, Charlotte, I can't give you a definite answer. The treatments we're using have worked many times for my patients, and Logan's condition today is a good sign. But I can't give you anything definitive. Will Logan be alright? Only God knows that."

The doctor leaves, and I close the door behind him. Feeling a bit weak, I lean against the door for support, my forehead pressed against the hard wood.

Behind me I hear footsteps, and then I feel strong arms wrapping around my waist. I can't help but melt into his embrace.

"Stop worrying, Rose," Logan whispers in my ear before delivering a small kiss to my neck. "I'll be alright. You heard the man." He's trying to inject strength in his voice, to soothe me, but I can still sense the uncertainty hiding in his words. The pain.

Fuck. It hurts. "I'll try not to," I say over the lump in my throat. I turn to face him, fighting back the tears and look into his face. "I just love you so much and want to see you get through this."

Logan squeezes me as tight as his diminished strength allows and returns my kiss. "I promise you, my Rose, I won't stop fighting. If there is any chance of me beating this thing, I'm going to fucking do it. For myself, but most of all, for you."

The tears can't be denied, they flow down my face in a torrent and I collapse against Logan, sobbing. Fuck this. Fuck life. Fuck everything.

"I need you to be strong for me, Rose," Logan urges me, kissing my hair and rocking me gently. "Everything's going to be okay, and even if it's not, I'll always be here for you." I cry harder, big hiccuping sobs, until I'm gasping for breath. Logan continues to rock me, comforting me, holding me, loving me, until I'm all cried out.

"I'm so sorry," I lament when it's over, sniffling and wiping at my nose. I feel slightly embarrassed. Breaking down like that isn't going to make anything better. But I needed to get that out since I've been holding the pain inside for days now. "You're right. I need to be strong."

He rests his forehead against mine and says, "You are strong, my Rose." He kisses me sweetly and I mold my body to his. He takes my hand in his and raises it above my head, all the while kissing me. But it's awkward, it feels weird and I don't know what he's doing. I break the kiss and look up as he's slipping a golden engagement ring sparkling against the light onto my ring finger.

My heart stops in my chest and my mouth falls open. He releases my hand and pulls back slightly. *A ring.* I stare at my hand in disbelief.

"Oh my God," I gasp, clutching my hand to my chest as my heart skips a beat. Ordinarily, something like this would have sent me through the roof, but I feel like I've been punched in the stomach.

The tears are back, and I fucking hate it. I'm two seconds away from being a blubbering mess again and it's for all the wrong reasons.

"Marry me, Rose," Logan implores, his heart in his eyes. It tears at me. He can see my pain, and I can see his. "Marry me tonight." He pauses and says, "Or tomorrow at the latest."

I open my mouth to speak, but no words come out. This should be the happiest moment of my life. I should be jumping up and down with joy, yet all I can feel is a heavy, crushing pain that refuses to get the fuck off my chest.

The heavy feeling is compounded by the knowledge of why Logan wants me to marry him tonight.

Because he knows he might not be here tomorrow.

The thought is nearly enough to bring me to my knees and I sway like a leaf in the wind. Logan catches me before I can fall, and I hate myself for it. Here I am falling to pieces, when I should be strong for him. For us both. Logan continues the assault on my heart, though I know he doesn't mean to. "If something happens to me, I want you to have everything. The business, all my assets. Everything."

I shake my head, feeling like I'm being suffocated. "No, Logan. I refuse to accept it, and I don't- I can't marry you for that... That's not-" I shake my head, unable to accept this and unable to talk and my heart tries to leap up my throat. I can't take the thought of him dying. I can't bear it.

Logan continues to hold me tight and it breaks my heart because I know he's using what little strength he has to hold onto me. "I want you to marry me because I fucking love you."

The pain is surreal. I'm so choked up that it's hard to breathe, much less get out words. "Logan..." I croak.

Logan pulls me in tighter, kissing the tears staining my face. "Just tell me yes, Rose. I *need* this. Don't deny me, my Rose." He squeezes me weakly.

My words are choked and reflect the pain I'm in as I stare into his loving gaze. "Only if you promise to never leave me," I whisper, barely hanging on by a thread. I know it's a promise that Logan has no way of knowing he can keep, but I want it anyway.

Logan hesitates and it sends a sharp pain into my heart. In this moment, a promise is a hollow thing. We both know it. But I need to hear it. I need something to hold on to. "I'll do my best," Logan finally replies, and it doesn't make me feel any better. "I'll stick around forever... or for as long as I'm able to fight."

I can't take anymore.

Feeling like my heart is going to explode, I collapse against him and sob into his chest until I'm all spent.

Over and over I tell him, "I love you, Logan." I plead with him, "Don't leave me."

"I love you, my Rose," he says softly and with a sincerity I can't deny.

CHAPTER 34

LOGAN

"This is where he lives?" my Rose asks me as she slips out of the car. I have my hand held out for her, and although she rests her small hand in mine, she doesn't put her weight in it. I wish she would. I wish she wouldn't walk on eggshells around me.

It was better when I'd kept it hidden. When she didn't know about the cancer, and was blissfully unaware.

Things are different between us, and in some ways I hate it. Like this moment, when she didn't even want me to drive. Others are sweeter now that her walls have fallen down and she doesn't hide a thing from me. Those moments make it all worth it.

I stretch out and even though it's brisk in the early morning, the chill feels refreshing.

"Yes, it's been… nearly seven years now." I answer her question as she takes in the ancient stone building. I shell out a pretty penny for my father to live here, but it's the best service and quality that any place has to offer for him in his state.

My heart pains in my chest at the thought; I almost had myself admitted to a similar environment.

I close the door with a heavy heart as Rose's heels click on the sidewalk and a breeze lifts the dried leaves off the ground, causing a soft rustling to fill my senses.

My body did not take the first week of radiation well. I was constantly nauseated and fatigued. And worried that the inevitable was going to happen. I wanted to send Rose away. I did try though, several times, and had I been well, she would have beat the shit out of me.

Five days on and two days off. That weekend I recovered well and Rose stayed by my side the entire time and told me to fuck off when I tried to send her away.

The thought brings a smile to my lips as I look up and watch her walking up the rough stone stairs of the building in her heels. She's gripping the railing and I'm quick to make my way over and hold her waist, helping her to balance.

She smiles sweetly, the chill making her cheeks flush a beautiful shade of pink. Her engagement band clinks on the metal railing as we walk up together, and the sound fills me with pride.

She's my wife.

I've never been so proud. I have yet to tell my father though, and Rose hasn't told a soul.

Legally we're married, but as far as everyone else knows, we're engaged.

She wants it to stay that way.

I open the door for her and she looks at me with exasperation. It's a heavy door and just climbing those stairs took a lot out of me, but I'm not going to just stay in bed everyday until I die. I want to be me. I want to live my life, and that includes opening doors for my wife.

It hurts me that she doesn't want to tell people. At first I thought she was ashamed. But she's scared of what they'll think.

She doesn't want the will changed either, but she has no fucking choice in that matter. That's already been done.

The warmth of the building cocoons us as we walk in. The front hall is open and spacious.

The deep red oriental runner placed down along the length of the hall muffles the sound of Rose's steps as we move from the stone floors to the rug.

She slips her coat easily off her shoulders and I move to take it. She looks up at me with worried eyes.

"It's only a coat, Rose; I think I can manage." There's a hint of admonishment in my tone and she purses her lips. She doesn't argue though, she doesn't like to as much now, knowing that I'm not well.

An asymmetric grin pulls to my lips at the thought; that is one benefit of being ill, I suppose.

"Logan," I hear my father's rough voice call out to me from the sunroom to our left, before we make it to the welcome desk. I lead Rose, splaying my hand on her back.

The sunroom has several tables and comfortable chairs. The stone fireplace is lit, and the heat feels welcoming.

As we get closer, I notice how my father's eyes are solely on Rose. She's walking a bit slower with her hands clasped in front of her.

Anger stirs in my chest.

I didn't bring her here for him to make her uncomfortable.

I wanted them to meet at least once, just in case, but I won't let him make her feel unwelcome. She's my bride, my wife, the love of my life. And he had better realize that and respect it, or we're going to have problems.

"Mr. Parker," Rose says in a professional tone I recognize from all of our meetings and presentations. She has an amazing ability to slip into a mask of ease when she's uncomfortable. I fucking hate it.

"Father, meet my wife, Charlotte Rose." I introduce them while staring hard into my father's pale blue eyes. They widen slightly, and his mouth falls open with surprise.

"Wife?" he asks with raised brows. Before I can answer he replies with disbelief, "I never thought I'd live to see the day." He looks at her stomach before reaching Rose's eyes.

My face heats with embarrassment. I don't want him to think I've knocked her up, although the thought makes my dick stir in my slacks.

"Fiancé he means," Rose is quick to reply smoothly, and my father's eyes dart to her ring finger before he nods his head easily, sitting back in his seat.

He's confirming her fears and I fucking hate it, although I suppose I can see his position.

"I see my son has been keeping secrets," he says as he eyes me and then holds out a hand for Rose. "At least he introduced us before you two tied the knot."

Their handshake is business at best, but Rose seems comforted by the warmer reception.

I take a seat, my body stiff as the anxiety of the two of them getting along grows.

"How did you two meet?" he asks Rose.

She smiles warmly, tucking a strand of hair behind her ear. She looks hesitantly at me and then leans forward and replies, "At a conference a few months ago."

My father nods, and then a smile suddenly appears at his lips. He raises his hand, pointing at her and nodding his head as he says, "Don't tell me, you worked for..." he snaps his fingers and my heartbeat picks up. "Armcorp?" he asks.

Rose's beautiful smile grows across her face as she asks,

"He told you?" Her brow furrows, although she looks pleased.

"Not exactly, but I had a feeling."

I huff a humorless laugh. My father has always struck me as intelligent, but I didn't think I was so obvious.

I sit back in my chair as the two of them engage in easy conversation.

My leg pains me again, reminding me that I have radiation again tomorrow. One more week, and then we'll see where I stand.

I ignore the pain and smile along with Rose's story of how I ruined her presentation.

She laughs and pauses to remember the rest of our story. I remember it, though I don't know if I remember it as clearly as Rose.

My father interrupts before she's able to continue, saying, "I'm proud of you son," and his voice cracks. He clears his throat and adds, looking back at Rose, "I'm happy for the two of you. I'm happy he found someone to love."

"Thank you," Rose says with a soft voice. I can tell she wasn't expecting it. I wasn't either.

My father and I exchange a silent nod. My heart is swelling in my chest at his approval. This is what I wanted. I wasn't sure if he'd understand. But it means the world to me that he does.

Rose nervously clears her throat and picks up from where she left off. Her hands wave in the air as she talks about how she was so nervous to meet her new boss.

My father's not watching her though, he's watching me. His eyes are filled with pride and glassy with tears.

I've never seen him so emotional before. Not since the day I told him I had cancer, although back then he was in disbelief. Now, his happiness is evident. It brings a warmth to my chest.

I can only hope I live to see the day that she proudly calls me her husband. I unconsciously take her hand in mine and kiss her wrist.

It makes her pause her story and her eyes soften with happiness, although her cheeks flush with a blush of embarrassment.

"I love you," I tell her easily.

"Logan," she says shyly, looking between myself and my father.

"Don't deny me, my Rose."

I can see her blossom with love shining in her eyes as she whispers, "I love you, too."

I know she does.

EPILOGUE

LOGAN

Remission is a beautiful word.

I'm still on edge most days, thinking the cancer will come back. But it's been a year and the scans show no visible signs of returning.

"Logan!" I hear Rose's voice from the other side of the penthouse.

The large doors are open and it lets in a cool breeze. It's getting late and I should shut them, but I can see the ocean from here and the palm trees are close enough to touch. It's a beautiful escape from the city, and our first night here. I was nearly asleep on the sofa, lost in work as usual. But it was only for tonight to wrap up a meeting I couldn't put off. And then no computer. Charlotte's orders.

I put the laptop on the coffee table, sliding it across the glass and stand up. Stretching out my sore muscles.

I crack my neck and sigh. It was a long ride on the jet. Nearly six hours. I shouldn't complain, after all, it was a jet, but I fucking hate traveling. You'd think I'd be used to it by now, but I'm not. I'm not sure I ever will be either.

"Logan," my Rose calls out again.

I take large strides to where her voice came from, the bedroom suite.

She's standing in front of the dresser, putting away the clothes from her suitcase. I don't know why she does these things, there's hired help here to do just that. But she always insists on doing it herself.

She bends down to put away whatever's in her hand into the bottom drawer. Her pale pink cotton dress slips up her thighs and just barely shows the curves of her ass. I have to suppress a groan of satisfaction. I fucking love that ass. I love every bit of her.

"Yes, my bride?" I ask her as I walk up behind her and wrap my arms around her waist, pulling her back into my chest. Her lush ass pushes against my cock and it already starts hardening for her. I want her now even more than I did when we first met. I have no plans for that to ever change.

She rolls her eyes and scoffs. "Just because we're on our honeymoon doesn't mean I'm your bride." She lays back in my arms and gives me a sweet smile as her baby blues find mine in the mirror.

I chuckle and hold her closer to me, loving her warmth.

"And whose fault is that?" I ask her. We've been married for nearly three months now, legally six, but my Rose insists on ignoring the online certificate. She didn't even wear the wedding band I picked out for her until we had the *real* ceremony.

Charlotte was so caught up in her work that she wasn't ready to take so much time off for a honeymoon. She's finally got the entire department running smoothly. She's always been good at what she does, and it makes me damn proud. I hadn't anticipated her being as much of a workaholic as I am though. Thankfully, we've started slowing down and hiring more people so we can do less.

It's time to enjoy life. I have one worth living, with a partner I want to enjoy.

"I was thinking…" I stare at her reflection in the mirror, but her eyes don't meet mine. She busies herself with folding a shirt that's on top of the dresser.

"What were you thinking, my Rose?" I ask gently, planting a small kiss on her neck.

She hums sweetly and leans her head against my shoulder with her eyes closed.

Her small, delicate hands find mine on her waist and she slowly opens her eyes to stare back at me in the mirror. "I was wondering," her eyes dart down, then back to me, "if we could make this a babymoon?"

My eyebrows raise comically as she says the word I assumed I'd be hearing on this little vacation of ours. Her friend Eva's recently gotten pregnant. Ever since she announced it, Charlotte has been all about babies and pregnancies.

She's more than hinted. And I'm taking it seriously.

My brow furrows. …wait.

"A babymoon?" I ask her, "Isn't that for when you're already pregnant?"

She nods her head with a twinkle in her eye.

Oh, shit. My grip on her loosens as my mouth opens.

"Oh no!" she says as she bends over slightly with a wide smile. She covers her face as she laughs at me. "No, no, not yet." She turns in my arms and I let out a breath I didn't know I was holding.

My heart slams in my chest and I close my eyes to try to calm down.

I guess I'm not quite as ready as I thought I was.

She places her hand on my chest and fiddles with the buttons on my dress shirt.

"I just meant, we could try. We have two full weeks."

She stands on her tiptoes and plants a small kiss on my lips.

I close my eyes, enjoying her touch. I love this woman so damn much.

I live for her. Only for her.

She pulls away slightly and when I open my eyes, she's looking up at me through her thick lashes with hope.

I grin at her. "I think we can try."

"Ah!" Her high-pitched shriek makes me close my eyes. She jumps up and down and wraps her arms around my neck, practically swinging.

I laugh and look down at the beautiful smile on her face.

I'll do everything I can to make her happy. And if that means we're going to have a baby, then I'll be the best father I can. Our children will never go without.

"I love you so much, Logan," she says before kissing me passionately.

I break our kiss, only to tell her what I've said every single day since I first confessed it, "I love you, my Rose."

The End.

THANK YOU!

Thank you for reading Simply Irresistible, a collection of books that we love!
We hope you loved these stories as much as we do!

Don't stop reading! We have added a Sneak Peek of our co-written novel Bought Highest Bidder Book 1. We hope you enjoy it!

Willow & Lauren xx

SNEAK PEEK AT BOUGHT

HIGHEST BIDDER BOOK ONE

Everything has a price ... and I'm willing to pay.

I trust no one. I thrive with control and I've learned to be ruthless and coldhearted. A love life? I'm not interested.

But I still have desires.

That's where Dahlia came in; my treasure. She had never been a submissive before and I was eager to train her.

When I saw her on stage at the auction, dressed in gold, I knew I had to have her.

She's mine for an entire month. I own her. But one lie changed everything.

She's going to pay for it. But I'm doing this for her own good. She needs this.

I'm going to make this right. I'm going to heal her.
If it's the last thing I do.

***Bought is a full-length standalone romance with an HEA, no cheating, and no cliffhanger.**

Want more? Join our mailing list to receive bonus deleted scenes! (If you're already on our lists, you'll get this automatically).

PROLOGUE

LUCIAN

I slowly pace the room, letting the sound of my shoes clacking against the floor startle her. My eyes are on Dahlia, watching her every movement. Her breathing picks up as she realizes I've come back for her. With her blindfold on and her wrists and ankles tied to the bed while she lies on her belly, she's at my complete mercy, and she knows it.

The sight of her bound and waiting for me is so tempting. I force my groan back.

Her pale, milky skin is on full display as she waits for me. I've left her like this deliberately, in this specific position. She knows now not to move, not to struggle. She knows to wait for me obediently, and what's more, *she enjoys it.*

The wooden paddle gently grazes along her skin, leaving goosebumps down her thigh in its wake. They trail up the curve of her ass, and her shoulders rise as she sucks in a breath. Her body tenses and her lips part, spilling a soft moan. She knows what's coming.

She's *earned* this.

She lied to me.

And she's going to be punished.

She doesn't know this is for her own good. She should, but she hasn't realized it yet.

I'm only doing this for her. She *needs* this.

She needs to heal, and I know just how to help her. The paddle whips through the air and smacks her lush ass, leaving a bright red mark as she gasps, her hands gripping the binds at her wrists. I watch as her pussy clenches around nothing, making my dick that much harder.

Soon.

I barely maintain my control and gently knead her ass, soothing the pulsing pain I know she's feeling. "Tell me why you lied to me, treasure," I whisper at the shell of her ear, my lips barely touching her sensitive skin.

"I'm sorry," she whimpers with lust. I don't want her apology. I want her to realize what she's done. I want to know why she hid it from me all this time. She'll learn she can't lie to me. There's no reason she should.

Smack! I bring the paddle down on the other cheek and her body jolts as a strangled cry leaves her lips, her pussy glistening with arousal.

"That's not what I asked, treasure." My tone is taunting. She needs to realize what I already know. She needs to admit it. To me, but mostly to herself.

I pull away from her, just for a moment, leaving her to writhe on the bed from the sting of the paddle.

I didn't anticipate our relationship reaching this point.

In the beginning, I thought this would be fun. Just a form of stress relief for me.

But things changed.

I bought her at auction, and now she can't leave. She's mine for an entire month. But the days have flown by, and the contract is almost over.

I need more time.

I'm going to make this right. I'm going to heal my treasure.

If it's the last thing I do, I'll give her what she needs. What we both need.

She parts those beautiful lips, and hope blooms in my chest.

Say it, tell me what you desperately need to say.

But her mouth closes, and she shifts slightly on the sheets before stilling and waiting patiently for more.

I pull my arm back and steady myself.

Soon, she'll realize it. My broken treasure. Soon she'll be *healed,* but that won't be enough for me anymore. I want more.

Smack!

CHAPTER 1

LUCIAN - A FEW WEEKS PRIOR...

I stare at my jacket, laying it over the arm of the tufted leather chair in the corner of my office. I need to leave this fucking building and get home, but I don't fucking want to. It's not like I have anything waiting for me. Nothing to do but more work.

I've spent a fortune on my home. I built it from the ground up, painstakingly choosing every piece of hardware and meticulously designing each room myself. But I couldn't give a damn if I go back there anymore.

It's cold and lifeless. Empty.

My brow furrows, and a frustrated sigh leaves my lips. I could keep working. *There's always more work waiting.*

I clench my jaw and type the password to unlock my computer, the gentle tapping of the keys soothing me. It's a comforting sound. But only for a moment.

As the screen lights up and I glance at the window of emails left on the desktop, I seethe and remember why I'm in such a horrible fucking mood. My eyes focus on the lawyer's name attached to the most recent email. This is why I'm so damn pissed and aggravated.

I'm fucking tired of leeches always suing me. Trying to take a piece of me they haven't earned. Most of the lawsuits don't bother me. It comes with the territory. But my *family,* and my *ex-wife*? It fucking shreds me, and I hate that I ever felt anything for them. At some point in time I had feelings for them, emotions I've long since grown cold to.

Now there's only anger.

I steady myself, knowing they've tried this before and failed. They'll keep trying, and it's aggravating, but I refuse to give them anything. I've learned my lesson the hard way. I know better now.

My eyes widen as a new email pops up.

From Club X.

It's been a long time since I've seen an email from Madam Lynn. And an even longer time since I've set foot into the club. The pad of my thumb rubs along the tips of both my middle finger and forefinger, itching to see what's inside.

Images flash before my eyes, and I can practically hear the soft sounds of the whip smacking against flesh and a moan forced from the Submissive's lips. Never to hurt, only for pleasure. Whips aren't my tool of choice, nor what I've been known for in the past. But nonetheless, the memory kicks the corners of my lips up into a grin. I tap my fingers on the desk, debating on opening the message before moving the mouse over to the email and clicking on it out of curiosity.

Check your mail, sir.

I huff a laugh at the message and immediately hit the intercom button on my desktop phone for my secretary. It's not yet five, so she better fucking be at her desk still.

"Yes, Mr. Stone?" she responds, and her voice comes through with a sweet and casual air.

"Could you bring me my mail, please?" Although it's poised as a question, it isn't one. There's only one correct response, and she knows that.

There's no hesitation as Linda says, "Of course." Her voice is slightly raspy. Linda's old, to put it bluntly; she should retire.

If I was her I would, rather than putting up with my arrogant ass.

I'm happy she hasn't though. Every year I pay her more money to stay. A hefty raise, a gift here and there. It keeps her happy. Finding a good secretary is more work than it's worth. It was a pain in my ass when I started. Linda's the first I've been able to keep for more than two months and now that she knows what she's doing, with more than four years of working for me, I have no intention of finding a new secretary. So when I make a request, I say *please*.

I go through the emails remaining in my inbox, waiting impatiently for her soft knock on the door to my office. Usually I don't bother with the paper mail. Just like most of these fucking emails, they're junk. She knows what to do with them. So I leave it to her to organize and sift through it daily. She hands over the personal mail at her discretion, usually waiting until the end of the week to bring it all by, but this particular one I want right now. I'm not interested in waiting.

The light knocking at the door echoes in the small room, and I look at the clock. It's only three minutes later. *Not bad, Linda.*

"Come in," I call out and she does so quickly, closing the door behind her. She walks straight to my desk, not wasting any time. Her pink tweed skirt suit looks rather expensive. It's a Chanel, if I'm correct. I see she's putting that last bonus to good use.

"This is from today," she says, placing a compact stack in front of me, "and this-"

I stop her, waving my hand and pulling out the small, square, deep red envelope. "No need."

She collects the remaining mail, tapping it lightly on the desk to line everything up together and asks, "Anything else, sir?"

The use of sir catches me off guard, and for a moment I wonder if she knows who the sender of this particular piece of mail is, but her face is passive. And it isn't the first time she's called me sir. Most of my employees do. Linda just happens to use it less often than most.

I shake my head and say, "That's all." The lines around her eyes are soft, and her lips hold the faintest form of a smile. Linda's always smiling despite having to deal with me. She takes my hot temper in stride. That's one of the reasons I'm eager for her to stay.

She nods her head before turning on her heels. I wait until she's gone to open the envelope.

I watch her leave and listen to the door click shut, leaving me in my spacious office alone and in solitude. Just the way I prefer it.

I finally open the envelope with the letter opener on my desk, avoiding the black wax seal embossed with a bold X entirely.

The thick cream parchment slips out easily from the elegant envelope, and the handwritten message is in Madam Lynn's beautiful penmanship. If nothing else, I admire her flair.

I can practically hear her sultry voice whispering in my ear as I read the sophisticated script.

Dear Sir,

An auction is to be held and I personally wanted to invite you, Lucian. It's been far too long, and I know you're in need. Renew your membership first.

I'll see you soon,

L

An asymmetric smile plays on my lips as I take in her message. I may be a Sir, but she is certainly a Madam. I sit back in my leather desk chair and tap the parchment against the desk as I debate on whether or not I should attend.

It's been nearly a year since I've been to Club X. Even longer since I've had a Submissive, and only one of those was purchased at one of the monthly auctions. She lasted the longest, but only because she was required to.

It would be a nice distraction from the mundane. I muse, staring absently at the back wall lined with black and white sketches from an up-and-coming artist.

Before I can decide, my desk phone rings, bringing me back to the present. I lean forward with annoyance and answer it.

"Stone," I answer.

"Lucian," my sister's voice comes through the line. It's bright and cheery, everything my younger sister embodies. Bubbly is what she likes to be called.

But her happiness doesn't rub off on me. Not after reading the fucking emails from our parents' lawyer. I doubt she knows, and it's not her fault.

She reminds me of them, though. I wish it wasn't like this. I wish I could separate the two, but I can't. They manipulate her, and it's only a matter of time before they'll come up in conversation. Shit, our parents could be why she's calling now.

"Anna, how are you?" I ask her casually. I trace my finger along the wax seal of the envelope as I listen.

"I've been good, but I've been missing you..." she trails off as her voice goes distant. I don't respond. I don't care to admit my feelings either way. Yes, there's a bit of pain from losing contact with my sister, but she chooses to keep in touch with them. She made that decision. And I refuse to have any contact with them.

"It's been too long," she says in a sad voice and then her tone picks up. "We should do lunch sometime soon."

I take in a long breath, not wanting to commit to anything. Lunches are quick unless it's a business meeting. Then they aren't really lunches. But beyond that, I don't have much to tell her. I'm certainly not going to be telling her what she wants to hear.

"Maybe soon," I finally reply.

She huffs over the phone, "You say that when you really mean no." Her voice is playful and forces a rough chuckle up my chest. She may only be nineteen, but Anna's a smart girl. I can't deny her. No matter how much I wish I could, I have a soft spot for her.

I lean forward and pull up my calendar. "I can do Thursday."

"Deal," she quickly agrees, and I can practically feel her smile through the phone. It warms my chest that I can make her happy. Unlike the rest of them, she doesn't take, take, take from me. She truly just wants to see me.

"I've missed you, too, Anna."

"Well you won't have to, since I'll text you and see you on Thursday," she says confidently.

"I will. I'll talk to you then." I'm quick to end the call before she can drag me into a longwinded conversation. She can do that on Thursday for all I care.

"Talk to you then. I love you," she says brightly.

"Talk to you then," I answer and hang up the phone.

As I do, my eyes catch sight of the card and I pick it up and rise from my desk, slinging my jacket over my arm and thinking about the last time I was there.

It's been a long time since I've set foot in Club X.

And a visit is long overdue.

CHAPTER 2

DAHLIA

God, I wish I could wear this color, I think to myself as I slowly slide my fingertips over the rich, velvety purple fabric that lays across my desk. A fabric that will hopefully be turned into an award-winning gown. I suck in a breath, holding it and hoping that I'll be able to contribute to the design.

It's the new in vogue color this season, and it's only a matter of time before models will be flaunting it down the runway. I just hope that I can eventually be one of those fashion designers that proudly walks the runway at the end of a successful show. One day.

I like purple; it's probably up there with red and black as one of my favorite colors. I just don't look good wearing it. I gently lay the fabric down on the desk, thinking. Black suits me better, and it's probably why nearly all of my closet consists of black and greys. Even now, sporting dark silk slacks, a blouse the color of midnight and a cropped black leather jacket with my dark brown hair pulled up into a sleek ponytail, I look like I'm modeling for the grim reaper.

I think I need to stop wearing so much black, I tell myself, *maybe then I'll stop being so damn depressed.*

I take a deep breath and shake off the thought, taking the advice from my therapist to focus on the positives in my life. Black may be slimming, but it doesn't do the spirits any good. I just read a study on colors and the effects they have on the psyche and mood. I huff a small laugh. It was an odd thing to be tested on in my History of Fashion Development class, but it was eye opening.

Today has been wonderful, though. Actually, the past two weeks have been a dream come true. Growing up, I was heavily intrigued by fashion. Christian Dior, Gucci, Prada, Michael Kors, you name it. If it had a name, I wanted to wear it. I dreamed of cutting fabrics and sewing them into gorgeous gowns. One of my favorite gifts my mother ever got me was a drawing pad and a huge set of colored pencils for sketches. I filled the entire book up in only a month.

Over time, my obsession morphed into a lifelong dream of wanting to work in the fashion world, and up until several weeks ago, it looked like that fantasy would never come to fruition. But I finally got my foot in the door, and I'm not going to let this opportunity slip through my fingers.

Now I'm sitting here with my own office on the top floor of Explicit Designs, working one of the most coveted internships in town, living out my wish. It's unbelievable. Seriously, I absolutely love this job. I get to see all the latest designs and in-style fashions, meet quirky, interesting people and be involved in the entire creative process that goes into making these magnificent creations. It's funny how things turn out.

Especially considering how I'd almost given up.

A surge of anxiety twists my stomach, and I frown. It

chills me to know how close I'd been to abandoning everything, how close I'd been to letting the darkness overwhelm me. Thinking about it makes me shudder, and I try my best to push the unwelcome thoughts away. It's a constant battle. Dark thoughts always seem to be waiting in the shadows of my mind--stalking me, haunting me, and then pouncing right when I think things are going good.

But things are better now, I try to convince myself. *And I need to focus on being happy.*

A clinking sound pulls me out of my reverie and causes me to look up. I see my boss, established fashion designer Debra Ferguson, through the glass window of my office, gathering her things and getting ready to pack up for the night.

This is the one thing I don't like about the floor I work on. The whole area is a large open space with floor-to-ceiling windows surrounding the offices, and there's virtually no privacy. Everybody can see everyone else. I suppose it isn't so bad, but I do miss my privacy.

I watch as Debra, who's clad in a fashionable red dress that hugs her matronly frame, slings her oversized Prada purse over her right shoulder and slides on her Gucci shades. For a woman in her late forties, she exudes the kind of sex appeal you would find in someone half her age, and it's one of the reasons why she's so popular. To me, she embodies everything I want to be when I'm her age: intelligent, confident, sexy and in complete control of her destiny.

As she makes her way out of her office, she doesn't bother looking my way. For a moment, I wonder if I should step out and tell her goodbye before she leaves. It would be the polite thing to do, yet I stay rooted in my seat.

I shouldn't, I tell myself, feeling a sense of self-consciousness wash over me. *I'll probably just annoy her.*

I don't know why I think that way. Debra has been mostly gracious to me. I suppose I'm intimidated by her. At least that's what I think it is. I'm new, and still trying to learn my place. There are only a dozen or so people working here, and everyone has their own routines. I need to learn mine.

Feeling conflicted, I watch as she walks out of the large room and disappears from view. I let out a slight sigh when she's gone. I don't know why I get like this, why I let my own self-doubts cause me to miss out. It's infuriating. And it's a wonder I've even landed this job with all the insecurities weighing me down.

After gently folding and putting away the purple cloth before making sure everything is in order, I grab my vintage Chanel purse and sling it over my shoulder. The purse is a hand-me-down from my good friend and coworker Carla. We shared a class two semesters ago, and I know it's only because of her that Debra even considered me for this position. I owe her so much already. *But wow, this purse.* I run my hand along the plush quilted leather, still in disbelief that it's mine.

I nearly died when she gave it to me, as I'd never owned anything so expensive before. Let alone *vintage Chanel.* For the longest time, I refused to use it, scared I would somehow lose it or someone would steal it… or worse, I'd get wine or lipstick on it. Instead, I let it collect dust in my closet. I only started using it after Carla scolded me and said to stop being so worried about it. In her mind, it was just a purse, and what was the point of having it if I was never going to use it?

I'm about to walk off when my phone dings. Quick to see who it is, I whip it out. *It's Mom,* I think anxiously. *She finally responded to my text.* Instead, I'm greeted by a message from my roommate Callie.

Calgurl182: *Gonna be studying hard for my exams. Please be quiet when you come in from work. Thx*

I grin at the message. When I need to get a paper done, I study hard, but Callie takes studying to a whole new level. And with exams coming up, I know Callie's level of anxiety must be through the roof. I can totally relate to her not wanting to be disturbed.

After making a mental note to be quiet as a mouse when I enter our tiny apartment near campus, I flip over to my last text with my mom and my grin slowly fades.

> *Hey Mom, I know I told you about landing my dream job recently, but things are really tough right now financially. I've had to pay for so many things, a used car, clothing, rent, tuition... all these things have left me a little strapped and I'm not sure how I'm going to afford to pay for my next semester. I hate to ask, but can you help me out? I'll pay you back as soon as I get the chance.*
>
> *Love you,*
>
> *Dah*

Staring at the blank space where her response should be, I feel dejected. I wasn't expecting much from her, but she could have at least responded and let me know that she cared, even if she can't help me out financially. I've had to pay for college myself. Which was fine when I had a job, but this internship doesn't pay anything, and I couldn't keep my retail job and also work here. I'm fucked. I was hoping my mother would be able to help me out. But this is the third text I've sent about money, and she hasn't responded to any of them. She sure as hell reminded me that she was going on vacation with her new boyfriend though.

It makes me feel like I'm low on her priorities. But maybe she just can't handle dealing with added stress right now.

She's been distant lately, and I know even before she started dating this current boyfriend she was having a really rough time. The last few years while I've been at school, my mother has grown apart from me. I can't help but wonder if it's because I remind her too much of my father. I hope not, because it'll only make me feel worse, maybe make me resent my father more, if that's even possible.

Just thinking about him sends a shiver of apprehension down my spine. I don't know if I'll ever forgive him for ripping our family apart. For letting what *happened* to me, happen. Even now, I still can't fathom it. My father was supposed to be my protector, my guardian. *He let him hurt me.* That fact shakes me to my very core, and occasionally, I suffer nightmares over it.

It's been better lately though. I swallow thickly and grab my coat.

Stop bringing this up. I've had a relatively good day, and I don't need to screw it up by living in the past. I'm never going to get over it if I keep wishing things had turned out differently. What I need to do is quit worrying and figure out a way to pay for my tuition next semester. I square my shoulders and nod my head at the thought, feeling my confidence come back. I'm going to make this work and have a life I'm proud of.

Just thinking about my money woes stresses me out. I can't help but think I'm going to be worn thin by having to work in order to pay the bills on top of doing this internship. That's not even factoring in the time I'll need to study for school.

I need to figure something out by next month. After

finals, there's the holiday break and I can do something then. I'll find a way to keep this internship *and* pay for my classes.

Steeling my shoulders with resolve, I walk out of the office as I think to myself, *One way or another, I'm going to find a way to make some money on the side. Even if it kills me.*

Bought is available now!

ABOUT THE AUTHORS

Want more? Join our mailing list (http://eepurl.com/csrkNv) to receive all sorts of fan extras!
(If you're already on our lists, you'll get this automatically).

Willow Winters
View her entire catalog on her website:
https://willowwinterswrites.com/reading-order/

Like her on Facebook:
http://facebook.com/authorwillowwinters

Lauren Landish
View her entire catalog on Amazon.
https://www.amazon.com/Lauren-Landish/e/B00SNT0Z0U/

Like her on Facebook:
http://www.facebook.com/lauren.landish

Have a sneak peek at some of our cowritten novels!

Highest Bidder Series:

Bought
Sold
Owned

Given
From USA Today best selling authors, Willow Winters and Lauren Landish, comes a sexy and forbidden series of standalone romances.

Bad Boy Standalones, cowritten with Lauren Landish:

Inked
Tempted
Mr. CEO
Three novels featuring sexy powerful heroes.
Three romances that are just as swoon-worthy as they are tempting.